JUST FRIENDS, JUST WAR

JUST FRIENDS, JUST WAR

a novel by

Korinthia A. Klein

DEDICATION

This book is dedicated to my husband, who is more than just my friend.

CHAPTER ONE

The day Alex was officially introduced to Claire, she nearly broke his arm.

He had seen her around the dojo before; he'd just never been paired with her in class until that cold January in 1995. It was hard not to notice the only girl in jujutsu at the time. There were more later, and a couple in the black belt classes, but when Alex signed up for beginner lessons during his junior year of high school, the girl with the mousey brown hair and hazel eyes was the only one who crossed his path back then. Women had the option in their martial arts school of wearing a red belt or a green belt once they passed their first test. Men could only wear green, so Claire's red belt against her black gi made her stand out even more.

She was a few levels ahead of him—already into the advanced wrist escapes and throws—and he was still on basic wrist locks. Alex was feeling cocky after having passed the first two levels with little effort, and their teacher didn't appear pleased with that attitude. Sensei seemed to want to put Alex in his place. After they had finished their warm up stretches and done push-ups

1

and crunches and a few hundred blocks and strikes, it was time to partner students for practice. Sensei paired Alex with Claire. He was grooming her to teach, and asked her to review the basic throws from sixth kyu, a level she had passed months ago, so she might be better prepared to demonstrate in an upcoming class.

She was about a head shorter than Alex, and she smiled sweetly as they bowed to each other. She didn't look like much, but he should have taken her more seriously right from the start.

They were instructed to take turns going through their kyu levels, both left side and right. Claire was supposed to do one of her techniques, then Alex one of his, and back and forth until they'd gotten through everything in their respective levels. Since Claire outranked Alex, she was standing on the right side of the mat to indicate her superior position to him in the dojo. Alex couldn't quite admit this bothered him, but he decided girl or no girl, if she was going to do jujutsu, he wasn't going to show her any mercy. She could go off and cry in her room when she got home if she couldn't take grappling with guys.

The first technique Claire was working on was a basic hip throw. Alex got into the traditional starting posture of grabbing her by the lapel (*high* on the lapel, he had to remind himself, when working with a girl) and the sleeve near the elbow. She carefully went through the motions of positioning herself with her back to him, lifting him up, and twisting to drop him quietly onto the mat in a side breakfall. He should have appreciated the skill it took to do such a thing so gracefully. It was more like a dance than fighting, but Alex was there to learn combat, not to waltz around the dojo with a girl in a gi.

When his turn came and she grabbed him slowly, he responded with an inappropriate amount of speed and force. She slapped her free hand against her thigh quickly as the sanctioned signal to stop applying pain. He did his technique on both sides, and then she gently did one of her own, and then Alex brutally executed his next wrist lock. The black belt assigned to run the class hadn't noticed Alex's first turn at his wrist locks, but at his second go the Sensei with his fourth-degree black belt did hear the frantic level of Claire's slapping and came over to investigate.

"Alex?" he asked, sounding slightly amused.

"Hai, Sensei?" Alex responded dutifully.

"What do you think you're doing?"

"I, uh...I guess I don't know, Sensei."

"No, you clearly don't. First of all, your technique is sloppy. You are applying pain, but not in the most direct and controlled way. You're only hurting her because she's letting you."

That confused Alex and he saw a hint of a smirk on Claire's face.

"Hai, Sensei," he acknowledged.

"Claire?" said Sensei.

"Hai, Sensei?"

"Can you please show Alex how this technique is done?"

"Hai, Sensei." Claire smoothly guided Alex's body through the lock and took him to the ground where he slapped out when she applied a twinge of pain.

Sensei studied Alex carefully. "We always reflect back the energy presented to us in this space. If she grabs you at a gentle speed, you have to respond in kind." There was something slightly resentful in Alex's face that caused Sensei to add, "And Claire? If he oversteps his bounds like that again you have my permission to throw him for real."

"Hai, Sensei," she said.

She carefully ran through both sides of her next

technique and could feel Alex's embarrassment manifesting itself in anger toward her. She could take it. Guys always thought being a guy was enough to entitle them to some claim on physical dominance. That was true in many circumstances, but not in the dojo. In the dojo, technique was everything, and hers was very, very good.

When Alex's turn came again, he started off gently enough, but in the last moment of the second side he chose to wrench on her wrist a little more to let her know who was still the guy in this dance they were doing on the mat. Claire gave him a tiny smile that told him exactly what was coming but there was nothing he could do about it.

Faster than Alex could register, Claire turned herself under his arm, hoisted him onto her back, and slammed him to the floor. Everyone else in the dojo stopped to look. He was barely aware of what had happened as he lay gazing up at her, but she wasn't going to let him off that easy, and she braced the arm she was still holding against her leg and rotated her wrist. It wasn't an official part of the technique, but she didn't think Sensei would mind at that moment. The pain was ridiculous and Alex forgot about slapping out. Claire gave his arm one last, sharp crank right as he started smacking the floor in desperation, and Alex seriously thought another second more and he'd have been in a cast.

She waited politely for him to stand again, and she bowed. How could he not have wanted to be friends with Claire?

She didn't remember it quite that way. She remembered Alex being petulant, and she remembered feeling satisfied about being able to execute a hard throw, but she didn't remember any specific turning point where he wanted to be her friend. Claire seemed to recall him avoiding her for about a month at least, but Alex always said that was simply the luck of how the classes were organized at the time. When they eventually were paired together again it was in preparation for Alex's test. He was gentle and precise that time around, and he asked if she would be his partner for the actual kyu level test the next day. She didn't have anything going on, but she said it would depend on whether she could get a ride.

"I could come get you," Alex offered.

"You have your own car?" she asked.

"Yeah, I go to Kennedy High and it's kind of a long way from my house, so my parents helped me buy it last year when I got my license." He surprised himself with the length of his answer since "yeah" would have sufficed.

"Huh. I go to Andover."

"Hey, we beat you in the division finals last year!" said Alex.

"You didn't beat me at anything!" said Claire.

That made Alex smile, and he got her phone number and directions to her house so she could help him test. The beauty of having someone as talented as Claire be the recipient of the technique—or his "uke" in Japanese—was that she made him appear better than he was. Alex passed his test and got a second stripe on his belt. Claire had four on hers and was ready to test for her fifth.

Alex offered to take her out for a celebratory lunch afterward.

"How can you eat right after a test?" Claire asked. "My stomach's usually still in knots for an hour after testing."

"I dunno. I can always eat," said Alex. "Where you want to go? You made me look fucking great on that mat, so you pick."

5

"You're paying?"

"I'm paying."

"Then that gyro place with the good cheese fries down that way." She pointed sort of ahead and to the right.

"Yeah, that place is good," said Alex approvingly.

Then he glanced at her sidelong in a way that made Claire say, "What?"

"Nothing. It's just I can't believe you actually picked a place."

Claire laughed. "Why not? You asked!"

"Yeah, but girls usually say something like 'Oh, where do *you* want to go?' and then it goes back and forth and it's stupid. Even my mom does that. Not that my dad really asks, he usually just decides, but probably because he got tired of not getting a real answer."

"Huh. Everyone in my house just answers, so I don't know how special I am."

Alex was starting to think pretty special.

They paired with each other whenever the opportunity came up after that. It helped to have someone you knew to work with when learning the basics of a technique. At some point it was better to start applying your moves to other people so that you could be assured of being able to execute them in other circumstances, but Claire and Alex had a good rapport in class that helped them both. Alex appreciated that she was direct and honest, and only praised him if he deserved it. Claire liked that he could make her laugh, and that after that first unfortunate incident together, he'd been nothing but respectful.

The rest of the dojo simply assumed they were dating, which was their first experience with what was to become a perpetual problem. They were just friends and that was fine for them. It did not seem to be fine for anyone else.

The first time the dating issue arose was right at the beginning of a class before the official warm up started. Stretching next to Claire was a woman in her early forties who had recently started classes at the dojo. She was chatty and pleasant and interested in all the young people, and asked many questions. When she found out Alex and Claire went to different high schools she was intrigued.

"That's unusual! How did you two meet, then?"

"Here," said Claire, tilting her head sideways to look at her while bent forward to put her palms flat on the ground. Alex on the other side of her tried to duplicate that stance with less success. He wished he were as flexible as Claire.

"Isn't that sweet! Finding love in the dojo of all places."

Alex's eyes flew open wide, and Claire stood up straight again and said, "No, Kathy, we're just friends."

Kathy didn't seem to have heard and simply went on, "You could go to junior prom at both schools that way, I suppose. I'm sure your parents would be glad to get their money's worth from the extra use out of your dress."

This was the first any of the other people in the dojo had heard about the specific status of Alex and Claire's relationship, and they appeared to find it interesting. It was even interesting to Claire when Alex explained that he already had a date for his prom, and her name was Lindsay.

"Oh, dear, I'm sorry! I just assumed...."

"That's okay," said Claire, and then the black belt bowed onto the mat and the official stretches began, ending the casual discussion. But then for the next twenty minutes Claire found herself stealing glances at Alex and thinking, *Who the hell is Lindsay?* She and

Alex only really saw each other twice a week at class and she liked him a lot, but hadn't really given whatever it was they had much thought. He was okay-looking. She'd had to work closely enough to him that she'd noticed flecks of green in his blue eyes. His sandy hair was a bit scruffy, though, and she decided he was not as cute as some of the other guys she had crushes on at her own school. The idea of kissing Alex was too odd to contemplate. She couldn't picture it, and her gut reaction when trying was a simple "no way," so she didn't force it. She decided being friends was plenty, but friends who actually knew their respective dates' names would be better.

Claire had three older brothers and was comfortable with the kind of pal-around interaction that that involved. She'd learned from them that boys were generally cocky and crude and had surprisingly fragile egos. Well, Jason and Derrick had taught her that, anyway. The youngest of the boys, Ben, was gay, and had come out when he was about her age. She'd learned different things from him, primarily about the bravery it takes to be yourself in a potentially unkind world. Any kids at her school now who might be gay were firmly closeted.

She had girls in her life that she did things with, but those friendships were more of a long-standing habit left over from grade school. She liked them, but no single one of them would claim Claire as her best friend. Alex was different. And different in a way she felt completely at ease with. Could you have a guy as your best friend? Claire didn't see why not. It would be like an extra brother, but one she didn't have to fight with for time in the bathroom in the morning. That element of her life had dramatically improved after Jason and Derrick had moved on to college, but Ben was commuting to a local technical school to learn television editing and still lived at home. He easily took twice as much time in the bathroom as she did.

Alex was also mulling things over during that stretching session. Did people really think he and Claire were a couple? It made sense, he supposed. If he were watching the two of them talk and laugh and pair up at every opportunity at the dojo, he'd have probably reached the same conclusion. But she was not his type. He was attracted to blondes and redheads who dressed cute and liked to flirt. Claire was okay, but on a dating level there was nothing there for him. He was fine with them being friends—she was incredibly cool and they liked a lot of the same things—and he was worried now she might want something more. Of course, she had spoken up really quickly that they were just friends, so he trusted that was what she actually thought. Besides, the idea of dating someone who could snap one of his limbs off was not appealing. He would stick to girls like Lindsay who wore makeup and thought shopping was exercise.

Kathy apologized to Claire again after class in the changing room.

"You two are so darling together, it seemed obvious, but I know that must have been embarrassing and I'm sorry."

"That's okay, really! I only ever see Alex here, and some days like today he gives me a ride, so I didn't even know about his prom date."

"And that doesn't bother you at all? I'm sorry, I'm being presumptuous again," said Kathy apologetically.

"Why should it? We really are just friends and that's fine."

Kathy slipped her shirt over her head and then reached for her coat. "Well that's very modern of you. I don't personally know any women who have a man for just a friend, other than married couples who get along, but that's different. Good luck with that."

Claire was glad to get her own coat on to leave, but she still had to wait for the men to change so Alex could give her a ride home. She hoped it wouldn't be a weird ride home.

The discussion among the guys in the changing room was rather different.

"We thought you were banging her or something," was the general consensus, and it annoyed the hell out of Alex.

"Okay, one, she's not my type, and two, what the fuck is wrong with you guys? You can't think of any reason to hang out with a girl unless you're planning to bang her? Come on!" Alex had a twelve-year-old sister named Pamela (who everyone called Pammy). He was becoming more sensitive to the way guys around him behaved out of protectiveness over her as she was starting to look less like a little kid. He knew from personal experience how much of what guys said was all talk, but some of it wasn't, and he didn't want any of it around his sister. Or Claire, for that matter. What had she ever done to deserve assumptions made about her like that? He wondered if any of these guys would still be standing if they had the guts to speculate about Claire in front of her. He preferred the idea of being on Claire's side.

"Aw, you know how it is," one of the guys said. "She's cute and she'd probably let you get somewhere."

"Shit, you'd have to be *sure* though! That girl could twist your fucking balls off and hand them to you if you caught her at a bad time of the month."

One of them laughed and added, "Man, I couldn't screw someone that much tougher than me. At the rate she's going she'll be testing for black belt easy before she graduates high school."

"Yeah, but that bitch is flexible! When she does

10

those splits—"

"Okay, shut the fuck up about Claire already!" said Alex. "Sensei hates this kind of trash talk down here anyway, so unless you want to do nothing but wind kicks and two-finger push-ups for the next month and a half I think you shouldn't risk he might walk in here and catch you at it."

"Hey, sorry, you're right. Claire's okay. We're just, you know...."

"Yeah, I know," said Alex. Sometimes he wasn't all that proud to be a guy.

The drive back to Claire's was awkward, but not for long. They started off in an uncomfortable silence, and then Alex gave a forced laugh. "Did you know they all thought we were a couple?"

Claire cleared her throat. "No, I really didn't. I guess it makes some sense, but...."

"But what?"

"Well, I don't think of you like that. But I really do like you as a friend, so if that's okay...."

Alex looked relieved. A little too relieved in Claire's opinion, but she'd remember to throw him extra hard next time she had the chance in order to make up for it.

"That's cool, because I really like having you as a friend, too, and I don't want anything to get, like, strange or something between us," said Alex.

So, it was officially decided. They were just friends and it made them happy. They started doing things together outside of the dojo, and discovered quickly that their new arrangement didn't seem to make anyone else happy. Among the people their relationship didn't make happy was Lindsay, who wanted to know why Claire's name was ahead of hers on Alex's speed dial list on the phone in his room. (He simply switched the order and couldn't figure out why that didn't make it instantly better.) Also not happy

11

were their respective parents, and for opposite reasons.

Claire's dad didn't trust boys around his daughter, period. But this particular boy who claimed not to be interested in "that way" he declared disingenuous, and therefore even less trustworthy. His only daughter kept trying to explain they were just friends, but he kept repeating that he didn't believe Alex wasn't up to something. Mr. Walker didn't bend his strict rules when Alex was over, no matter how much Claire said they should treat him like any of her other friends who happened to be girls.

Things were reversed at the Sullivan house. Alex's mom adored Claire, and proclaimed her an improvement over the sort of girls her son was usually interested in. She couldn't understand why the two young people weren't dating, and chose not to apply their normal house rules for taking out girls when it came to Claire.

The only time that became a problem was when Claire was over one Saturday evening to watch a *Monty Python and the Flying Circus* marathon on the big TV at Alex's house. She and Alex both loved *Monty Python* and could recite some of their favorite sketches together by heart, so they set themselves up with a pizza and watched late into the night. They lost track of the time and ended up falling asleep together on the couch. Claire was in a ball at one end and Alex was splayed out at the other. They weren't even touching, but that didn't matter when Mr. Walker called to angrily ask why his daughter had been kept out past her curfew, and Mr. Sullivan had to explain that he simply hadn't paid any attention to the kids all night without somehow sounding negligent.

Claire's dad came and got her at what he kept referring to as "an absurd hour" and lectured her the whole way home about respecting rules and how they had been worried sick. Claire listened and was irritated, but didn't feel like combating her father while he was sleep deprived and mad. The next morning she suggested he talk to Alex directly.

"Please, Dad? If you'd only talk to him you'd see there's nothing to worry about. Please?"

"But I'm not interested in learning anything about Alex, I'm interested in trusting *you*. And missing your curfew to be out with a boy is—"

"But he's not a *boy* boy. He's Alex, and it's him you don't trust. We fell asleep watching TV, Dad. It's not that terrible. I'm sorry, okay? Can you please just talk to him?"

Her dad agreed, and Alex came over, but only after Claire begged him for over half an hour on the phone.

"I don't want to talk to your dad! He scares the shit out of me, Claire!"

"Don't be such a wuss! He's practically ready to forbid me from even letting you drive me to the dojo now, so get over here and show him you're not a jerk. And remember not to swear. He finds that 'vulgar and intellectually lazy' or something."

Alex had no clue what he was supposed to say in his defense, but the talk at the Walker kitchen table alone with Claire's dad went unexpectedly well. He reminded Mr. Walker that Claire outranked him at the dojo by several levels, and she was quite capable of beating him to a pulp. He even rolled up his sleeve at one point so Mr. Walker could see all the bruises up his arm from working with the man's sweet little girl. Then Alex showed him a picture of himself and Lindsay at the junior prom that he kept in his wallet, and explained she was the one he was interested in dating.

"Then why are you with Claire on a Saturday night instead of with your girlfriend?" Mr. Walker wanted to know.

"I usually am with her, but my girlfriend doesn't like *Monty Python*, and that's the night it was on. Some things you just want to do with a buddy, and that's Claire. It's nice to hang out with her and not have to worry about anything. With Lindsay, I don't.... I feel like I have to do everything extra right in front of her, you know? Claire's just my friend so it's not a big deal when we get together. She's fun, but in a guy way, kind of. Not that she's a guy, I know that, but I don't think of her like a girl because she's not like any other girl I know. I'm not going to try anything with your daughter."

Mr. Walker calmed down after that, but did insist if Alex and Claire wanted to hang out late, they do it at their house. He didn't like how lax things seemed at the Sullivan home.

Alex wished things were as loose at his own house as Claire's dad thought they were. He was seldom allowed to take Lindsay upstairs, and making out with her while doing things like watching TV was hard because there was an open-door policy, and Pammy or anyone could walk in at any time.

Overall, Alex liked how things were going with Lindsay. The two of them hung out together at school, and kissed by her locker until teachers walked by. She was one of the prettiest girls in his grade, and she liked that he had a car. When school first let out she wanted to do things almost daily. Alex thought that was excessive but tried to accommodate her. He only ran into real trouble when she decided one day she wanted to watch him at the dojo.

"Please, Alex? I want to see you do all your karate stuff! I'll bet you look cute in those black pajama things you keep in that duffle bag."

"It's jujutsu, not karate, and the uniform is called a gi, Lindsay. Why can't you ever remember that?

Anyway, I don't think it's a good idea. It's not a good place to be distracted, and you're distracting!" He pulled her toward him playfully, trying to disrupt her train of thought with repeated soft kisses.

Lindsay smiled but was not deterred. She gently pushed his lips away from hers enough to say, "But I want to go! They have seats there, right? I'll be quiet and promise not to get in your way at all."

Alex wasn't crazy about the idea, but he agreed and told her he'd pick her up right after he picked up Claire on the way to class on Tuesday night.

"I didn't know you drove Claire," said Lindsay. Her smile was still there, but now seemed pasted on.

"That's right, you haven't met her yet, have you? I don't drive her all the time, but lately it's been every Tuesday, and always when we test so we can grab lunch after."

"You go to lunch?" asked Lindsay, her pasted smile starting to look even less real.

"Uh, yeah, 'cause food. Tell you what, how about I take you somewhere next time? Where do you want to go?"

"Oh, I don't know. Where do *you* want to go?"

Alex rolled his eyes which left Lindsay pouty, but he didn't know what he was supposed to do about it.

That Tuesday he picked up Claire and told her Lindsay was coming to class, too.

"Huh. I guess it'll be nice to finally see what your famous type is!"

"Ha ha! Just be nice to her, okay?"

"I'm always nice."

"Yeah, tell that to the bruise on my shin."

Claire laughed.

"It's not funny!" said Alex. "That thing is in Technicolor! Sensei lets you get away with murder sometimes. If I cracked into you like that he would twist me down so fast I wouldn't even have time to blink."

"That's not true! Besides, I gave you ample warning to move."

"You gave me that one stupid grin that you always think I'll know what to do with!"

"Hey, if you can't read the warning...."

Alex shook his head. "You're insane, you know that? When you get your black belt someone should lock you up before you hurt somebody."

They enjoyed their usual pre-dojo banter for a while, but then they picked up Lindsay. Claire asked if she would rather sit up front next to Alex, but she said she was fine in the back. Lindsay made a big show of leaning up front to give Alex a kiss before he started the car again. Claire's expression showed she clearly thought it was funny, and Alex shot her a look that said, *You promised you'd be nice*, so she was somber for the rest of the drive.

In the dojo, Lindsay found a seat on the futon by the window with a good view of the mat. She appeared delicate in her cute outfit and earrings, and her long blond hair was arranged carefully. Claire didn't wear makeup, and before stretching would usually yank some of her hair back in a barrette without checking a mirror. She looked alert, solid and at home, while Lindsay seemed fragile, a little bored and clearly out of place. Alex glanced over his girlfriend's way nervously once or twice, but eventually he became absorbed in what he was doing and forgot about her.

Alex and Claire were paired together after the warm up and were told to work on their traditional techniques. At the end of the list of new skills required to pass each kyu level was an ancient technique that was rather stylized. Even the bow for those techniques was more elaborate; it involved facing each other while

16

going down on one knee, reciting a phrase in Japanese, and a slap to the ground. The traditional techniques were tricky to master, and to execute them properly required understanding on both the part of the attacker and the defender. It resembled a dance, but started with a punch or a grab, and took concentration as the two people involved moved on the mat together as seamlessly as possible.

The one Alex was working on was actually more complicated than the one Claire was doing, but his big problem was that he kept leading with the wrong foot, and it would screw him up early. Claire wanted to slap his knee every time he goofed, but the techniques were too dignified for that kind of horseplay. She instead told him quietly that she would raise an eyebrow if he was starting to move the incorrect foot. It was probably cheating, but it helped him get through the class.

It was a productive session, and after they bowed out and Claire was sent off into the dressing room to change first, Alex was feeling energized and happy and went over to sit with Lindsay.

"What did you think?" he asked.

"I don't know," she responded in a cool tone.

"It can be hard to follow if you don't get what's going on, but I can walk you through it if you want."

Lindsay wasn't smiling. "So, do you always work with Claire like that?"

"Like what?"

"Like, having to hold onto each other that way the whole class?"

Alex didn't like what she was implying. "You mean like the rest of the class was doing too?"

"Yeah, but, Alex, she's the only girl!"

"So, you'd be happier if I was grabbing a guy all evening?" He was trying not to draw attention to himself as the next class was filtering in, but he was getting pissed and it was hard not to raise his voice.

"You know what I mean—you've got her, like, in your arms and you're holding her down, and, God! What am I supposed to think?" said Lindsay, clearly flustered.

"It's jujutsu, not a make-out party! Did you see me slapping the ground every time she got me down? That means, 'Stop, I'm in pain!' She's not doing something nice to me over and over, she's twisting my fucking arm."

"Yeah, but you seemed to like having her hurt you! What is that about?"

Right then Claire appeared, and the men started filing downstairs to change. Alex didn't move. He decided he'd rather leave in his sweaty outfit and take it off at home.

The drive was quiet all the way to Lindsay's house. When she was leaving the car, Lindsay hesitated about giving Alex a kiss, but then she glanced over at Claire and laid one on him with a lot of tongue.

As they backed out of the driveway, Claire finally burst out laughing. She knew it was rude, but she couldn't help herself.

"What?" Alex was now annoyed with two girls in one night and it was aggravating.

"I'm sorry, but I have never been more flattered to not be your type!"

"What does *that* mean?" asked Alex defensively.

"Well, geez did she smile even once? And how long does it take her to get her eyeliner like that? She'd be a blast on a camping trip. And I can't imagine her getting through any part of the warm up routine. By the time we got to advanced push-ups she'd be a pretty blond corpse."

"You're just a goddamn comedian tonight, aren't you?"

18

"Oh, come on, Alex! I hope she's a good kisser because as company on a drive she's a pain in th—."

"Hey! You're not seeing her like she normally is. She was a little, I don't know.... She didn't understand what we were doing."

"What does *that* mean?" asked Claire. It was her turn to sound defensive.

"She doesn't.... I guess we do have to touch each other a lot and I never thought about it."

"But you know it's not like that! It's—I—"

"Yeah yeah yeah, I know." Alex wasn't sure what to do about any of it, but he was done with the issue right then. He was more upset that Lindsay had intruded upon Claire's life than the other way around.

Claire knew by his tone that he was done talking, which worked out fine since they were at her house.

She got out and leaned back through her open window long enough to say, "Nice shoulder lock tonight, by the way. I think you've finally got that one down."

"Thanks," said Alex with gratitude.

Claire walked up to her front door and let herself in. Alex turned on the car radio so he wouldn't have to think on the drive home.

Claire walked into the kitchen and started pulling her gi and the matching black t-shirt she'd worn underneath it out of her bag so she could make sure they were washed by class time on Thursday. Her mom was at the table working on cutting up apples for a pie for Ben's birthday dinner the next night. He liked his apple pie with dried cherries in it, and those were already in a dish by the crust which was waiting to be filled. Claire popped one of the dried cherries in her mouth before her mom could say no.

"How was class tonight?" her mom asked.

"Good, I guess."

"What was wrong with it?"

Claire sat down across from her mom and frowned. "It's, well...I met Lindsay tonight."

Her mom raised an eyebrow and seemed as if she were trying not to look too interested. "What was she like?"

"She's...." *How to put it?* "She reminded me of an overpriced cupcake."

Her mom smiled to herself and kept working on her apples. "Sounds like the kind of girls Jason was always interested in at that age," she said.

Claire thought back to her oldest brother's prom date when she was ten and Jason was eighteen. She'd thought the girl resembled the Barbie dolls her friends played with. Claire never owned any Barbies.

"I don't get it, is all. I mean, I don't like him like that, but he's such a great guy and what does he see in someone...."

"Who's not like you?" asked her mom.

"Kind of. Is that weird to think? 'Cause if I put it like that, it sounds as if I want him to like *me* like that, and that's not what I'm saying."

"I know what you're saying," she said. "When your brother started bringing home girls I couldn't relate to, it made me think he didn't really like me. As his mom I felt a bit rejected. I wanted to see something of myself in those girls so I would feel reassured that he loved and admired me, too. Imagine how I felt when Ben brought home John!"

Claire laughed. "Well, none of us love and admire you more than Ben, so I guess you're right. The two things don't have to be connected. Do you want help with those apples?"

Her mother slid the bowl over so she could help herself, and Claire got up to find a knife. They sat together and worked on Ben's pie and talked. Her mom listened as Claire excitedly told her about how her techniques were coming along and that Sensei thought she was gifted. He was considering putting her in charge of the new beginners-only class he was forming, and they'd be able to deduct her pay from her other tuition, so it would be like attending the dojo practically for free.

"That sounds like a wonderful opportunity, Sweetie," said her mom. "I hope that will mean even more opportunities like it ahead."

"I hope so too," said Claire as she reached into the dish for another dried cherry. Her mother scowled but Claire knew she was teasing.

They put all their apple slices into a bowl, added the dried cherries, and mixed them together with cinnamon and sugar before putting all of it into the pie crust. Then Claire's mom set to work on cutting out letters from more dough to spell out a birthday message for Ben that she would then arrange on top of the pie.

Claire watched her mom for another moment and then said, "Mom, why do we do pie for birthdays instead of cake?"

"Why, would you rather I make you a cake next year?"

"No, I still want that chocolate pie you do, I'm just wondering why we're different."

Her mom smiled as she continued to cut out her letters. "You don't need a reason to be different." And she stopped her work for a moment and looked her daughter in the eye and said, "Just be who you are. And if that means your right-hand man is an actual man, that's okay."

Claire laughed. "Geez, Mom, I was only asking about pie!"

"I know. Still, you take your parenting moments

when you can get them."

Claire gave her a small hug, then gathered up her dojo clothes to put in the laundry room. She was looking forward to the next class. One with less Lindsay in it.

CHAPTER TWO

Aside from the one and only time Lindsay visited the dojo, that first summer Alex and Claire spent together was one of the best ever. Neither of them had anything going on besides their jujutsu classes, so they hung out, and even signed up for a weapons class on the weekend which was challenging and fun and gave them even more to practice jointly. Without school there was time enough for everything, so Alex took Lindsay to movies he hated and rented other ones with Claire that he actually wanted to see.

Summer was unstructured, which let them be themselves in a manner that wasn't particularly scrutinized by anyone other than their families. And their families, for the most part, got used to their relationship. Alex still wasn't allowed up in Claire's room, but he didn't feel like her dad wanted to clobber him when he walked into their house anymore, which was an improvement.

At Alex's house they included Pammy while they hung out and watched TV or joked around, and Pammy cheered Claire on as she watched the two friends toss each other around the backyard lawn. Alex only got annoyed with his sister's presence when Pammy made some crack about how Lindsay would never have put up with the grass stains involved in such an activity, and Alex told her to leave his girlfriend out of it, and to stop campaigning for him to put Claire in that role. Pammy ceased dropping hints about her preference after that.

The one person who held onto hope that Alex might actually want to date Claire was his mother. She laid out an irresistible lunch for her son one afternoon, and when he sat down to enjoy it she started her interrogation.

"So why don't you simply go out with Claire?" his mother asked again.

Alex glanced up from the nice lunch she'd prepared for him and realized it was only civilized looking bait. It didn't quell his appetite any to know that, so he picked up the sandwich and took a big bite while he gave her an irritated look.

"Mom, it's not like that," he said with his mouth still full.

"Chew first, then explain it to me," she said, and sat down across from her son.

Alex swallowed and then shifted uncomfortably in his seat. "She's not my type. She knows that, and she's fine with it, so why can't you let it go?"

His mom shook her head. "How much more of your type does she need to be? The two of you can talk about anything, you make each other laugh, she's cute as a button…. Just because she doesn't have the right hair color doesn't seem important compared to all of that."

"She's my best friend, Mom."

"Yes, and wouldn't it be nice to be dating someone who is also your best friend? Wouldn't that be ideal?"

"Is Dad your best friend?" Alex asked, reaching for some potato chips to add to his plate.

Her hesitation before answering said all Alex needed to know. His parents' marriage was the only one he'd seen up close, and it wasn't supposed to be based on friendship as far as he could tell. His parents each had their own set of friends outside of their marriage, and as husband and wife they formed a team that negotiated to make their family work. They didn't make marriage look fun, so he didn't think it was supposed to be. Besides, even if he were attracted to Claire, if they tried dating and it went badly, they couldn't go back. She was too important to date. End of story.

"Mom. Thanks for the lunch, but I'm done with your version of the Spanish Inquisition, okay? It's tasty, though, I'll give you that." And he kissed her on the cheek as he grabbed one last handful of chips to take along with the rest of his sandwich as he left the room.

Splitting time between Claire and Lindsay wasn't much of a problem for Alex in the summer. There was a lot of time to go around, and when Lindsay wanted to be with her friends and shop and do whatever else groups of girls did (Alex imagined makeup was involved, but he really wasn't sure), that left him long stretches to hang with Claire. When senior year started, however, free time got tighter. And when Lindsay became aware of how much of his summer Alex had actually spent with his friend, she wasn't pleased. Especially since with their new schedule he saw Claire outside of school more than he saw her.

"It's too much!" she complained after classes as they walked to his car. "Two nights a week and every Saturday afternoon is too much!"

"Christ, it's all dojo stuff! It's the same two classes a week it's always been, plus now the weekend weapons class. What possible difference does it make? I would be there doing jujutsu anyway if Claire was around or not, so why does it matter?"

"It just does! I only see you once on the weekends if I'm lucky!" argued Lindsay.

"This isn't a fucking custody battle! Besides, I see you at school and at lunch and I drive you home.... I barely even get to talk to Claire lately. Most of the time I spend with her, she's trying to cut off my air supply or take me down with a hanbo or something. I spend way more time with you where I get to do all kinds of fun things I never do with Claire."

Lindsay looked sullen. Alex leaned into her against his car, hands on her waist, lips pressed gently on her neck, and with each slow kiss he said, "Like this...and this...and this...." He kissed her until she giggled. He smiled and gazed into her eyes. "You know you're adorable, right? Why would anyone as pretty as you think she had anything to worry about?" She kissed him back and got into the car.

Alex understood that Lindsay didn't like the situation, but most of the time she was easy to distract. Which was good, since he couldn't imagine what she expected him to change. She wanted him to take her to homecoming, however, so she didn't have much choice but to let the matter drop.

As they got further into senior year they applied to colleges. Claire decided to go to a small school in central Pennsylvania because her mother was an alumna. This made Claire eligible for a sizable scholarship, which was impossible to pass up. She had no idea what to major in, but it was important to both her parents that she simply have a degree of some kind. Sensei agreed to provide her with a job every summer when she was home, assuming she earned her black belt before year's end, and of that he expressed no doubt. It worried her that she was looking forward to summers more than to school.

Alex set his sights on the large state university nearby, and was attracted to engineering, although he hadn't decided what specialty. He had long talks on the phone with Claire concerning their fears and expectations about living away from home, and they agreed to write to each other when the time finally came to move. The school year plodded along uneventfully. Then came prom season.

Alex's school held their prom three weeks before Claire's did. Lindsay spent long hours hunting for the perfect sexy dress with her bored boyfriend in tow, and excitedly told Alex that she'd talked her parents into letting their whole little group of her three friends and their dates get a hotel room after the dance. It made Alex anxious, but he only shared that with Claire, and even then only after a couple of different phone calls where he didn't have the nerve to bring it up.

"So what's the deal with you, anyway?" Claire asked.

"Why?"

"'Cause I feel like something's on your mind and you're not saying it. Tell me and get it over with! Sometimes just getting something off your chest is enough to help, and you can tell me anything."

"You won't laugh?"

"I didn't say *that*." She could tell Alex was scowling at his end of the phone. "I'm sorry. Just tell me. And I won't laugh."

"I'm...I've never.... This is impossible! I can't tell you this!"

"Because I'm a girl or because you have lost the power of speech?"

Alex paused. He really wanted to talk to someone, and Claire was it, as much as he wished there were another option.

"I think Lindsay is planning for us to have sex after the prom and I'm not sure I want to. There, okay? And

I know guys are always supposed to want to or something, but I don't feel prepared or ready or whatever and, and I don't know."

Claire didn't feel like laughing. The idea of sex scared her, too. Only one of her group of friends at school had done it, and that person seemed to kind of regret it.

"Huh."

"Huh, what?" asked Alex.

"I don't know. I guess I just always assumed, you know, since you guys have been together this long and all, that...."

"Yeah, well, everyone always assumes stuff but that doesn't make it true."

"I guess. Gosh, Alex. Can you talk to Lindsay?"

"God no! She's all excited and organizing things and I.... Is something wrong with me?"

"I doubt it. I remember when Derrick walked in on Jason and his girlfriend in his room one time and he was totally freaked out. It kind of turned Derrick off dating for most of high school."

"How come Jason was having sex in your house and I've never even seen your room?"

"Where do you think the rule came from?"

Alex laughed. It was a relief to laugh. "So, Claire, I don't know if it's too weird to talk to you about this, but I'm really not sure what to do."

"I don't think it's weird. I mean, who else can you talk to? We all have to talk to someone or we'd go crazy."

"I guess." He was feeling better.

"And I think you should go with your instincts. If you get there and you want to say 'no' say 'no.' If you want to try it, just be safe about it or whatever. I don't think the universe will come crashing down either way. And if you get further than you feel like, and you want to turn Lindsay off, pretend to call her my name by mistake and it will be like tossing her in a cold shower, I'm sure."

Alex laughed. "Thanks, Claire."

"No problem."

The prom went fine, and the time in the hotel horsing around with everyone turned out to be fun. Alex did sleep with Lindsay, which went better than he expected, although she had to leave the bed and throw up afterward because she'd had too much to drink.

About a week later, Claire had her own prom-related crisis. Alex came to pick her up for the dojo and she wasn't ready. Her mom said she was up in her room and wouldn't come down.

"Can I please go up and see her?" he asked.

"You know the rule, Alex."

He looked at her and then glanced up the stairs. There was concern on his face as he turned to her again and said, "Please? You know nothing like what everyone keeps thinking is going to happen. I know it's a rule you guys have, but right now it's not a helpful rule, Mrs. Walker. If I can help Claire I'd really like to. Can I please try?"

She thought about it, and agreed he was right. The rule wasn't helping anyone at the moment and deserved to be set aside.

"It's the second door on the left," she said.

Alex set his duffle bag down in the front hall and went up the stairs. He found Claire's room and knocked.

"I told you, not now!" said Claire.

"Claire? It's me, Alex. Can I come in?"

There was a pause. "Does my mom know you're up here?"

"Yeah. So, can I come in? Are you decent or whatever?"

That made Claire laugh reluctantly. "No, I'm having some quality naked time alone with myself. Just, come in already."

Alex carefully opened the door and glanced around the room. It was the least girlie room he had ever seen that had an actual girl living in it. There was nothing pink or frilly. It was simple and decorated mostly in green, and there was a Bruce Lee poster on the wall. She had a desk with photos in little wooden frames on it. One was of the two of them that had been taken at a tai kai, which was sort of like a martial arts convention. They were smiling and he had an arm around her shoulder, and they were sweaty from the workout.

"So, what's going on?" he asked.

She appeared as if she might have been crying, but it was hard to tell now.

"I really don't want to talk about it."

"But you're the one who told me that's what we're supposed to do. And you were right, Claire. I mean, why don't you want to follow your own advice?"

"I just don't."

"Well, I'm not leaving until you tell me what's up." Alex sat down on the end of the bed and kicked off his shoes as if he were preparing to stay a while.

"Fine! Stay! But I'm not talking about it."

"Fine. Be a hypocrite. Do you have any snacks up here?" he asked.

"How can you always be hungry?"

"How can you be such a fucking hypocrite?"

"Shhh! I don't want my mom to hear how you swear so much!"

"Well, start talking or I'll tell her I learned it from you."

Claire realized he really wasn't going to give up. Once Alex got fixated on something it was hard to shake him.

"Okay. But it won't sound like anything to you, and then I'll just feel more stupid."

"I won't make you feel stupid. Much. Just talk to me."

Claire sighed. "I've been seeing this guy at school named Matt."

Alex looked surprised. "Huh."

"Yeah, I...I didn't let my parents or anyone know or anything. I just wanted it to be private."

"I'll say. Why?"

"I don't know, it seems funny to have everyone know your business like that."

Alex couldn't relate. Part of the fun of being with Lindsay was being seen with Lindsay. If he had to keep her a secret it wouldn't be worth the trouble, most likely.

"Anyway," continued Claire, "I guess you could say he dumped me today and I wasn't expecting that."

"I'm sorry. That sucks."

"Yeah," Claire sighed. "We even talked about going to the prom which is in two weeks, and I got tickets, and that's all dumb to be upset about because it's not my kind of thing anyway. Matt made it sound like a good time, and I.... Anyway, at least now I don't have to worry about any of it. I'm out some money, but, hey, maybe there's a market for scalped prom tickets, what do you think?"

"I think you should still go to the prom."

Claire stared at him. "Weren't you listening? The whole date thing is blown! Who goes to a dorky dance like that alone?"

"I can take you."

Claire stared at him again. "No, Alex, that's nice of you but...it's not something I should have thought about doing to start with. I do tai kais, I don't do proms."

"Yeah, well, I do both and I think we should go. Come on, Claire, it could be fun. You might like getting all dressed up for a change."

Claire was kind of torn. It would be better than taking Ben, and she'd already bought the tickets....

"What about Lindsay?" asked Claire.

"What about her?"

She gave him an exasperated look. Alex shrugged. "Hey, she's already had a real prom and a real hangover and, well, everything she wanted. I can't imagine she'd care."

But Lindsay cared a lot. She was furious when he told her about the second prom while they were standing on her front porch the next evening.

"But you can't!" she wailed.

"Why not? She's just a friend and she got dumped and I want her to feel better."

"Why is that your job? What about how I feel?"

"It's not like we're going to a hotel after or anything! It's only the dance and home again. We're even just going in my own car."

"But Claire is not your girlfriend! I am! And you can't do things with her that you're supposed to only be doing with me! Do you want me to be your girlfriend anymore or not?"

"Lindsay, that's not fair. I don't try to control anything you do with any of your friends."

"Well maybe if you had guys for friends like a normal boyfriend it wouldn't matter, would it?"

"I'm taking Claire to her prom."

"No. You're not."

"That wasn't me asking permission, that was me stating a fact, Lindsay. You're just going to have to deal with it."

"No, I'm not. You go, we're through," she said, seeming positive that he wouldn't call her bluff.

"Well, it's been nice knowing you," he said.

Her jaw dropped. "You are going to pick her over me?"

"No, I'm just being me. You're the one who decided that you don't want me, simply because you don't like me helping my friend."

She looked enraged and started pummeling his chest with her fists. All Alex could think was how ridiculous it was that all his jujutsu was worthless against a skinny girl who couldn't throw a decent punch, because if he did anything but take it, he would be labeled some sort of batterer. He let her scream and cry and eventually she stormed inside her house and he left for home.

He called Claire when he got there and told her about the breakup.

"God, Alex, I'm sorry! I really don't care about the whole prom thing if you feel like going back and telling her that it's off."

"No. No, I don't think there's a way to undo it. I think I want to get drunk. I've never done that before— you want to try it with me?"

"No, I really don't."

"Huh. This just seems like the perfect excuse. Maybe another time."

"Yeah, well, don't call me then either."

Alex laughed. "But you could be my designated driver! By the way, I have a question."

"What?"

"How did you expect to get away with going to the prom without letting your parents know you were even dating someone?"

"I.... Well, I guess I'm an idiot, because I hadn't thought that far ahead."

"Hm. Well, start thinking ahead now, because you're going to need a dress."

"Oh, shoot. I forgot about that."

"I had a feeling. You are like the only girl on the fucking planet who bought tickets to the prom and didn't worry about the dress."

"Can't I just wear a tux, too?"

"No! I'm taking you to the prom but you're going to dress like a goddamn girl for once, okay?"

Claire smiled. "Okay."

Claire went out with her mom that weekend and found a dress. It was awfully late in the season to be shopping for prom, but most of the girls wanted slinky things, and some of the more elegant (and modest) dresses were still available. Claire found something she liked in a deep blue that made her hair seem less mousy somehow. It was long and had a single strap over the right shoulder that angled high across her chest. There were tiny crystals in it here and there that reflected the light like stars. She usually hid her athletic figure under jeans and baggy shirts, and her mother expressed surprise at how mature her daughter looked in the beautiful dress.

Claire didn't have pierced ears and wasn't used to wearing any kind of jewelry, so despite her mother's urgings to accessorize, she decided the dress was enough. She also didn't want to do anything new to her hair, short of actually checking it in the mirror before she left, but her brother Ben wasn't having any of that, and made sure to be home the night of the dance.

"Here," he said, "let me part it on this side so it will look fuller, and show off more of the left side of your face. That's your good side."

"I have a good side? What's wrong with the other side? And how do you know anything about hair styling? You do television production!"

Ben said, "Please! It's in the gay stereotype handbook somewhere. Besides, anyone knows more

34

about it than you. We could give the brush to Alex and he'd do a better job on your head than you're willing to do."

Claire was agitated.

Ben gave her a critical look. "Oh, come on, Claire, what's wrong now?"

"I don't know. This whole thing just doesn't feel like me. Is it too late to back out?"

"Uh, yeah. I'd say so." Ben started running the brush through her hair again. "But why wouldn't you want to go? I would have loved to have gone to my prom! If John and I hadn't broken up before tickets went on sale I would have bought some and forced a big scene and probably been on the national news and I would have done all my interviews in my tux."

Claire grinned. "That would have been cool!"

"Yeah. Or maybe the school wouldn't have even cared, who knows? But, I'll simply have to make a scene and get interviewed in a tux on another occasion. So what are you worried about?"

"I just...I don't want to dance with Alex."

"I would! He's got a nice butt, and his arms are to die for."

Claire cracked up. "Don't say that around him, okay? He would freak!"

"Oh, I know. He always looks at me like I'm going to bite him if I get the chance. Maybe I should! Then he'd see my gay powers don't turn him into one of us under the full moon." He made one last pass with the brush. "There. How's that?"

Claire studied herself in the mirror and thought she looked rather good for a change. "Thanks. That *is* better. Are you free every day for this?"

"Yes, for an insanely huge fee. So why don't you want to dance with the boy? You touch him and move around with him all the time. When I've watched you guys do those routines of yours in the living room, you've always got your hands on him and you pick him up or he picks you up and you end up tangled together on the floor a lot. If it weren't for the pain thing, I'd sign up for jujutsu."

"This is different. Jujutsu's not supposed to be romantic. Dancing is, and I don't want to do it with Alex."

"Then don't dance! It's *your* prom. Do what you want. You get to decide what it is. If you want to jump rope all night, do that. And don't worry about Alex. He's only going in order to make you happy. If dancing won't make you happy, then he's not going to do it, okay? In the meantime, you're gorgeous! Why aren't you wearing any jewelry, though?"

"I don't have anything that's right."

"Well, I'd have gotten you something if I'd known, but it's too late now, isn't it?"

Claire went downstairs and her mother tried not to make a fuss and embarrass her daughter, but she seemed like she might cry. Her dad got worried all over again about Alex, and Claire told him to relax.

When Alex pulled up and came to the door in his tux, she was surprised at how handsome he looked.

He was startled that she answered the door herself. In his experience girls usually liked to make more of an entrance when they dressed up, but he reminded himself it was just Claire. She looked pretty, and not like someone a month away from testing for black belt.

"You clean up nice!" he said. She smiled and started to move out the door, but he caught her lightly by the elbow and said, "Boy, you haven't done this before, have you?"

"Why?"

"Parents want pictures, Claire."

"Of us?"

"No, of the fucking Easter bunny. Moms get super sentimental and want pictures, so we have to wait a minute and get that out of the way."

"My mom didn't say anything about—"

"Just trust me on this," and he led her back inside the house.

Sure enough, her mom was busy fiddling with her camera in the living room when they got there, and Ben was suggesting some pictures by the staircase might be nice. Claire thought she was going to die.

Alex felt her tense up and he got her attention again. "Hey," he said quietly. "It's still just us. This makes them happy and it will be over in a minute. Then we'll go have a dinner we didn't get through a drive-through window for a change, and we'll come home, and it will be fun, I swear."

He didn't mention dancing anywhere in there and Claire felt better.

"Oh, hello Alex," said Claire's mom when she finally noticed they'd come in the room.

"Hi, Mrs. Walker. I promised my mom you'd take some extras for her, okay? She wanted us to stop by our house so she could take some, but I told her I didn't think Claire would appreciate that."

"Of course I'll give her some. Why don't you stand over here, first, by the fireplace."

Claire looked miserable. Then Alex had a moment of recollection and said, "Oh, hey, I have something for you." He reached into his pocket and pulled out a small item. "I knew you wouldn't want some kind of corsage, so I got you this."

It was a simple necklace lying in a jumble in his palm. Claire picked it up and untangled it. It was a silver chain with a round silver pendant, and on the polished surface there was an engraved Japanese character. She only recognized the ones for kicking and punching and numbers, so this one was unfamiliar.

"What does it say?" she asked.

"Friend," he answered.

It was obviously not an expensive necklace, but she decided at that moment it was the nicest piece of jewelry she might ever own. She put the necklace on and stood for pictures.

Once they got in the car and started talking like themselves, the evening wasn't weird at all. Alex still swore too much, and Claire still threatened to knock his head off, and the next thing they knew they were giving keys to the valet at the elegant hotel downtown. Claire knew a lot of people had gotten rooms there for afterward, but she was glad to know she'd be going home at the end of the night.

The ballroom was beautiful and the music too loud.

"Better than the music that was playing at my prom," he said as they walked in the door.

"You like Boys II Men?" asked Claire with surprise.

"Better than all the Hootie and the Blowfish our DJ couldn't stop putting on. Do you think we'll escape the night without the fucking *Macarena*?" said Alex, and Claire shrugged as he moved on to asking, "Hey, how long before you think they bring out food?"

"Geez, Alex, didn't you just eat a whole bunch of those Dunkaroos that were lying in the backseat of your car?"

"Yeah, but that was way back in the car. Let's go find a table already."

When the food arrived it was pretty good, and the two of them laughed and talked while they ate as easily as they normally did despite the new setting. Alex kept singling out different people from Claire's senior class and trying to guess things about them.

"Chess club president, for sure," he said, pointing to a skinny guy with glasses.

"No! That's Bobby Sykes. He's on the track team—high hurdles I think."

"Really? No wonder we always beat you at those meets. What about her? She must have some student class council type position."

"Yeah, senior class VP, actually. How'd you figure that out?"

"I don't know. The way she's working the crowd, I guess. What does a class vice president do, anyway? And how often do class presidents get assassinated that you even need one?"

"I think she attends funerals for the biology frogs when they're done being dissected."

"I can see that. Okay, those two are cheerleaders."

"Right again! How'd you know that?" asked Claire.

"I just know cheerleaders." Alex surveyed the room a moment and then said, "Hey, would you like some punch?"

Claire laughed. "That's the first time you've ever asked me that where I don't have to prepare to defend myself!"

Alex smiled. "How do you know you don't?"

Claire grinned happily. "Punch sounds good."

Alex got up and crossed the room to the table with the punch and the ice sculpture. As Claire was was admiring the room a couple of friends came over to sit with her a moment.

"We're so glad you came, Claire! This is normally not your thing, so we weren't expecting you," said Mary.

Jennifer said, "Yeah, there's an after party at my house later if you and—who is that, anyway?"

"That's Alex. The guy I do the martial arts stuff with."

Both girls studied him a moment. Alex was talking with a small group of guys gathered at the punch bowl.

"That's Alex? That cute guy is the one you don't want to date?" asked Jennifer.

"Why not, Claire? He seems nice," added Mary.

"Well, yeah he's nice. We're just friends, though." Claire felt as if she should simply have that tattooed on her forehead to save time.

"But...." started Mary. They both turned to look at Alex by the punch bowl again. "I mean, why?"

Claire was seriously contemplating telling people Alex was gay from then on. Life would be so much easier that way, but Alex would probably kill her. He'd try, anyhow.

"You know what?" said Claire. "I'm going to go get myself that punch since my friend the date seems to have gotten stuck."

She got up and walked over to where Alex was laughing with Tim and James from her history class. She took the extra glass of punch from his hand when she reached him.

"Claire!" he said when he saw her there. "How come no one here knows what you can do?"

"Huh?"

"Yeah, we didn't know you were testing for black belt!" said Tim.

"I, uh...it just doesn't come up in class I guess," said Claire.

"Can you do something?" asked James.

"Like what?" Claire was a little embarrassed and she couldn't imagine what she was expected to do in that unlikely atmosphere.

"Guys, she's in a fucking prom dress. And it's not like jujutsu's a party trick or something," said Alex. "But you should see how high she can kick! It's really cool."

"Isn't there something you could show us?" asked Tim.

Claire shot Alex a look that said, *What have you gotten me into, you dork?* and he smiled broadly at her. He took her glass back.

"Try to grab her by the wrist," Alex suggested.

"Is that okay?" James asked Claire.

She shrugged. "Sure. I guess I can't get my dress all messed up that way."

James grabbed her tentatively around the wrist with one hand and she turned her own hand and easily slipped out of his grasp.

"No, you have to do it harder than that!" said Alex. "Trust me, you're not going to hurt her."

Claire shot him another look, and by that time Tim had circled around her and tried to grab her from behind. Without thinking she cracked him in the ribs with her elbow and started to turn when she realized how restricted she was in her dress. It seemed crazy to her that women were already at a disadvantage compared to men in terms of general physical strength and height, but then they were expected to hinder themselves further through their clothes. Their shoes were designed to hobble them, skirts and dresses limited their movement and dictated how they could sit or walk, and the cut of a shirt or blouse could make life more complicated if they needed to bend forward or raise their arms. She wondered if the dress made her appear pretty only because it made her look incapacitated. She couldn't wait to get out of it.

Alex was pissed. "Hey, what the fuck? Not cool. Sorry, Claire."

Tim apologized and winced as he rubbed his side. "Yeah, Claire, I just wanted to see what you'd do. Trust me, it will not happen again. Christ that hurt!"

James seemed impressed. "Can I grab your wrist again?" he asked.

"I guess once more."

This time he grabbed her tightly with two hands. She stepped into him, reached in to grab her trapped fist with her other hand, and pulled it free while stopping her elbow inches from under his chin so he could see how easily she could have clocked him.

"That is so cool!" he said appreciatively. "What happens if I try to—"

"Guys, I think Claire said she was done," said Alex.

"Actually, I don't mind too much," said Claire. This was starting to be fun. Much better than dancing. But they were starting to attract a small crowd.

"Well, if you want to use me to show off some moves, I don't care," said Alex. "Just don't screw up the tux so I can return it tomorrow, and I'm good."

Claire tried to think what they could demonstrate where she didn't need her legs too much. "We could do some wrist locks maybe," she said. Those were small and contained and less likely to draw more attention.

"Sure!" said Alex, as he set both their glasses on the table. He evaluated her outfit and noticed she had neither a sleeve nor a lapel to grab. "You have to do everything from a punch, I guess."

Claire laughed as she realized Alex was about to be the best dressed uke in town. "Can you imagine if we showed up at the dojo in these clothes? But you know, the tux in weapons class might look good. Very James Bond."

"You guys do weapons?" asked Tim.

"Yeah, mostly with a short staff called a hanbo, but some sword work too," said Alex.

"It's fun," said Claire. "You should come by and try a sample class or something."

"Maybe I will," said James.

"So, what are you going to do?" asked Tim, as his date appeared by his arm asking what was going on.

"Ready?" asked Alex.

Claire nodded and he tried to punch her in the face. She turned slightly, grabbed his extended hand and performed a basic lock. He came at her faster than he would have in class, and she responded automatically with the same amount of force, so he went down onto his knee quickly and grimaced as he slapped out.

"Whoa! Can you show me how to do that?" asked a guy named Carl who had been watching from the sidelines.

"You know, you really need the training that comes before it to do it right, but I can show you an escape if you want." She showed the small crowd how the weakest part of someone's grip was where their fingers met, and how if you turned your wrist the narrow direction you could slip through that spot. She described what a difference your hips made in directing the power of your whole body, and how you could use that to help free yourself.

Alex loved watching Claire teach. When she got her black belt she was going to be a great instructor, but they wouldn't be paired in class anymore and he was going to miss that. At least until he got a black belt of his own, but he doubted he was going to make it before he left for college in the fall.

Claire started specifically showing the girls who had joined the gathering by the punch bowl how to get out of various grabs. They were amused and eager to learn, and after a few minutes there were several pairs of elegantly dressed teenagers practicing wrist escapes. There were more people doing that than there were on the dance floor at one point.

Eventually Claire felt she was at the limit of what she could responsibly show anyone, and she didn't like the feeling of being sweaty in her dress, so she picked up her punch and asked Alex if he wanted to take a walk. They strolled around other parts of the hotel to see what was there, and found a karaoke bar, a gym, and a laughably small swimming pool. Claire decided she was about done with what the hotel had to offer, and as they headed back into the ballroom to get their things, Alex spotted the professional photographer set up outside the door.

"Hey, Claire, I think we should get a real picture."

"Why?"

"Well, just because. You're probably never going to wear a dress again if you can help it, and it might be nice to have later. We can laugh at our hair or something in twenty years."

"What's wrong with my hair?" asked Claire a little defensively.

"Nothing *now*, but people always look back at old photos and laugh at their hair. Besides, it might be nice when you go off to school to have a picture of us where we're not sweatballs in jujutsu clothes. That way if you want to set me up with any of your cute college friends you have something better to show them."

Claire laughed but looked dubious. "I don't know...."

"Hey, I'll pay for it and give one to my mom for her birthday, okay?"

Claire wasn't crazy about the notion, but she agreed, and they waited their turn in the short line for pictures. When they got up in front of the shimmery backdrop together, Claire couldn't decide how they should stand. The photographer wanted her to have her back to Alex and his arms around her waist, but she wasn't sure.

Alex said, "Hey, it's what prom pictures are like. Just pretend we're doing a setup for defense from a body choke."

That made Claire smile and the photographer caught it. They collected their things and said goodbye to a few people, and then Alex started to drive her home, when he got an idea.

"Wait, Claire, how much time do we have tonight? You don't have your normal curfew, do you? Not on prom night, right?" he asked hopefully.

"I'm sure my dad will wait up until I'm back no matter what, but yeah, Mom got him to keep it sort of open-ended."

Alex smiled broadly and said, "Well damn, Claire, we've got one more place to go then! After a quick stop at my house first to grab some stuff, okay? And I think I'll change out of my tux real fast."

"That's not fair if I'm still stuck in this dress!" objected Claire.

Alex thought about it for a second and then asked, "Can I grab you a pair of my sweats and a t-shirt or something to borrow? Because if we stop by your house to change your dad's not going to let you back out with me."

Claire wasn't ready to let the evening end, and she was incredibly curious where Alex wanted to take her so late at night. "Yeah, I guess. I really want to get out of this thing."

So Alex, still grinning, drove them to his house where everyone was asleep. He disappeared into his room long enough to change into jeans and a sweatshirt, and came out with some sweatpants and a dojo t-shirt for Claire. She changed in the downstairs bathroom where she had to roll up the bottoms of the sweats so she wouldn't trip in them, and looked like she was swimming inside the shirt, but she didn't care. She felt more like herself in Alex's clothes than she had in the dress she owned.

Alex was waiting for her by the door, holding a backpack, and they went out to his car again. He looked the happiest she'd seen him all night as he started driving.

"Can you tell me where we're going now?" asked

Claire.

"Uh, somewhere where you'll have to walk a bit, so I grabbed you my mom's sneakers since you're still wearing shoes that are stupid for walking in," said Alex, who rummaged in his backpack with one hand and pulled them out for Claire to put on. "I hope they fit. Otherwise I could piggyback you if I had to."

"No, these are okay," said Claire, slipping the dark blue Keds onto her feet, and glad to be rid of her useless kitten heels.

They drove past the edge of town and up into a hilly area that was famous for the colors of its leaves in the fall. Eventually Alex pulled over into some kind of parking area set aside for hikers, and shut off the engine.

"Now's the part where we walk, but I promise it's not too far," he assured her.

They started their assent up a path that Claire was finding hard to navigate in the darkness, but Alex seemed confident about where he was going, so she simply stuck close to him. They walked for about ten minutes when Alex finally turned to her proudly and said, "We're here."

"Where is here?" asked Claire, glancing around a small clearing high above the town. The view down below was almost hypnotic. To see your whole world condensed into a living picture you could block out with your hands was a little disconcerting.

"No, you're looking the wrong way! Turn around and look up," instructed her friend.

Claire did as he suggested and was speechless for a moment. That high up and facing away from the city, the stars were brilliant. The longer she looked the more there seemed to be.

"Isn't it amazing?" said Alex.

"Wow," said Claire. "How did you find this spot?"

"There's this guy at my school who is going into astronomy, and he told me about it one time. I was asking him about certain constellations, and eventually he told me this was where he comes with his telescope sometimes to scan for comets and stuff."

Alex loved the stars. He'd never given them much thought until someone told him that the view from the southern hemisphere was completely different. The night sky had always looked like a random assortment of decorative lights with no order to him before—like lights thrown onto a Christmas tree. Once he started seeing patterns it was different. And the patterns on top of patterns intrigued him. The fact that certain things were always visible while others were dependent on the time of year set his mind spinning, trying to picture in three dimensions how everything in the universe lined up to create the scene before him. The first time he went on a camping trip far from the city lights he was dumbfounded by all the stars. And when he realized the swath of stars stretched out across the sky in front of him was an arm of the Milky Way, and he was a part of that, it made him feel insignificant and meaningful all at once.

The minutia of actual astronomy when he tried to study it didn't hold his attention very well, so he never considered going into it as a field to call his own, but as something that excited his interest on the side, it never left. He was always trying to remember different constellations and finding new ones in books, and then hunting for them himself on a clear night. Alex wanted to share some of them with his best friend now that he finally had her with him up so late.

He unzipped the backpack he'd lugged all the way up the hill and pulled out a blanket. He laid it down and stretched himself out on it facing away from the town below. Claire lay next to him in his baggy sweats and propped herself on her elbows behind her, head tilted toward the sky. After a second Alex sat up and started fishing in the bag again.

"Here," he said, and handed her one of two flashlights that he'd also dragged along in his backpack. Claire sat up and took it.

"What's this for?" she said, flashing it on and off in his face a moment to bug him a little.

"Stop that! My eyes will have to adjust all over again!" Alex swatted at her arm and turned his head.

"Sorry."

"Yeah, anyway...flashlights are the easiest way to show things to someone in the night sky. From your perspective if I point with my finger it could look like anywhere, but the light beam reaches higher and makes it easier for you to follow where I'm actually pointing."

Claire turned her flashlight on again and pointed it up toward a small cluster of stars. "So you can see where I'm pointing?"

Alex switched on his own flashlight and matched the direction of her beam. "Right there. That little group of four near the Big Dipper?"

"That's pretty cool!" she said appreciatively.

Alex smiled. "Okay, so, you know the Big Dipper, right?"

"Yeah, that and Orion's belt are about it, though. Where is that, now, anyway? And is there anything else to Mr. Orion? Does he have matching pants?"

Alex laughed. "It's hard to see this time of year. Easy in the winter. It won't be out for a while. And, yeah, he has legs and arms and a shield and sword. But you see this group down here?" as he traced along a string of stars with his light.

"Yeah, what's that?"

"Scorpius. He was the slayer of Orion. Stung him

dead."

"Hmm," said Claire. "Not sure I'm seeing that, but okay. What's this?" She swung her own beam up and over.

"Draco."

"Okay, explain that one."

"Draco the dragon was considered the guardian of Polaris, the one star that never moved." And Alex laid out all the important features of the constellation, sketching around carefully with his beam of light as Claire followed.

"Whoever came up with these would have done a pitiful job designing dot-to-dot books. Very vague. Whereas, here?" she said, pointing up and farther west than they had been looking. "This is a raccoon."

"What?"

"See? These little rows make the stripes on the tail, and these are the feet...and here is the nose...and ears..."

Alex gave her an odd look. "You can't just make up your own constellations!"

"Why not? Someone else made up the ones you're showing me! They're not real, they're just agreed upon. If I want to call that star 'Bob' and can get the rest of the world to agree, then it's 'Bob.' That doesn't mean it was always 'Bob' or even has to stay 'Bob'."

Alex was sort of stunned by the idea. It was obvious when Claire said it that the names were arbitrary and not actually connected to the natural universe, but he'd spent so much time learning the proper designations for the things he saw in the sky that he felt a little lost for a moment. He knew the star she was pointing to was called Antares. The name had anchored it for him and had given it a place. But she was right. It didn't know it was or wasn't Bob.

"Now I think this one's a cobweb," said Claire,

pointing again with her flashlight.

"That's Pleiades." But Alex did have to admit the faint clump of stars reminded him of a cobweb. Those stars appeared as if they had settled into a soft, neglected corner of the dark, and they seemed fragile at the impossible distance he was viewing them from, no matter how immense and fiery they really were.

"Does this one have a name already?" asked Claire, as she traced around in the dark with her flashlight.

"Actually, you're overlapping two different ones." But the distinction was already seeming less important to Alex. He and Claire owned the stars as much as anybody. They could name them as they pleased.

He showed her what the two separate constellations were, but then he thought about it for a moment, and declared that the area of the cross-section Claire had pointed out could be a shoe.

"A shoe? I'm not seeing a shoe," said Claire, laughing.

"Not like a sneaker, like one of the girlie shoes you wore tonight. One with a high heel." And he moved his flashlight around.

"I do see it!" She smiled and propped herself up on her elbows again and gazed upward, entranced and happy.

Alex lay back and they both quietly took it all in for a while. But then Alex found himself studying Claire instead. She had a look of wonder and delight on her face that was almost childlike. Maybe it was a result of all his mom's prodding, but for the briefest of moments he pondered if they really should be more than friends. There was something beautiful about her face tilted up toward the stars. Something about her expression was perfect at that moment, and it spoke to part of him in a way that felt like yearning. But then she started talking to him again and the spell was broken. It was the voice of a friend.

"Make up another one!" she said.

Alex smiled and searched around the sky, trying for a change not to see the things he'd taught himself to find.

"Uh...how about a frog on a skateboard?"

Claire giggled. "Oh, I doubt it. How are you putting that together?"

Alex traced along the stars, sketching out the board and two wheels, and then the basics of the frog hunched over on top of it.

"Huh! Not bad! Although, honestly? It could be a hedgehog on that skateboard. Or a beehive."

Alex laughed. "Or a Northern Blue. Beautiful plumage, ay?" he said in a bad British accent.

Claire lay back down and laughed. "But he's dead! He's a late parrot!" she said in her equally bad British accent.

The two of them faithfully ran through the entire *Monty Python* pet store routine for the millionth time.

When they got back to concentrating on the stars again, Claire asked questions, and when Alex knew what something was, he told her, and when he didn't, he now felt free to make something up. Alex was starting to think he had a knack for it. He always came up with something that made Claire laugh.

"You know the coolest part?" asked Alex after a while.

"What's that?"

"That looking up at the stars is looking back in time."

Claire glanced at him quizzically. "What do you mean?"

"Well, think about it. They are so big, and to seem so tiny they have to be a ridiculous fucking distance away. In the daytime, whenever you look at the sun, what you're seeing is eight minutes old because it takes that long for the light to reach us. Many of these stars have been dead for a long time, but the light is only reaching us now."

Claire hadn't been much into science in school, and other than making a model of the solar system in fifth grade she didn't remember ever learning much about space. What Alex was saying was an amazing idea, and one she wished she'd been told earlier in life so she'd have had more time to ponder it.

"That's mind-boggling," she finally said, and she marveled up at the shoe Alex had found for her, and tried to grasp how it wasn't really there on so many levels. It occurred to Claire that for anyone staring back at them from near one of those distant stars, she might not even exist yet. Her planet could appear new and devoid of life, but somehow, there she was anyway. It was an interesting thought that long after she was dead, she might live again if viewed from a great enough distance. But that probably only worked for heavenly bodies, and hers was quite down to earth.

Alex was glad he'd brought Claire. It hadn't gone the way he'd imagined, but things with Claire seldom did and that was why he liked her. She kept him thinking.

"Hey, Alex?"

"Yeah?"

"Thanks for this," said Claire, tilting her head back up. The only constellations she could still find were the ones they'd just invented. She couldn't even remember the parts of Draco or Scorpius already, but the shoe was still there, as was one small duck and a pair of glasses.

"You're welcome." He looked up at the sky he now felt part ownership of. Leave it to Claire to change the way he saw the whole universe, he thought with a smile. Now that was a friend worth keeping forever;

not someone to date and, by extension, risk losing.

After about an hour of gazing at the stars, Claire was feeling cold in her borrowed t-shirt and they decided to call it a night. They returned everything to the backpack, made the short hike down to the car, and Alex drove her home where the light in the living room was still on. Claire had a brief moment of dismay when she realized she was carrying her dress and shoes and wearing her date's clothes, but whatever lecture she faced when her dad saw her was worth it for the night they'd had.

Claire asked, "Assuming you're not banned from the house after my dad sees me wearing your pants, want to come by tomorrow? I picked up that ninja movie from Blockbuster that Sensei was telling us about last week."

"Well, my social schedule is wide open now so I'm definitely free. Want me to bring a pizza?"

"I'd love pizza," said Claire, feeling a bit bad as she let herself out of the car. She leaned back in the window a moment and added, "Alex?"

"Yeah?"

"Thanks for everything tonight. I had a really good time."

"I'm glad. I did too!"

"Good enough that it was worth losing your girlfriend over?" she asked skeptically.

"Oh, hell yeah. There will be other girlfriends, but only one prom where I got to try and punch my date." He smiled. "See you tomorrow, okay?"

"Okay. Bye Alex."

"Bye."

She went inside and called to her dad that he could safely go to bed now, and she ran up the stairs before he could see her carrying her dress. She changed into her plaid pajamas, and before climbing into bed, she picked up the picture of her and Alex on her desk and studied it a moment. Sensei had taken it after a particularly fun workout session with the Grand Master on one of his visits from Japan. Alex was leaning down into her to fit in the picture, and the two of them looked really happy, but also sweaty, and her hair was messily clipped in a barrette. She loved that picture. But it might actually be good to have a real photo for when she went off to college in a few months. If all she got to take with her of Alex was a picture, it may as well be a nice one.

She slept in her necklace, even though she was fairly sure it would turn her skin green.

CHAPTER THREE

For Claire, the last few weeks of school after the prom went better than usual. Not that school had been bad before; she'd always gotten along fine. Claire was never particularly picked on or ostracized, but she wasn't much of a joiner, either, so she never felt specifically a part of the scene at school. She did what interested her and didn't fret about the rest. The closest thing she'd had to a trauma was her breakup with Matt, but that had led to something better anyway. She couldn't imagine the prom would have been any fun without Alex.

After the prom, Claire seemed to enjoy a sort of minor celebrity status. People she'd never talked to before came up to her in the halls and wished her luck on her upcoming black belt test. At least half a dozen people, including James, did decide to sign up for classes or sample lessons at the dojo. Now there was the matter of actually passing that test.

She practiced with Alex at home, but for the real test she was going to be paired with someone named Rob who was also testing for Sho-dan. Sho-dan was the official name for a first-degree black belt, and it meant "beginner." It was humbling to know that the years of work she had put in at the dojo, and the countless hours of training, all added up to merely a place to start the real lesson. She was scared.

Alex thought she was ridiculous for being nervous.

"You'll be fine! There isn't anyone anywhere who doesn't think you'll pass."

"It's not that I don't think I'll pass. I'm just scared of what it means to really be a black belt."

"What are you talking about?" Alex thought it would be cool to be a black belt and didn't see any kind of down-side.

"There are expectations that go with it, and I don't think I'm up to them. Plus, like when Tim tried to grab me at the prom to see what I'd do? That's not good, Alex! I don't want people thinking of me as someone they want to test to amuse themselves. I don't want someone to hurt me purely for the bragging rights."

"Tim was just screwing around," said Alex.

"I know, but either someone is screwing with me to see what happens and I hurt someone by mistake, or I'm in actual danger and the skills don't work. Who would I ever hit for real, Alex? How am I supposed to know what I can count on when there is no way to test any of it? "

"Well, your groin kick works, so when in doubt use that." Alex winced a little at the memory of when she had miscalculated her distance from him and kicked him for real. He didn't get up for over five minutes, but at least he'd gotten some decent sympathy from her for a change, and she'd bought him lunch four times in a row before she decided her penance was paid.

"That's true. Sorry, again, by the way."

"Yeah, well.... Anyway, I think the test will be fine and you should relax and worry about the after effects or whatever later. Oh, uh, can Pammy come? She's asked me like a hundred times if she can sit with me to watch you test."

"I don't mind. My parents actually want to come, too."

"Really?" He knew Claire's parents had mixed feelings about her involvement in jujutsu. They never would have told her she couldn't do it, but it was obvious it made them nervous. They were supportive, but wary, and he could tell they didn't like watching their little girl get thrown around. Of course, with as much sparring as he and Claire did in the house, he would hope some of their fears had been mitigated by witnessing up close that she gave as good as she got.

"Yeah, and Ben's coming, and Jason's coming to town and will be bringing Danny with him." Claire hadn't seen her nephew, Danny, in a while and was looking forward to the visit. Derrick and his girlfriend were thinking about getting married and Claire hoped more nieces and nephews weren't far behind. She loved being an aunt.

"Isn't he too little to sit in on something like that?" asked Alex.

"Jason can handle it," she teased.

"Yeah, funny. No, Danny—how old is he now?"

"Almost two. We'll have to find a babysitter if Jason wants to come."

"I'd do it if I didn't plan to be there, too. Can Pammy and I come by after and play with Danny some? I'll bet he knows a ton of new words," said Alex.

It was amusing to Claire how much interest Alex always took in her nephew. She had never known another guy, aside from Ben, who was so entertained by small children, and she found it incredibly sweet. He would have made an excellent babysitter, but people didn't trust a boy in that job. It struck Claire as both a shame and unfair, since she knew girls who babysat purely for the cable and cookie privileges, and Alex would have actually paid attention to the kids.

"Sure," said Claire. "I can't see why not. If you want, I can ask my mom if you and Pammy can stay for dinner."

"That'd be great! What kind of pie does Jason eat again?" Alex knew Claire's mom always made the favorite dessert of whatever family member was visiting.

"Pumpkin."

Alex looked happy. "Cool. Yeah, I'll be there."

Claire hadn't learned much in life yet about getting guys, but she knew that once she had one, the way to keep him was apparently pie.

The morning of the black belt test Claire didn't feel well. She made herself eat a little oatmeal so there would be something in her stomach, but she didn't want it. She reviewed her notes and recited the long Japanese phrases she was supposed to use during the meditation period before bowing in. She worried that she might forget the names of the techniques, or how to move, or that she might screw something up for Rob who was testing with her.

Claire had her mom drop her off at the dojo early so she could take her time stretching. She listened to the sounds of the traffic passing on the street rather than concentrate on any of the stray thoughts that kept coming into her mind and threatened to make her jittery.

Sensei set up the video camera and made sure everything was in order. He would administer the test and tell her if she had passed, but it wouldn't be official until the tape was reviewed in Japan by the Grand Master, who would make the final decision. Claire didn't like having her picture taken, and cared even less for being videotaped, so the camera added to her agitation.

Rob showed up, changed, and bowed in to join her on the mat. He appeared even more nervous than she did. Claire knew he had more reason to be, since she had seen him draw a blank during practice sessions, but she was prepared to help him as best she was able.

Eventually people started arriving at the dojo to observe. Alex and Pammy sat up front. It was odd to see Alex there in his regular clothes and with nothing expected of him. Claire's parents and Ben took their seats in the row behind. By the time everyone gathered who wanted to watch, there weren't any seats left, so a few spectators had to stand to the side by the radiator.

Sensei turned off the phone and put the closed sign on the door so no one would walk in and cause a distraction. He started the video camera. He bowed and stepped onto the mat and faced his anxious students. He led Claire and Rob through their meditation, they bowed in, and the test began.

They alternated techniques, much the same way they would have in class, but with a new, serious efficiency. There was no talking except for Sensei requesting in Japanese the performance of each technique. There were ten Sho-dan techniques, all of which had to be done on the right side and the left, and then all nine of the traditional techniques they had been working on since the beginning of their training. All of the techniques were as physically challenging to submit to as to perform, and by the end of the test the audience had observed a total of fifty-eight attacks followed by techniques.

For the people testing it was nerve-wracking and exhausting. Rob stumbled twice, and briefly blanked on a technique once, but overall did very well. Claire was nearly perfect. Toward the last dozen or so techniques, she was sloppier due to fatigue, but only

Sensei and Alex noticed. When they were done, they sat in silent meditation for a minute, and bowed out. Sensei turned off the camera, shook their hands and congratulated them both.

Everyone looked happy except the two new black belts. Claire was bewildered. She had expected to feel a variety of wonderful things from elation and triumph to relief and serenity. Instead she felt dazed and shaky and...sick. She ran down to the bathroom and threw up. Rob didn't go that far, but he sat with his head between his knees for a while before he was ready for his friends to take him home.

When Claire came back upstairs she was embarrassed, and her parents were worried. Sensei looked at her with tender concern and put a hand on her shoulder.

"How do you feel?" he asked.

"Awful, Sensei."

He gave her a knowing nod. "Everyone feels bad after they test for black belt. You're not the first student to be sick after that ordeal and you won't be the last. Don't worry about it. Go home and get some rest and maybe have some tea. I'll see you next week and we can talk about how you want your name to appear on your new belt when I order it."

Claire said quietly, "Hai, Sensei." He gave her shoulder a small squeeze and released her to her friends and family.

She hugged her parents and they headed for the car. She stopped to talk to Alex on her way out.

"You did great," he assured her.

Claire wanted to smile, but couldn't quite manage it.

"Are you all right?" he asked.

"Yeah. No. I guess I'm just really tired."

"You mind if Pammy and I come over still?"

"No, that's fine. Thank you guys for being here. I

guess I'll see you at the house in a few minutes."

Claire puzzled the whole drive home why she felt the way she did. Part of it was exhaustion. That was a long stretch to go without a break, concentrating the whole time, being physical and performing under stress. Part of it was recognizing the sheer number of mistakes that accumulate after so many techniques in a row. Claire knew she passed and did fine, but there were small things all along the way that she wished she'd done better, and they were all caught on tape and would be viewed in Japan. Another part of it was the realization that the new magic title of black belt didn't feel deserved because she was still only herself and didn't know if she were truly as capable as she was expected to be.

When they got home, Claire decided to run upstairs and take a shower. She dashed past Jason who tried to ask her how the test went, but she didn't want to think about it anymore, so she simply shouted, "Fine!" from the top of the stairs. She gathered a change of clothes and went into the bathroom. She could hear Alex and Pammy arriving as she stepped into the shower.

Claire didn't want to be rude and spend too much time away from everyone, but the water felt unbelievably good. It amazed her when she thought about it that anyone had the will power necessary to leave the shower ever. She washed her hair and used the body wash sample that had come in the mail. It was nice and clean, not flowery, and she decided maybe she might ask her mom to buy her some for real. Her mother always thought she should do at least a few things more like a regular girl, so she would be pleased to see Claire want to pamper herself that way.

She finished up, got dressed, ran a brush through her wet hair without bothering to do anything else to it, and reappeared downstairs. Ben was helping their mother set the table, and her dad and Jason were having a heated but good-natured discussion in the corner about some sports-related issue. Alex and Pammy were taking turns tickling Danny as he ran back and forth between them in the living room.

"Cwaire!" screamed Danny when he spotted her. He ran over and threw his little arms around her knees and when she bent down to hug him, he laughed and patted her hair and said, "Wet! Wet!" She rubbed her damp head into his tummy until he wiggled free and ran back to Alex, who hoisted him up and made him squeal with delight. It hit Claire right then what a remarkably good dad her friend was going to make one day. She could see that clearly in his future. She was looking forward to meeting those lucky kids of his and hearing them call her "Aunt Cwaire."

Mrs. Walker called them all in to eat. She'd put the leaf back into the kitchen table the way they used to use it as a family of six. She'd made a wonderful meal with several of Claire's favorite things, but Claire still wasn't hungry yet. She picked a little at her chicken and had a token scoop of garlic mashed potatoes, but that was about it. Alex, sitting next to her, dug in, and occasionally broke off bits of his biscuit to feed to Danny every time the toddler climbed onto his lap.

The general level of noise and activity at the Walker table was much different from what Alex and Pammy knew in their own house. The Walkers talked all through meals and the siblings were used to teasing each other and no one was afraid to voice an opinion. Most of the time to Alex it felt like a free-for-all, and he tended not to participate on the occasions he was over. It was not unusual at the Sullivan table for nothing to be said that did not relate specifically to the passing of salt or butter. His father thought order was more important than banter.

Claire was reluctant to recount anything about her test to Jason, but almost none of the other people at the table were. Pammy spoke with great admiration about how Claire had been able to take a guy down who was bigger and stronger than she was. Her father was proud, Ben joked he was going to stop stealing her ice cream out of the freezer now that he'd seen a sampling of what the consequences might be, and her mom talked about how graceful and confident she'd appeared.

"Not bad, Sis! Good reviews all around," said Jason approvingly. Claire didn't blush because she never blushed. The only one who hadn't said anything yet was Alex, and Jason finally wanted his opinion, too. "You know better than the rest of us whether she's really any good at this jujutsu stuff. How do you think she did?"

Alex swallowed the bite he was chewing and said seriously, "Claire's as perfect as it gets. She's going to run that dojo someday." And he helped himself to another biscuit while Danny started scrambling into his lap again. Alex was a good observer of other people but was often oblivious to how people reacted to him, and he missed entirely the collection of looks around the table. Pammy gazed at him curiously. The two brothers weren't used to paying their sister compliments so plainly over a meal and appeared surprised. Mr. Walker looked at Alex with a certain kind of respect, and Claire's mom pushed more potatoes his direction. But the biggest impact his small statement had was on Claire.

It got her thinking about something she'd never considered before. She was all enrolled in her little college for the fall, but she really didn't know what she was planning to do there. She was glad her parents wanted her to have a degree and a college experience, but beyond that Claire had no vision of her future. She had signed up for basic classes that would cover the essentials required by any major, but now she had a picture in her head. She would like to run a dojo. The idea excited her, and she started wondering what sort of business and Japanese studies classes her school had to offer. She would check out the course catalogue after dinner.

Jason broke her train of thought by saying, "Well, I think it's very cool that the next time I need help collecting payments from a client I can take my little sister along to rough 'em up. Good job, Claire."

"Thanks! Are you sufficiently scared enough of me now to tell me where Mr. Bunny Face is?" she asked.

"Never!" said Jason.

"God! Let that go!" begged Ben.

"What's a Mr. Bunny Face?" Pammy asked Claire.

"It was a small, stuffed toy I had as a kid that Jason and Derrick kidnapped and then promised never to reveal its whereabouts," explained Claire.

Ben said to Pammy, "It comes up at every family gathering, I'm afraid. But you know, it ends here! I am sick of hearing about Mr. Bunny Face!"

"Don't you tell!" said Jason, laughing.

"Claire, they tied him to a bottle rocket and blew him up the day after they nabbed him. Fluff and stuff everywhere. Not pretty, but there is nothing left to return," said Ben.

"Jason!" said their mom, appalled. "You blew up your sister's toy?"

"Only a few of them. Derrick's not here, so I'm going to say it was his idea," said Jason.

"I think you should apologize to Claire," said their mom.

Claire shrugged. "Mom, I don't care anymore. I barely cared at the time. If I had wanted revenge, I would have made sure you found those magazines Jason kept in his closet."

"What magazines?" her mother asked, eyebrows raised.

"How did you know about those?" asked Jason.

Ben started cracking up and helped himself to more green beans.

Eventually Mrs. Walker started clearing the table to make it ready for dessert, which was two delicious looking pumpkin pies and Claire's favorite chocolate pie, along with fresh whipped cream on the side. Alex looked so happy, that Mrs. Walker smiled at him and said, "Alex, I have to say, you are very satisfying to feed."

"Does that mean I get a slice of each?" he asked hopefully, and she smiled again as she started cutting into the first pie.

"So how is Sara?" Ben asked Jason.

Jason shrugged. "Good."

"Where is she again?" their dad asked.

"Oh God, at some makeup extravaganza convention thing down in Dallas!" complained Jason. "It's ridiculous how much of our lives is dominated by all of that nonsense. She is still working toward that pink Cadillac—at least, I think it's a Cadillac. Who the hell still gets excited about a Cadillac?"

"Does she have a chance at it?" asked his mother.

"Who knows? I try not to pay attention. That's her fool project. I mean, the truly stupid thing? Is that she doesn't even use the stuff! All that crap she puts on her face she pays too much for at the mall. It's like an anti-testimonial or something. At least it keeps her from spending too much of my money, since she seems to make something for all her effort."

Ben rolled his eyes in annoyance. "How is her thing any more stupid than your landscaping business?"

"'Cause my thing is a real job and her thing is messing with makeup."

"Jason, you are so lame, sometimes," said Claire.

"Hey, you of all people should be on my side," said Jason, laughing. "You never wear makeup! I'll bet you didn't even wear any to your prom."

"No, I didn't, but I accept that I'm strange," replied Claire. "You, however, like women in makeup. I'll bet you wouldn't recognize Sara without any on, and who do you think supplies it? Women are somehow supposed to magically be made up to please you, but no one is supposed to worry about manufacturing it or getting it out there? How is that not a real job?"

"Tell you what, when her lipstick brings in as much as my office park account, I'll give her a standing ovation."

Alex kept casting his eyes over at Danny (who had crawled up into his grandmother's lap) during that whole conversation. He was quiet, and at first looked as if he might not finish his pie, but when Pammy asked if she could have the rest of his piece, he took notice of it again and polished it off.

While Ben helped his mom load the dishwasher and clean up the kitchen, everyone else filtered into the family room where the sliding door to the back yard was opened. Some people stayed inside to talk, and Danny went to run around outside in the hopes of being chased. Alex did jujutsu rolls in the grass to make Danny laugh, and the tiny boy loved hiding between Pammy's legs. At one point, Alex lay down on the lawn and balanced Danny on the soles of his feet straight up in the air, which scared Claire a little. Alex promised he was being careful, and Danny had never looked happier, so she left it alone. After the toddler ran off to spin with Pammy, Claire lay down in the grass next to her friend.

"Are you feeling better yet?" asked Alex.

"Yeah. Yeah, I'm going to be fine. Now I'm just starting to feel sore all over."

"I'll bet." They were quiet for a minute, and then Alex asked, "Do you ever worry that Jason and Sara are going to get divorced?"

Claire was surprised and sat up a bit. "Why are you asking that?"

"I don't know. It just...it never sounds good when he talks about her and I keep thinking about Danny."

"What do you mean?"

"I just don't think people with kids should get divorced," said Alex.

"Well, gosh it would be great if no one got divorced, but just because it happens doesn't mean it has to be the end of the world. Besides, I may not be crazy about Sara, but they've stuck it out this long, so I don't see anything changing now."

"Good."

"Good? You don't care if they're happy together or not, so long as they stay married for Danny's sake?"

"Pretty much."

"Well, that's kind of dumb," said Claire.

"Why is that dumb? Kids need their parents. If you're going to make kids, you should give them what they need."

"Well, that's very judgmental and absolute of you."

"Thanks."

She shook her head and lay back down to study the leaves against the sky above her. She was starting to feel like herself again. Extra sore, but Claire.

After many rounds of spinning on the lawn, Danny led Pammy back into the house to get a snack, and Claire and Alex were left alone lying side by side. It was blissfully quiet after all the noise. After a few minutes Claire realized Alex had fallen asleep. That happened to him sometimes after pie. Claire thought of pie as kryptonite for mortal men.

She lay there a moment and studied him peacefully sleeping there. Claire thought about how much he had physically changed in the past year or so. There was stubble on his face now, and he'd had to start dutifully shaving every day since the beginning of his senior year. His shoulders had gotten broader in that time, too, which made a difference in how she grappled with him.

Claire tried to imagine kissing him. If she crawled on top of Alex at that moment, would he be disgusted, or simply succumb to something so primal? She decided she didn't know, and she didn't want to find out. It was too weird. Claire abandoned any stray curiosity she might have in that area. It didn't matter what anyone else thought, that was not who they were to each other.

She suspected that their friendship status would be what kept them together in some capacity in the long term. There were too many things that they differed on that she couldn't imagine putting up with in a real partner. Claire was getting more and more interested in politics and couldn't wait to vote in her first presidential election in the fall. She was hoping to help get Clinton reelected, but she knew Alex felt differently. There was a conservative streak in him that went hand in hand with his tenacity and his snap judgments, but in a friend she could deal with that. She was not going to kiss a Republican no matter how nice a date he had been at the prom.

When she realized the light was fading, and Pammy would need to get home soon, she gave Alex a poke in the ribs. He jerked awake.

"Hey!" he cried. "Why can't you be nice?"

"I'm always nice," she said standing up. But she

regretted a little waking him so rudely. She offered a hand to him. He took it and let her help him get to his feet.

"Race you back to the house?" he asked, but she started running before he finished the sentence and they arrived at the door together.

Alex and Claire each attended the other's high school graduation. Alex graduated in the top ten percent of his class, and Claire somewhere nondescript in the middle of hers. A couple of people from Claire's school remembered Alex from the prom and were happy to see him again. He made her point out Matt, the guy who'd dumped her, and when she finally did, he scoffed and told her she could do better. The only person who might have recognized Claire at Alex's school would have been Lindsay, and luckily they didn't run into each other.

The rest of the summer was bittersweet. At eighteen they didn't feel like kids anymore, but they hadn't tried living as adults yet, and it made them anxious. Alex was not looking forward to doing his own laundry and he was going to miss his mother's cooking. Claire was used to having her own room and was scared of getting lost in a strange town and not knowing anyone. They talked about their fears on the phone late at night, each telling the other they would be fine, but not believing it for themselves when they heard the same words back.

They used as much of that time as they could to play since they didn't know when the chance would come again. Alex and Claire threw each other around on the grass and stayed up too late watching movies and arguing about politics. Pammy had joined a summer softball league and Claire and Alex attended all her games and took her out for ice cream afterward every time. They tried to assuage Pammy's fears about being the only child left at home.

Alex worked hard at jujutsu but had lost hope of testing for black belt before leaving for school. He made it all the way to first kyu, the last level before Sho-dan, but didn't get to test for it. Claire encouraged him and said he could test next summer when he came home if he stayed in practice, but the dojo wasn't as much fun for Alex since they seldom saw each other there. They didn't overlap anymore because Claire was in black belt classes now.

But every once in a while, when one of the instructors needed a sub, Sensei would ask Claire to take over, and she had run a few of Alex's classes. At first she thought that might be awkward having Alex call her 'Sensei,' and that they would have trouble keeping straight faces, but it was no big deal. Alex was respectful and disciplined and took her instruction carefully. She realized he'd matured a tremendous amount since they'd first met on that mat at sixteen. She hoped she had, too.

Alex still hadn't decided exactly which area of engineering he wanted to go into at the large university, but the whole idea of combining his math and science skills and applying them to some practical design field interested him. His school started a couple of weeks earlier than Claire's, so he had to pack up and leave first.

Alex was not a good packer and had Claire help him. He knew his mom would have done it, but there was something less emasculating about having Claire do it instead. However, there were different frustrations working with her.

"You really want to take this stupid t-shirt?" she asked him in the middle of folding a stack of his clothes.

"What's wrong with it?"

She rolled her eyes and finally pointed out that as

far as "bikini watcher" t-shirts went, this one was particularly ugly. "Besides, it has a hole," she said.

"No it doesn't."

She frowned at it a moment, then put a bit of the fabric between her teeth and pulled. There was a small tearing sound and she said, "Well, it does now," and tossed it into the wastepaper basket by his desk with perfect aim.

"Hey!" he complained. "Okay, fold my pants instead for a while. I don't think there is anything offensive in that pile and I can't start wasting textbook money on new shirts right now. Maybe I should help you pack early so I can toss out every other one of your socks."

"They're all identical gym socks, so good luck having an impact with that strategy," she said. "Anyway, I just don't want people there thinking you're some kind of sexist dweeb."

"I appreciate that, but keep your choppers off my clothes, okay?"

"Fine."

They packed in silence for a while, and Claire finally spoke up as she was nearing the end of her task.

"Alex?"

"Yeah?"

"You'll write to me, right?"

"Sure, I already told you I would."

"I know," said Claire. It was verbal stalling. She hated the idea that he was leaving in the morning. She felt as if she'd never see him again, which was silly since they'd both be home for Thanksgiving, or at the very least Christmas. Claire zipped up the big bag she'd finished packing and stared at it.

Alex taped up his last box, then stepped back and looked at all the things he was taking and couldn't tell if it was too much or too little. He'd find out soon enough, he supposed. He finally glanced over at Claire and realized she was noticeably sad. Not in a weepy way, but distant, and a little wistful. Sad in a Claire way.

"Hey, I promised my mom I would spend dinner and all of tonight with my family, so I better walk you out," said Alex.

"Okay."

She followed him down the stairs and said goodbye to his parents and to Pammy who was helping set the dinner table. Claire was secretly glad not to be staying for dinner, even though Alex's mom was a good cook. Claire always found herself trying to start conversations that didn't go anywhere, but eating in silence made her ill at ease. Alex walked her out to her parents' car. Claire stood by the car door, not quite ready to get in.

"Hey, I'll give you a call later this week and tell you what it's like so far, and if my roommates are cool and all that," said Alex.

"Sure."

"Hey Claire?"

"Yeah?"

"I'm going to miss you."

Claire smiled up at him. "I'm going to miss you, too. I'll only have Ben to beat up on for the next two weeks."

Alex grinned. "He punches more like a girl than you do."

Claire pretended to be offended and went at him with an exaggerated right hook. Alex caught it and pulled her in for hug. They stood that way for a moment, their arms around each other, but neither of them trying to inflict pain for a change, and then Alex let her go and started jogging back toward the house. "I'll call you soon, I promise!" he said.

Claire watched him and didn't say anything. She

didn't like goodbyes.

She spent the next two weeks making decisions about what of her own stuff to pack, and enjoying time with her family. Her parents surprised her with a new Compaq desktop computer to take to school and she was thrilled.

Alex did call after a few days and said one of his roommates was great and the other one was a little annoying, and that it wasn't all as scary as he had expected. Everyone else was also pretending not to be nervous, and it kind of leveled the playing field more than he had anticipated. He sounded busy and upbeat.

As Claire packed for college she found herself feeling depressed. She knew she was ready to move on and explore things on her own, but she was going to miss having her brother down the hall and her mom to talk to and her dad to look out for her. She was going to miss her routine at the dojo. She already missed Alex. What if being in different states caused them to drift apart? She'd spent too much of her life without a best friend, and now that she had one she couldn't imagine going back. She needed him and wondered if in his new college life he'd still need her.

She opened the top drawer of her desk to see if there was anything in there she might want to take, and to her surprise she found a flat box wrapped in simple red and green paper that appeared left over from Christmastime. Claire was perplexed and searched for a card, but there wasn't one. She tore through the wrapping and discovered the card was inside the box. It was from Alex. How had he gotten the box into her room? The front of the card had a picture of Bruce Lee doing an impressively cool kick, and inside Alex wished her luck at school, told her to write him at the address on the back of the card, and requested that if she had a pretty roommate who

73

thought he looked cute to please explain he was really available. She pulled back some of the tissue in the box to find the picture from her prom. It was five by seven in a simple silver frame. They looked nice all dressed up with his arms around her waist.

She smiled, put the tissue back in place, and packed the whole box carefully in her suitcase. She had nothing to worry about. Alex would always be her friend.

CHAPTER FOUR

Claire and Alex enjoyed their respective colleges. Claire liked her small campus in the quirky town, but found it a little hard to adjust to all new people. Alex thought the opportunities presented by the huge institution he attended were amazing, and immediately found a new girlfriend.

They wrote each other real letters often, even though e-mail was easier, primarily because it was nice to have a reason to check the mailbox. Sometimes Claire would carry one of Alex's letters unopened in her back pocket for most of a day, and when she found a moment when she needed a lift, she would pull it out and smile to herself as she read about whatever goofy stuff her friend was up to. Alex usually read Claire's letters while still standing at the mailbox in the dorm lobby. She always made him laugh, even if she were writing to gripe about things in her life that weren't going well. She had a way of describing her personal angst that was still designed to be funny, even as he felt bad for her.

Claire lived a little too far away to visit, but since Alex was still in their home state, it wasn't hard to arrange for her to go see his campus. When Claire came home for winter break, his school let out a week later than hers, so he invited her up for a few days. She had Ben drive her there, and Alex would bring her back after finals.

Alex lived in a large dorm complex that was segregated male/female by floor. There were three people in a room, and three rooms to a suite that shared a bathroom. Each three-person room had a sleeping area and a separate study area with desks and a couch.

Alex had first thought Claire could take his bed and he would take the couch, but decided as much as it made him feel like her overprotective dad, he wasn't comfortable with her sharing a room with two guys she didn't know. He also didn't like the idea of her on the couch, which was too easily accessible to the rest of the suite if they forgot to lock the door (which was all the time). Alex had no doubt that Claire could knock the snot out of a guy if he tried something and was unarmed, but if a group of drunken idiots stumbled home and pulled some stunt, he wasn't sure. He decided she should sleep on the couch in his girlfriend's study area the next floor up.

Claire wasn't crazy about the idea, but Alex had made up his mind on that point, and there was no persuading him of any other option. Rather than spend her whole visit banging her head on the Great Wall of Alex, she gave in and met Tracy.

Tracy was blond and intimidatingly pretty. She was the first person Claire had ever met who she thought might have fake boobs. She couldn't imagine anyone could be as thin as the midriff-baring outfits she wore (*In December?*) proved her to be, and still have breasts that large without surgical assistance. Tracy looked like a pinup, but she was also smart and majored in communications, and at least made an attempt to be nice to Claire.

Tracy didn't ask her any of the usual questions, but her roommates certainly did when they were alone with Claire in the evening before going to sleep.

"So you guys really were never involved?" Mindy asked.

"Nope," answered Claire, trying to sound bored enough that they would drop it, but they couldn't seem to.

"But he has, like, a prom picture of the two of you," said Samantha.

"Yeah, but he just took me as a friend. It doesn't mean anything like that."

"Christ, leave her alone, already!" said Tracy, coming back into the room in her pajamas having brushed her teeth and removed her makeup. "If they want to say they didn't date let them say whatever they want! I don't buy it, but he doesn't ask about who I dated or didn't date in high school either, so why should I care?"

"I just can't picture if they hung out while he was drinking that Alex didn't try something," said Mindy.

"Alex doesn't drink," said Claire.

The three girls looked at her for a beat and then burst out laughing.

"Are you kidding me?" asked Samantha.

"No, I mean, at least in high school he didn't drink," said Claire.

"Well, he does now!" said Tracy. "And he's quite grabby after his fourth beer so that's why no one believes you. But hey, if he was sober the whole time with you anything's possible." And the three of them started laughing again.

It made Claire uncomfortable, and she didn't like that Alex had been keeping something from her. She knew that drinking parties were a big part of the college lifestyle, and she'd had a beer at a gathering in her dorm, but she had no interest in getting drunk, and she didn't think Alex did either.

But then she realized that wasn't true if she were being honest. Claire was projecting things onto him she wished were true. Alex had been curious about drinking in high school, he simply wasn't hanging with a crowd (namely her) who did that. Alex was probably embarrassed because he knew she'd disapprove, but she didn't appreciate not knowing what kinds of things he was really up to. She asked him about it the next day after one of his early finals.

"So, apparently you're some kind of party guy now?" said Claire, when he came by Tracy's room to pick her up for a walking tour and lunch.

"What? What has Tracy been telling you?"

"Just that you guys all go out to some bar called Hammered every weekend and that you can chug an entire pitcher at a sitting."

Alex seemed bothered and didn't look at her as they walked. "It's not *every* weekend," he offered up lamely.

"Oh, well, then never mind. As long as you've got your binge drinking on some kind of biweekly schedule...."

"It's not binge drinking," argued Alex.

"Please! Then what is it?"

"It's just drinking! Everybody does it like that."

"Not everybody," said Claire. "Justin doesn't." Justin was the roommate that Alex wrote her was annoying. She'd had a little time to chat with him the night she arrived. Justin was pre-med and nice and studied hard. He had a girlfriend back home, so wasn't interested in much of what passed for the social scene in his dorm.

Justin and Claire had had a fun conversation until

he discovered she was there as a friend of Alex's. He'd looked taken aback and shook his head, and informed her that her friend was a jerk. That had really disturbed Claire. She wasn't sure what had happened in only a few months to turn her friend into someone she wasn't sure she wanted to know.

"Oh, don't fucking talk to me about Justin. He never wants to do anything and he complains if the rest of us want to have any fun," said Alex.

Claire didn't know what to say to that. She was feeling out of place and unhappy and was starting to wish she hadn't come.

Alex didn't want to disappoint Claire, but he didn't want to feel guilty either. He felt entitled to experiment with certain things since his home had been pretty strict. That was part of what college was for.

They stopped at the oldest building on campus. It had a bell tower, and a sweeping staircase that predated any thought of wheelchair access. They sat silently at the bottom of the steps and watched students hurry by in the cold.

Alex finally said, "Look, Claire, I'm just trying some stuff, okay? I still study, I still get my work done, I go to all my classes.... I just want to have some fun, too. Is that so terrible?"

Claire looked away from him and pulled her arms around herself a little tighter. Eventually she said, "I just don't like finding out that you're keeping stuff from me. I feel like I don't even know you right now."

Alex was hurt. They sat quietly again for another moment. Alex didn't notice the cold anymore.

Eventually he sighed and said, "Hey, really, can you blame me for not wanting to tell you? I mean, you're acting like I killed somebody or something. Or took up kitten juggling."

Claire smiled to herself at his reference to *The Jerk*.

She recalled leaning against him the afternoon they watched it at his house as they ate stale popcorn left over from the earlier part of their Steve Martin movie marathon from the night before. Maybe she was being overly judgmental. Sitting with him so close he still felt like Alex, so maybe she should trust that and give him a chance to explain himself better.

"Anyway," he continued, "I still want to show you around, and there's a great sub place on the other side of campus that I want to take you to for lunch, so can we not do this now?"

She looked at him skeptically, and then Alex said, "The sub place has cheesecake brownies."

"Cheesecake brownies?"

"Uh-huh. With mini chocolate chips in them."

Claire thought about it and stood up. "Well, then let's get on with this tour already." He was her friend and deserved a little slack. As long as he also sprung for brownies.

Alex smiled. One of the things he had always liked about Claire was that since she worked out so often, she ate like a real person and not a rabbit.

He showed her the huge and elegant library, and took her by the sculpture garden near the art complex, and pointed out every building he had a class in. It was a good walk, and by the time they got to the sub shop they were both ready to eat.

They laughed and talked and felt like their old selves, and Claire started wondering all over again why Alex thought he needed to drink to have a good time. She asked him about it more diplomatically as she split her brownie with him, and Alex sighed.

"You get that my house wasn't all that fun, right?"

"So?" said Claire. "What does that have to do with making bad decisions here?"

"So, now I'm out of there, and I want to try stuff.

Without anybody thinking they know better and telling me what to do. Please don't be one more person telling me what to do."

Claire slowed in her chewing of her brownie as she studied him. Then she gave him a combination of a small shrug with one shoulder and a nod that meant she would let it go for the moment.

He understood why Claire didn't get it. She liked remaining in control of herself at all times, and the idea of purposefully dulling her senses or making herself physically vulnerable like that was unthinkable. Alex wasn't in the same kind of danger if he got drunk, so he didn't worry about it. He was having fun. He was a social guy who liked having people to do things with, and drinking had eased the feeling of isolation he'd felt on the big campus when he'd first arrived. When Alex didn't know anyone, drinking together created common ground. In one night you could invent an instant stupid history to look back on and laugh about.

And drinking was what the girls all wanted to do. He'd first kissed Tracy during a drinking game at Hammered. Alcohol simply made everything seem more fun, and he liked not feeling inhibited. Although when he was honest with himself, he did know better even when he was drunk. It simply provided a plausible excuse for reckless behavior, and he took advantage of that. Still, he wanted Claire to loosen up and see it wasn't a big deal, so he invited her to go out with a group of his friends after his last test the next day. She reluctantly agreed.

Not all of Alex's regular friends were available to go out because a few of them still had exams in the morning, but Tracy and Samantha wanted to go, as did another girl from their suite and three guys from Alex's. A couple of the guys had started drinking before they even left for the bar, but Alex didn't seem to care.

Hammered was a dark, scuzzy bar with two floors and a dance area. The music was techno and too loud, and the beer overpriced. The big appeal of the place was that women got in free, and you only had to be eighteen to be allowed inside. Anyone under twenty-one was stamped on the backs of their hands so they couldn't buy alcohol, but no one monitored who actually drank it.

They nabbed a big table by a heavily tinted window, and the one guy in the group with a passable fake ID got them several pitchers. Alex and Tracy were seated together toward one end in a corner, and Claire was wedged between two guys by the window. Samantha started digging in her purse and saying she wanted to play quarters.

Tracy was laughing a lot, and wanted Alex's attention since they weren't going to see each other for a few weeks when he left for winter break in the morning. But Alex was too busy watching the guy sitting next to Claire. The guy was already drunk and had put one arm behind her, and Alex didn't trust where that guy's other hand was under the table.

Claire was doing as minimal participation in the game as she could get away with, and Alex didn't feel like drinking much at all. He didn't want to get drunk in front of Claire. It did feel stupid with her watching. But Tracy was happily getting drunk and falling all over him and everyone else seemed to be laughing at nothing. The guy with his arm behind Claire had slipped it down behind her.

"Alex!" Tracy said, pulling his face toward hers and his gaze away from Claire's direction. "Alex, come on, you haven't even finished your first glass! How are we supposed to get through these pitchers without your help, huh?" She laughed and gave him a wet kiss that didn't quite land on his mouth properly because he was already turning away again. His attention had been caught by Claire muttering something to the guy next to her about keeping his hand off her ass.

About the point where Alex realized he was deeply unhappy and wanted to leave, there was a surprised grunt and a hard thud accompanied by the clinking sound of all the glasses on the table jumping slightly. Claire was holding the hand of the guy next to her under the table somewhere, and had forced his chin straight down onto the surface in front of him. Alex wasn't sure which lock she was doing, but it was a doozy.

Everyone at the table was silent except for the guy who was repeating, "Ow ow ow" over and over, and Claire who was saying calmly, "What part of 'no' aren't you getting? My crotch is not a public hand warmer!" She gave him one more slam into the table, and then she stood. "Thanks for inviting me out, but I think I'm done. See you back at the dorm."

Alex got up to go with her and Tracy looked pissed. "Hey, just because she's going doesn't mean you have to!" she protested. "The girl can obviously handle herself, so what does she need you for anyway?"

Alex watched Claire head out the door, and he was frustrated at being boxed into the corner with no one moving to help him get out. He finally stepped up onto the table and walked over it to get to the door. He caught up with Claire as she was crossing the street to head back toward the campus.

"Claire, I'm sorry. I shouldn't have suggested you come to the bar. You're right, it *is* stupid, but sometimes when you're not around I just want to be stupid, okay?"

"Alex, I don't care what you have to say about it right now," said Claire miserably. "I'm tired, I smell like cigarette smoke, and Mr. Grabby Hands has been driving me crazy. I just want to take a shower and maybe hang out with the Trekkies in the lounge and watch the latest episode of *Deep Space Nine* when it comes on in an hour."

They stood there on the sidewalk opposite the bar facing each other for a few moments, and then Alex simply apologized again. She accepted his apology, and after walking past a few more buildings and nudging her in the side a couple of times, she finally smirked, and Alex believed he was forgiven. He put his arm over her shoulder as they walked across the snow-covered expanse behind the law building.

About halfway back to the dorm Alex asked, "So which lock was that?"

"This one," said Claire, as she deftly turned while strategically slipping her hands around the one he had been resting on her shoulder. She applied just enough pain to guide him most of the way to the ground before she released him.

"Fuck, I can't believe I walked right into that!" laughed Alex as he rubbed his wrist, glad at least she hadn't face-planted him into the snow. Although he probably deserved it that evening. "Good choice, by the way."

"Why thank you. It's an oldie but a goodie." She was smiling now as they continued on their walk.

No one was home to let Claire into Tracy's part of the suite, so Alex lent her a towel and some shampoo and soap and found her some clothes of his to wear that didn't smell like smoke. She rinsed off quickly in the men's shower while Alex guarded the door. After Claire put on sweatpants and a t-shirt that seemed even bigger on her than the similar ensemble she'd donned at the end of prom night, she and Alex headed downstairs.

Justin was in the lounge among the collection of

guys assembled specifically to commandeer the TV for their Star Trek viewing. Claire waved to him (despite a look of objection from Alex), and he gestured for her to take the seat next to him. Claire was the only girl in the room, and really didn't want to sit next to strangers again, so she gave him a grateful smile.

"Hey, you're into *DS9*?" Justin asked her, not really acknowledging Alex to her right.

"I'm more into *Voyager*, but I really like Odo."

"Oh, you'll love this one! Odo and Quark are stranded together on a planet and—"

"Wait," said Alex, "Is this a rerun already?"

"Yeah," said Justin, finally looking at his roommate. "It's the one from the end of last month. No new episodes due out in December until after Christmas, so it's this one again."

"Oh, I'll totally watch this one again," said Alex. "Quark fucking kills me."

Justin looked confused. "Why don't I ever see you down here when it's on?"

"I'm usually in Tracy's room, so I watch on Samantha's TV."

"Huh," said Justin. "Well, what did you think of the B plot with Jake and—"

"Wait!" interrupted Claire, "I haven't seen it so stop giving it all away!"

"It's starting now, anyway, so I'll shut up," said Justin.

But he didn't really shut up because the enjoyable part of watching TV in the lounge with a show's fans was the community participation. People jumped in with jokes and observations all the way through, which added to the entertainment. And there were criticisms about plot details and discontinuity that caused lively debates during commercials for 1-800-COLLECT (to help you save big on long distance!) and the Army

85

Reserve suggesting you should "be all you can be."

It was a great time, and when the hour was up and they were leaving the lounge, Claire spotted the ping-pong table across the room.

"Hey, I've been playing a lot of ping-pong in my dorm with the girl across the hall, so I'm getting pretty good! Let's play!" said Claire.

"I really should study," said Justin tentatively. "I have one last exam tomorrow."

"Oh, just for one game, okay?" said Claire. "Then we'll leave you alone."

Justin glanced at Alex, who gave him a resigned shrug as an invitation, and he went with them to the desk to check out paddles and the few balls that weren't dented yet. They ended up battling it out in an alternately silly and intense ping-pong showdown that lasted until past midnight before Justin eventually headed upstairs. Claire and Alex took a break for a delivered pizza before continuing to play until nearly three in the morning. They had more fun than either of them had had in a long time. They laughed until they were worn out and then headed up to sleep.

Tracy's room was still locked, and it seemed too late to start pounding on the door. Alex decided to have Claire sleep in his bed, since one of his roommates was missing and, well, apparently Justin wasn't so bad after all. Alex slept in his clothes on the couch in the study area, and as he was drifting off thought to himself he should really give Justin a fair shake the next semester.

In the morning, Claire went up to get her things, but Tracy wasn't letting her in. Alex came up and went back into her bedroom to argue about it. Claire could hear them from the hallway, Tracy saying how dare he leave her like that and what kind of crappy boyfriend was he, and Alex saying that was stupid and what did it have to do with Claire's stuff anyway. Samantha finally couldn't stand it anymore and simply came out into the hall with Claire's bag of things. She told Claire it had been nice to meet her, and she hoped to see her again sometime.

"And, by the way? Whatever that was you did to Josh? That was great!" she added.

"Was that his name?" asked Claire.

"Yeah, and I wish I had a move to stop him cold like that when he gets all gropey."

"Let me show you...." said Claire, leading her through a couple basic defense techniques that were easy to remember.

After a minute of laughing and being absorbed in what they were doing, they realized Alex and Tracy were standing in the doorway staring at them. Tracy looked irate, as if her roommate were fraternizing with the enemy. Alex seemed worried that Samantha might be learning something that could get used on him if he wasn't careful. Samantha thanked Claire, and headed back to her room with Tracy behind her as the roommates started to argue. Alex and Claire wanted no part of that, and quickly went back down to his floor.

"Soooo...." said Claire after she'd changed and gotten her things together to leave, "Did I just screw something up for you again?"

Alex shook his head and zipped up his own bag. "Oh fuck no. Don't worry about it. I think she was hoping for an excuse to end it anyway. I'm pretty sure she's interested in the bass player from this band she likes to go see all the time, and now she's free to do what she wants."

"I don't know, Alex, I've got a bad track record at this point. I'm like your own personal relationship destruct button."

"That sounds fucking handy, actually," said Alex, unconcerned.

Claire bit her lip as she hoped it was possible for him to find someone whom she didn't irritate so much, and they could break this pattern. Of course, Alex would have to make an effort to choose more wisely. About lots of things.

Claire said goodbye to Justin and she and Alex drove home. They didn't talk much, but eventually Claire felt they needed to clear some things up or it would bother her.

"Alex, are you going to keep drinking like that?"

He continued to look down the freeway as he drove. "Yeah, Claire, I am. For now."

"But why? You still have fun when you're not drinking."

He cast her a brief glance before putting his eyes back on the road and said, "No, I have fun with *you* when I'm not drinking. I don't have what we have with anyone else. It's different when you're not around, Claire. Anyway, I promise not to keep it from you anymore if you don't lecture me."

"Well, that's something, I guess. Have you ever blacked out?"

"Only once, and it was in the dorm, so it wasn't a big deal."

Claire looked out the window. Finally she turned to him and said, "Do you promise me at least that if you see this start turning into a problem you'll stop? I mean, if it affects school or anything you're actually there to do?"

Alex thought about it. "Sure," he said. "If it gets to be a problem like that then it wouldn't really be fun anymore."

"Okay," said Claire, "then I promise not to bring it up again unless you seem to be telling me something that seems over the line."

"Sounds like a plan," said Alex, relieved that

discussion on the topic seemed to be closed.

After break, they each returned to school with the feeling of a fresh start. Claire had experienced ambivalent feelings about drinking in college before visiting Alex, but now she was resolved not to let that become part of her life. She didn't want it and she didn't need it. When people offered her something at a party and she said she didn't drink, contrary to all the talk of peer pressure, no one ever made her feel bad or left out. Half the time someone usually said, "Oh, I wish I could do that!"

Alex did manage to patch things up with Justin by convincing the rest of the suite not to blast music or be too disruptive during study hours. Justin was a decent guy when Alex got to know him, and eventually they became good friends and remained friends after everyone else from Alex's drinking crowd had drifted off.

Toward the end of his freshman year, though, the drinking did turn into more of a problem. Alex was honest about what he was doing in his letters to Claire, and she appreciated it, as much as some of the things he was describing were a little painful to know. But at one point he was going out at least three nights a week, and when he e-mailed Claire that he had missed a couple of classes and a quiz because he was too hung over, she called him and told him it was time to stop. He agreed. He cut back to only drinking in the dorm at gatherings there, and never let himself get more than a little buzzed.

Alex's first year of college was his year of excess and overindulgence. Claire found it interesting that by the time her friend turned twenty-one and could drink legally, it had lost nearly all of its allure.

Their sophomore year, Alex took an American History course that included a trip to Gettysburg. The

Civil War battleground was an easy distance from Claire's school, so she caught a bus and met up with him there on that Saturday of the trip. Alex got permission to have Claire join them on the tour. It was a chilly, fall day at the historic site, and there were moments on some of the hills overlooking the battlefield where the wind cut right through Claire's light jacket, but she tried not to look as if it bothered her.

The tour was more engaging than Claire had anticipated. To be in such a peaceful setting while trying to imagine so much death having happened right where they were standing was peculiar and unsettling. The professor explained how harrowing it must have been to be a soldier on that spot, and to be able to see the enemy approaching around the hill they were facing, but to know your weapon didn't fire that far. You could merely watch the danger approach and imagine your fate.

There was a War College of all things, that shared the town with Claire's little school, and it unnerved her when she passed it. Alex's view on war in general was different from hers. She saw it as the ultimate expression of human failing. He saw it as the necessary correction of injustice on a large scale. The only middle ground they could find to share was in mourning the loss of life and limb involved, but it was another topic they had to agree to disagree on in order to put their friendship first.

There wasn't a lot of time to really talk to Alex on that field trip since he was expected to stick with the group, but it felt good to walk with him in that sacred space. He seemed more self-assured to her than he had the year before.

Alex was glad that she'd stuck it out while he'd gone through a stupid phase, and liked spending time with

Claire where he didn't have anything to be ashamed of. He gave her a hug before he got back on his bus. She smiled when she heard him explaining to somebody before the doors closed that, no, she was not his girlfriend.

Claire liked her liberal arts and business classes. She found various people to hang out with during her time in college, but nobody special. College was strangely crowded but lonely in her experience. She made some effort at dating and got over her worries about sex, but didn't find anyone worth mentioning to Alex in her letters until Doug her junior year.

She had been immediately taken with Doug, who was handsome and well-dressed, because he took command of their study group in a way that reminded her of how a black belt runs a class (but without the threat of push-ups). He was older and majored in political science, and he seemed knowledgeable and confident.

The first time they stayed late after the rest of the study group had gone, Claire listened transfixed as he spoke with authority about the breakup of the Soviet Union coming up on a decade anniversary. She started to add something about watching the Berlin Wall coming down on TV when she was eleven, when Doug interrupted her to say how irresistible she was and leaned in to kiss her.

Claire's first instinct was to put him in a choke hold, but he gave off the impression he could have anyone he wanted, so she was flattered when he wanted her. She admired his intelligence, and liked being seen with him, and somehow didn't notice that he never really listened to her. All she knew was he dominated a space carved of loneliness and it was comforting. Although, she started to question things when after a few weeks of dating she was finally able to get a word in edgewise and tell Doug about her black belt.

He was somewhere between intrigued and amused by the idea. That bothered Claire, since that information wasn't something she shared easily. Telling people about her martial arts training was like asking for trouble, and she really wasn't interested in testing her skills in the real world if she didn't have to. But Doug seemed to be factoring her into elements of his future, so it was something he needed to know. Especially since her goal was to run her own dojo one day.

"Well, you would run it, but have real people do the instruction, right?" he'd asked.

"No, the point would be one day I would like to be qualified enough to be the head instructor. I know that's a ways off, but—"

Doug laughed as he drank his beer in the restaurant they were in. That part of the country was strange when it came to alcohol. You could only buy it from state liquor stores, and if you wanted to take some home from a restaurant you could only do it in large quantities, which didn't make any sense to Claire if the goal was to make overconsumption more difficult. Restaurants that you wouldn't expect to do a good business in a college town did fine on Friday nights if they served beer. Where Alex was you could get alcohol easily at the grocery store and there was an entire block of bars catering to college students. She wondered how different hers and Alex's experience with drinking would have been if they'd each been in the other's shoes where the rules were so different.

Claire frowned as she ran her fingers along the cold glass of beer her boyfriend had ordered for her, but that she hadn't drunk from. "I'm serious. Why don't you believe that's something I do?"

Doug gave her a playful tap on the nose and leaned

in close. "Because your beauty is lethal enough. Combine that with any more power and what chance do the rest of us have?"

Claire had never been told she was beautiful before, other than by her parents, or Ben when he was trying to talk her into some favor or another. It felt good. Good enough that she was willing to overlook the way he seemed to be planning ahead for them without consulting her much, if at all.

Doug smiled at her, and Claire was charmed as always by the dimple in his cheek.

"You'll love living in Rhode Island," Doug told her. "I've got connections in the legislature and have an internship lined up after I graduate this spring, and when we move—"

"But I have another year of school left after you graduate," said Claire. "So you mean after that. We'd have to be long distance for a year."

Doug cupped her face in his hand and smiled again. "But I'd miss you too much. How am I supposed to go without you? No, if you still want to finish school you could transfer. How about that?"

"I don't know. I like where I am and don't really want to feel like I'm starting over in my senior year."

"But isn't love more important? Why would you want to hurt me?"

Claire didn't want to hurt anyone, and particularly not the man who had made her feel needed and desired in a way she hadn't before. "No, of course I don't. I just think—"

Doug interrupted her with a kiss and said, "Don't think so much. You need to trust your heart more. And to trust me more." And in that moment Claire felt safe in how certain he was, and it was a relief compared to her worries about someday being an adult alone in the real world.

They had been dating for about five months when Alex was finally able to come out for a real visit. His school was on a different schedule, so their breaks didn't overlap, and he decided to spend his time off in March with Claire instead of going to see his parents. She couldn't wait to show him around the pretty little campus that she'd been calling home for the past few years.

Claire figured it would be fine for Alex to sleep on their floor. Her roommate's boyfriend spent half his life in their room, so she'd be a hypocrite to object. Stepping over an engineering major camping out in a sleeping bag hardly seemed to compare with the kind of uncomfortable evenings Claire had been made to endure that semester. She had considered setting Alex up in Doug's apartment, but it was bad enough she still had classes during his visit. Claire wanted all the time with her best friend she could get, even if most of it was spent asleep.

The first day or so with Alex in town was great. He did most of the talking, and he told her all about what interesting teachers he had that term and how much he liked his electrical engineering classes. He wasn't seeing anyone for a change, although she knew he'd gone through quite a string of girlfriends that year, and that he thought weekends on the big campus were not as much fun without a date. Once they were on the topic of dating in general, he finally asked Claire about Doug.

"So your letters have been...." His brow was creased, and his hands were forced deep into his pockets as they walked together. "I don't get the stuff about your boyfriend. It's like you think you're sharing details but they aren't really details so it winds up being kind of vague."

"How do you mean?" asked Claire.

"Like, you said at least twice that he's polite."

"What's wrong with polite?"

"Um, it's not a thing. I mean, it *is* a thing, but not something worth mentioning in boyfriend material," explained Alex.

"Well maybe it's a thing to me."

"No, it's a red flag."

"How is being polite a red flag?"

"It's not under normal circumstances. But if it's something you feel like telling me to sell me on someone you're seeing then something's off. How serious is this guy, anyway?" Alex asked.

They paused to sit on a bench along the path, where they were overseen by the trademark mermaid atop one of the college's buildings. March was an unpredictable month, but Alex had lucked out in terms of weather. Tulips and daffodils were starting to come up, and it was a pleasant temperature if you stayed out of the wind.

"Actually, Alex, I guess you'll be the first to hear that we're kind of pre-engaged."

"*Kind of* pre-engaged? What the hell is that? How can you water pre-engaged down any further?"

"Fine! Just pre-engaged then, are you happy?"

"I don't think so." He frowned a minute and glanced up at the mermaid, which based on his expression apparently had gone from whimsical to plain stupid in his mind.

"What is wrong with you?" complained Claire. "You're supposed to be happy for me!"

"Well let me meet the motherfucker first and then I'll tell you what I'm supposed to be, okay?"

"Why are you mad?" asked Claire.

"I'm not mad! I just...Claire, there is nothing you have written me in either letters or e-mail that led me to think you'd found the right guy for you. I figured when you did, I'd know."

Claire felt defensive. "What can you think you'd possibly know or not know just from my general letters?"

"I'd know."

"Well that's the dorkiest thing I've ever heard. I'm the one who's supposed to be saying whether or not I know. Why do you think you have a vote?"

"I'm not saying I get a fucking vote," complained Alex. "I'm just saying I'd know, and this doesn't feel right. Based on the stuff you've written, he's not interested in being a part of your life. He's, like, trying to remove you from it and put you in his. It's fucked up."

Claire had no idea what to make of that. Sometimes with relationship issues it seemed Alex was either overly sensitive or a total blockhead, and this had a foot in each camp.

"Well, can you at least wait to meet him before you make up your mind like that? I don't even know if I want you to meet Doug now."

"Oh, I'm going to meet him," said Alex matter of factly. "And I will try to be objective, but he better be great enough *I'd* want to date him."

"He's not your type," said Claire with a smirk. Alex thought it was funny how much he had grown to treasure that smirk considering how much it needled him back when he was sixteen.

The three of them got together for dinner a day later after Claire's last class. Doug kept an arm firmly around Claire for as much of the evening as possible. She beamed at what she apparently regarded as a grand display of devotion, and Alex recognized as a guy simply marking territory in a way that was both annoying and unnecessary. Doug ordered for Claire, and then pressured her into having wine which Alex was sure she didn't want, but Doug made it sound as if she were being unsophisticated if she didn't.

Alex was perplexed. He had to admit the guy was unusually handsome, but so what? Was that important to Claire? He honestly didn't know. His friend seemed unduly distracted by gestures that looked like caring but were more for show: pulling out her chair, standing when she stood, making a big deal about catching all the doors for her—as if Claire couldn't open her own damn doors. Was she so disconnected from being treated like a regular girl that she couldn't tell an act from true affection?

As they ate, Doug didn't converse so much as think aloud in front of them about his honors thesis, and then went on a tangent that landed them on the topic of women's rights. Doug was all for them. In theory. But then he started saying something about how it was a recent phenomenon due to economic circumstances, and the invention of the pill, that had led women to the point where they were no longer able to enjoy not having to be employed, and Alex couldn't contain himself any longer.

"Claire, what the fuck is he saying? I mean, I'm all for girls being fine to stay at home if they want to and it sounds good to me, but he's making it sound like down through time they had a choice about it. You're the one who got me to stop and realize it was like a system of free labor that's not respected very well."

Before Claire could respond, Doug said to Alex, "Women were very happy being treated with reverence, and not being burdened with the option of any taxing ambitions."

Claire looked startled, and she glanced at Doug before she turned to Alex and said, "I think what he means is—"

But Doug spoke over her to add, "There is ample

evidence that women today are less happy than in an era when they were given preferential access to lifeboats on sinking ships and having doors held open for them."

Oh, the damn doors, thought Alex. Fuck the doors. "You can't make it sound like women throughout history had a choice. They couldn't get jobs if they wanted to, they couldn't own property, they couldn't vote for fuck's sake back when my grandma was born, and hell, my mom couldn't even get a credit card without my dad's signature when they first got married. That's not reverence, that's a con job."

Doug smirked as if he were listening to something too far beneath his pay grade to bother with. Claire shifted uneasily in her seat and stole odd glances at Doug as he turned his attention back to his meal.

Tired of listening to Doug, Alex decided to salvage the rest of the dinner as best he could by only talking directly to his friend.

"Whatever, dude. So, Claire, when I was checking out some of the facilities here on my self-guided walking tour, I noticed they have a martial arts club. You never mentioned that. Have you checked it out at all?"

Claire was relieved at the change of topic. "No, not yet. I keep meaning to, but I've been so busy! I try to review my old kyu levels regularly in the gym here as best I can without a partner, but with classes and studying that seems about all I can handle most of the time. It does look fun, though. I don't know, maybe I should check it out, make some new friends."

"I think it's tae kwon do, but I'll bet they'd take you in. Could be an interesting comparison to try it, see how Korean and Japanese techniques differ, and it would keep you in some kind of the right mindset when you're ready to test again next summer," said

Alex.

Doug looked perturbed and forced his way back into the conversation. "Claire doesn't need more friends. And she certainly doesn't need to be doing that kind of dangerous activity. She might get hurt or bruise those pretty cheekbones of hers."

Alex stared at him. Then he sat back and said, "Yeah. Hey Doug? I'd like you to meet Claire? She's the black belt you keep putting your fucking arm around, and the only reason you have that arm is that she lets you keep it."

"Alex!" Claire was embarrassed and Doug appeared angry.

"Hey," said Doug "I don't know what your problem is, but I think I know Claire better than you do, and I've never seen her do anything to suggest she isn't anything other than the sweet thing I see before me."

Alex folded his arms tightly across his chest and raised an eyebrow at Claire in a way that asked, *Why don't you deck this guy?* Claire shook her head at him. But she found herself suddenly wondering what *was* she doing with this guy? Whenever they talked about the future—their post-pre-engagement future—it was always about him and how well she would fit in with his plans. Those plans never accounted for her family or her friends. Alex was right that Doug's plans all seemed intended to isolate her from them. That had sounded nice to be wanted exclusively like that, but the person he wanted wasn't really her. She did jujutsu, and it didn't matter if he could picture it or not, it was a necessary part of who she was.

"You don't know her at all," said Alex.

Claire wondered if this was one of those moments where having a guy for a best friend was not the most useful thing. She felt maybe a girl would have come along, made minute observations, and shared them in private afterward. But not Alex.

"Excuse me," started Doug. "But if you thi—"

"Yeah, no, fuck that. I am done with your arrogant bullshit for tonight. Claire can make up her own mind and do what she wants, and I'll support her no matter what, but I can't do this anymore right now." Alex got up to leave, tossing some money on the table to pay for his part of the meal.

Doug started to put his arm back around Claire while saying, "Good riddance, asshole. Claire doesn't need you."

But Claire stood up to follow her friend out of the restaurant saying, "Uh, yeah I do."

Doug watched her leave with a look of fury on his face that scared her. Claire felt she was getting a glimpse into something dangerous she hadn't recognized before. She caught up with Alex who was waiting for her a little ways up the street. They walked in silence as Claire shuddered slightly, and eventually when they were almost back to the dorm Claire blurted out, "Fine! You were right, okay? I see it now! So, gloat away!"

Alex stopped and waited for her to face him. "I don't want to gloat."

Claire shot him a knowing look.

"Okay, so I do a little," Alex said, as they started walking again. "But not until later when you'll be fun to tease about it. Not while you're hurt or something." They walked another moment in silence along the dark sidewalk, and Alex finally asked, "I mean, come on, Claire, what the fuck? Why him?"

"He...he made me feel special."

"You *are* special, so what's the big deal about that?"

"Yeah, well, you say that, but it's hard to find someone else who thinks so," complained Claire.

"That's fucking stupid. The only reason you're

100

having trouble is you deserve someone really great, and maybe that will take a while to find. In the meantime, don't settle for arrogant fuckers like Doug. You deserve someone more like...."

"Like you?"

Alex said seriously, "No, you deserve someone better than me."

Claire didn't know what to make of that, but she said, "Well, there isn't anyone better than you out here, so I am really stuck."

"Look, I don't normally go for that whole 'there's someone for everyone' nonsense, because I don't believe that. I'm way more worried about there being too many guys out there who aren't worthy of you who will see a good thing and try to snap you up, and then you'll be stuck with some loser and only he gets the good end of the deal in the long run. You need to be patient and a lot more discriminating, Claire. There's a decent guy out there for you and you'll know it when you meet him."

Claire couldn't figure out why Alex didn't apply such wisdom to himself. She had never thought anyone he dated made any sense for him. But what did she know? She'd been perfectly happy feeling swept away by Doug because she liked the idea of it so much, and as soon as she saw him through her friend's eyes she realized it was absurd. Claire was actually feeling painfully embarrassed by then, and kind of wanted to go hide somewhere.

They had reached the walkway near the entrance to her dorm. There was light from the building, but where they were standing was still fairly dim. They stood there in silence for a moment, and Alex finally said, "So, is the Doug thing over, you think?"

"Yeah," said Claire quietly. "Yeah I think the Doug thing is pretty much history. I'll tell him after you go."

Although something in the way Doug had looked at her when she left the restaurant made her wonder if that was wise. Maybe she should avoid a confrontation and let any items she'd left in his apartment go. It was a confusing mess and her head was starting to hurt. Then she glared at Alex a little and said, "Remind me not to invite you to my wedding one day if I've already put down all my deposits."

Alex would have expected any other girl to cry about deciding on a breakup, but that wasn't Claire. She merely looked as if she wanted to hit him, which from her truly meant something.

Alex gave her a grin, and then he moved to do a leg sweep on her. Claire's eyes flew open wide, and she sidestepped it and tried to get him in a choke hold. He laughed and did the appropriate counter move, and Claire laughed herself as they fell into a familiar sparring routine. She hoped briefly no one would think it was a mugging or an attempted rape happening and get the campus police involved. They were laughing too much by the end of it to worry about any outsiders misunderstanding.

Claire had missed having someone around to throw punches at, let alone whom she could really talk to, and who actually cared. It was hard to see Alex leave when the week ended.

Alex's big discovery the summer before his senior year was that he had a knack for carpentry, which he tried his hands at for the first time when Sensei needed help constructing a new weapons wall for the dojo. Alex was surprised to learn he loved woodworking. He loved the tools, he loved the planning aspect of it, he loved the smell of sawdust. He loved all of it.

Most of what Alex was learning in school involved a computer, and there wasn't much in his life that was hands-on in any satisfying way. Carpentry was satisfying. He got a part-time job at a custom cabinet making shop for the summer, and he learned a great deal in a short amount of time. He went back to school wondering if he really wanted to be an engineer after all. He still liked it and didn't plan on dropping out or anything—Alex's parents would have killed him before that could happen—but he tried to think of an active way to include his newfound interest into his life that had more significance than a hobby.

Claire went back to school feeling sad that it was her final year. She was going to miss the area which was so beautiful, and the town full of oddities that she'd become accustomed to. The stores kept inexplicable hours, the signals at the intersections allowed pedestrians to cross diagonally if they chose, and there was local food she was sure they didn't have in the Midwest that she would probably crave. She wondered how many of her new habits would fade from memory once she left the only place where they applied.

Alex and Claire both graduated with honors from their respective schools, but the timing of the different ceremonies overlapped in such a way that they couldn't attend each other's event. They didn't care about that as much as they cared about coming home and starting their post-school lives. After so many years of being apart, they were looking forward to living in the same city again.

CHAPTER FIVE

After graduation, both Alex and Claire moved back home, but Alex was anxious to have his freedom again. He'd grown accustomed to living on his own and didn't want to be in his parents' house. He worked diligently every day applying for engineering jobs in the area, and he got a response quickly from one of the local engineering firms that paid well. The minute he had enough saved up for first and last month's rent, he set himself up in a small apartment in the city six blocks from the dojo.

He was still interested in doing something serious with carpentry and started looking into the Army Reserve. If he joined the local engineering battalion, he knew from someone he'd talked to at school in ROTC that they did carpentry work there. It was appealing, but Alex wasn't prepared to enlist right away. Primarily because it required a stint of a couple of months of basic training somewhere, followed by the Army's special training for what he was interested in, and he didn't think that was fair to his new employer. He decided he could do that later, and also some carpentry on the side at some point. He pictured a house one day with a shop in the basement, where he could make his own furniture or cabinets on the weekends, and simple toys for the kids he hoped would be running around his legs.

Claire's house felt more accommodating to returning children, especially since Ben had never left, and Claire wasn't in such a hurry to figure out what she was doing. As much as she loved her teaching job at the dojo, it didn't pay well enough for her to afford her own apartment yet. She decided to stay home and save some money, and when she found a way to earn the extra bit of income she needed to sustain an independent lifestyle, she would move out. But Claire got lazy in that arrangement, and Alex thought she needed to get out of there.

"You can't keep living with your parents like you're in high school!" he complained one afternoon when they were having lunch together near the dojo.

"Well I don't have a big shot engineering job like you do, so what kind of options do you think I have?" asked Claire in frustration.

"You could move in with me."

That startled Claire. "Are you crazy?"

"What? You're an adult! You should be out of your parents' house and doing your own thing without having to report back to them all the time."

"It's not like that."

"Oh no? Well, how about I drop by tomorrow night and go straight up to your room?"

Claire got his point. She was still living like a kid with a kid's rules in a lot of ways. She knew when Ben wanted to be out all night he always called home to let their mom know, and he never brought guys home, not even to the first floor. He'd simply made that arrangement seem comfortable, but maybe she should talk to him about getting out of the house, too.

"How would that even work? Do you have enough space?"

"Sure. I can sleep anywhere, so you can take the bed for all I care. I'm fine with crashing on the couch because then I can fall asleep to the TV if I want. I do that half the time now."

It was tempting. It was more than tempting because he lived close enough to the dojo she could even walk to work. She still didn't have her own car, and sharing expenses with Alex might finally enable her to get one.

"Hm. What about dating? Wouldn't it crimp your style to bring someone home and have me taking up all the bed space?"

Alex shrugged. "I'm not seeing anyone right now. If someone comes along we'll deal with it then."

Except for the mental picture of her father hitting the roof, Claire was sold. It sounded both practical and like a lot of fun.

Within the week, Claire had argued with her parents (who didn't object as much as she expected, since the idea of their daughter living all alone in the city scared them more than her technically cohabiting with a man) and packed up her things and set herself up with Alex. His place was a basic one-bedroom apartment on the third floor with laundry facilities in the basement. It was in a more urban, interesting part of town, and the mix of tenants in the building ranged from elderly people who had been there for decades, to students who liked that the building was on a bus line to the university north of there.

Alex cleared out three drawers and half his closet and bought a spare comforter and pillow to use on the couch. He really was fine with that. He'd have slept in the bathtub if it meant having Claire to come home to each night after work. As roommates, they were comfortable enough with each other that small issues that could have led to problems got settled early. Claire never waited in silence hoping Alex would figure out what she wanted. She knew he was too dense to pick up on small signals, so she was blunt with him about doing dishes or dipping into her ice cream.

Alex simply liked having someone else around, and arguing with Claire was always interesting. He might not have agreed with her politics, but she never sounded ridiculous when she argued her side of an issue. She wasn't afraid to challenge him, and she really listened to his side of things, which was not his experience with the liberals he'd known in college.

Unfortunately, with the election looming in the fall, there was more tension than usual in that area, and their arguments started sounding less thoughtful. Claire was an active Gore supporter, and Alex made it quite clear he was planning to vote for Bush. Claire's clock radio went off every morning set to NPR which drove Alex crazy, but not quite as crazy as his car stereo being set to Rush Limbaugh drove Claire.

"How can you listen to that crazy fat man?" she would say whenever Alex repeated something from the program to try and support an argument he was making.

"Ad hominem attacks don't fucking support your side very well," he would complain.

"What? He *is* fat! And he *is* crazy! Okay, so maybe fat isn't relevant, but come on Alex! It's all so, so...slanted!"

"And you don't think NPR is slanted?"

"But they make a real attempt at simply presenting information and balance. Rush is masquerading as information and shouts his bias from the rooftop."

"But, see, he admits that. You know where he stands and that's honest. Why should I trust a source that pretends not to have a bias when that can't possibly be true?"

"I don't even know where to start with that kind of logic," said Claire. "I want to hear facts presented clearly so I can decide for myself what to think about them. Rush tells you how to think. You don't find it creepy when people call him and say 'ditto' like they're programed to agree?"

"What's wrong with agreeing? Why do you even bother to talk to me about certain things if you're not hoping to get me to agree?"

"I want you to agree because you think my argument is sound, not because you don't want to bother to think it through yourself."

"But you know I do think things through myself, so what difference does it make where I get the information? It's all the same information," said Alex.

"But opinion isn't the same thing as information! He's an entertainer, not a reporter."

"How is that different from you watching the Daily Show?"

"Yeah, but Alex, I don't get my news from there. They do funny stuff with the news, but they expect you to know the headlines already before they comment on them. It's not the same."

"I don't see the difference, and anyway, Gore is going to lose so get used to it."

"He is not going to lose!"

As much as such arguments got heated and more frequent the closer the election became, neither of them took it personally. It was one of the biggest advantages of having always remained just friends. As a romantic couple, it likely would have proved too much. Such disagreements would have felt like attacks on their individual characters if the two of them were on a more intimate level, but as friends it didn't matter. If anything, it clarified the relationship they did have even further, satisfying each of them that they were not right for one another beyond close friendship status.

One of the few real conflicts they ever encountered during the time they lived together had to do with Ben, because in that case it did have personal implications. The Walker house had to be fumigated for an infestation and the whole place was going to be tented and clouded with poison. Claire's parents simply planned the whole event around their vacation and used the opportunity to take a cruise and declare it a second honeymoon. Ben was stuck, so Claire invited him to stay with her. She didn't think much of it because it was family and it was only for a week, but Alex flipped out.

"But I can't live here with him for a week!" he insisted.

"Why not?"

Alex gave her a look, and she knew what it meant, but she was going to make him say it. Claire waited patiently with her arms crossed in front of her.

"Fine! You want to hear it? Because he's gay, all right? I don't want to live in an apartment with a guy who's gay."

"Alex, it just doesn't make any sense. What are you really afraid of?" Claire wanted to know.

"I'm not afraid," he protested.

"Well, what else is it? Hate and discomfort and all of that all come from some level of fear."

"I don't hate anybody!"

"I didn't say you did! You're in the discomfort category and it's still a fear-based reaction."

Alex did not want to be talking about this, but Claire was not going to let it go. It mattered to her in a way it didn't to him because it was personal, and he could appreciate that. He sighed, and decided it was a conversation he'd better simply get over with.

"I can't think the gay thing is weird without it being somehow hateful?"

"Sure, you can think it's weird all you want. The problem is when it affects your behavior and makes you treat people unfairly."

"I treat Ben fine."

"Yeah, if I'm right there and you have an escape route clearly envisioned. I'm just saying that if it were Jason or Derrick you wouldn't care about one of them staying here for a week, would you?"

"Probably not," he admitted.

"And even if it were a girl friend of mine, like Mary or Jennifer, you still wouldn't have a problem."

"Well, no. Especially not if it were Jennifer."

"Okay, so the problem is with you, not with Ben, because Ben's relationship to you is about the same as you to any of those other people. None of those people —including Jennifer, by the way—are attracted to you."

"But, see, if Jennifer were, it wouldn't bother me."

"So what? You can't control what people are thinking. Who cares what a gay guy might be thinking about you?"

"But, Claire! You are not being fair about this, because I don't feel comfortable around someone who...." He didn't know how to finish the sentence.

"Who what? Who might be attracted to you but you don't like back? Come on! Ben is not going to rape you or something."

"I know that, but if a guy hit on me, I just...I don't know what the fuck I'm supposed to do."

"Oh, I didn't realize you were God's gift to everyone attracted to men, so that is a problem. God, Alex, get over yourself!"

Alex was annoyed. "I'm serious! I don't want some guy coming on to me."

"This is ridiculous anyway," said Claire, "because

you are not his type."

"What do you mean?" asked Alex in surprise.

"You mean besides the fact that you're straight? That's big right there. Kind of a deal breaker, really, if you thought about it for two seconds. And he likes blondes with a lighter build than you've got. You are way too bulky for him. Trust me, you are not on his radar screen."

Alex was genuinely taken aback. He was certainly not disappointed, but there was something about being lumped in with a whole category and flat out rejected that was disconcerting. For the first time he considered what it probably felt like to Claire when he spoke about what his type was and how she wasn't in it. On one level it didn't matter, but rejection was rejection.

"Also," said Claire, "you can't be worried about what other people are thinking anyway. Do you think every woman you look at and have thoughts about would be pleased to know you're doing it? No way! But you're entitled to your thoughts and so what? If a gay guy sees you and has thoughts of his own, you can't control that, so forget about it! It only concerns you if someone acts on it."

"But why isn't that something to be legitimately worried about?"

"Look," said Claire, "If I asked you out what would you say?"

"I would say 'no' and 'what have you done with Claire?'"

"Right. And if Ben got hit on the head and woke up attracted to straight guys with less fashion sense than I've got, and asked you out, you would just say 'no' and that would be the end of it."

Alex thought about it. That made sense, and he'd turned girls down before, but the idea of a guy looking at him that way made him shudder.

Claire studied her friend carefully a moment. "You want to know what I really think?"

Alex looked at her quizzically.

"I think straight guys who are afraid of gays are really afraid of being looked at the same way they look at women, because they know they have something to be ashamed of there."

"Oh come on!"

"Sorry! But I think you know how guys think, and you feel that's okay for you directed outwardly, but the mere idea that you could be the recipient of that same treatment—even just in someone's head—is upsetting, and frankly kind of revealing. Every guy I know who treats women well, and is secure in his masculinity, does not have a problem with gays."

"I treat women fine!" protested Alex.

Claire studied him a moment in a way that made him feel exposed. "What about in your head? I think your drinking phase a few years back showed a lot of what you would do if you could. Sure, you're a perfect gentleman now, but in your head are you still all grabby? Why should you be allowed out in society if you're going to subject women to that?"

"What? How did I end up getting accused of something, here? You're going to hold me accountable for any stray thought that doesn't...? That just because a woman who wouldn't want me looking at her that way is.... It's not fair to me that...." And Alex stopped as something clicked.

Claire sighed. "Ben's a good guy, Alex. I love him. If you'd just talk to him like a person and stop thinking about yourself for a change, you'd see that."

"Yeah, well I'm still not crazy about the idea, but I guess he can stay for a week. But he's staying in the bedroom with you! And I might not shower the whole week so be prepared for that."

"You are such a moron," said Claire with a small grin.

"Hey, I just gave you what you wanted!"

"I'm eternally grateful, but you're still a moron."

The week with Ben turned out to be enjoyable, as much as Alex almost hated to admit it. Ben was an excellent cook and decided to earn his keep by taking over the meals. He even called Mrs. Sullivan and found out what Alex's favorite foods were, so instead of their usual fare of ramen and frozen pizza, they were treated to meatloaf and baked mac and cheese and chicken Kiev and Swedish meatballs with mashed potatoes. For breakfast there were banana pancakes every morning. By the third day Alex was making sure to get home early enough from work to eat while everything was still hot. And he did shower, but he got fully dressed in the bathroom, which Claire found hilarious since he occasionally wandered around in his boxers if only the two of them were home.

In addition to being a good cook, Ben was funny. He always told a good story, and Claire knew from experience that sometimes he exaggerated for effect, but usually he was just being keenly observant about absurd details. Instead of turning on the TV while he ate, Alex would sit at the small table and laugh with Claire and her brother. It was fascinating for Alex to watch her with someone she had an even longer history of inside jokes with, and they were constantly having to fill him in on background to certain references.

"Claire never told you about the skunk?" asked Ben incredulously.

"What skunk?" asked Alex.

"No! Don't tell that one, or I'll tell about when Dad caught you in Mom's shoes!" said Claire.

"Tell away! I have nothing to be ashamed of because I looked great in those shoes," said Ben. "Anyway, we were on our annual death march in the deep woods that Dad always thought would make a man out of all of his kids—it only worked on Claire—and she was trailing behind as usual when all of a sudden she was talking about some kitty."

"Hey, is it my fault that he drags us into the woods without telling us anything about what we might find there? Besides, I was what? Like, three?"

"Sweetheart, you were at least six because I was in second grade and I did a story with illustrations about it with stink lines over you and everything."

Alex laughed. "What did she do?"

"She wanted to pet the nice kitty with the white stripes up its back, and cornered the damn thing up against a tree! We heard this horrible screaming and Dad—who was surely worried about self-preservation because coming home to Mom with one fewer kid was not an option—bolts into the woods and runs smack into stinky, here."

"God, that smell was like pain," said Claire wrinkling up her nose at the memory.

"Tell me about it," said Ben. "It was too late to go home and dunk Claire in a tub of tomato juice, so she got the tent all to herself and the rest of us had to sleep out under the bats."

"Why wasn't Claire outside since she could have used the airing out?" asked Alex.

"Did you miss the word 'bats'? We were near some bat-tastic location and they fluttered around all night and Claire was a total spaz about it and wanted to be in the tent."

"I forget, did we have to throw that tent away?" asked Claire.

"God, no! We got that new one for the next year because Mom finally agreed to come along and wanted one she could stand in, but that other one resurfaced in all its stinky glory when I needed it for Scouts."

"You were in Scouts?" asked Alex with surprise.

"Not for long, because I ended up in theater and A.V. club which sucked up all my after-school time, but it wasn't bad. Compared to Dad's camping excursions it was downright dainty."

"Huh," said Alex. "Yeah, I nearly made it to Eagle Scout but I kind of lost interest halfway through high school."

"You never told me you were in Scouts!" said Claire to Alex.

"I didn't?"

"No! How can I have known you all this time and not known that?" she asked.

"I have no idea," said Alex with a laugh.

"Well, see, there's always something to learn," said Ben. "Even for the Bobbsey Twins."

"Who the hell are the Bobbsey Twins?" asked Claire.

Alex shrugged while Claire cracked up and Ben rolled his eyes.

The nicest moment for Claire out of that week was the Saturday when she came back early from the dojo. Originally when she went off to teach for the day, Alex had planned to clear out so he wouldn't have to be alone in the apartment with Ben. But after their morning pancakes, Alex wound up hanging out and helping with the dishes.

Alex was still on a bit of a hair trigger, and if he'd caught Ben checking him out or doing anything he considered weird, he would have bolted. However, getting to know Ben as Claire's brother, instead of Claire's gay brother, had been enlightening. Alex was starting to feel a bit ashamed because there was nothing not to like about Ben when he really thought about it. Alex had simply dumped all of his preconceived notions about what gay men were like onto him, and he was starting to realize how stupid that was. And what was he scared of? He decided Claire was right when she said on some level his discomfort was based on fear, but he still hadn't quite sorted out why. One thing he did know for sure was that it was nice to spend time with someone who never asked why he and Claire weren't a couple, and Alex told him so.

"Please," said Ben, passing a freshly washed dish into Alex's hands to dry. "I knew before that prom you were not right for each other."

"What makes you say that?" This was new. Most people seemed resigned to Claire and Alex's reality, but no one had ever endorsed it before. Alex was intrigued.

Ben paused in his dish washing and looked at him seriously. "Have you ever seen her cry, Alex?"

Alex shook his head.

"Me neither," said Ben. "Not even when that skunk blasted her in the face as a little kid, she did not let anyone see her cry. The right guy for her is the one she feels safe enough with to finally cry in front of when she needs to."

"But I make her feel safe," said Alex, a little confused.

"Yeah, and so do I, and so does Mom, and so do a lot of people in a lot of different ways, but not in the one way she needs. She needs you, Alex, but I'm holding out hope she'll find that other guy she needs, too."

"Huh."

That was the moment Claire happened to return to the apartment. She'd forgotten her student roster in her room and come back to fetch it. She had no clue what Ben and Alex had been discussing, but it made her happy to see the two men she was most crazy about in the world at the time, standing side by side in the kitchen in a real conversation. It was a big improvement over the skittery Alex from the beginning of the week. He wasn't ready to attend a gay pride parade, but he wasn't going to have to hold her hand if they passed a building with a rainbow flag on it either. It was progress via one gay brother at a time.

Alex and Claire shared the apartment happily for a half a year, and more happily once they survived the 2000 election debacle and its peculiar aftermath. The two of them passed out on the couch together with a bowl of popcorn while awaiting the infamous returns from Florida, and couldn't believe in the morning that it still wasn't over. Alex was enough of a gentleman not to rub Claire's nose in the results when they finally came since she was bitterly disappointed, but they found a way to put it behind them and move on. The two of them figured if they could survive that contentious event as roommates, they could survive anything. Then Beth moved in down the hall.

Alex didn't even notice Beth right away, but she apparently noticed him because she started talking with him one day by the mailboxes, and worked her way into his life from there. Beth was blond and trendy and not shy. Alex thought she was pretty and enjoyed flirting right back, which seemed to be fine with Beth until she noticed Claire coming in and out of the same apartment.

Alex was talking to Beth outside her door one afternoon as Claire dashed out of their door with her dojo bag slung over her shoulder, and Beth finally said, "So, who is that, anyway?"

"That's my roommate."

"But these are all one-bedroom apartments."

"Yeah, I sleep on the couch."

"Because, you're like, in trouble or something?"

"What?" asked Alex, not understanding.

"Like, when you fight with your girlfriend and end up on the couch."

Alex sighed. "Yeah, no, I said roommate, not girlfriend. She's just my friend. She's got the bedroom and I always sleep on the couch."

"But, she's a girl."

"I noticed that. Although apparently that's sexist or something, and I've been recently informed I'm supposed to be calling her a woman now since she's not twelve."

Beth started to frown but then seemed to think better of it, and instead smiled at him as she twirled a bit of her long hair. "But, like, how do you have a girl for a friend?"

"She's around and we do friend stuff. I'm not sure how it's that complicated."

"Well, I don't get it. When I'm around a cute guy I want more, so...."

"Do I qualify for more?" asked Alex with a grin.

"Maybe," said Beth, coyly. "I'll let you know." And she headed back inside her apartment.

All Claire knew for a while was that the new girl down the hall cast her strange, dirty looks that also seemed smug for some reason. When Alex finally mentioned her one day it made more sense.

"So, are you guys going out or something?" Claire asked.

"Not yet, but she kissed me down in the laundry room yesterday."

"Huh."

"What?"

Claire wasn't sure what to say. She didn't trust Beth, but she didn't have any logical reason not to, so she was stuck. "Nothing. I guess, um, we should have that talk about the apartment and dating and all that, finally."

"Oh. Huh. Well, I don't see any reason anything has to change," said Alex after a moment. "I mean, Beth's right down the hall in her own space, so why would that affect you? I still want you to stay."

"Are you sure? Because, I got that raise recently and I've been saving up, so I could get out on my own at this point pretty much any time."

"Nah. Besides, I like having a clean bathroom and your tolerance for it getting fucked up is way lower than mine."

"Yeah, I think you just like using my body wash and are too macho to buy your own."

"I do not use your body wash!"

"Oh, sure, that's why I'm using it up at twice the rate I was before I moved in."

"Okay, trying the damn stuff once or twice is not the same as using it."

"Well, remember that next time I borrow your razor to shave my legs."

"I thought you said you didn't use my razor!"

"No, I tried it once or twice, which is apparently not the same thing."

Alex smiled and threw an exaggeratedly slow punch at her face which she smacked away with a little more force than necessary. He rubbed the spot where she hit him admiringly and went to see if Beth was home.

Once they started officially going out, Alex tried to explain to Beth at greater length about his friendship with Claire. She didn't get it. That didn't surprise Alex, since no one ever got it, but he didn't care. If Beth wanted him, great. If not, it was no big deal. But Beth did want him.

One afternoon, on a day when she knew Alex usually came home first, Beth met him at his door and invited herself in. After a few minutes inside she tried to lead him toward the bedroom, but Alex stopped her and said, "No, Beth, that's Claire's room."

"Well, where do you want to do it?"

"Do it? How about in your apartment?"

She ran her hands up his chest and down both arms and kissed him.

"But wait, Beth, seriously, why don't we go down the hall to your place?" Alex was befuddled, but the way she was touching him wasn't helping him think straight.

"I don't know," she said vaguely. "Don't you want me, Alex?"

"Well, yeah, but...."

And she pulled him on top of her onto the couch.

When Claire got home, she started to get out her key when she heard the amorous sounds from behind the door. Actually, all she heard was Beth, who she thought was being exaggeratedly loud, but she assumed Alex was involved in there somewhere, and she turned back around and decided to have dinner out. She only wished she'd brought a book.

When she got home later that night, no one was there. She wondered what they should do. Claire knew Alex really did want her there. She was the person he counted on to talk to, and she loved his company, so it was easy to imagine their current arrangement continuing indefinitely. She suspected Beth wasn't as supportive of that concept, especially after what Claire assumed was some kind of territorial display.

Alex didn't return to the apartment until he came home to shower in the morning. Claire lay in bed and listened to the water running, wondered how much of her body wash he was using up, and after he'd had sufficient time to dry off, she called out to him.

"Alex?"

"What?"

"Come here a minute."

He appeared in her doorway in the same pants and undershirt from the day before, still toweling off his hair, which was getting pretty shaggy. "What?"

"Alex, we need to talk about the apartment. I don't think it makes sense for me to live here anymore. I could start looking for someplace new this afternoon when you get back from work if I can borrow your car. I'm thinking if I can be out by the end of the month that would keep the rent thing easy to square away—no funny overlap to calculate or something."

Alex looked surprised. He came and sat on the bed across from her. Claire sat up and hugged her knees.

"But I thought we were okay."

"Well, I'm okay, and you're okay, but from the sounds of Beth screaming to her creator yesterday, I don't think she's okay."

Alex cringed with embarrassment. "I'm sorry. That was dumb, I just...."

"Yeah, yeah, I know what you just, but I really think our cohabiting stint has run its course and it's time to do something else."

Alex glanced down at nothing in particular for a moment. Claire recognized he was sad. She was a little sad, too, but as much as having her best friend so close was great, it was complicated in their case. And she realized she should be trying to form some sort of social life apart from Alex. Having him at her disposal all the time for companionship had caused her to neglect looking anywhere else, and that wasn't good. Even without Beth in the picture, it made sense to move on.

Alex looked at her earnestly. "I can promise that won't happen again, Claire. You don't have to leave."

Claire sighed. "Yeah, I do. I might actually find someone myself, you know, and how crowded is that going to seem?"

Alex glanced at his watch and frowned. He got up and reached into their shared closet to pull out a fresh shirt, which he put on and buttoned quickly as he realized he had to go. "Can we talk about this for real after I get home from work? What time do you get back from the dojo today?"

"There's no weapons class, so I'm done teaching at four."

Alex was still frowning. "Well, I'll see you when I get home. Don't start packing or anything yet, okay?"

Claire smiled. "Okay."

She spent the morning circling apartments she could afford in the local listings since there was nothing available in their current building, then went off to the dojo. Since she still didn't have a car it would be nice to stay in the neighborhood, but it wasn't going to be easy. She was in for a long walk wherever she ended up, most likely. But right as Claire resigned herself to having to break down and buy a car so she could still get to work once she moved out, Alex came home with news.

"So, assuming you're still intent on us not living together anymore, I think I have a solution," he said.

"What's that?"

"I mentioned it to a friend at work, and he told me he's actually looking for someone to take over his place at the end of the month when he gets transferred. It's furnished and has a big TV and it's way closer to my job."

"So you're leaving me here with Beth?"

"No, I'm leaving you here near the dojo. If Beth still wants to go out, I know where to find her. Besides, I'll be able to visit my best friend and my girlfriend in one trip."

"Yes, the girls you pick always love that concept, don't they?"

"Come on, Claire, I'm still fine with staying here, but if you don't think we should be sharing a space anymore, this makes the most sense. We'll go get your name put on the lease and you can have all the furniture and the extra drawers and closet space, and your life won't have to change all that much."

"I guess." Claire was having second thoughts, but it was probably fear of being alone. She was going to have to get over that sometime. She and Alex needed separate lives, but at that moment she didn't like the idea of not seeing him every day. Even if she did have to fight him for time in the bathroom the same way she used to with her brothers.

"Good. Let's go out and have a celebratory dinner or some fucking thing, okay? My treat."

"In that case, anything as long as it's expensive."

Alex smiled. Big TV or no big TV, he was going to miss her a lot.

They ended up at a small place within walking distance called *Pasta Amore*. Claire had always wanted to go there, but it was out of her price range and was considered a romantic place to take someone, so she'd been out of luck on either score. It was cozy and pretty and set up for couples, and was known to serve some of the best desserts in town. Alex looked fine since he'd come from work, but Claire was underdressed. Claire was chronically underdressed. They were tucked into a corner and regarded a little suspiciously since they were the only people there not holding hands, and occasionally they'd kick each other under the table.

Despite her threats, Claire did not order the most expensive thing available. They each ordered the lasagna and had salads and breadsticks and water. They laughed and argued, and by the time Claire's seven-layer chocolate dessert with raspberries came they were rather full, and she offered to share it. They lingered over the dessert, and Claire cocked her head when they were about halfway through it and said, "Do you ever wonder where we'll end up?"

"What do you mean?" Alex was hesitating over his next bite, contemplating if this was too much chocolate to cram into one dessert, and worrying he might go into a diabetic coma if he ate any more of it. Claire was taking small bites but looked determined to polish it off.

"You know. Like in ten years will we each have houses and kids...."

"By then? God, I fucking hope so."

"'Cause I'm thinking that depending on who I end up with, I might need you to help my kids with science things when it comes up."

Alex laughed. "That's thinking awfully far ahead, isn't it?"

"I like thinking far ahead. And anyway, no matter how far ahead I look, I don't get any better with math or science, and even if you get worse you'll still be ahead of me, so my kids will need you."

"What if you marry a rocket scientist? Then you won't need me anymore," said Alex.

"I'm not going to marry a rocket scientist."

"How do you know that?"

"Where would I run into a rocket scientist?" asked Claire.

"The dojo, probably. That one guy...um...Craig! Remember Craig?"

"The guy who kept forgetting the number five every time he was supposed to count in Japanese?"

"Yeah, him. He went into rocket science."

"Well, that doesn't speak well for the field, so I may have to set my sights higher anyway."

Alex laughed and officially put down his dessert fork. Claire kept working.

"In that case," said Alex, "I promise to help your kids with their science projects or whatever."

"Good! I feel better about reproducing someday. And I'm not going to meet anyone at the dojo."

"Why do you say that? That's where you spend all of your time, and new people keep coming through. Maybe if you started wearing lipstick there you'd have better luck," he said with a grin.

Claire tried to kick him again, but he anticipated it was coming and got her first in the other leg. "Ow! No, everyone is too scared of me there, and I need to maintain that or no one will take me seriously. It takes a lot to be a small to average-sized woman and command respect in that kind of place. I can't see some new guy saying to himself 'Yeah, the girl who knows that whole list of choke holds—she's the one!', no."

"At least you know all the steps for reviving someone if you do those techniques too hard."

"Oh, yes, that's sexy. Can't believe I forgot that."

Alex sat back in his chair and looked thoughtful. "It'll happen, Claire. No, I think in a few years we'll both have established ourselves better in what we do, and we'll find the right people and hang out as couples and carpool all our kids somewhere someday. And when our spouses die we can go find some old age home where we can do tai chi together until we fucking croak."

"Boy, and I'm the one who thinks too far ahead?"

Alex chuckled and signaled the waiter for the check.

CHAPTER SIX

Alex moved out at the end of January. Ben, having been inspired by his talks with his sister, decided to finally move out of their parents' house not long after that, and in with his serious boyfriend of several months. The boyfriend was a kind and affable guy named Jacob who lived on the opposite end of town. Fine for Ben, but now Claire's two main sources of transportation if she needed it were effectively unavailable. She would have to break down and buy a car.

Claire didn't need a car to do much aside from grocery shopping and certain errands, but after about a month of trying to bum rides from inconvenient sources and taking the bus when necessary, she decided it was time. The idea of being able to get around on her own was appealing, and she'd been saving her money. Claire did some research, decided what makes and models she was interested in, and felt prepared to go out and find what she wanted. Then one of her friends suggested that if she went to a dealership to check things out, it would help to bring a guy.

"What for? My money's as good as any guy's," said

Claire.

Jennifer shook her head. "No, when I went shopping for a car for college? They wouldn't even look at me. I finally had to send in my dad or I'd have been walking to the West Coast."

"But that's insane!" Claire could not accept that in this day and age a salesperson would be so ridiculous as to do something so sexist. It also seemed weird to ignore the customer you planned to eke extra money out of, so none of it made sense.

"Insane or not, take your dad unless you want to be out some money."

But Claire couldn't bring herself to do that. She was not going to run to her dad. She talked with Alex about it on the phone one night as they ate dinner together in separate apartments. Alex had grown accustomed to the Walker family style of conversing during meals, and now eating by himself seemed lonely.

"Yeah, Pammy had the same problem," he said. "She had to shop around for a dealer who would give her a fair shake when she got to Arizona and it took time."

"Well, I hate this!" said Claire.

"I don't blame you, but I think it's a case of it being an industry made up mostly of guys and they assume women don't know enough and are easier to take advantage of. I'm sure some women know what they're doing, but I'll bet a lot are more interested in the color or something, and that makes 'em easier to screw with."

"But not every guy knows stuff either."

"Yeah, but on average they're probably right to make the assumption guys know more. I know more about cars than you do," said Alex. It wasn't a challenge; it was a statement of fact and Claire took it that way.

"Well, what if we went and looked at the same thing but not together. I just want to see if you really do get a better deal."

"You mean like a sting?"

"No, I...I just want to know."

So they arranged to get together on a Saturday afternoon when Claire wasn't teaching, and Alex was planning to meet Beth for a date later that day anyway. Claire had done her homework and decided she wanted a used Honda. She knew the blue book prices and what range she was looking in. Alex parked a block away from the dealership and Claire walked up to the place alone and located the car she was interested in. After a ridiculously long time she was finally approached by a salesman. He was pleasant and seemed honest and helpful. Claire liked him. She got a price quote that sounded good to her, and feeling happy, she told the guy she would think about it and get back to him soon. She returned to where Alex was waiting for her, leaning against his own car and reading a book.

"That took a while. How'd it go?"

"I think okay," said Claire. "The sales guy was named 'Stephen' and this was the deal he quoted me on the blue Civic at the end of the lot." Claire handed him the piece of paper. Alex considered it a moment then told her to wait there.

Alex got onto the lot and started looking at the couple of sports cars they had to offer. 'Stephen' stepped up to him immediately. They chatted and joked around for a minute or two, and then Alex said he really should be considering something more practical, and after being shown several things they finally reached the Honda that Claire wanted. Alex and the guy talked it over and they haggled a little, and when he returned to Claire and handed her his slip of paper her jaw dropped. The price quote was nearly nine-hundred dollars less. And he'd thrown in floor mats.

"*What?*" was all she was able to say over and over.

Most of the time Alex didn't buy that women suffered much unequal treatment in society, although he'd come around after years of listening to Claire to understanding at least historically how unfairly women had been treated in the past. From where he was standing in the here and now, women seemed to have more options, frankly. If a woman wanted to be strong, great, and if she wanted to be weak, that was fine too. He felt men were under a lot of pressure to simply be strong, and it forced them into roles that didn't always fit. However, this was a glimpse into something else and it pissed him off.

"But he seemed so nice!" Claire said.

"All good salesmen seem nice. I suppose women think because a guy acts nice he *is* nice. I don't think that, especially not in a situation where someone wants something."

Claire stared at the paper a moment and clenched her teeth.

"Well, what do you want to do?" he asked. "Should we try someplace else, or—"

But Claire started marching back to the dealership. She glanced around until she spotted Stephen and smiled. She handed him the slip of paper that he'd given Alex and said, "Yes, I'll take it, please."

Stephen seemed pleased until he looked at the slip, and realized what had happened.

"But, what I quoted you—"

"Was apparently a mistake."

Alex then appeared behind her and the salesman got defensive. "Hey, I don't know what the two of you think you're doing, but I don't have to do business with either one of you, so—"

"So, what do you think, Alex? Should I call my brother and see if he can get a news crew down here Monday?"

Alex smiled. "That's right, he edits that whole 'consumer gotcha' segment every week for Channel 6 News, doesn't he?"

"I'm sure he'd pull a few strings for me, since I'm his favorite sister and all."

Stephen seemed uneasy. "Is that some kind of threat?"

"Some kind, yes," said Claire looking him straight in the eye and not blinking.

"But everyone knows that—"

"No, everyone doesn't, but they will on Monday," said Claire, "You might want to pick a better tie for the cameras."

The salesman cast a look akin to betrayal at Alex. "So I give you this price and you're out of here?" he said still looking at him.

"No, look at *me*," commanded Claire. "*I'm* the one with the checkbook who wants a car, not my friend with the y-chromosome."

So he repeated his question, this time careful to look directly at Claire.

"Yes, I will take the car at the guy price and then I'm out of here," she said.

"And don't forget the floor mats," said Alex.

"And I'm keeping the pen I sign the papers with. And maybe a stapler if I spot one," added Claire.

The salesman didn't seem anything like the sweet, smiling person Claire had found appealing when she first got there. He walked them silently to the office and started drawing up paperwork. Claire didn't act giddy or even smile. She simply signed what she needed to, got out her checkbook, and arranged for temporary tags. She took her keys and her pen and her stapler and walked out to get her new car. Alex went with her, and she drove him the block to where he was parked.

"Thanks for your help, Alex," she said as he got out.

"Not a problem. Thanks for having me along! I don't get to watch you do jujutsu that often anymore and that was about as good."

Claire smiled. "Have a nice time with Beth. Oh, and call me before next weekend! *Life of Brian* is showing at the campus theater and I thought we could go."

"Sounds good," said Alex as he waved goodbye. He smiled to himself as he got behind his own wheel again. Thinking about the stunned and defeated look on Stephen's face he decided it was probably similar to how he appeared when Claire threw him and cranked on his arm that first time they were paired at the dojo. Alex was glad he knew better now, and hoped the sales guy had learned his lesson, too. He headed off to have dinner with Beth.

Beth wasn't quite as amused by the story, especially when Alex was telling it for the third time.

"Why didn't she just take her dad? Why did she have to bug you?" Beth poked listlessly at her salad with the dressing on the side. She shot what Alex thought was an almost accusatory glance at the steak on his own plate. He could never figure out why Beth always requested he take her to expensive restaurants if she never ordered anything more than salad off the menu.

"She didn't bug me. I wanted to go, and taking a friend is better than feeling like you're running to your parents for every little thing."

"What's wrong with running to your parents? That's what they're for," said Beth.

"Yeah, but you're only in your third year of college

and your parents pay for your apartment and everything still. I mean, that's kind of like being at home."

Beth looked offended. "It is not! I take care of myself and it's not like they are doing my fashion design homework or anything!"

Alex shrugged. "You can think what you want. But I liked being able to help Claire today."

"Well, I think it would have been easier to simply tell her parents she wanted a car and be done with it," said Beth.

It seemed like an awfully juvenile attitude toward money in Alex's opinion, but he wasn't there to cosign a loan with Beth. He was there to have fun, and as long as Claire didn't come up, they did. Beth was pretty and she laughed at his jokes and she didn't seem to care if he couldn't spend the whole night if he had to work the next day. She was fairly standard girlfriend material as far as he was concerned, and the six months or so they'd been together had been a good time. He figured he had years left to play before he had to worry about what he needed in a serious relationship.

But in early September things changed, and the first person Alex called was Claire.

"I'm getting married."

"Married?" Claire wasn't sure how to react to that. There was a twinge of jealousy that he would be getting married first, but more than that she was concerned. "To Beth?" she asked.

"Well, yeah, to Beth! Who do you think?"

Claire had always assumed Beth was one more cute passing diversion that Alex would tire of eventually, and then he would find someone decent. Someone maybe Claire could talk with, too. Someone who at least didn't glare at her like she wanted her to get hit by a bus.

"I didn't.... It seems awfully soon, Alex. I mean, why now?"

"You can't just be happy for me?" he asked, sounding annoyed.

"Yeah, like you were for me and Doug?"

There was silence on the other end.

Claire started in with, "It's just that you and Beth don't—"

"She's pregnant, Claire," Alex said before she could get to any of the points he knew she wanted to make. None of those points made much difference anymore, and he didn't want Claire to put her foot in her mouth.

It was Claire's turn to be silent for a moment.

"Claire, we just found out, and she wants to keep the baby and I can't see letting my kid down, so I...I asked her to marry me last night and she said yes."

Claire's brain was having trouble processing so much new information at once. "Pregnant?"

"Yeah."

"Well, how did that happen?"

Alex was irked. "Well, how do you think it happened?"

"It's just, why weren't you doing something to, to...."

"I thought she was on the pill, so when—"

"You *thought* she was on the pill?" Claire couldn't believe what she was hearing. What kind of mess had he gotten himself into?

"Look, it doesn't matter now anyway, does it? She's pregnant, she's having the baby, we're getting married, so just be happy for me already! Jesus, Claire! I'm going to need you there to get through the wedding and all without passing out or something so, you know, get on the same page as me and at least pretend you can deal."

Claire was torn. The first thing she wanted to do was yell at him for being anti-abortion, and then not being more responsible about where he put his dick, but she knew he wouldn't see it that way since he thought he *was* being responsible by sacrificing everything for the baby. And then she wanted to say to him that marriage was not some kind of magic solution to the problem. That there were other arrangements or possibilities or something that didn't result in him tied to Beth for life. But Alex had made up his mind, and she knew he couldn't be swayed. Anything she said now would be something uncomfortable that sat between the two of them forever, so she should keep it to herself.

"I'm happy for you and I can deal," she said.

She could sense some of the tension leave Alex over the phone. "Thanks, Claire."

That was September 10, 2001.

The next day, both Alex and Claire awoke on a beautiful Tuesday morning in their respective apartments to the news that terrorists had hijacked planes and were crashing them into buildings.

Claire had switched on the TV as she walked to the kitchen to get some cereal, but didn't glance at it until she realized she was hearing the voice of Peter Jennings, the evening anchor. That meant something was horrendously wrong. The network didn't pull out his reassuring presence that early in the morning unless there was a very good reason. She backed up and looked at the pictures of smoke pouring out of the World Trade Center. She forgot about her breakfast and stared at the screen.

Alex had been brushing his teeth when he flipped on Fox News and saw the same images. There was speculation about whether it was an accident or not, until a second plane hit the other tower and the word terrorism began getting tossed around. He felt his gut tighten and he couldn't take his eyes from the set.

Eventually he felt like he should go to work, but it seemed pointless. He experienced a strange combination of emotions that didn't seem to work together: a sort of hopelessness and a steely pride all mixed up. He drove to work while riveted to his radio, and arrived at his office to find a solemn atmosphere, and people glued to TV sets and nothing productive happening.

Claire had gotten up to organize things that needed to be photocopied for the dojo that day, but she didn't want to go out. She didn't want to do anything. When the first of the twin towers collapsed, she burst into tears and sank onto the couch. It took a lot to get Claire to cry, but that was all she really did that day. She called in to the dojo and found that Sensei had decided to close it until Wednesday. She was glad, although she couldn't imagine wanting to teach jujutsu on Wednesday, either.

Claire felt scared in a way she had never known before. She had found much to criticize in her country that she thought it needed to improve upon, but living in the strongest nation on earth had made her blind to the benefits of feeling her homeland was invulnerable. That strength had given her a backdrop of confidence to work from that she'd never taken notice of.

She called Ben, but he was freaking out over friends he had in New York that he couldn't get through to, and her mom called to see if she wanted to come and be with them for dinner that night, but Claire didn't feel she was done crying, so she declined. She went to bed feeling worn and not looking forward to another sad day in the morning. It might have helped her to know Alex was down the hall, but she didn't find that out until well after the fact.

Alex had driven straight from work to Beth's apartment. He meant to stop in on Claire, too, but Beth was waiting for him out front when he got there, her eyes red and puffy, and they went directly to her place. He held her, and felt frightened about what kind of world his child would be entering. Alex felt the weight of responsibility layered on top of all his sadness, and it made him alternately numb and determined. He would fix things for this baby, but he had no idea how.

Of all the hundreds upon hundreds of stories there were to dutifully suffer through after that horrible day, the one that haunted Alex's thoughts the most was a firefighter's account of a pregnant woman who had jumped from one of the towers and hit the ground outside the window in front of him. He said she split open like a melon and the baby burst out. Alex could picture it and he wished he couldn't.

But the next day, with an eerie stillness in the sky due to the grounding of all the nation's airplanes, everyone who had watched the tragedy from a distance and still felt it as their own loss, wearily got to their feet and went through the motions of normal life. Claire taught class, and no one whined. Alex went to work and solved problems that now felt meaningless. It was hard to picture feeling light again. But Beth didn't have time for an extended period of national mourning.

As inappropriate as it seemed to nearly everyone, Beth wanted to get on with planning her wedding. And despite her decidedly unholy knocked-up condition, she wanted it to be a big church wedding. She told Alex she wanted it soon, so the expensive form-fitting white dress she desired would still look good on her in the photos. In two months the wedding was going to happen, and Alex was trying to help in the scramble to put it together. Unfortunately (or fortunately, depending on how much it bothered him to be involved) Alex was only an accessory to the event at hand.

Beth picked out his tux and the hall and the cake and the flowers and the invitations. She and her mother dragged him along to look at china patterns and crystal and things he couldn't care less about. He was a good sport about all of it, really, until the question of the attendants came up.

"She cannot be your 'best man,' Alex!" said Beth angrily.

"Why do you get to decide that?" It was bad enough that he didn't feel like participating in something so unnecessarily showy or frivolous at a time when no one felt like celebrating anything, but he wasn't getting any say on the parts that mattered to him.

"Because I don't want a woman standing up on your side at my wedding! It looks stupid!"

"No, what looks stupid are all those bird-of-paradise arrangements you want at the reception. I haven't had much of a say in anything, Beth, and it's supposed to be my wedding, too, isn't it?"

Beth pouted and tried to pretend the pregnancy was making her feel frail and sick, but Alex wasn't buying it. She kept saying she didn't like that the timing of the terrorist attacks had interfered with her big day, but she didn't have a lot of choice. She was pregnant and that dictated her timeline. Beth even tried to convince him that it might be patriotic to stick it in the face of the terrorists and have a party despite what had happened. She was having the wedding she wanted and that was that, and neither terrorists nor Alex would stand in her way.

"Alex," she tried to say sweetly, "I've dreamed my whole life of the perfect wedding, where I get to be a princess in a white dress surrounded by my friends who look like roses, and I stand in front of everyone in the church and the organ plays and—"

"I thought I said no organ," interrupted Alex.

Beth shot him a look and continued, "—and the bells ring and it's all beautiful. I want what I pictured, and that picture doesn't include Claire standing on the groom's side."

"Does your picture include me?" asked Alex.

"What kind of question is that? You're the groom!"

"Yeah, but am I the groom first, or am I me? If you're marrying me, Claire is the best man."

Beth looked cross but finally had to accept that Alex wasn't going to budge on that point. He was obstinate about certain things, and she sometimes muttered that she was going to have to do something about that, but not until after the wedding, and Alex ignored it.

"Well, I don't want her in a tux because that looks stupid, too."

"I'm sure we'll figure something out."

Beth toyed with the idea of adding Claire to her line of bridesmaids, but there were already so few men to go around on Alex's side that there would be no way to balance that out. They ended up having Claire wear a simple black dress that blended in nicely with groom's side of the altar.

Claire was glad, because the puffy-sleeved magenta dresses on the other side gave her a headache. The idea of paying for one of those sartorial monstrosities would have been too much to put up with, even for Alex's sake. The whole thing seemed like a child's idea of a wedding to Claire, and she wondered how many of the choices had been made while flipping through magazines in the late eighties and early nineties with giggling girls munching on snacks in what she pictured as a cloyingly pink room.

Beth announced that the bridesmaids would walk up the aisle unescorted, primarily because she didn't want to deal with Alex's idea of a best man walking alongside the maid of honor. So Claire simply came out from the back by the choir area with the minister and the rest of the groomsmen to stand with Alex, and watched the whole thing unfold from by his side.

Alex looked nervous and proud and was handsome in his tux. Claire had told him before they walked out that he "cleaned up nice," and he smiled and squeezed her hand briefly. It pained her to see anxiety on his face as he waited for his bride to appear.

Claire wanted to report to him all the stupid chatter in the bridal party dressing room, and let him know how little he meant to the whole proceeding. It was all about the dress and the hair and the makeup. There was giggling and gossip, and his name didn't come up once except in Claire's own head. She wanted to take Alex's hand and run, and find him someplace to hide until it was all over, but he'd made up his mind. He was getting married to Beth, and the way Alex worked, that wasn't going to be undone.

The music started. It was the only element of the ceremony, aside from Claire's presence, that reflected Alex's wishes. He'd put his foot down about wanting a string quartet to play for the prelude and the march. He always thought an organ sounded hokey at weddings and he wanted something elegant and peaceful. He'd found the group himself and booked them before Beth could have any objection. The quartet played beautifully, and had a soothing effect on both Alex and Claire.

By that time in November, the nation had begun to heal in a way that celebrating a wedding didn't feel so unseemly after all. The bridesmaids walked up the aisle, beaming. Beth followed them with her parents, and smiled in her perfect makeup and carefully done hair. The morning sickness had been bad enough that she hadn't gained any weight in her pregnancy yet, and her dress fit beautifully. She air kissed her parents and came to stand by Alex. Claire felt conspicuous standing on the other side of him, and wondered if she shouldn't be there, despite what Alex wanted. Because the truth was she hadn't worked out in her mind what supporting her friend in this circumstance really meant.

The wedding was long, with several of the standard bible readings from Corinthians, and Pammy stood up to read the Apache Wedding Prayer. She was in her second year as an anthropology major, and her contribution was the only non-Christian element Beth had agreed to.

Alex was nervous during the whole ceremony in a way only Claire could see, both because she was standing close to him and because she knew him so well. She noticed he had the same set to his jaw that he did before so many kyu level tests which he never felt adequately prepared for. She saw his hand shake a little when she handed him the rings. Beth looked nervous but in a fluttery, excited kind of way. She smiled the whole time. Claire wanted to be happy for them, but when they were pronounced husband and wife and walked back up the aisle to music and applause, she felt something closer to apprehension and sorrow.

Directly after the ceremony were pictures. Claire was included in one large group photo and then informed she wasn't needed for any others. She did get to stand with Pammy for a moment, where Claire took the opportunity to hug her old friend and tell her she thought she'd read well.

"It was a lovely choice, your reading." said Claire.

"Thanks," said Pammy. "But I have to tell you, it's a fake."

Claire gave her a questioning look, and Pammy seemed sheepish.

"There are real Apache wedding prayers," she explained, "but that one that you hear at a lot of weddings these days is from some old movie. We refer to such things in the field as 'fauxlore'."

"But you picked it to read anyway?" asked Claire.

"I did," she said, casting a look toward Beth and her brother who were being directed this way and that by the photographer. "I just... I don't know, Claire. I'm looking forward to being an aunt, but everything else about this...."

Claire didn't know if it was a good thing or a bad thing that they couldn't continue their conversation, but Pammy was called away to pose with her family, which now included her new sister-in-law. Claire watched as Pammy stood where she was told and smiled for as long as she was instructed to. She wished she could simply go with both Alex and Pammy out for ice cream the way they used to half a decade ago.

The reception was long and overdone, and Claire felt exposed up at the head table. She didn't like being on display, and was horrified when she realized she was expected to give a toast. Somehow not actually being a man had left her with the sense that some of the duties of the best man role would not be expected of her. She had kind of lumped the toast in her mind in with the bachelor party that didn't happen on her watch, so when the microphone was handed to her and everyone quieted down, she had a moment of panic unequaled by any she had experienced in the dojo. Alex held his new wife's hand and looked at Claire expectantly.

She stood with the microphone and tried not to look at the roomful of people. It was one thing to be the center of attention and be asked to do something physical. Public speaking was another matter. She took a deep breath and calmed her mind enough to collect her thoughts.

"I know the best man toast is supposed to be funny —and I could tell all kinds of embarrassing stories about Alex if I really wanted to. But today, I don't really want to. I think...I think it's enough to note here that I can't imagine anyone making a better husband and father than Alex will be. I can assure Beth she is a lucky woman. I wish with all my heart that their lives together will be long and happy." She raised her glass, and as she saw Alex and Beth smiling up at her, all she could think was *Please, God, let this woman be worthy of my friend.*

The food looked better than it tasted but the cake was delicious. Since the bride and groom were so young the average age of the guests was pretty low, and a lot of people started drinking early. Claire decided to take a walk around the hotel rather than watch the first few dances, and to her surprise, Beth's older brother, Jeremy, caught up with her.

"Hey, you're going the wrong direction!" he said as he reached her.

"Why's that?"

"Because they're about to throw the bouquet."

"Then I'm going exactly the right direction," said Claire.

Jeremy gave her a funny look and laughed. "In that case, you mind if I join you?"

Claire shrugged and said, "Sure, I guess. I'm not headed anywhere special, I just wanted to get out of there for a minute."

Jeremy nodded and fell in step next to her as she proceeded toward the lobby. He squinted at her toned arms that were well displayed by her sleeveless black dress. "So, do you work out a lot?"

Claire considered saying something snarky, and instead simply said, "Yes."

They walked in silence for a few more steps as he eyed her up and down. "So, Alex's best man, huh? That's really unusual for an ex-girlfriend to want to do that."

Claire felt part of her mind switch over into autopilot so she could have the same tired conversation while continuing to think about other things. "No, we never dated. We're just friends."

Jeremy appeared surprised and started to respond in some typical way, when Claire couldn't help herself and added, "You know, because Alex is gay."

Beth's brother appeared genuinely alarmed and Claire regretted her joke. "No! Jeremy, I'm teasing! Alex is obviously not gay, okay? It's just that I get asked that a lot about being just friends and there are times I feel like saying he's gay so people won't keep on about it. I'm sorry."

Jeremy looked as if he were trying to figure out why that would be funny, and then said, "Yeah, anyway, we should really be getting back in there, don't you think? My sister's going to be pissed enough that I missed the whole garter thing, and you were probably missed at the bouquet throwing, so why don't we go back and be in hot water together? The bar's open, I could get you a drink."

"No thanks—about the drink, I mean. But sure, we can go back in together. I think I'll make one last appearance and then head out of here. It might be nice to not walk back in there all alone."

They returned to the reception where the music was blaring, and he talked her into doing the next slow dance when it came up. Claire waited and felt out of place as Jeremy got himself a tequila, and eventually led her onto the dance floor. They'd only been on it a moment when Claire realized she'd made a mistake. Jeremy's hands repeatedly dropped inappropriately low no matter how often she redirected them.

At about the point where she was considering which way to simply break Jeremy's hands, Alex appeared.

"I'm cutting in, Jerry," he said.

"Why? You didn't want her," he sneered.

Claire narrowed her eyes, and Alex slipped between the two dancers, cutting Jeremy loose before she could get in something like the groin kick Alex knew his new brother-in-law was in for in another second. As Jeremy sulked away, Claire said, "Thank you."

"Sorry about that," said Alex. "He's a bit of a weasel. I got nervous when I saw him go after you when you ducked out before."

"Yeah, well, I can take care of myself."

"I know, but you shouldn't always have to."

"Well, thanks."

They didn't say anything for a moment, and then Claire realized to her astonishment that they'd been dancing. It wasn't as weird as she always imagined. Like almost anything they did together it seemed to come naturally. She decided to enjoy herself and not dwell on the idea too much. Alex actually looked the most relaxed she'd seen him all day. He held her comfortably and was light on his feet.

"I liked your toast, by the way," he said. "Short and not stupid."

"Good. I'm glad, because I meant it."

He smiled down at her. "You really think I'll be a good dad?"

"Like that's a hard prediction to make! Of course you'll be a good dad."

"Honestly? It makes me feel better to hear you say that. My Dad...I love my Dad, but he wasn't exactly fun. I want to have fun with my kids but still keep some kind of order and I'm not sure I know how to strike that balance."

"Oh, you'll figure it out," said Claire as they continued to move easily along the dance floor. It was strangely like jujutsu, judging and adapting to the direction and energy of the person you were handling. It always amazed her in what unlikely contexts her training came in handy. "My Dad was strict but we had a lot of fun growing up."

"Well, that's good to hear. And, just so you know, if this baby's a girl? That 'no boys upstairs rule' of your Dad's is starting to sound less crazy to me."

Claire laughed. "Oh no! We've lost you to the dark side already!"

Alex smiled and spun her around once extra fast right as the song was ending. He let her go slowly and said, "So, I'd better get back to my wife. The OB said some champagne wouldn't hurt the baby, but I'm going to see if I can keep Beth away from it anyhow."

"Yeah, well, I'm going to head out. You're taken now, which makes Jeremy the next best prospect, and that's way too depressing to contemplate."

Alex laughed. "Well, run while you can! Seriously, though, thanks for being here for me today. It meant a lot."

"Sure. It's part of that whole friend deal, so don't think anything of it."

He took her hand and gave it a squeeze. "You're the best, Claire. See ya soon, okay?"

"Okay. Bye, Alex."

But Alex didn't get to see Claire again for months. After he and Beth went on their honeymoon on a cruise ship for a week, there were thank you cards to write, and after that their focus turned to preparing for the baby now that the wedding was done.

They were living in Alex's apartment, and it was filled with gifts they didn't know where to put. The clutter was even getting to Alex who wasn't famous for being neat. He didn't understand why Beth had registered for half of the things they got and tried to convince her they should donate some of it, but she wanted it all and said she'd figure it out.

Alex dutifully unwrapped boxes and read Beth the names on the cards so she could make a list of exactly what they got from whom. She was happiest when people stuck to what was on her registry and didn't appreciate when people deviated from her selections in order to be creative. So when Alex got to Claire's gift, at first he only mentioned the cookie jar she had gotten for them that Beth had picked out herself. He wasn't going to say what he found inside, except it made him laugh and Beth wanted to know what was so funny.

"Nothing. It's kind of an inside thing, so I don't know if you'd be interested," he said.

Beth frowned at him from her spot on the floor where she was surrounded by tissue and boxes and lots of kitchen supplies. "But what is it? And why wouldn't I be interested? I'm your wife for God's sake."

"It's just...it's silly and I don't think you'll get it."

"Fine. So, I'm not as fun as Claire. I still need to put whatever it is on my list."

"That's not what I meant! And it's not true. You two find different things funny is all." Alex thought this was not an auspicious beginning to their life as a married couple. "Here," he said, handing over the cookie jar.

Beth took it and lifted the lid. Inside was a stuffed, toy bunny. "What's so funny about that? It's probably for the baby."

"It probably is for the baby, but it's also for me. You have to open its mouth."

Beth slipped her finger between the plush toy's jaws and pulled them apart. The bunny's eyes began to blink a menacing red and its mouth was full of fangs. "What the hell is that about?" she asked, with a look on her face that told Alex she didn't want to prove him right, but that she really was a bit horrified that someone might want to present such a thing to a newborn.

"It's from a *Monty Python* movie we used to watch together all the time. There's a part in it where some people get a warning that death awaits them with big pointy teeth, and it turns out to be this innocent-looking rabbit that isn't so innocent."

"That doesn't sound funny." Beth pulled the rabbit from the cookie jar and handed the offending toy back to her husband.

"But it's a real bloodbath, and this super fake-looking rabbit is flying around with sharp teeth, aiming for people's necks and—"

"Yeah, Alex, it's not sounding funnier," she complained. Alex had only ever taken Beth to romantic comedies that she was interested in. He realized she had no idea what movies he actually wanted to see.

Alex opened the rabbit's mouth again and chuckled to himself.

"I don't want that thing near the baby," said Beth, eyeing it with distaste.

"I'm sure Claire assumed it would be up to our discretion. If you don't like it, fine, but I want to hang onto it for a while."

"But, Alex, it—"

"Hey, it takes up a hell of a lot less room than all of these bowls, and whatever all that mixing equipment is over there. We can even leave it in the cookie jar for now until you learn to actually, you know, bake something."

Beth scowled at him and wrote "obnoxious fanged rabbit" by "cookie jar" on her gift list under Claire's name. "Next box, please," she said. She was clearly done with this conversation.

Alex wedged the rabbit, mouth tucked closed,

between his leg and the arm of the chair he was in. It made him smile a little every time he glanced at it, but it also disturbed him in a way he couldn't place. Something about it being cute from the outside, but that it wasn't what it seemed.

He was bad at metaphor and analysis because he preferred problems with clear and concrete answers. He didn't like questions where multiple people could come to different and sometimes opposing conclusions, and somehow they were all correct. During college when he'd had to do papers along those lines for certain classes, he'd called Claire and had her guide him so he could complete his assignments.

Alex wanted to make the eyes on the bunny glow again, but he didn't dare with Beth in the room. He pushed whatever disquieting thoughts he had aside and got on with helping his wife sort the gifts. A bunny could just be a bunny.

CHAPTER SEVEN

The main effect the September 11th attacks had on Alex was to finally push him into joining the Army Reserve. It was something he'd looked into and seriously considered, and had eventually planned to do, but the direct attack on his country compelled him to sign up at a time he might otherwise have been too distracted to bother. Alex loved his country and the things it stood for, and he was concerned with a baby on the way that its home was being threatened. He wanted to contribute and make things safe for his family, even if this meant being away from them for a while. Individuals making sacrifices for the greater good had always been a concept that made sense to him. He wanted to help.

Alex didn't tell Beth where he was going the day he enlisted in late February of 2002. Before he put his signature to the government papers, he arranged that he could do his nine weeks of basic training soon so he would be home in plenty of time for the birth of the baby in May. Alex was bright and strong and motivated and exactly the kind of person the recruiters were looking for.

Before going home he decided to find Claire. He hadn't seen her since they parted on the dance floor at his wedding, and he missed her. He loved Beth—at least, he felt he should love Beth—but she wasn't exactly easy to talk to about things that mattered. He thought she liked the idea of being married better than the reality. It was all still so new it was hard to tell.

Beth had wanted a house right away, because she told him married people had houses, not furnished apartments. He wanted to make her happy, and it did make sense to get a house before the baby arrived and needed room, so they'd hunted in the dead of winter for something they could afford. There wasn't much, and Beth had gotten pouty when she realized they were not going to have a two-story home in a nice suburb like she had grown up in.

They settled on a small one-story house with an attached garage out in an old farmland area. There was not a lot around it, but Alex hoped one day someone would want to buy up the land in that area to develop into homes or an office park since it had easy access to the freeway, and they could sell at a good price and find something bigger and closer to town. His parents helped them with the down payment, and Beth's parents arranged to have it all painted and decorated once the place was officially theirs.

Alex was shocked by the effects of pregnancy on his wife's body. Beth was young and healthy, and everything was going about as smoothly as her doctor said it should, but pregnancy was more complicated than Alex would have imagined. There was a lot of vomiting the first few months, and apparently the term "morning sickness" was a misnomer, because Beth was sick all the time. He'd always pictured one day running out for ice cream or something in the middle of the night for his pregnant wife (several years in the future, but he tried not to dwell on that), however, Beth didn't seem to have cravings. She had aversions. She could smell things in their home or on his clothes that would send her running to the bathroom or the sink. Once he'd been treated at work to a lunch of garlic bread and pizza, and when he tried to kiss her when he got home, she practically broke her ankle trying to get away from him.

Beth was cranky and miserable, but she didn't believe she was behaving that way. If he told her he wanted to do something to cheer her up, she would act hurt and insulted that he thought she needed cheering up. Her moods were everywhere. She kept getting urinary tract infections and whimpering that she couldn't take anything for her headaches. Currently she was in a phase of excruciating leg cramps at night, and she had terrible heartburn that made it unpleasant for her to lie down. Not that the baby let her sleep if she did. Whoever was in there moved all night long and would apparently be a good candidate to join the dojo one day by Beth's account of its kicking ability. Pregnancy was no joke, and to dismiss any of it as some basic natural process with no adverse effects on the mother was, at best, unreasonable.

It made him rethink some of the arguments about abortion he'd had with Claire. He'd never considered pregnancy a hardship and didn't used to think its consequences had a place in the discussion, but maybe it was something to factor in after all.

Alex was staunchly pro-life, and Claire was as solidly planted in her pro-choice stance. Each knew the other could not be persuaded to switch sides, so the discussions didn't come up often, but when they did, the two of them really went at it with guns blazing. Alex was of the firm opinion that a baby was a baby, and no one had the right to kill it. For Claire the issue had to do with control over her own body and women being allowed to make their own decisions. The most unusual outcome of one of those arguments was when Claire managed to convince Alex to move even further over to the right.

"But it's not really about the baby, it's about judging the behavior of women!" Claire had insisted. At the time, Alex was trying to measure out the pieces of pine he was going to cut for the new weapons wall, and Claire was supposed to be helping. But somehow they'd gotten onto the messy topic and Alex had simply put down his measuring tape and pencil and prepared to verbally spar in the same space they were used to doing so with their bodies.

"No, I don't care how the baby got there, it's just that once it exists it should get a chance! If the woman doesn't want it she can give it up, so what's the big deal?"

Claire shook her head and said, "You make it sound like pregnancy is easy or something! It's not a small thing to go through all that, and if you don't want to, you shouldn't have to."

"Then don't get pregnant," said Alex.

"See, that's where the judgment comes in. Are you for an exception for rape or incest?"

"Well, yeah. That just doesn't seem fair."

"Then it isn't about the baby. You just said you don't care how the baby got there."

"Yeah, but isn't it punishment enough to have to go through something like that and—"

"So a woman who gets knocked-up by some other means and possibly—God forbid—enjoyed herself, deserves the *punishment* of pregnancy?" asked Claire.

"Claire, I don't think it's fair to have to carry a rapist's baby."

"But only if she's somehow absolved of making it."

"What does that even mean? Of course she's absolved if—"

Claire raised an eyebrow at him and said, "What if a woman consensually sleeps with a guy and gets pregnant and then finds out the next day on the news he's been arrested as a serial rapist. Does she still have to carry the rapist's baby?"

"Well, I think she does in that case, because she wasn't raped."

"Then what matters to you is the woman's behavior, not the baby. You want to decide for her what situation is upsetting enough to make a difference. A rapist's baby is still a rapist's baby no matter how it got there. You're saying in one case you can imagine being upset, so an abortion is okay, but in the other case she brought it on herself."

"I didn't say that, exactly," replied Alex. But she was confusing him. He had a hard time seeing the connection between the rights of a baby and the rights of women. Claire seemed to feel taking away a woman's right to an abortion led to women having no rights at all, and he didn't see how she could make that leap.

"Then what exactly are you saying?" she wanted to know.

Alex thought for a second. She was correct that it was inconsistent to believe a baby had rights but only dependent upon how it was conceived. "I guess I'm saying you're right. To not be hypocritical I have to be against any exceptions based on rape or incest."

Claire had never expected to be told by Alex she was right on anything to do with this topic. It was vexing to then find herself also disappointed by the fact.

"Are there any exceptions in your mind?" she asked.

"Well, now that you've convinced me to give up that one, I guess not," said Alex.

"What about the life of the mother?"

153

"That's just a given, Claire."

"Not to everyone! I talked to people on campus who felt that was God's will, and if she dies she dies."

"Yeah, but that's fucking crazy! Don't lump me in with that!" complained Alex.

"Why not? It just means you're on a slightly different place on the slippery slope."

"I'm not on the slippery slope! I'm pretty clear about what I believe, and you just clarified it more."

"Don't remind me. And the only people who are standing firmly on the bedrock at the absolute bottom of that slope are the crazy 'let the whore die' people. You are one step up, but on the slope."

"Fine, but that doesn't make where I'm standing slippery," insisted Alex.

"Sure it does. If you have room for one exception there could be more."

"Well, there aren't any more, okay? End of story!"

"So, if I got raped by my Dad—"

"Claire—"

"Just hear me out! If I got raped by my Dad and got pregnant with a two-headed baby without a brain in either head and no donatable organs, and the whole pregnancy was going to be a painful nightmare that kept me in bed the whole time throwing up in a bucket, you'd make me go through with the pregnancy?"

"Claire, that's stupid."

"No, that's an extreme scenario, and you have to make policy with exceptions in mind or else the most desperate cases fall through the cracks and suffer."

That didn't make sense to Alex. He felt policy should reflect the general sense of things. He trusted people found ways of dealing with the exceptions, but the exceptions shouldn't dictate what the basic law was for most people.

Claire studied him a moment and then said,

"Seriously, Alex, I want an answer. Do you think you or anyone else has the right to tell *me* I have to suffer like that to no useful end?"

Alex wasn't sure what to say. He would trust Claire to make a good decision. He didn't believe she would ever have an abortion—given a normal scenario. He simply didn't trust other people to do the right thing all the time, and felt there should be laws in place to keep things the way they should be—to keep women from killing babies he would raise if they were handed to him.

"Claire, if I have to think about your insane scenario, can you at least think about your own slippery slope when it comes to at what point a baby is a baby?"

"What do you mean?"

"If you were pregnant and you wanted that baby, then in your head you would think of it as a baby right from when you found out, wouldn't you?"

"Probably, but I don't have the right to tell someone else to think about it that way."

"Why not? Either it's a baby or it's not a baby. The second it's born you wouldn't say it's okay for someone to kill it, even if it were a hardship on the mother to let it live. What if she doesn't want it because it has something wrong they didn't catch in the womb? She can kill it before it's born because she can't deal, but not after? It's not the baby's fault. How is that fair?"

"But that's not how women make those decisions and—"

"How do you know? What about those extreme exceptions you were talking about? If a woman thinks what she's carrying is a baby until she gets a job as a bikini model, and then decides it's not a baby so she can kill it because it will screw up a photo shoot, then *that's* okay? Don't we need to protect babies from the

155

rare psychopath who wants to do that?"

"It's tragic, but that's the risk for making sure women maintain autonomy over their own bodies."

Alex shook his head. "That's a sacrifice, not a risk. A human sacrifice. There are problems either way, and I'm saying I'd rather err on the side of not killing babies."

Claire scowled as if she'd have to think about that one a little longer. "You still haven't answered whether or not you'd tell *me* what to do.

Alex threw up his hands. "God, Claire, just help me measure the fucking wall again, okay? I don't want Sensei thinking he can make me do push-ups simply because this isn't done when I promised."

Claire had reluctantly gone back to work and they didn't talk the rest of the time. They did, however, think loudly enough at each other that it didn't feel like silence.

The really interesting thing to them was how often over time they found themselves resorting to the very arguments they'd fought so hard against when with their own crowds. In a women's studies class, Claire had been the focus of great scorn when she insisted that people who were pro-life didn't necessarily want to oppress women. She found herself repeating verbatim things Alex had said in his own defense, because she knew how he meant them, even if she didn't agree.

Alex once had a similar experience during an engineering study group when someone had slammed all pro-choice advocates as baby killers. He felt personally responsible for defending Claire even though she wasn't involved, or even in the room, and they'd given him hell. He found himself at one point saying, "But you're a guy and it's not a decision you'll ever make, so why do you get the final say for someone else?" and thinking how strange his voice sounded in his ears saying such things. His arguments with Claire were heated, but constructive, and never devolved into something petty.

That was the trouble for Alex about disagreements with Beth. Any argument turned into a fight. She wanted the two of them to agree about everything or it meant they didn't love each other, apparently. Alex knew that wasn't true, because his feelings for Claire never changed no matter how hard the two of them argued. It usually felt good to be challenged like that, even if half the time it gave him a headache. Beth did not like challenge.

So on that day when Alex enlisted, he drove by the dojo to tell Claire first, but someone else was teaching. Next, he tried Claire's apartment, but she wasn't home. He decided to wait out front for a while and see if she showed up. He leaned by the doorway and watched people walk by. At one point, he observed a pair of men in Army fatigues and wearing berets and felt a sense of pride that he would soon own such a uniform. He pondered as he waited in the cold how to best tell Beth and his mom. He was not looking forward to it. He hoped Claire might understand better, since what she did for a living was like being a soldier in training. That or she'd hate it. Probably both.

After about half an hour when he was ready to give up and go home, Claire arrived with a small shopping bag. She was so surprised to see him there she almost didn't recognize him.

"Alex! Hey, come on up! You can talk to me while I chop stuff."

Alex smiled, and tried to peek in her bag while she fumbled with her keys. "What do you have?"

Claire laughed as she pushed open the door to the apartment building. "Nothing in here for you! But I've got sandwich stuff in the fridge if you want."

They walked up the three flights to the apartment they used to share and Claire let him in. He tossed his coat onto the couch and made himself at home. He decided a sandwich did sound good, and pulled out a tomato and some lunch meat and mayonnaise, then found the bread in the cupboard. It took him a second to locate, because Claire had rearranged things onto lower shelves after he'd moved out. Claire proceeded to pull an assortment of fruit from her bag and then got out a cutting board and a knife. She put some strawberries in a strainer and rinsed them off, and got to work cutting them up after giving Alex a second with the knife to cut some slices off the tomato.

"What are you making?" asked Alex as he slapped his sandwich together.

"A fruit salad for dessert tonight."

"Since when do you eat fruit for dessert?"

"Since I've been seeing a guy who doesn't eat refined sugar," said Claire.

Alex gave her a funny look and asked, "What's wrong with him?"

Claire grinned. "Other than thinking sugar is poison, not much so far. He's coming over in about an hour or so, and we might see a movie or we might hang out here, but he said he'd bring by some kind of vegan dinner if I made dessert."

Alex smiled and said, "Oh yeah, that's going to work. I see you lasting about a week without tacos and Oreos."

"Actually, weirdly enough, Oreos are vegan, believe it or not. Although the refined sugar I guess nixes them anyway. But I've gone two weeks so far and I'm still standing."

Alex looked at her knowingly and stopped chewing for a second.

"Fine!" said Claire, laughing. "Busted. I make sure to grab a cheeseburger before I see him so I can function."

Alex snorted and took another bite of his sandwich. "Seriously, it sounds like a match made in food hell. Or at least food purgatory. I mean, you like meat. And sugar. So why are you interested?"

"He's fun. I got paired with him to walk up the aisle at Jennifer's wedding and we had a good time."

"Jennifer was able to talk you into wearing that floofy blue dress? How'd she do that?"

"It was periwinkle, and yeah, sometimes you have to go above and beyond for a friend and do things that are painful, like those shoes. Anyway, with this guy, it doesn't have to go anywhere, but it's nice sometimes not to go to a movie alone. I mean, for those of us without a legally binding date for life we have to keep trying things." Claire slowed in her slicing as she realized then it was odd for Alex not to be home with his wife at that hour. "Why are you here, anyway?"

Alex had been so quickly lulled into their old routine that he'd completely forgotten why he'd stopped by. "Oh yeah. Uh...I guess I just wanted to tell you I joined the Army today."

Claire narrowly missed nicking herself with the knife she was using. She stared at him with her mouth open. "What? Now? You joined the Army *now* while we're bombing Afghanistan and troops are going over there? Are you crazy?"

"No, I'm not crazy! I felt like it was something I should do. Besides, it's the Reserve."

"Why do you think that makes any difference? You think they'll only ship you off one weekend a month, and two weeks in the summer? Alex!"

"Claire, I don't know why you're getting so upset! It's not like—"

"It's not like what? Like you'll be going off to war? That's exactly what it is!" Claire didn't know if she thought her friend was brave or an idiot. The line between the two things often seemed hard to draw.

"I wanted to feel like I was doing something, Claire. I hate feeling helpless about things, and it just seemed like a positive contribution to make."

She searched his face another moment, then turned back to her chopping. She was attacking the strawberries rather viciously and the pieces were getting kind of small, but she didn't seem to care.

Alex ate his sandwich and watched her. He knew she would forgive him because she didn't have a choice. Claire moved on to cutting up a small pineapple. She chopped off the spiky top with such force it made her bowl on the counter jump a little.

"Claire—"

"What?"

"Just don't cut off one of your fingers doing that because you're mad at me. You need your hands."

She sighed and looked him in the eye. "I don't...Alex, I hate this. I don't have a good feeling about it."

"Well I do, and I think it will be fine," he said.

"Yeah, but Alex, you shouldn't be trusting some of your instincts."

"What does that mean?"

"Never mind. Forget it. You'll make a great soldier and they're lucky to have you."

Alex felt like he'd been maligned in some way, but couldn't place exactly how. He decided to let it go and figured he should finally face Beth. At least with Claire there were no tears and he'd gotten a sandwich out of sharing his news.

"Hey, I have to run. Good luck with your date, and maybe we can all get together and chew on some

160

unsalted tree bark sometime, okay?"

Claire didn't smile, but she stopped what she was doing to walk her friend to the door. He slipped his arms into his coat but didn't bother to zip it. Claire fought the urge to do it for him.

"Alex, I...I need you to stay safe, all right?"

"I'll be fine! Basic training in Oklahoma is not the end of the world."

Alex gave her a small hug and waved as he headed down the stairs.

Claire didn't feel like chopping fruit anymore. But she also didn't want to disappoint her date, so she went back to making perfectly good fruit smaller.

When Alex got home, he discovered Beth was not as annoyed with the idea of his being in the Reserve, as she was with the fact that he'd be leaving her alone while pregnant for nine weeks, and then again sometime in the summer for a couple of months for specialized training when the baby was still little.

"You're abandoning me to go play soldier?"

Alex was insulted, and really didn't want to fight with his pregnant wife, but no matter what he did that seemed to be happening more and more. In his mind, the time apart might be beneficial and give them some breathing room. Apparently this was not true from Beth's point of view.

"I'm not *playing* soldier. I *am* a soldier. Or going to be, anyway. Why do you have to be so negative?"

"Because you are leaving me all alone, and already planning to do it again when the baby's here!"

"You can go stay with your parents if being alone makes you nervous! Jesus, I don't even know what you do here all day while I'm at work. It's not like you need to be in the house while I'm gone, so go wherever you want and call it a vacation while I'm in training!"

Beth looked incensed. "Don't know what I do? I

have picked out the theme for the nursery and am putting that together, I keep the house in order, I do the laundry and all the shopping, I do all the cooking for you, I—"

"How much time does it take to make spaghetti? And you act like I never lived on my own and don't know what the chores are or something. I handled all of that while working full-time for years so it's not like I—"

"But that wasn't in a house! And when the baby comes—"

"When the baby comes we'll figure it out. I promise. I'm not abandoning you. And look, this is going to bring in extra money which you've been wanting. This is a way I can do that since I'm not due for a raise yet, and maybe you can get the bassinet you were telling me about that I said we couldn't afford."

Beth paused. "The mahogany one with the ruffles?"

"Sure. That shouldn't be a problem now. And just think of this as an extra job where I have to travel sometimes. It will be fine."

As Beth got used to the concept, she did admit she liked the idea of seeing him in uniform, and the extra income was appealing. Alex couldn't tell if the peace they made on the issue was a sign of Beth's approval, or resignation that it could not be undone.

His mom was worried and his dad was proud. Pammy sounded like a carbon copy of Claire over the phone. He explained his plans at work, and they obligingly gave him the time off they were required to by law.

Basic training wasn't quite the ordeal Alex had expected, but it wasn't easy. Fort Sill, Oklahoma wasn't too hot at that time of year, but was barren and uninspiring. This was where he was supposed to begin what the Army referred to as the "soldierization process." Drill sergeants yelled at him to do everything faster, including eat, but they still didn't make him do as many push-ups as Claire used to when she thought his class was complaining too much. He was ordered to sing while he ran or walked, and he was surprised how many people around him couldn't carry a tune. (He was amused that the Army, of all places, was where they were going to learn.) It was arduous at first being up before dawn every day, but he got used to it. Alex got used to a lot of things, and returned home about two weeks before the baby came.

He returned to an extremely uncomfortable Beth and was glad that at least he was there to tend to her those last couple of weeks. She seemed more appreciative than she had been back when she took his presence for granted. She told him she liked his short haircut and was impressed with the level of shape he was in after so many weeks of more intense exercise. Alex liked the way he felt and made a promise to himself to keep it up. Instead of vague workouts whenever he could get them in, he made himself get up early every day and run two miles, and alternated days with push-ups and sit-ups so that passing the PT tests the Army required would continue to be easy.

Beth started having contractions in the middle of the afternoon one Thursday, but they were far enough apart that when she called Alex at work, she told him not to come home early. He stayed at work, but was no use to anyone the whole time. He finally went home early, and found Beth watching TV and timing her contractions with the pretty wristwatch she'd had Alex buy her for her birthday. He hated waiting around, but Beth seemed fine. The contractions hurt but weren't debilitating, and they were regular but far apart.

Things started speeding up around midnight and they finally went to the hospital. After about twelve hours of labor, Beth gave birth to a perfect baby girl. They hadn't wanted to know the sex of the baby beforehand, and Alex thought it would be worth the wait to be surprised, and he wasn't disappointed. Not about any of it.

Claire got the call from Alex later that day and thought he'd never sounded more tired or more happy. She hadn't seen him since before basic training, and now they had lots of catching up to do. Alex wanted her to see the baby right away, but Claire said she would wait until he called her when they returned home.

Claire always figured Alex would be a great dad, but his devotion to a kid that was actually his own was stunning. As much as Claire had unfortunate feelings about Beth, once the baby arrived in the world she could understand how Alex had come to the decision he had. He adored that baby, and anything short of marrying Beth would have kept him from her.

Caitlin Ashley Sullivan was as cute a baby as anyone could ever dream of. Claire went over to their tiny house in the middle of nowhere about a week after the baby was born. She didn't feel comfortable going to the hospital, since most of the people were there to see Beth, and she knew Beth didn't want to see her. But Alex had called her up once they were home again and said Beth would probably be resting in the middle of the day, and that Sunday would be a good time to come out and meet his new daughter.

Claire pulled up in front of the house to see Alex waiting for her on the front step with a little swaddled bundle in his arms. He had the biggest grin on his face she'd ever seen. He stood and met Claire halfway up the walk and turned so she could see the little scrunchy face nestled in the blanket. Caitlin was awake and had a comically concerned look on her face, as if there were sounds in the distance she didn't approve of.

Claire laughed. "Oh my God, Alex! She's beautiful!"

Alex smiled proudly. "She's so good, Claire. She almost never cries, and she sleeps for good stretches already, and she recognized my voice right there in the hospital that first day."

"Why, were you swearing?"

Alex laughed a little and said, "Yeah, I guess I'm going to have to cut that out, now, huh? Right Caitlin?" The baby gazed at him like she didn't believe a word of it. Alex and Claire both cracked up. Caitlin had a startled reaction, but she didn't cry.

They sat together on the front step and started filling each other in on how their lives had been going. Claire was most amused when Alex told her about the joys of doing push-ups in the rain. She laughed and suggested she might add that to her classes if the students got too whiny. Then Alex offered to have her hold the baby.

"Oh, can I? She's not too little to get passed around?"

"Hey, of course you fu—oh, yeah, the new swear-free me. Of course you can," he said.

She held out her arms as he transferred his baby over to her, and Claire was entranced. Caitlin was so tiny and cute. She even smelled good. Claire was genuinely happy for Alex at that moment and hoped it would last. She worried about his happiness.

They had a pleasant time on the step, until they heard Beth inside.

"Alex?" she called from somewhere inside the house.

"What?" Alex called back.

"Do you have the baby?"

"No, she just flew out of the bassinet. Of course I have the baby! And Claire's here."

There was no response to that, and a moment later

Beth was in the doorway in her robe looking tired. She seemed embarrassed to be seen in her still-bloated postpartum condition, but she'd put some blush and eyeliner on. She blinked at Claire a second, and then shifted her gaze toward Alex and said, "Did she wash her hands before you gave her Caitlin?"

"No, but she didn't touch the baby's face or anything. She's only touching the blanket."

"Well the pediatrician said—"

"I know what the pediatrician said. I was right there. It's fine. If I thought Claire was posing some kind of danger to the baby, I would do something about it, don't you think?"

Claire watched something silent pass between Alex and his wife that she couldn't read, and then Beth said, "Well, I want my baby back, now."

"It's *our* baby, and why now?"

"I need to feed her."

"But she's fine right now," protested Alex.

"Yes, and she'll stay fine if you give her back to me so I can feed her already!"

Alex reluctantly took the baby from Claire's arms and handed her over to Beth, who disappeared with Caitlin inside the house.

As they sat there, Claire wanted to ask about how things were going with Beth, but that was exactly the kind of thing she knew Alex's wife would see as meddling. Claire didn't think it was fair that merely because she was a woman it made Alex coming to her with his concerns a problem. He needed someone to talk to, and she could see it was stressful for him to be all boxed in. Claire was not a scheming kind of person, but she suspected Beth was. That made Claire wonder if Beth could only imagine motives of the type she was capable of herself, which meant Claire would remain untrustworthy until Beth changed. That wasn't going to happen anytime soon. Which meant certain conversations were off limits.

She squeezed Alex's knee and said instead, "The baby is beautiful."

He smiled to himself and then turned his grin toward her. "Yeah. Yeah, I go back and forth between not wanting her to change at all because she's so cute right now, and wishing she were already like, nine or something, so we could play catch or go to the fu—go to the zoo. Golly gosh darn this swearing thing is going to be hard to lick!"

Claire laughed. "You should get a rubber band to put around your wrist and snap yourself every time you slip."

"Sheesh, I'll have no wrist left."

"Oh, I think you'll be fine. I'm impressed you're making any attempt at cleaning up your language."

"You know, when I held that little girl in the hospital the first time, I promised her I would do anything for her. The least I can do is give up a few words I don't really need anyway."

"Well, I think you're great, and Caitlin's a lucky little girl."

"Thanks, Claire."

They sat in silence for a while and simply enjoyed the comfortable sense of each other's body so close by for a change. The two of them had always had a very physical if platonic relationship, but it had seemed odder once Alex had stopped working on his jujutsu and gotten married. They were both trying to negotiate some new boundaries but they hadn't figured them out yet. Beth finally called from inside the house again.

"Alex!"

"What?"

"I think I want to go out to my Mom's today! Come help me pack up some stuff."

"What? Why? Excuse me, Claire." Alex got up, clearly annoyed.

She listened uncomfortably for a minute as Alex and Beth argued inside, Alex insisting that she had said they'd be home the whole day and that she knew he wanted to see Claire. Beth said she didn't feel well and that she wanted to be where her mother could pamper her a little since Alex was no good for that.

Claire wondered if she should go, but it was rude to Alex and played too well into Beth's hands. She tried to study the clouds instead. It was hard to convince herself of shapes in them now using adult eyes. She questioned if as a child she really had seen fanciful things more clearly, or if she had been better at making herself believe she had. It made her wonder if she'd still be able to find the constellations she and Alex had made up that night they'd owned the stars.

Alex finally came out and apologized. He appeared tired and frustrated.

"That's okay," Claire said. "I didn't expect to get to stick around for very long, anyway. You know, people with new babies—not famous for having much social time." She could tell he didn't want her to go, but he put an arm around her and walked her to her car.

"Thanks for coming out here. Maybe when the baby's bigger or something, I can find some time to bring her out to you."

"Sounds good," said Claire. "Anything you need, you know I'm only a phone call away, right?"

"I know. It's...there's a lot to adjust to. We'll be fine."

"Okay. Bye, Alex."

"Bye, Claire."

She got into her car and watched him head back toward the house in a way that was an odd combination of graceful and lumbering. Like an exhausted dancer. Observing his body, she realized it had been a long time since they'd done any sparring. He was so broad and strong now, she wondered how much harder it would be to throw him. Despite the height difference, they had been a much more equal match physically in high school. She used to touch him all the time. The idea of having her hands on his body like that currently felt a little foreign. She still hoped someday he might find the time to get his black belt, but that was looking less and less likely the way his life was going. He had graduated to modern martial arts, and that involved signing your life away and using an M-16.

Alex and Claire weren't able to see each other often, but they tried to stay in touch. If Beth had made Claire feel welcome at their house things would have been different. Claire would have liked to have seen the baby as she grew, and to have talked with her friend face to face, but that wasn't possible. Alex called her, usually when he was up late at night with the baby when Caitlin was restless and Beth was asleep. He would fill her in about work and everything Caitlin was doing, and he loved hearing about the dojo, even though he was feeling less and less in touch with everything and everyone there. Claire would tell him funny stories from the classes she was teaching, and about her preparations for her next level black belt test.

Right after the fourth of July, Alex went off for two months of training in Missouri for his MOS ("Military Occupational Specialty," he explained to Beth—where he would get trained in a skill). He had specifically signed up to be a carpenter in the Army Corps of Engineers, but the official title for that was Carpenter/Mason, so he also learned about pouring concrete and laying block, in addition to framing a building and hanging doors. Fort Leonard Wood in Missouri was not as taxing as Fort Sill had been, but he still slept in a barracks and had to go on group runs. There were very few breaks and the days were long. The thunderstorms at night were like nothing he'd ever seen before. He wrote to Claire that it was better than the finale at a fireworks display. Most of the time it didn't even rain, but the lightning seemed close enough he was surprised it wasn't taking out nearby trees.

Claire didn't get his letters until he was practically back, because the opportunity had come up to attend a seminar in Japan. She was able to tour Tokyo with Sensei and two other black belts, and even got to work in the Grand Master's space for a week. It was a remarkable experience and she felt she had a much better understanding of her art having seen where it developed. Claire found Japanese culture inscrutable and marvelous and wished she could really speak the language. She only knew the words for things like punches and kicks, along with strange jujutsu phrases such as "crushing the devil"—none of which were too handy in a restaurant or when searching for the bathroom.

The two friends had a lot to share when they returned from their respective trips, but Alex's life as a married man with a child made any real contact nearly impossible. He still called Claire at night if he was up alone with the baby, but he didn't get to see her. That changed a little when he and Beth found themselves in a baby-sitting crisis almost a month before Caitlin's first birthday.

Beth's parents were having a formal party on a Sunday afternoon in celebration of their 30th wedding anniversary. Everyone, including Alex's parents, was invited except for children under ten, and Beth was looking forward to wearing nice clothes and not lugging around the baby. She told Alex she wanted to be seen with him in a nice suit with no spit-up on his shoulder. Unfortunately, all the relatives they generally left Caitlin with would be there, too, so they had to find someone new. They asked around until they found a seventeen-year-old who said she could do it, but then the morning of the party, she canceled to play in a soccer game. Alex couldn't figure out how a soccer game could sneak up on someone so that they didn't have more notice, and Beth started frantically calling all of her friends, none of whom were either home or available. She was upset, and Alex said he didn't have a problem with missing the party to stay home with the baby himself, but Beth wasn't hearing of it.

"I could try Claire," he finally offered.

Beth looked irritated at the suggestion, but the closer the departure time got, the more it apparently wasn't sounding so bad. They were in a bind, so Beth relented. Alex called Claire.

"I have plans with Ben, today," said Claire. "I don't want to bail on him with no notice."

"But you're my last hope, Claire! What am I supposed to do?"

Claire thought about it for a moment. She did want to help, and they really had to be desperate if Beth was agreeing to ask her.

"I guess I could do it if I can bring Ben along with me."

"Great! Sure! Bring Ben! Have a party! Can you be here in an hour?"

"I'll do what I can."

"Thank you! You're the best, Claire," he said, which earned him a dirty look from his wife that he chose to ignore.

Claire and Ben drove up as Beth and Alex were ready to rush out the door. The young married couple were dressed up and looked lovely, and Alex carefully handed Caitlin over to Claire.

"There's instructions on the fridge about how to do her bottles. Diapers and stuff are in all the obvious places, if she starts rubbing her ears it means she's tired and might go down for a nap—don't let her go to sleep with a bottle even though she'll want to—and, uh...I don't know. Don't let her run with scissors. Okay?" said Alex.

"Got it. Bottles, diapers, scissors," said Claire.

Beth glanced skeptically at Claire, but Ben delightedly gave the baby his finger to play with and said, "Don't worry. I've got her covered. Cute belt, Beth —did it come with the outfit?"

Beth looked pleased for the first time since Claire and Ben had arrived and said, "Thanks, no, I found it at a vintage store."

"The one on Clement?" asked Ben.

"No, the one a couple blocks past that."

"Oh, you're good! You have to have quite an eye to find anything as nice as that over there."

Alex and Claire were out of their element and shared a look, and then Alex reminded Beth they had to run.

"Okay," she said, and then to Ben added, "If you need anything, my cell phone number is on the list in the kitchen."

Ben and Claire had a great afternoon watching the baby. They originally had planned to get together at a coffeehouse to talk about the possibility of Ben and Jacob going up to Vermont for a civil union ceremony, and he wanted to run some ideas by Claire before presenting the notion to the rest of the family. However, all talk of Ben's life went out the window while Caitlin was awake and available to play with. At eleven months, Caitlin was on the verge of walking alone and wanted to hold onto someone's hands so she could tour the house in her wobbly way. She laughed and clapped. She had a dimple in her right cheek.

Claire was mesmerized the same way she had been the first time she saw Caitlin. She'd only had the opportunity to see Alex's baby on a few brief occasions, usually at the dojo when Alex would stop by while doing errands and wanted to show Caitlin off. For Claire to actually hold her and see her move and hear her babble was almost unreal. She hoped she would have a baby as sweet someday.

But in the baby-sitting department, Claire was merely an assistant to Ben. He'd gone out to help Jason when each of his kids was born and was natural with babies in general. He talked to Caitlin as if she were an adult and she loved it. She kept grabbing his nose and laughing, and when he did peek-a-boo with her, she acted as if it were the greatest comic routine ever.

Eventually Caitlin started rubbing her ears and climbed into Claire's lap. Within a matter of minutes the baby was passed out there, and Claire thought it was the most wonderful feeling having the weight of that sweet trusting little person in her arms like that. No wonder Alex was smitten and didn't get out much.

The baby rested for about an hour that way in Claire's lap, and Ben found some cookies and milk to snack on while they chatted over the sleeping girl. He told Claire about how he and his boyfriend were planning on buying a house together soon.

In a perfect world, Ben and Jacob would get married and adopt kids, but for some reason too many people in power believed that the nation would crumble and all would be lost if such earth-shaking events were to transpire. The closest they were going to get was the civil union ceremony Vermont offered to gay couples, and the rest they would figure out over time. Ben was not a political person, and Claire knew he hated that by simply trying to do the most basic things that others did, he was making a political statement. All he wanted was a family of his own. A wedding could be a start. Ben asked Claire if she would be his best man.

"You know, since you've had practice at it," he said, biting into his cookie.

Claire laughed quietly so as not to wake Caitlin, and said she'd be honored. "Can I wear a tux at yours?"

"God no! I'll find you something cute once we pin down color schemes and all that."

"How can you do a gay wedding and be that traditionally conformist by making me wear a dress?"

"Because it's my day to be the princess and you have to do what I say."

Claire laughed again and Caitlin stirred in her arms. She kissed the sleepy girl on the forehead. Claire wished she would finally find someone. It was hard to have all the men in her life paired off and to still be alone herself. She was going to be twenty-four in a few days and it was sounding old to her, even though she knew that was probably silly. But it was the oldest she'd ever been, so she couldn't help it.

When Alex and Beth returned they seemed happy and uncharacteristically relaxed. They didn't get out much alone, and it had been good for them. Alex wondered if they got out like that more often if they would fight less when they were home.

Caitlin was up by then and clinging to Ben. Beth didn't seem to care, but Alex was a little hurt that his baby was torn between coming to him and staying with this new guy she'd only known for a few hours.

"She's a total doll!" said Ben, holding her hands and walking her over to her dad where she finally let him scoop her up and nuzzle her cheek. Alex kissed Caitlin in the palm of her hand and wrapped her fingers around it, which made her laugh.

Ben and Beth took a minute to finish their earlier conversation about vintage clothing stores in town, and Alex and Claire went out on the front steps with the baby.

"She's amazing, Alex. I'm glad you called me."

Alex was pleased and grinned happily. "I'm glad you finally got to spend some time with her. I honestly can't imagine my life without this little girl."

The two of them sat and played with Caitlin, who climbed from one lap to the other, and eventually Ben emerged from the house to drive Claire home. In the car, Ben told Claire that Beth wasn't as bad as she'd made her out to be.

"Are you blind?"

"Well, Claire, of course she's uncomfortable around you. She's a bit young, and insecure, and from where she's standing you look like a threat."

"But I'm not! I wish she would see that already and let it go."

"She's not crazy, Claire. She knows Alex is not going to cheat on her or something. God, that boy's as loyal as a dog. But I think she wonders if the house were on fire which one of you he'd save."

"Caitlin."

"Well, no kidding. He'd drag himself over a mile of broken glass for Caitlin, but beyond that? Sweetheart, it's a coin toss."

Claire considered it for a while. Ben didn't sound wrong. Maybe she should have a little more sympathy for Beth's position. Maybe.

It did help considerably as far as Claire was concerned that Beth actually liked Ben a great deal. The most interesting result of the last-minute baby-sitting decision was that Ben made it onto Beth's go-to sitter list. When Alex and Beth decided they did need to get out as a couple, and if they wanted to see to a movie in the middle of the week when it was harder to find a relative to watch the baby, they'd call Ben. If his boyfriend were scheduled to work anyway, and Ben would have otherwise been at home alone, he preferred going over and caring for Caitlin and didn't charge them.

In the meantime, Alex was enjoying the Army Reserve. When he reported to his new unit after his training at Fort Wood, he was offered the opportunity to become an officer since he had a college degree. Beth told him at first she thought he should, because it sounded prestigious and paid better, but then she found out it would require another two months of training somewhere and nixed it. That suited Alex fine since he wasn't interested in the added responsibility, and the officers didn't get to do the kinds of hands-on things that interested him anyway.

His early drill weekends were spent learning to drive different military vehicles, and a couple of times a year they worked on marksmanship, which he was good at. His unit at one time did interesting projects in the local area, such as building structures for city parks and the like, but with troops being called up, those projects had gone by the wayside.

Alex guardedly waited for something to happen with his unit in terms of deployment, but nothing out of the ordinary did. He got to work on the Alaskan road project during his two weeks of annual training in 2003, and he liked the easy schedule of one weekend a month of training close to home, but when the President decided to invade Iraq and still nothing much happened with his unit, he wondered why not.

Initially his unit was designated as a donor group, and certain individuals were plucked out and used to fill gaps in other units around the country that needed more people in order to be deployed. As time dragged on, and Alex did more annual training in 2004 (this time at the less scenic Fort McCoy, Wisconsin), he was starting to resent being passed over, even as his wife, mother, sister, and best friend breathed a collective sigh of relief each time he was. He could understand Beth's apprehension since she was due with another baby that July, but from everyone else it felt like a lack of confidence in him.

Claire was doing heavy campaigning for the democratic presidential candidate, John Kerry, for that fall's election. Between that, and preparing to test for her third-degree black belt, she didn't have much time to keep in touch with Alex. She reserved her efforts for big moments, such as when she came out to meet the new baby when he was born, this time at the hospital because Ben came with her. Conner James was a fairly easy delivery and quicker than the prior one, and Caitlin was almost as proud to be a big sister as Alex was to be a father again.

It was difficult for Alex to talk to Claire at that time anyway, because she was so angry with Bush and so opposed to the war, and he didn't like the level to which he felt she got carried away. The problem was, he had trouble refuting most of her arguments. It did seem that all the reasons the administration had laid out initially to justify such an action had systematically fallen one by one. All Alex was left with was the fact that what was done was done, and they had to finish what they started. He believed the lives of a billion people in that region hung in the balance, and America could have a hand in making the future better for them and the world at large, or it could leave a disaster that would haunt his children and his children's children. He believed they still had a responsibility there, no matter how right he thought Claire might be on many of her points.

The funny thing for Alex about the upcoming election was that he was genuinely torn. He told Claire he couldn't bring himself to vote for Kerry, but he didn't want to vote for Bush this time, either. He had too much information from the military perspective to find the President trustworthy anymore, and it frustrated him. He'd had conversations with people returning to his unit about what a mess things were, and how badly certain things were handled, which was unfair to the individual soldiers who he knew worked hard.

He still sided with Republicans on most social issues, except for one important one, and sadly it was on that point that the two candidates seemed to agree. Gay marriage somehow found its way to the top of the agenda that year, and Alex had completely reversed himself on that compared to the last election. Unfortunately (to Claire's great dismay), Kerry also claimed to oppose it.

The thing that had turned Alex around was watching Ben with his kids. He had never met another guy who showed as much genuine delight in kids as he did himself. Alex usually felt lonely in the joy he got from children, because it was not generally something men expressed any passion for, and he worried that people might misinterpret his own interest as pedophilia or something disgusting along those lines. It was nice when he finally had children of his own to lavish attention on and have it be considered acceptable. Ben wanted children, too, but in his case it would always be deemed suspicious or condemned by someone.

That struck Alex as tremendously unfair. Ben was great with kids, and Alex trusted him completely with Caitlin and Conner. When he sat for them, Ben made sandwiches cut into cool shapes, got down on the floor to play silly games, and could read them the same book a dozen times and never seem bored. As far as Alex was concerned, any kid would be lucky to call Ben "Dad."

Alex now saw the Republican platform as it related to gays as intrusive and punitive to no productive end. Ben adopting a kid that someone else didn't want or couldn't raise was win-win as far as he could see. Especially when Alex considered the opinion he shared with his party on abortion, it seemed insane not to open the adoption pool to as many qualified candidates as possible willing to adopt the children who would result from such a policy. But Democrats were only marginally better on gay rights, declaring loudly and often that gays shouldn't marry. For all intents and purposes, their offerings of rights for Ben were merely lip service if they couldn't grant him something as basic as marriage, and empty promises were not enough to sway Alex's vote.

When he stood in the voting booth that November, he stared for a long time at the presidential choices, and finally left that section blank.

CHAPTER EIGHT

Claire was torn about the idea of air conditioning in the dojo. Sensei had been putting her in charge of more and more decisions concerning the business and the classes, and so many of the students were coming to her about air conditioning that she was trying to make up her mind before talking to Sensei about it herself.

On the one hand, the August they were in the middle of was particularly hot, and potentially that could make it tougher to attract new students into a space that was sweltering. On the other hand, jujutsu wasn't supposed to be easy or comfortable. Their little space was so much more agreeable and inviting than anyplace she'd trained in Japan. It got unbearably hot there, too, and she was given only hot tea to drink on her breaks. You were supposed to acclimate and endure, which were necessary skills in jujutsu and in life. That was a good lesson, and she didn't know how much air conditioning undermined it or not.

From her own personal point of view, she didn't need it. Claire liked to sweat. She liked knowing she was working hard, and the heat didn't bother her. She accepted she was hot and got over it. But there was attracting and retaining students to consider, and so many of her students were whiney. When they grumbled as she led them through all the push-up variations, they didn't seem to realize that she did them with every class. They may be doing fifty push-ups they didn't like, balancing themselves on their fists and on the backs of their hands, but Claire was doing them for three classes in a row, and by her 150th push-up for the day she wasn't complaining. She figured that was why she was there, to get stronger and improve.

It still bugged her that even though she could do the advanced push-ups on her thumbs or the tips of a few fingers, she wasn't strong enough to do them with one arm at a time. Alex could do that, and made it look easy. She wished he would get back into jujutsu. Claire thought of him every time she stepped into that space to stretch, even though it had been years since she'd worked with him there.

As she ran through her last class of the evening, she decided almost sadistically against the air conditioning. As the group of mostly white belts did their kicks and sweated and looked annoyed, all she could think about was how easy their lives were if this was the toughest thing in their day and they were paying for the privilege. Claire tried not to take for granted that she never went hungry, never wondered where she was going to sleep, and didn't live in fear for her life or safety in more than the most abstract of terms. A little sweat wasn't going to kill them, and next month would cool down considerably anyway.

She chose to distract her students from the heat by using the end of class to do what they called "fencing." Everyone sat at the end of the mat, and then Claire selected two students to come up and face one another. She handed each a foot-long section of foam rubber tubing that they were supposed to treat as knives.

The rules were simple: no hitting to the face, no stabbing (only clean slashes), and you had to kiai (make a deliberate sound such as "Ai!") when you struck. Claire would position them to start, tips of their "knives" touching, and standing far enough back from one another that each person had to make a deliberate advance on their opponent in order to land a strike. Claire would signal when they could start, and make the call when she thought someone scored a point. Best two out of three won the match and remained standing to face the next opponent.

Claire was always fascinated by which students had a knack for the fencing exercise. Rank meant very little. She found scoring a point on Sensei nearly impossible, and most students found it difficult to land a blow on her, but that had certainly happened. Often white belts were best at the fencing exercise. They had little experience and nothing to lose. They were unpredictable. Claire had often told Alex that white belts were the most dangerous people in the dojo.

The exercise went well and had the students so energized they did forget about the heat. Fencing was one of the few sparring opportunities that got Claire working on that same level, so she decided to take a turn with the student left standing once they'd all had a try. She picked a white belt to make the call as to when they should start, and she positioned herself with her foam knife tip to tip with her opponent's. He was a young guy named Zach who had gotten his green belt only the week before. He was 17 and not much taller than she was, but strong. He was nervous to the point of almost appearing scared.

Claire kept her face clear of any expression. As the match started, and they pulled their knives in toward their bodies defensively, they began circling each other on the mat. The adrenaline rush in that moment always amazed her. It was the closest thing in her life to understanding real panic, and she was interested in controlling it. She found if she didn't fight it, or obsess about it, and simply let it run its course, she could use the extra clarity and quickness it provided to her advantage. Most students used it to their detriment by acting impulsively and leaving themselves vulnerable by mistake. Claire made a couple of false lunges to get him to back up where she wanted him, and got in an easy and sound swipe to his thigh.

For round two, she pulled back from their neutral position and simply stood there. Zach waited for something to happen and appeared confused, and the other students were rapt. Claire remained expressionless, and slowly raised her knife straight up above her head. She resembled a black belt version of the Statue of Liberty. She waited. Zach looked as if he couldn't imagine what he was supposed to do because if he approached her, she could swing her arm down and get him easily, as if he were on a chopping block. But Claire merely waited. She wanted to see how much nerve he really had, and she wanted to see how predictably he might strike her across her body.

A lot of martial arts worked like a magician doing a trick. There were a million variations on how to dramatically present someone with the card they selected, but it all hinged on how well the magician forced the mark to pick the right card at the start. You could eliminate a lot of uncertainty in a fight by simply making your opponent strike at the place you were prepared for them to go.

The smart thing for Zach to do would be to be brave enough to aim for her arm, or maybe her ankle, but everything about the way she was presenting herself said to hit her straight on. Eventually he got up the nerve to step forward, and she let him get in a slash across the torso. She praised him, because the strike took guts even if it was predictable. At that point, Claire realized she was tired and decided to get in her last point quickly so she could go home.

They faced off, but this time when the signal came, instead of pulling back she took advantage of the slow way Zach always pulled his knife in, and she leaned forward just enough to slide her weapon straight down along his and across his wrist. He would have had nothing left with which to hold a knife if they had been using real blades. Zach looked surprised, then bowed, and they all took their places in order to bow out together.

As she was shaking the last student's hand and sending the two girls in the class downstairs to change, Alex walked in. Claire lit up. It was a welcome surprise.

"Hey, when did you get here?" she asked happily. The male students waiting for their turn to go downstairs glanced at Claire with curiosity, since she was smiling in a way that was simply sweet and not a disguised warning. She heard one of them speculate quietly to another if the muscular guy who'd entered the dojo was her boyfriend, and if it was freaky to date a girl who could knock you over. She shot the student a smile that was decidedly less sweet, and he shut his mouth quickly and shifted his gaze toward the ceiling.

Alex grinned and walked over with Claire to a spot more removed from where the students were standing. "I was watching the last couple of fencing rounds through the window," he said. "You must be tired to have gone with that wrist slashing move. Kind of ends things quick."

Claire laughed. "Yeah, well, they only fall for that once, so I'm in for a longer fight next time."

Alex's grin faded a little as he asked, "You busy now?"

"No, once everyone gets changed and out of here, I just have to sweep up and I can go, too."

"I still remember how all of that goes. Want help?"

"Sure!" said Claire. "I'd like that." She didn't know why he was there, but she didn't care right then. She simply liked having him back in the dojo.

The girls came up and left, and the boys went down to change, and Alex kicked off his shoes and grabbed the broom from by the radiator. He started carefully sweeping from the back corner of the mat to the front as Sensei had at some time or other instructed every white belt how to do. Claire retreated into her own private area and changed her clothes. She put her gi into a bag so she could bring it home to wash right away. By the time she was done, everyone was out of the dressing room below and was putting on their shoes and heading out. Alex put the broom and dustpan away and Claire got the lights and locked up.

Once they were on the sidewalk in front of the dojo, Claire wasn't sure where they should go because she still didn't know the reason for his unexpected visit.

"Are you hungry?" she asked. "'Cause I'm starved and I was thinking of grabbing something from the Greek place on the way home." One of the nicest things about that area of town was the wide diversity of ethnic food. The best sushi around was only a few blocks away, and there was a Middle Eastern restaurant close by that she'd always meant to try.

"I can walk you there, but then I have to get back home," said Alex.

They walked slowly under the light of the street lamps and Claire started to become nervous.

"So, what is it you don't want to tell me?" she finally asked.

Alex smiled to himself, knowing he was busted. He looked at his feet as he placed one in front of the other and said, "I'm getting deployed this fall."

Claire came to a dead halt. "You're getting what?"

"Deployed, Claire. My whole unit has been called up. I have to go out to Camp Atterbury in Indiana for a while, and then I'm going to Iraq."

"No."

"No?" That actually made Alex laugh unexpectedly. "What do you mean, 'no?'"

"You can't go!" said Claire. "You have little kids and a life and, and—"

"And so does practically everyone else over there. You know that."

Claire shook her head. "But, you can't go, Alex! If you get hurt or—"

"I won't get hurt. I promise," said Alex. Her face was tipped down, so he lifted her chin up gently with his right hand and made her look at him. "Do you hear me? It's going to be okay, Claire."

She nodded. There were no tears. Alex could always trust that with Claire there would be no tears.

Alex said, "I need you to do something for me. I need you to check in on my mom once in a while. She and Beth don't really get along and, well, talking to you would be a big help to her, I'm sure. I think she likes you better than she likes me."

"I doubt that," said Claire quietly.

"Hey, Claire, you can write me letters or send me e-mail—I'll have my laptop with me. I'll only be gone a year, maybe two tops, and—"

"Only? *Only* a year or two? Oh my God, Alex, what —"

"Come on Claire, I'm counting on you to be the tough one here. Remember? I'm the wuss in this relationship."

"That's the problem! How am I supposed to survive here knowing you are out there with someone trying to literally kill you every minute and I can't—"

"I'm sure not every minute, and besides—"

"Yes, every minute! And this war is wrong anyway and you shouldn't be there and I—"

"Claire, I don't approve of how we got there either, but it needs to be resolved and I don't have a problem with being a part of that. How many times do we have to go over this?"

"Enough that it keeps you here."

"Well, that's not happening. I got the call from my captain back in April and—"

"You've known since April? Why am I just hearing about this now?" Claire was trying to keep calm, since she didn't want to appear upset, and she knew Alex didn't need to see her that way, but it was difficult.

"Yeah, well...Beth kind of freaked out and wanted to wait before telling anyone in case something changed. We've had a couple of false alarms before and it's stressful, so it made sense to wait a little bit and see if it would pan out. And then in late May when it all seemed a go, you were in Japan and it didn't seem like the right time to tell you as soon as you got back, and we each had family stuff in July.... I'm sorry, Claire. I should have found a way to tell you sooner, but...."

Claire started walking again. She wasn't hungry now, but heading toward the restaurant gave her something basic to focus on. Alex walked beside her and didn't say anything.

"So, what can I do?" she asked. "I feel like I should be helping with something."

"I told you what you can do. You can check in on my mom while I'm gone. She's not taking the news well at all, and I expect it will get worse for her when I actually leave."

Claire thought about it. "It doesn't seem like enough."

Alex walked quietly next to her for a moment and then said, "You know how to bake your mom's cookies, right? You used to do that at our apartment when you were bored. Send me some of those."

"Okay."

"Claire, I'm going to be fine."

"Sure."

"Claire?"

"Hm?" She stopped walking again to look at him, but felt as if she were having trouble really seeing him.

"I have to get going. I'm supposed to be home in time to read a story to Caitlin and I don't want to break my promise. There's time before I go to Camp Atterbury, so I'll make sure I see you again. I still have to train the guy they're hiring to replace me at work while I'm away, and, you know, just stuff. But we'll get together, okay?"

"Okay."

He gave her a hug, and as he started to release her she hung on extra tight, so they simply stood there a while. She was scared that it might be the last time she felt his arms around her like that. She was afraid to let him go if it meant he had to go to war. But Claire did finally let him go. His daughter was waiting, so Claire relaxed her grip and watched Alex leave. She walked straight home and put herself to bed and waited a long time to fall asleep.

Alex felt terrible leaving Claire like that, but there really had been no good way to tell her. He knew all too well her feelings about their country's involvement in Iraq, and there wasn't anything more he could say to assuage her fears. She'd be okay, though. Alex was more worried about his kids and Beth. Claire was tough, his wife wasn't, and he had no idea about his kids in this situation.

Over the next couple of months, Alex prepared his

family for his departure and got Beth acquainted with the appropriate people in the family readiness group associated with his unit. He arranged for a yard service so Beth wouldn't have to worry about chores that were generally his. He made sure his will was in order. He taught his wife how to handle the finances and do their taxes and find the fuse box. Alex didn't know how much of those things she was really going to do, and how much she would get her dad or brother or friends to help with, but it didn't matter. As long as everything ran smoothly without him, he was fine.

He trained his replacement at work, and his colleagues there treated him with great reverence and respect. People with opinions on either side of the conflict tended to be unnervingly solemn with him. Much of the time they approached the topic of his upcoming deployment as if he had a terminal disease, which irked him. He came to think of it as the "cancer look." Alex knew everyone was worried, but he was not envisioning his assignment in Iraq as a dire circumstance. It was an opportunity to test himself and put to work all the training and expense the government had seen fit to invest in him. He was ready and he wasn't scared.

The only thing that didn't happen before he got on the bus to Camp Atterbury was getting together with Claire again. Beth kept coming up with one more thing she needed him to do or get or arrange, and by the last couple of weeks all he really wanted to do was be with his kids. Caitlin was three (and a *half*, she liked to remind him frequently) and said something surprising and new every day, and Conner was sixteen-months and running nonstop.

Alex experienced brief moments of doubt here and there when his kids would do something particularly adorable, and he would realize how much of their lives he was going to miss. If he was away from them for an hour it felt like they'd grown and changed noticeably in his absence. He expected to be away for a period of time equivalent to Conner's entire life so far, and what would they be like then? Would they even remember him? The thought panicked him a little if he let it. He wanted to see Claire, but time with his kids was more important. She didn't like goodbyes anyway, so he put a package together for Claire instead, and arranged for Ben to get it to her.

But the thing about Claire was that even when she wasn't there, she was still kind of there. It didn't matter how long a stretch they were apart, they always picked up where they left off, and she was part of his daily thought process so she never felt far away. He especially felt her with him the day Caitlin found the bunny.

"Daddy, what's this for?" she asked, pulling the neglected stuffed rabbit out from the back of Alex's closet. He'd been sorting through everything and putting things in a pile for Goodwill that he didn't think were worth Beth putting into storage while he was gone. There was a lot of stuff that was too small on him now, including his gi, sadly. He'd been a skinny thing in high school, and when he'd tried the top of his gi on for the hell of it, it didn't want to close enough across his chest, and it was way too tight in the arms. At least his waist wasn't that far off.

He'd hesitated with the gi over the Goodwill pile, and then folded it up to put into a box instead—the one at the very back of his closet, with his prom picture and his defunct Blockbuster card inside. There was also a bottle cap from the last beer he ever drank that made him black out. He was holding it when Claire had called and told him to stop his excessive drinking, and he had, but he'd carried that bottle cap in his pocket for years as a reminder. Most of the printing was worn off from rubbing it with his thumb on many a night when things got hard and he wanted to keep his promise. That was something Beth knew nothing about. There were lots of things in the box he didn't want to explain to Beth. Things that she'd probably want to fight about. Like the bunny.

"Oh, Caitlin, that was actually from Aunt Claire for you, but your mom worried it was a little scary."

"But I'm not scared."

"I know you're not. You're my super brave girl, aren't you? But this bunny isn't exactly what it seems."

Caitlin looked at the bunny and back at her dad, not understanding. Alex smiled and pulled both her and the bunny into his lap and showed her how to reveal the fangs in its mouth. Caitlin's eyes went wide and she laughed. "It's like a secret bad bunny!" she squealed.

"Yes, it kind of is," he said, grinning. "Except the battery must be dead because its eyes are also supposed to glow all red.

Caitlin got excited. "Can we make them glow? Please?"

"I guess. Let me see what kind of battery it needs and then you can find a match in the drawer in the kitchen."

"Mommy doesn't like me in that drawer. She says I mess it up."

"It's a junk drawer, Honey. You can't mess it up. There's like, a key we don't know what it goes to, and like, a million rubber bands, and we may have to try a few of those batteries in there until we find one that works, okay?"

"Can I have the key?" asked Caitlin brightly.

Alex laughed. "Why do you want the key?"

"Because you have keys so that could be my key."

"Hm. Well, let's wait until Conner is older and not

putting everything in his mouth and then yes, you can have it."

Alex had finally fished the battery out of the hidden compartment inside the rabbit and showed it to his daughter. "See there? It's a triple-A."

"I only know regular A," explained Caitlin.

"Yeah, this isn't a new letter, it's the regular A three times. Triple means three. It starts with the same letters as 'triangle' and remember how a triangle has three sides?"

Caitlin nodded seriously. "Yes, and a square means a triangle with *four* sides," she said, carefully holding up 4 fingers for him.

Alex smiled. "You smarty-goof, where did you learn that?"

"I figured it out," she said proudly.

"Did you? Well you're awesome." He scrunched up his face a little to let her know a challenge was coming. "How many sides does a circle have?"

Caitlin sat blinking a moment and then told her dad, "The inside and the outside."

Alex let out a surprised laugh while tickling his daughter enough to make her squeal. "I like that. It may not get you through geometry very well, but that's how I will think of a circle from now on." Caitlin grinned.

He gave her the old battery to compare to ones available in the kitchen drawer and continued his sorting while she went off to look. She returned with four triple-A batteries and the key.

"Honey, I thought we were going to leave that in the drawer until Conner's older, remember? He could choke on this or get lead poisoning or something."

"You said it was mine now."

"I did, but I also said it needs to stay in the drawer."

"But I don't want it in the drawer, I want it with

you."

Alex was confused. Nothing gave him more pleasure than trying to follow his daughter's train of thought, but this one was getting away from him.

"But I have keys, remember? So why do I need this key?"

"Because you said it was my key."

"Caitlin, I'm not following."

Caitlin looked at him as if she felt bad she had to explain something so obvious. "For your Army sleepover. I can't go with you, so if you have my key it's like I'm there too because the key is mine."

Alex swallowed a bit and couldn't say anything. He showed her he was putting "her" key safely in his shirt pocket and then he set to work replacing the battery in the bunny. It took until the third battery to find one that worked, but when it did he was greeted with an expression of such pure delight on his daughter's face that it would have been worth trying a thousand batteries to make those bunny eyes turn red.

"Ahhhh! Daddy! My secret bad bunny glows!" She hugged it tightly and laughed and then camped out on the floor next to him playing with it until he was done going through everything in his closet.

"Daddy, it needs a name."

"What, Honey?"

"My secret bad bunny needs a name."

Alex got down on the floor with her and took the bunny in his hands a moment. Damn, it did make him smile, thinking of it peeking up at him from that cookie jar the first time.

"Well, it's based on a bunny from a movie, but the bunny in the movie didn't have a name, they just kept describing it as death awaiting people with big pointy teeth."

"The people had pointy teeth?"

Alex laughed. "Dang, I have to keep my grammar straighter with you. No, the bunny had the big pointy teeth, and it flew all over the place and killed a bunch of soldier kind of people, which was a joke because nobody normally would be scared of a bunny."

"Can I see the movie?"

"I would love for you to see the movie, but it's not a kid movie, so you have to grow up a bit more. But not too fast, okay?"

"Do I name the bunny 'Death With Pointy Teeth'?"

"Um, no. Better not. But that would be super funny."

Caitlin beamed at her dad.

Alex wracked his brain for anything innocuous enough to maybe counteract the displeasure he knew the toy was going to elicit from Beth when she realized it had resurfaced. "How about... Mr. Bunny Face? Or at least maybe call him that until we think of something better?"

"Mr. Bunny Face! Because he has a face!"

"He does! So it works great, huh?" God that girl was funny. What was he supposed to do without her in Iraq?

From that moment on Caitlin and her bunny were inseparable, with the exception of one unpleasant incident. Alex was in the basement trying to repair a chair in his shop (one of many chores he was trying to complete before he had to leave) when he heard a shrieking from the kitchen that made his blood run cold. He arrived at the top of the steps in two bounds to find Beth holding the bunny pinched in one hand out of Caitlin's reach. His daughter was screaming and crying and desperately trying to grasp her toy.

"What the—?" started Alex.

"Daddy! Daddy, he was in the garbage! I woke up and he was gone and I looked and looked and then I

194

saw him in the garbage!" Tears were streaming down his daughter's face, and he shot a glare at Beth that immediately wiped the smirk off of hers.

"What. Were. You. Thinking," he said with a forced calmness designed to not frighten Caitlin while still getting Beth's attention. He wasn't playing.

"I—I didn't think she'd really miss it and it's old and —And none of this would have happened if you were better at taking the garbage out on time," Beth said defiantly.

Alex carefully took the bunny from her hand, inspected it, took it to the sink to clean a little bit of yogurt from one of its paws, dried it on his shirt, and handed it back to his daughter who was still crying but starting to calm herself. He bent down to look Caitlin in the eye and said, "You go play, Honey. Why don't you read Mr. Bunny Face a book? I got you some new ones from the library yesterday. They're still in that bag by the door."

Caitlin wiped her eyes and said, "Will you read one with me? I can only read the ones with the Green Eggs and Ham."

"I bet you can read more than that, so we'll do that together when I'm done with the chair, okay?"

"Okay," she said. "You still have my key?"

Alex patted his pocket. He always had her key. Caitlin ran off while making her bunny fly, pretending it was attacking people with its big pointy teeth.

"Now look," said Beth, when Alex stood up and turned his attention back toward her. "You know I don't think that's an appropriate toy. I can't believe you let her have it without talking to me, and—"

"Beth. I don't care what you thought. How is Caitlin supposed to learn to respect our things if we don't respect hers?"

"But—Alex, I hate that—I hate—"

"Well, there's your problem. Stop hating whatever. Love Caitlin first, okay? That's our job. If you start to do something, and you can picture it heading toward another scene like that, just stop."

Beth burst into tears. Alex sighed and walked over to her and took her in his arms.

"I don't want you to go," she finally said, her face buried in his chest.

"I know."

They stood that way for a long time in the kitchen until they could hear Conner on the baby monitor waking from his nap. Beth dried her eyes and headed that direction, while Alex decided they could live with one fewer chair and went to read all the new books with his daughter.

It was snowing lightly that day in early November 2005 when his company of over a hundred people climbed onto the buses for Camp Atterbury. There was a news crew there. The soldiers and their families said less than private goodbyes, and then the buses left. Claire watched the footage on the morning news, and again when they repeated it at six. She could spot Beth holding the baby, and Alex's mom keeping track of Caitlin, but Alex was harder to see. He blended in so much with all the other uniforms that it was like watching a shell game. It made her uncomfortable that her friend who was unique could seem to be so easily reduced to one of many cogs in a wheel.

For the first several weeks of Alex's absence it wasn't too bad. He was in Indiana, and there was little to be scared of there that anyone knew of. He was missed, but safe. He e-mailed people about his training and there was not much to worry about or obsess over. But when Alex actually boarded the plane that flew him to Kuwait, that changed.

Ben told Claire about how he'd helped Beth box up

most of Alex's things to store in a closet, because she felt their house was small enough as it was without tripping over stuff no one would be using. Beth didn't want reminders that her husband was missing by coming across his running shoes or his spare razor. For herself, Claire wished she had more reminders.

Claire, who until the day Alex left had been an insatiable news junkie, stopped listening to the news altogether for a while. It was too hard. Every time a reporter calmly stated how many soldiers were killed by roadside bombs that day in Iraq, she found herself hoping it wasn't Alex. Then she was left feeling ashamed because the flip side of that meant she was hoping it was someone else's "Alex."

On days she missed him most, Claire wore her friend necklace, and the t-shirt Alex had left for her. The shirt had been included in a box Ben brought by a couple of days after Alex shipped out. It was a small box with only a few things in it, but it meant everything. There was a copy of Alex's official military portrait in his dress uniform, a drab looking t-shirt in her size with the Army insignia of his battalion and its numbers on the front, an old mangled spiral binder, and a card. The card had been made by Caitlin and had elaborate scribbles in various colors on both sides and the envelope. Inside Alex wrote:

Dear Claire,

I'm sorry it didn't work out to have a real goodbye, but we've had lots of goodbyes before and you never liked any of those anyway.

Hope you like the picture, and that the t-shirt fits. The notebook is something I came across while packing and reorganizing some things and I thought you'd get a kick out of it. It's got all my notes from jujutsu that I took back in high school. I hadn't realized how much of it turned into a journal of sorts and it brought back a lot of memories, a lot of which are yours, too, so I thought you should have it.

And when I said we've had lots of goodbyes before, I want you to remember the most important thing they all had in common: They weren't the end. I'll come home and I'll see you again, so try not to worry too much. (Or at least enough that you send those cookies.)

—Alex

Claire read through Alex's old notebook for hours. They were definitely the notes of a future engineer—detail-oriented, with words such as fulcrum and torque to describe certain techniques. Everything was dated and included notes about who was teaching the class and the different people he worked with. There were simple sketches here and there, and lots of extra words scrawled in the margins.

The technique descriptions were pretty good, and it was funny to remember people she hadn't thought about in years. The most interesting part was that the margin scribblings were all editorial comments. Apparently working with Jim was annoying because the guy couldn't refrain from making sound effects under his breath. Paul grabbed from the wrong side every time, and Chris had unbearably sweaty hands.

Then a few months in, her name appeared. There were maybe three lines on the page about how to do a particular wrist lock properly, and the rest of it was about how underestimating a girl could be a dangerous thing, and how cool he thought it was that Claire had nearly broken his arm, and what was that throw? He wrote that he hoped she didn't think he was a complete jerk because she was obviously good, and he could learn a lot if they were paired together again.

The next few times they worked together he wrote notes about how he wanted to roll as quietly as she did, and have as much control. Eventually working with her became old news and didn't merit much mention in the margins (aside from occasionally noting with pride that he'd managed to make her laugh particularly hard that class). However, the day Lindsay had come to observe, there were all kinds of angry-looking scrawled words about why did his girlfriend have to be that way and how he was never letting her within five hundred yards of either the dojo or Claire again.

The notebook made her unexpectedly nostalgic. It was certainly Alex, but a more innocent version that she'd forgotten. It was so strange to think about the ways in which people change and the ways they don't. It was hard to remember with any accuracy how one really used to be, because the changes were so gradual as to be rendered imperceptible. Claire wished she'd kept any sort of journal so she could have a snapshot of her thoughts from back then.

Or maybe she didn't. Maybe it was better to live with the illusion of having always possessed a certain maturity so she could have a sense of continuity, and maybe retain some dignity that the truth would quickly rob her of.

CHAPTER NINE

Not long after Alex was deployed, Sensei introduced a new project to Claire at the dojo. She really didn't want more on her plate, but he suggested it could be a good distraction if she chose to get involved.

The dojo was putting together a collection of short films, some of which were designed to go on the website, and the rest were for a nebulous promotional idea. A professional photographer and videographer was hired to take all the footage, and was being given general access to the dojo over the course of several weeks.

The first time Claire ran into him, he was looking through the viewfinder of his large digital camera at the doorway of the back room as she stepped out of it. He was clicking away much to her annoyance.

"Hey!" she snapped at him, holding up her hand in front of her face and scowling. "What are you doing?"

He was a man about her age with a slight build, dark hair and olive skin, and he lowered the camera quickly as he said, "Oh, hey, I'm sorry. Mr. Lee, uh, 'Sensei' I guess, said I could start by getting some stills for—"

Claire was embarrassed. "Ohhh. Oops! Excuse me, I totally forgot that was coming up. It's really the twelfth already?"

He nodded.

"So, uh...."

"Eric."

"Yeah, Eric, I've been distracted lately, and this film/photo thing Sensei set up slipped my mind. I'm sorry. I know you're doing your job. You took me by surprise is all."

He seemed somewhat flustered and finally said, "Hey, no, I'm sorry. Do you mind if I get some shots of you leading the class? If today is bad...."

"No, it's fine. Like I said, you just took me by surprise, and I shouldn't have been so grouchy. Hey, I'll even do my entrance again, okay?" Claire gave him a mischievous sort of look and went back through the doorway. Then she stepped out again appearing serene with an amiable smile. "How's that? Better?"

Eric grinned and snapped a picture. "It's perfect."

Claire was pleased to be forgiven, and then ignored him in order to make preparations for class. She had both a general class and a weapons class that evening, so she checked the number of hanbos available against the number of people on her roster, and wondered if she should go back out to her car and grab a spare one out of her trunk. Usually not everyone showed up like they were supposed to, so it might not be necessary.

She bowed onto the mat and started warming up her body with some basic stretches. She heard clicking. Claire looked at Eric upside down from between her legs.

"You're going to take pictures of me now? Before class?"

"If you don't mind," said Eric. "It helps me later to have lots to sort through."

Claire raised an eyebrow at him, and went back to stretching her hamstrings. As the class filed in there were lots of people to observe and photograph, and Claire learned to block out all the clicking.

Eric started taking video during classes, and Claire knew he was reviewing the footage with Sensei on the weekends. After the second week of looking at Eric's video work, Sensei took Claire aside once everyone had left and gave her a heads up that he had given Eric her phone number.

"Why?"

"Because you're not seeing anyone right now that you've mentioned, and I think he needs to ask you out before I end up paying for an all-Claire documentary."

Claire was confused. "What are you talking about? He points that damn camera everywhere."

"And somehow it only finds you."

She hadn't taken any special notice of Eric to speak of after that first day, so she wasn't sure what to do with this information. Claire looked at Sensei more critically for a moment. She'd known him for over a decade, and his hair was greying. His face was more lined than when she'd first signed up for classes, all worried that he'd give a girl a hard time about joining, but he hadn't batted an eye. He'd never given her a reason not to believe the things he told her. She trusted him.

Sensei studied her in turn, a hint of a smile on his face, and said, "It took me a while to find who I thought was the right person for this project. I think if Eric gets up the nerve to dial that number, you should consider getting to know him better."

"I can't believe you gave out my number."

"I know, it was presumptuous. There have been others over the years who asked for it and I never even considered giving it out. Eric was never going to ask so

I thought he should have it."

"Is that some sort of Zen dating concept?"

"Some sort."

Claire sighed. "Well, whatever happens, don't do that again, okay?"

"No, I'm sure I won't," said Sensei as he gathered up the last of his things and held the door for her as they stepped out onto the street.

But Eric didn't use her number. And three days after talking with Sensei about it and hearing nothing, Claire was about to shrug it off completely when Eric caught her outside the dojo early in the morning. He was sitting on the stoop when she arrived. There were no classes before lunch, but many days there was clerical work to do while the building was quiet. Claire laughed in her head at the idea of Eric there to get footage of her tapping away at her laptop. But Eric didn't have any equipment in his hands or strapped over his shoulders for a change.

"Hey, you're here early," she said. He stood up and moved aside as she pulled out her key and went to step past him toward the door. "Do you need something?"

Eric looked strangely exposed without his camera, and his hands moved around awkwardly until he finally shoved them both into his pockets. "No, yeah, I have to be at another job in a bit, but I'm shooting some more stuff here this afternoon and was wondering, um, if you don't already have a plan or whatever, if you'd want to grab lunch first? With me?"

Claire stood there with her hand still on the knob of the open door and considered him as he alternated between looking at her face and averting his eyes.

"I mean," he said, "I figured you have to eat, and I have to eat, and there's this great place I go all the time that's a block over so it's convenient and obviously you don't have to but if you want to, you know...eat...."

Claire couldn't help but smile a little, and Eric looked relieved. "Well, you've certainly done your research because I do, in fact, eat," she said. "No, that sounds good. I'd love company for lunch. Is 12:30 okay?"

Eric looked at her the way Alex looked at pie.

"12:30 is great!" he said. "I mean, I'll meet you there at 12:30. It's the Middle Eastern place on 5th in the middle of the block."

"Yeah, sounds fun. See you later."

"See ya," said Eric. He smiled at her as he walked backward briefly up the deserted sidewalk before turning on his heel and heading for his car. Claire didn't get as much done on that laptop as she had planned that morning because she kept checking the time more than usual.

When she arrived at the restaurant, Eric was camped out at a table with all of his equipment in cases at his feet. He stood up when she walked in. She smiled as she came over, pulled out her own chair, dropped her bag next to one of his and took off her coat.

"So...hi," she said.

"Hi," said Eric. "I'm glad you could come."

"Well, as we established, I do eat," she said.

"Yeah."

They sat for a second listening to the busy lunchtime activity in the restaurant and then Claire said, "Um, Eric?"

"Hm?"

"I've never been here before, so I don't know what to order. I mean, there was a falafel cart on campus that I used to grab lunch from back in college, but that's where my expertise ends."

"Okay, well, how about I go up and get a sampling of things you might like?"

"That sounds good." Claire waited while Eric went

to the counter. She watched him speak casually in another language to the older woman behind the cash register who beamed at him. He was cute, actually, when he was relaxed like that, and not hidden behind a camera or indecisive about where to rest his gaze. He reminded her of a grown-up version of Ralph Macchio's character in the movie *The Outsiders*, which was one of the few things she'd picked up repeatedly at Blockbuster back in high school that she hadn't watched with Alex. She and her friends couldn't get over how many cute boys were in one film the first time they watched it at Jennifer's house one night. The movie was ten years old at the time, so they declared the boys to be "vintage cute" and each picked a favorite. Hers was Johnny.

Eric came back with a receipt and said they'd hear their number called shortly. He and Claire sat across from each other for a moment with no idea what to say, so finally they started with easy things, and talked about the dojo and how his work was coming and how long Claire had been doing jujutsu.

"Since I was 15," she said. "Well, close enough to 16 I should probably say that, I don't know."

"Wow, when did you know it was something you wanted to do?"

"My brother, Derrick, tried it first. He didn't stick with it, but I used to go watch his classes because it looked so cool. And one time I went to watch a class and Sensei came up to me afterward while people were getting changed and showed me some basic wrist escapes. I had people grabbing at my wrists the whole next week at home because it was so much fun to know how to get out of. Derrick ended up quitting before the tuition payment was used up, so I asked my parents if I could go in his place, and they thought that was fine, and I've been doing it ever since."

"Well, I think you're amazing. In the dojo, I mean," he added quickly. "You're a lot of fun to watch there. Because, you know, you move so well. And you, um, make it look easy, which after watching the other people it's obviously not."

"Thanks," said Claire. "So, photography, huh?"

"Yeah. I drew a lot as a kid, but the first time I got a camera in my hands, that was it. That was all I wanted to do. My parents helped me set up a darkroom in the basement and I still use it sometimes for personal projects. Like, um, wait a second...."

Eric started rummaging around in the cases on the floor until he found a particular camera that he pulled out and turned on so she could look at some images on its small screen. "This isn't that great to look at here, but the prints are at my parents'."

"What am I looking at?"

"So, our neighbor was in hospice about a month ago. Cancer. It wasn't a surprise or anything, and he was old, but when it came to the end he wanted to be at home and, like, all of his family came from everywhere to spend time with him. The amazing thing to watch was what it meant for them all to spend time with each other since that was kind of rare, so they were glad to be together even though it was a sad occasion."

He started pushing buttons in order to scroll through the photos he'd taken. There was a hospital bed that looked incredibly out of place in the cluttered living room. The man in the bed looked weak and as pale as his bedsheets, and with him was a woman whom Claire assumed was his wife. There were pictures of small children and various adults, and they were caught at moments that suggested all kinds of stories. There was one photo in particular that Claire asked to look at longer of a young woman playing a violin for the man in the bed as he held his wife's hand.

All the faces in the man's line of sight were smiling, and the ones just out of his view were crumbling.

As Claire studied the photos in silence, Eric began to shift in his seat a little, and said, "I mean, I guess it's depressing, but there was also really so much laughter in that house, and I've known them since I was little and I wanted to do something. I thought with everyone too sad to really process it all right then that maybe they'd want pictures to look back on someday when it hurts less. So I took these."

Claire sat back as she got to the end of what was on the camera and was lost in thought.

Eric shifted in his seat again and said, "You know, I don't know what I was thinking, I just grabbed the first thing that was meaningful to me, but I guess it's pretty sad really, and—"

"No, they're beautiful."

"Yeah?"

"Yeah. Thank you for sharing them with me. And they're not just sad, they're...complicated. I've never seen a hospice situation in person, and I would assume it was kind of all sad all the time, but now I know it's more than that, so thank you."

Eric had an expression on his face that she would have also classified as complicated, because his brow was creased but he also looked pleased. Then he brightened and said, "Oh wait, I know what I should show you!"

He rummaged around again among the different cases, produced another camera, but this time they were rewarded with pictures of the most adorable cats and dogs Claire had ever seen.

"Oh how cute!" she said, and Eric smiled.

"Yeah, I got hired about a six months ago to do photos for an animal shelter for their website. They've been trying to reduce the number of animals that get put down, and when they have really attractive pictures of the dogs and cats online the adoption rates go way up. This cat?" he said, stopping at a particularly pretty tabby with green eyes, "This cat was the hardest to get a picture of because she was so sweet she just wanted to be in my lap the whole time. I had to use a different lens and shoot her from across the room, but personally I like these unusable ones better. They capture her personality more."

Claire laughed as he showed her one picture after another that were only an eye or a blurry nose and one of a paw coming right at the camera. "Did she get adopted?" Claire wanted to know.

"Yeah, she did, almost immediately. Which is good, because I would have taken her otherwise and my building doesn't allow cats, so that would have gotten tricky fast."

"What other sorts of things do you photograph?"

"Well, spring and fall there are a lot of weddings. That's its own thing that takes a while to get the hang of. I freelance for the paper sometimes. I do a lot of documentation for artists, which is weird because someone can spend years making a sculpture, and then I have the copyright on the photo of it. Which makes sense, but seems unfair in a way, because if they reproduce that photo anywhere I get a line of credit, too, and my part was quick and their part took forever."

"Huh," said Claire, sorting through so many different images in her head. "Well, what is your favorite thing to photograph?"

Eric stared at her speechless for a moment, and started to say, "I, uh, I can't—" when their number was called, and he hopped up to grab their food. He returned to the table with a tray of plates containing things made from rice and vegetables and what she guessed was lamb and something else on a skewer.... It all smelled wonderful.

"Now, the plain rice is called 'polow,' but this here, this is 'adas polow' which is rice with lentils, dates, raisins and in this case some meat. This is a chicken kabob, so that shouldn't be too new. These are stuffed grape leaves—there's meat in there, too, so I hope you eat meat. I guess I should have checked first, huh? And this is 'ashe reshte' which is egg noodles with herbs. It's not actually on the menu but I found out they were having it in the back, and I asked if we could have some. My mom makes it better, but this is still pretty good."

"Where are your parents from?"

"Iran. They moved here right after the revolution, so I was born here, but most of what I grew up with at home was Persian."

Farsi, Claire thought to herself. *He must have been speaking Farsi.*

He glanced nervously at her shirt with the Army insignia on it, before he looked back into her eyes and said, "Now, this place is kind of a mishmash of stuff, since most people around here don't know one region in the Middle East from another, so even though the owners are from Tehran, the menu is like from everywhere and nowhere."

"Well, all of this looks great. What should I try first?" asked Claire.

"Um, go with the grape leaves. They're usually an appetizer, so that seems like a good place to start."

They shared the food on the various plates and there was nothing Claire didn't like, but she tried not to get too full before having to teach a class. She asked Eric more questions about his family and found out his parents were both professors, and that he had an older sister. Then she started sharing a bit about her own family. When she got to Ben, Eric looked surprised.

"Ben Walker is your brother?" he asked.

"Yeah, do you know him?"

"I went to the same technical school a few years after him and they were always using his work as an example in editing classes. He's, like, one of their big success stories, so everybody's heard of Ben Walker. I have an old high school friend named David who went out with him a few times and he kept promising me he'd introduce us, but that never worked out."

"Well, I can introduce you anytime you want. Ben would love to know he has a fan club."

"Really?"

"Sure."

"That would be great!" said Eric. Then his smile sort of froze as his gaze caught on the Army shirt again.

Claire wondered if she'd spilled something on herself. When she inspected the front of her shirt, he looked chagrinned.

"Is something wrong?" asked Claire.

"It's, um...I'm sorry, I guess I'm hyper-sensitive right now to anything that's got a military theme to it. It's hard to know with the war on what people are thinking. Most people don't see any distinction between Persians and Arabs, and if they *do,* they tend to bring up the hostage crisis, which was what? Like, the year we were born or something? And no one can tell if we're in Iraq to fight people there or help them so I get why they're confused, but I wish they wouldn't take it out on me or my family. I've had some uncomfortable run-ins with strangers and it always seems to be people with 'support our troops' stickers on their cars."

Claire's brow creased as she considered what he was saying. She felt like apologizing, but she wasn't sure for what exactly. "Wow," she said. "Well, I'm not like that and I don't know anyone who's like that. The shirt is from my best friend who is deployed over in Iraq right now. He's a carpenter with the local Army Reserve Engineering group and they called him up to help do construction near Bagdad. We used to do martial arts together, and I miss him, and I think about him all the time, and wearing this shirt he gave me makes it feel like he's not so far away."

"I'm sorry. That must be hard."

"Yeah, well...not much I can do from here. I join the protest marches when they have them on campus or downtown, but aside from sending Alex cookies from time to time I feel pretty helpless."

Eric thought about it for a second. "Can he watch a DVD if you sent one?"

"I think so. Yeah, you know, he has his laptop and I'm pretty sure he's watched movies on it before."

"We could make him a movie out of some of the spare footage I've got from the dojo. Maybe that could be a good reminder of home."

"You'd do that?"

"Sure. Are there other things he might like a video update on?"

"His kids," she said without hesitation. "But...."

"But what?"

"It's just his wife and I don't exactly get along, so...I don't know how that would work."

"Do you get along with his parents?"

"Oh, yeah. Just fine."

Eric thought about it while he popped a stuffed grape leaf in his mouth. Then he suggested, "We could ask them if they mind saying they asked me to get video of her and the kids to send to Iraq."

Claire thought about it. "That...that might work. In the meantime the dojo stuff might be fun for him." She thought about it for another moment then smiled.

"Wow, Eric, you know, that could be really good. It's nice to have an actual project to ponder, instead of feeling like there's nothing I can do for Alex."

"I'm happy to help." And she could tell he meant it.

They finished their lunch and wrapped up the leftovers to go, then walked together to the dojo. Eric was easy to talk to once he relaxed and was himself. He was attentive and funny and knew an extraordinary amount about film. He was appalled that she'd never seen *Citizen Kane* or *Chinatown* or even *Reservoir Dogs*.

"I've seen *Kill Bill, Volumes One* and *Two* about a hundred times. Does that count for something?"

"Well, yeah, for a lot, but that and so many other things are much better if you catch some of the film references they're alluding to. We'll find time and I'll start filling in the gaps in your film knowledge. I mean, that you haven't seen *Seven Samurai* is a crime, really. I've got a big DVD collection so we can start with Kurosawa and you can bring the popcorn...."

Claire smiled as he went on and on, and thought he'd gotten a little ahead of himself in terms of assuming how much time she wanted to be spending with him after only one lunch, but she didn't mind. Eric was pleasant company, and he made her comfortable in a way she hadn't felt before—not even with Alex. He explained articulately and with great passion about film noir and cinema verite. He was showing off, but not in a way that was obnoxious, and she was flattered and amused. He was cuter the more animated he got. She noticed he adjusted his pace to match the speed at which she wanted to walk.

They started meeting for lunch regularly, and Claire got to know every item on the menu of Eric's favorite place, along with more food that he always managed to coax out of the back that wasn't available to other customers. But one afternoon she went to meet Eric there, and found him on the sidewalk with his camera out taking pictures instead. Someone had smashed the glass in the front door, and spray painted "Go home Arabs" on the window. Eric had an angry set to his jaw, and he kept taking pictures even as she approached him.

"Eric?"

Eric lowered his camera for a moment but continued facing the restaurant. "Yeah, Claire, I guess we'll do lunch another time or something. I'm going to help out here. After I document it all first. I got some good shots from the inside but stuff from out here is more what the paper would be interested in. And then I'm going to stay until I get the last of that fucking paint off the window."

"Is everyone in there okay?" asked Claire.

Eric finally turned toward her. He looked worn. "Yeah. I guess. I mean, it's happened before, so...."

Claire waited next to him as he continued to take whatever photographs he needed to take, and then said, "So how can I help?"

Eric gave her an appreciative grin and said, "Can you handle a razor blade?"

"A what?"

"A razor blade. It's what you use to get the spray paint off. You hold it at a forty-five-degree angle and scrape with it, but you need to keep the surface wet or you could scratch the glass. Hang on a sec, they've got a box of them inside behind the counter."

Eric crunched through the broken glass on the sidewalk and into the restaurant. Claire watched him talk with the distraught older woman behind the counter, and then walk around to her side to give her a long hug. She then handed him a bucket and patted his cheek, and Eric came back outside and motioned Claire

213

over by the window.

"We'll get started over on this end away from the broken glass. At least this asshole was shorter than the last one and I don't need a ladder." He reached into the bucket of supplies and pulled out a box of razor blades and fished one out for Claire. He then grabbed one for himself and started spraying down the window with glass cleaner.

As Claire got to work scraping, the restaurant owner came out onto the sidewalk to grimly survey the damage. He came over to Eric and said something in Farsi, and Eric replied in English, "Yeah, I'm done getting all the photos and I'll make sure you have copies for the insurance agent, so you're safe to sweep up now. This is Claire, by the way."

The man smiled at Claire industriously scraping at the graffiti on the window. "You are a good young lady. Do you want a kabob? You like chicken or lamb?"

Claire was embarrassed. The last thing they needed to be doing was worrying about feeding her. "No, that's okay, I'm fine."

"Both then," said the man as he clapped Eric on the shoulder and headed back inside.

Eric sighed and applied more glass cleaner to the area of the window he was working on. "*Go home Arabs,*" he muttered under his breath. "They're not even Arabs. And they *are* home. Fucking assholes should at least do their homework." He glanced over at Claire scraping away. "You don't have to do this. I know you need to eat before class, so it's okay if you have to go."

Claire took the spray bottle from him to wet down her side of the window a bit more. "No, I'm good. Plus apparently I'm getting all the kabobs, so why would I go anywhere?"

Eric smiled as he took the spray bottle back. "Okay

then."

Once the owner got the all-clear from Eric to clean up, things went together rather fast. The glass was swept, a wooden board was fitted to the front door, and a colorful sign affixed to it displaying the restaurant's hours and menu. With Claire and Eric working together the window was clean in no time, and the place was back in business. If it weren't for the police officers there taking statements, Claire thought people would barely be able to tell something had happened.

They stopped back inside to return the bucket, and the woman came from behind the counter to hug them both. She pressed some small wrapped treat into Claire's hands and patted her cheek. "Gaz," she said. "You'll like it. It's sweet like you." And then she signaled for them to wait as she went in the back to grab them some food.

While she was out of sight, Eric slipped some money into the cash register. "She's not going to let us pay," he said to Claire quietly. And sure enough when she came out with a big bag of takeout and Eric asked for a bill, she simply kept shaking her head and pushing him toward the door and smiling.

"Goodbye, Mrs. Hashemi, I'll see you tomorrow, okay?" Eric called as they emerged onto the now glass-free sidewalk.

As they started slowly walking together toward the dojo, Eric looked inside the bag and said, "Or maybe not. There's lunch in here for like, three days. Kabob?" he said, handing one to Claire.

She took the skewer of chicken and gnawed at it while they walked. Eventually she said, "So, that was pretty awful. How often does that happen?"

Eric thought about it as he fished a stuffed grape leaf out of the bag. "It was worst right after 9/11, then things calmed down for a bit. The vandalism comes in waves. I've noticed a correlation with military death tolls coming out of Iraq, and weirdly when there are slow news cycles, like the assholes are bored or something. Who knows."

"I'm sorry," said Claire.

"Yeah, well, thanks for your help. It meant a lot. Can I treat you to a movie? You've earned it. *Yojimbo* is at the campus theater tomorrow night and you'd love it."

Claire did love it. Between the cinematography and the sword work they found an endless amount to discuss about the film. But at that point they seemed to have an endless amount to discuss about everything. It wasn't long before Claire discovered she didn't like having a day go by where she didn't see Eric.

At the end of a particularly busy string of classes, Claire had some odds and ends that needed to be taken care of before she could leave the dojo, so Eric stuck around to keep her company and offered to help. They were completely alone for a change, and as she was standing on the mat putting the last weapon away, Eric asked, "What does it feel like, anyway, that wrist thing you guys are always doing?"

"Those locks I was teaching tonight?"

"Yeah, does that really hurt that much?"

Claire smiled. "Well, take off your shoes and I'll show you."

Eric hesitated, and then he kicked off his sneakers and started to step onto the mat, but stopped and asked, "Should I bow?"

"Probably. Acknowledging the mat is a way of being appreciative that it protects your bones."

"Then I'd better bow." And he did so before walking over to stand in front of Claire. "So, what do I do?"

"Okay, place your feet like this to give yourself some decent balance, then very slowly try to punch me in the face."

"God, that sounds weird to have you ask that." But Eric positioned his body the way she'd shown him and extended his arm. "Like this?"

"Uh, yeah, get your thumb out of your fist. That's a quick way to break it if you actually hit something. Tuck it back along the outside of your fingers, see?" She held up her own fist for him to copy, which Eric dutifully did. "And then when you strike, focus your energy on making contact with the first two knuckles, not the lower ones. The lower ones are weaker, and you can hurt your hand that way, too."

Eric nodded, returned to his initial stance, and concentrated on throwing a slow but proper punch. Claire gracefully reached around his arm and took his hand in hers, then she changed her posture slightly and began to twist it.

"Holy crap, that does hurt," he said, smiling appreciatively. "And you're not even trying, are you?"

She grinned as she shook her head. "It actually doesn't take much. It's a really weak place on the human body, so you don't have to be that strong to inflict a lot of pain, as long as your technique is right. See?" She twisted a tiny bit again to make him wince before relaxing her grip enough to end the pain, but still holding his hand.

Eric didn't move to pull his hand from hers. They stood that way long enough that Eric finally seemed compelled to break the tension by saying teasingly, "So, that move is good, but what do you do about this?" He went at her with a slow, exaggerated punch with the other arm (his thumb outside of his fist, Claire noted approvingly) and she laughed and deflected it easily. He smiled and came at her a few different ways in a clumsy fashion but faster each time, and Claire would shift her body slightly and be out of reach in an instant.

Eric laughed and made one more attempt at a slow

punch to the head when Claire suddenly spun around and hoisted him onto her back before he knew what was even happening. She was only going to hold Eric there a moment and set him back down, but when she turned her head to ask him if he'd had enough, he kissed her.

Claire dropped him.

"Ow!" said Eric in surprise while lying in front of her on the mat and rubbing the back of his head. She'd forgotten he didn't know how to fall safely. Claire felt bad because it was a really good kiss, it had just startled her too much for her to react any other way.

"Oh, I'm sorry! Are you okay? Eric?"

He didn't move so she bent down close to him to see how he was doing. He rubbed his head and looked at her with a smile. "So, yeah, that was super dumb of me, like, for lots of obvious reasons. If I ask first this time can I kiss you again?"

Claire smiled. "Sure."

Eric sat up and leaned toward her until their lips met. It was the way Claire had always wished a kiss could be, all soft but certain at the same time. She allowed him to roll her onto her back on the mat, and he ran a hand into her hair as he kissed her more deeply. Claire hoped they were enough below the sight line of the windows that they weren't putting on a show. The dojo was kind of a fishbowl at that time of night when it was dark out and the lights were on inside. But then she decided she didn't care. She only cared about how much she liked Eric's weight against her, and how gentle but passionate he was.

"You, by the way," Eric said quietly at some point between kisses.

"Hm?"

"The answer was 'you', when you asked at that first lunch what my favorite thing was to photograph. You are the most beautiful thing I've ever seen through my lens."

Claire felt something inside her melt. She studied him carefully for a moment as he looked back at her with an earnestness that almost hurt, and she said, "Let's get out of here."

"What?"

"My apartment's really close, just...just come with me there."

"Are you sure?"

"I am," she said simply. They scrambled up off the mat, gathered their things, shut off the lights, and headed for Claire's. Apparently, it was possible to find love in the dojo after all. Now that she'd found it, she wanted to take it home.

Eric nuzzled Claire's cheek as she fumbled for her keys outside her apartment, and once inside the door Eric set his camera bag down without caring where as they kissed each other all the way to the bedroom. Eric kept asking, "Are you really sure?" and she kept repeating, "Yes yes yes yes yes stop asking, just come here." They mumbled quickly through negotiations and information about condoms and testing and Claire's IUD as they undressed each other on the bed. They moved together rhythmically and forcefully, and after a time when Eric lay in her arms looking spent and happy, he kissed her lightly and said, "So talk to me. What do you want to do, or have me do that would feel good?" Claire had never been asked that directly before. She wasn't sure how to answer at first.

"I guess I'd like to see what you can do with that tongue besides speak Farsi."

Eric smiled and started slowly moving down her body with his lips and said, "Or French."

"You speak French?"

"Oui. Tu es la plus belle chose que j'ai jamais vue. Et

219

vous avez un goût incroyable."

Claire had no idea what any of that meant, but she couldn't believe the way it made her feel along with everything else Eric was doing.

In the middle of the night, as they lay in the dark together and Claire thought Eric was asleep, she tried to slip out of the bed, but Eric's grip tightened around her body to keep her there.

Claire laughed. "I must smell awful—let me just get in the shower for a minute."

"Nuh-uh," said Eric, eyes closed, arms still tight. "I'd bottle the way you smell if I could. Just stay. Unless you have to pee or something, then go and come back and then just stay."

Claire laughed again and stroked his hair. "Fine. I'll stay. But if you're awake you have to talk to me in French some more."

Eric grinned, and said, "D'accord, mais je vais juste te répéter encore et encore que je t'aime et espère que tu ne pourras pas comprendre ce que je dis car tu deviendras nerveux et penserais que je suis fou."

Claire smiled and snuggled in closer under the covers. "Are you going to translate?"

"Nope."

"Fine then. When I tell you later in Pig Latin that you're good in bed, you'll just have to wonder."

Eric kissed her. "C'est totalement juste. Et je veux mentir ici avec vous pour toujours."

Claire closed her eyes and smiled, and felt for the first time in her life that she was exactly where she was supposed to be, whether she understood one word coming out of Eric's mouth or not.

She wrote Alex a few letters about Eric. She didn't find it necessary to mention that he was polite, but did say dating him was like having her own unlimited Netflix subscription, and that Eric had everything

Monty Python had ever done on DVD. She told him when he came home they could have a repeat of their *Flying Circus* marathon anytime he wanted, and that Eric could make some pretty amazing snacks to go with it. Claire told Alex about how she'd never considered photography as a way to have a real impact on the world, but now she knew better. She told Alex she couldn't wait for him to meet her new boyfriend, because this one would pass any damn test Alex felt like throwing at him, let alone get through a simple dinner without being a jerk. Claire was never sure if her letters reached Alex or not. Letters back were sporadic at best.

Claire was struck by how quickly she and Eric established a routine of being together as much as possible. He had a drawer at her place and she had a drawer at his. She taught him the entire stretching sequence they used at the dojo. He showed her what the myriad of lenses he used were for, and tried to teach her how to look at the world in terms of what would make a good composition inside a smaller frame.

Claire thought Eric took beautiful photos. He took lots of pictures of her that she was too self-conscious to put up herself, but that didn't stop Eric from hanging prints of her all over his own apartment. She had to admit she liked them, though. He somehow captured images of her the way she wished she could be.

She only had two of his prints hung in her place. The first was of Eric sitting on the floor starting to speak and looking amused that she'd snapped when he was trying to teach her something about using his equipment. The other was of her with her hand blocking her scowling face the day they'd met in the dojo. Both pictures made her laugh. Looking back on the earliest months of her relationship with Eric, it was all laughing and movies and sex and takeout. There was nothing not to like.

The problem was that part of her felt guilty, because she still worried about Alex and didn't know if it was appropriate to be happy when he might be suffering. Claire knew that didn't make sense, because someone somewhere was always suffering, and to deny herself any joy under such a premise was insane. Besides, Alex would be the first to say that by some rationale, her being able to experience such happiness and freedom was the whole point of his being over there, somehow. She still didn't grasp that concept, but he believed it, so that should have absolved her of some of her guilt. But it didn't.

When Claire talked to Eric about it, he suggested they finally get around to shooting that video of Alex's kids. So Claire brought it up on a visit with Alex's mom one evening.

Claire had kept her promise to Alex, and either called or stopped in on his mom every couple of weeks. Claire wasn't sure how much it helped, but they had a nice little routine going. It was odd spending time in that house again. It still felt the same as it had in high school, and she often half expected Pammy to come around the corner in her softball uniform, even though she knew Pammy was grown and living in the Southwest with some man in a small off-campus house. Mrs. Sullivan had a lonely look to her when she answered the door.

"So, have you heard anything from Alex recently?" Claire asked, after they were settled in at the kitchen table with some coffee and crackers.

"Nothing past that last mass e-mail that I'm sure you got, too."

"Yeah, he sounds okay, but it's hard to tell. When he complains about exercising in the heat or how sick he is of MREs for lunch, I believe that. But when he says those nondescript things about what he's actually doing, I feel like he's not telling us something, and it almost makes me wish he'd left that part out."

Alex's mom frowned. Claire didn't see much of Mrs. Sullivan in her son except when she frowned. They had the same pattern of creases in their foreheads when they did that.

"Did I ever tell you about when Alex got hurt as a little boy?" she asked Claire.

"I don't think so, but I imagine Alex probably managed to bang himself up a lot as a kid."

Mrs. Sullivan smiled to herself a little. She took a sip of her coffee and then cradled the cup in both her hands. "Alex was a wonderful little boy. For a few years it was only the two of us because his father worked long hours and we were living in a bigger city back then and I didn't have any family around. I used to take him out every day if the weather was nice and I'd push him in a stroller at the zoo or the museum. He was so bright and talked early, and he was my whole day every day for what felt like a very long time while I was living it. Now it seems like it went by so fast I question if it was even real."

She took another sip and appeared to forget Claire was there for a moment. When Claire reached for a cracker, Mrs. Sullivan glanced over at her again. "Anyway, one afternoon when he was probably about two or a little older, it was raining out, so we stayed in, and I...I lost track of him. He couldn't have been out of my sight for more than a second, and then I walked into the living room to look for him and he was halfway up the bookcase. I think I screamed or called his name or something along those lines, because he turned and was startled and that was the point where the whole thing came down."

"Oh my God!" said Claire. "That sounds terrifying."

"It was awful. I didn't know about bracketing certain furniture to the walls and all kinds of things. People are much better informed about all those sorts of safety issues these days, and Alex is up on all of that. Before Caitlin was even born he'd put safety covers on the outlets and bolted things in place and made sure all the household chemicals were stored up high. I feel like I barely protected him at all."

Claire smiled and took another cracker. "Seems to me like you did just fine."

"Well, on that day I didn't. That the bookcase didn't kill him is astounding to me. He got a nasty cut to the head near his eye that bled like the dickens, but other than that he was simply scared so he howled."

"Is that how he got that little scar over his right eyebrow?"

"Yes, that's the spot."

"Huh." Claire had asked Alex about that scar one time, and he said he really didn't know why it was there. It was funny for her to have that information all of a sudden and know he still didn't have that piece of his own story.

"Anyway, I rushed him to the emergency room where they checked him over and said he was fine. His father was furious at me when he got home and found out, and kept saying I needed to pay better attention to his son, but it's so hard to keep track of a boy every minute. You do the best you know how, but at some point.... I don't think a week goes by that I don't still think of that bookcase coming down on my baby. For me it's one of the most significant moments in my son's life, and Alex has no memory of it at all."

She sighed and looked at Claire. "There are days when I think of him in Iraq and get that same panicked feeling that I'm supposed to be watching him better.

There are some habits that don't fade with time very well."

Claire didn't know how to respond to that. She wanted to say that Alex was grown and strong and knew what he was doing, but such reassurances felt disingenuous. She was scared for Alex, too, and hated being told it would all be fine as if she had an overactive imagination and needed to snap out of it. Her friend was in danger, and that was real.

"Um, you know," Claire started, "I had an idea I wanted to run by you today."

"What's that?"

"Well, Eric, my boyfriend I was telling you about last time? He offered to make a DVD of Caitlin and Conner that we could send to Alex. I sent him one of some footage of the dojo not that long ago, but I know he'd really rather see his kids and Beth and home."

"That sounds like a wonderful idea. I'm sure Alex would appreciate that a great deal."

"Yes, well, see, the problem is, I don't think I can go to Beth and ask to film her kids. She probably wouldn't like the idea if it was connected to me in any way, so we were wondering if you could say you asked Eric to do it."

Mrs. Sullivan thought about that for a moment. "Yes, Beth is a force to be reckoned with, isn't she. I keep hoping as she gets older things will even out, but there's a ways to go." Then she looked dubiously at Claire and said, "Won't it pose a problem one day when Beth discovers Eric is your boyfriend?"

Claire hadn't thought of that. "Oh, I guess you're right. Ick. Well, let me talk to Eric. Maybe if we lent you a camera you could get some footage of Beth and the kids, and Eric could edit it."

"I'm not good with a camera, Honey. Why don't you just ask your brother?"

Claire's mouth dropped open slightly as the solution struck her as so insanely obvious. "Ha! Well, now that's an idea! Why on earth didn't I think of that? Good grief, thank you."

Mrs. Sullivan looked pleased to have been of help, and asked as she always did if Claire wanted to join her at one of the family support group meetings. Claire declined. She was too aware that those meetings were intended for families, and she didn't need one more place to try and explain her relationship with Alex.

Claire called Ben when she got home, and he was fine with getting some footage for Eric to work with. The following week when he went over to play with the kids while Beth had her hair done, he got lots of funny shots of them together and making a mess eating lunch, and alternately stacking and knocking over blocks. When Beth came back from the salon, she was feeling presentable enough to be filmed herself, and she blew kisses to her husband and told him he was missed.

Ben dropped the digital tape off at Claire's place that night, and stuck around for a while as he watched her and Eric make dinner. He insisted he couldn't stay and eat because he had plans with Jacob, but he did linger and observe everything from his seat at the counter.

When Eric excused himself to take a call for work, Ben gave his sister a big smile and said, "This is all cute!"

"What?" said Claire, filling the rice cooker. So many of Eric's mom's recipes called for rice that she'd finally decided a dedicated appliance for the task was the way to go.

"This!" said Ben, gesturing around at everything, and particularly at Claire. "He like, runs his fingers along your waist every time he passes behind you, and you're all like, smiley, and well, your happy self all the time. And not the pokey-jabby-punchy-self you are with Alex. You don't even get all embarrassed when he kisses you each time he's close enough to do it."

"I guess I don't," said Claire. "So are you giving me some kind of brotherly stamp of approval?"

"I was holding back judgement until I saw his work, because if he was good in bed, but bad in the other darkroom, then I don't know if I could live with that for the rest of our lives."

Claire snorted as she started brushing some of the stray bits of rice off the counter and into her hand. "Aren't you generous. So, does he pass?"

Ben looked at her seriously. "Yes, actually. He's really talented, Claire. I actually have some of his shots at home that I tore out of the paper that I didn't realize were his until now. His work should be in a gallery, not just in people's wedding albums."

"That's good to know," said Claire. "He'll be really flattered you think that."

"Oh, don't tell him I said so, it will go to his head. Plus I need him to stay in the wedding game long enough to do my ceremony in Vermont. We're going with green as the theme color, by the way, so that should bring out your eyes, and I've decided you can wear flats instead of heels as a compromise but I get to pick your jewelry, because your idea of jewelry is just, no."

Claire laughed. "Fine! Whatever you want, just so long as you're nice to Eric. I love him and I want him to stick around."

"You what?"

"I love him."

"Have you told him that yet?"

"Um, not in those words," said Claire.

"Well, those are the only ones that probably count

so maybe consider using them. And now I have to run and use all kinds of words on Jacob to help him get over that I should have been home half an hour ago."

Eric was coming back into the main room right as Claire was letting her brother out the front door. "You really can't stay?" he asked, looking genuinely disappointed that Ben couldn't stick around. "My adas polow is pretty good."

"I don't doubt it. How about you guys come make it at our place next week sometime and you can show me how you put together all that footage of the Sullivan kids? I'm really curious to see what you do with it."

"That sounds great!"

Ben smiled at him, gave Claire a kiss on the cheek and said, "Bye, Sis."

As Claire shut the door, she leaned against it and studied her boyfriend.

Eric looked back at her curiously. "What? Should I have asked you before accepting the invitation? Because I can't imagine your turning that down."

"You know I love you, right?"

Eric gave her the same speechless expression as he'd done the time she'd asked what he liked to photograph best. "I do now," he said finally, and smiled.

"Wait, aren't you supposed to say 'I love you, too?' Isn't that how this works?" asked Claire looking bemused.

"Yes, it is," he said, slipping his arms around her waist and kissing her as she was pressed up against the door.

"Wait, no!" she said laughing as he started doing something rather ticklish by her ear, "You have to say it back now! Because that's only fair!" She was laughing enough that she realized this was the best defense against any of her techniques she had ever experienced, because while she was laughing she couldn't remember any of them. "Eric!"

He grinned. "I think we should check the rice."

She laughed again and held onto his arm as he started to head for the kitchen saying, "Eric, come on! What are you doing?"

He stopped and faced her, his arms around her waist again. "I am trying to drag out this moment a little longer, because this is the only time I will ever ever *ever* have the upper hand in this relationship. Plus, I think if I start to say this particular something you want to hear, then all sorts of other things are going to come tumbling out about marriage and babies and a home, and it is way too soon to say any of that, and then I will scare you off."

Claire kissed him. "You can't scare me off."

"Fine then," he said. "I love you, too. I don't know how not to love you."

The DVD was beautiful when Eric finished with it. He dubbed in the right music to go with the scenes of the kids playing, and he kept the pace of the whole thing relaxed without it getting dull in any way. He made a copy to send to Alex, and extras for Beth's and Alex's parents. Ben thought it was perfect.

As Claire packed Alex's copy away carefully in a box with some cookies and a letter, she felt good. When she was done taping everything up and had put the address on the box in clear block printing, she curled up next to Eric on the couch where he was watching some strange black and white movie he'd recently gotten called *Freaks*.

"What is this?" she asked.

"It's a cult classic from the fifties. I saw it once back in high school, and I found a copy when I was poking around in the odd bins at the DVD place down on Cramer."

"The acting seems pretty bad."

"Yeah." Eric lifted a corner of his blanket so Claire could join him under it. She did, and laid her head on his shoulder while watching the peculiar images unfold on the screen. "Yeah, it was famous for using real circus freaks, not for any Oscar caliber performances. That guy there, with no arms and legs? He gets out a match and lights his own cigarette. Pretty amazing."

"Seems cruel to put them on display like that in a movie."

"No, the point of it is that they are who they are, and other people miss out by not seeing past the surface. The 'freaks' here are the decent ones. The beautiful woman who does the trapeze act—her, there, the one with the accent?—she's the real freak. She's evil, and in the end, they make her look on the outside like she is on the inside so others will know. They understand that's the only way she'll get what she deserves, since most people only react to what they see. People are too quick to judge by appearance most of the time."

Claire thought about that as she enjoyed Eric's warmth under the blanket. She wondered if he could even count the number of times he was judged too quickly on his appearance. She was often misjudged by hers in many ways, usually by being underestimated. Claire had noticed that, as a couple, she and Eric were looked at and treated differently than she'd experienced in her past relationships. It was hard to tell if Eric was too used to the slights to notice, or was simply good at taking things in stride. It bothered Claire that she was already worrying about defending their possible children from poor treatment.

Claire shook off those thoughts for the moment and focused on the movie. As she got into it, she was fascinated by how much people were able to do in a world that was not accommodating to their various deformities. The suggestion was that all it took to adapt was determination, and she wondered what became of those who lacked that kind of mindset.

By the end of the film, Eric had fallen asleep with his arms around her. Claire carefully disentangled herself and shut off the TV, straightened up the kitchen, and put her package by the door so she wouldn't forget to mail it first thing the next day. She shut off the lights and went back to Eric on the couch. Claire smiled to herself, and then ran her hands lightly through his dark hair and kissed him softly until he stirred.

"Time for bed," she said.

He mumbled, "Why can't I stay right here?"

"Because I'm going to be in *there*, and I know how to wrap both my legs behind my head."

Eric's eyes flew open and he got straight up. "You make a really valid point."

Claire laughed as he took her by the hand and started to lead her when she stopped him to give him a hug.

"Thanks again, Eric."

"For what?"

"For the DVD for Alex. It's really nice and I know it will mean a lot to him."

"Hey, any way I can support the troops without having to buy one of those stupid stickers is fine by me. Besides, I'd do anything for you. Anything! Let's go to bed and I'll prove it."

Claire laughed again and let herself be led this time. "I love you," she said. She liked that it was finally easy to say.

"Je t'aime aussi," said Eric, "means I love you, too."

CHAPTER TEN

The day the call came, Claire wasn't even home. She was at Eric's, and they were discussing the logistics of moving in together. They had decided his apartment was the better choice. It was bigger and was in walking distance of more necessary things, such as a grocery store and the studio where Eric did his film developing and editing. The only thing about her apartment in its favor was its proximity to the dojo, but she could drive there. Everyone else did.

It had been fewer than five months since they'd started going out, but the sheer amount of time they spent together was making rent on two places seem wasteful. Besides, whenever Claire pictured the future, she couldn't imagine it without Eric, so why put that future off?

She stopped back at her place after the dojo to pick up a few things before returning to Eric's, when she saw her answering machine flashing. It was full.

She pressed the button and listened to her mother say she needed to come home. There were many hang ups in a row, and then another message from her mom. There was a message from Mrs. Sullivan saying she was sure Claire had heard from her mom by then, and that she would get more details to her soon, she promised. Claire tried not to panic. She went into sparring mode and let her adrenaline run its course while she calmly collected her things and headed for her parents' house.

Her mom met her at the door as if she had known she was coming, and looked as if she'd been crying earlier.

"Mom?" Claire had never been so scared.

"Oh, Honey, I'm so sorry to have to tell you this but —"

"Is Alex dead?"

"No! No, Sweetheart, thank God, no, but, Claire, Sweetie, he's been badly hurt. He's coming home soon."

Claire remained calm. She prided herself on her ability to not publicly burst into tears. There were many painful moments at the dojo where that could have happened and she would have lost some of her authority. She didn't want to cry in front of her mom and be reduced to a child again, especially at a time when she needed to feel strong.

"What happened to Alex?"

"He...we don't have all the details, his mom got her information from Beth and we're not sure, but...."

"Tell me what happened to Alex!" Claire was starting to lose it. There was only so much you could control no matter how hard you tried.

"Honey, he lost an arm. There was a roadside bomb, and, well, no one was killed, but several men were hurt."

Claire felt weak. She came in and sat on the couch and tried to picture her best friend with his arm blown off. It was wrong. Alex wasn't supposed to get hurt— he'd promised. What kind of pain must that have been?

It was inconceivable. She knew those arms so well, the muscles and tendons and pressure points.... How could one simply be gone? They were a matched set. They were part of Alex. She thought she might throw up, but she breathed slowly until that feeling passed.

Her mom had tears in her eyes, and simply sat with Claire in silence. Eventually she started making sounds about dinner and asked Claire if she wanted to stay and eat and spend the night.

"No. No, I want to be with Eric, I.... Mom, when is Alex coming home?"

"I don't know yet, Honey, I'll call you as soon as I know anything, okay?"

Claire nodded and got up to go.

Her mom said, "Are you sure you are okay to get back on the road so soon?"

Claire nodded again and gave her mom a long hug. She didn't say anything because she was on the verge of finally crying and she didn't want to yet.

She pulled up in front of Eric's (soon to be "their") apartment and saw him in the lit window on the second floor. He was happily sifting through papers on the table.

Claire let herself in with her key and Eric turned to greet her with a smile which left his face quickly when he saw her expression.

"What's wrong, Claire?" he said as he walked over to her.

When he was close enough to catch her, she fell apart.

*

Alex was in a hospital in Germany at that moment. He was heavily sedated and disoriented. They were preparing to ship him quickly to the Walter Reed Army Medical Center in Washington D.C. where the real recovery process would begin.

234

His dreams were a confusing blend of being in Iraq and being home. The worst ones involved being on a convoy and spotting his kids running and playing by the side of the road. He kept screaming at them to go home to their mom, but they wouldn't listen or couldn't hear him and then the bombs would go off. Sometimes he woke up at that point, but depending on the medication they were pumping though his veins, sometimes he was trapped there and had to watch.

Alex was confused when the doctors kept saying something about his right arm being gone. In his dreams he had two arms, and he spent more time closer to sleep than wakefulness, so he couldn't understand what they were talking about. He was in pain, but the way the medication worked he wasn't concerned about it; the pain was there, but it didn't matter.

He wanted to go back to his unit. Part of him was convinced that once they patched him up or bandaged whatever needed bandaging, that they would send him back out to finish the job he had come to do. But that didn't happen. Alex was going home whether he wanted to or not.

He didn't remember much about the plane ride, other than a doctor who was kind to him and strapped Alex down for the flight. The doctor distracted him by asking questions about his kids, and talking about Caitlin and Conner always made Alex happy. Although, he knew his information was out of date. He'd been unnerved by how much his kids had changed in a relatively short amount of time when he saw them on the DVD Claire had sent. He couldn't tell if he'd simply forgotten how they moved, or if they were different. He'd only been able to watch the DVD in small segments at a sitting because it made him cry if he wasn't careful. Even the footage from the dojo was difficult to watch, because it was disorienting to feel himself in that place, only to glance up and suddenly be in the desert again.

Most of his experience in Iraq had been a peculiar combination of boredom punctuated by fear. Alex was amazed at how quickly people could adapt to new circumstances and simply live in a new way when they had to.

The heat was insane. When they had landed in Kuwait the temperature was well over a hundred degrees, and stepping off the plane was like walking into an oven. The heat hit you like a wave and didn't leave. It was one thing to have someone tell you it was hot there, but until you experienced it, and knew what it was like to wear heat like a jumpsuit all the time, you didn't really understand. The heat was an overbearing presence more than a circumstance.

The thing that surprised Alex most about being at war was the waiting. They were always waiting for something or word from someone, and there was a lot of time spent simply hanging out with the other soldiers in the company. He knew as an engineer and a carpenter that the amount of down time he experienced was small compared to many soldiers there, but any time spent waiting in the heat was excruciating. Despite the heat they exercised. There were card games. He read whatever was around. Most of the people he worked with he liked, but he found the officers frustrating and was glad not to have joined their ranks when given the opportunity.

Packages from home were like gold—or more appropriately, water. He e-mailed when they were in places where establishing a connection was possible, but he wasn't supposed to reveal information that was too specific about where he was or exactly what he was doing. He wrote mass notes to family and friends mostly assuring them he was fine, which he knew was all they really cared about. Both his mom and Claire sent boxes of cookies which he tried to be generous about sharing, but it was hard to let anything from home go so quickly. Beth sent pictures of herself and the kids about once every two weeks, but the way the mail worked they sometimes arrived in a pile all at once. Beth told him they were fine, and they missed him, and there was something about being interviewed briefly on the local news for a story about spouses of soldiers enduring their absence.

He enjoyed the letters he got from his mom and Pammy, and even got one from Mrs. Walker that he appreciated, and one from Ben. The most diverting ones were from Claire. She sent him clippings from the satirical paper *the Onion* that she knew would make him laugh, and of course the DVDs. And her letters were interesting. She was scared to pieces for him and was trying not to let that come through, but it was impossible to help.

And Claire had met someone. She sounded content and settled. She didn't go into too much detail, but something was definitely different this time. Alex had a good feeling about it, and he was glad she had something going on that kept her from worrying about him every minute. He was looking forward to meeting the guy someday.

It was strange to Alex that he was living in a foreign country, but the only people he got to know were the people who had traveled with him from his own. There was surprisingly little contact between soldiers and actual Iraqis. He didn't get to eat the local food or see much of what the local people did. He saw a lot of American Army facilities where they had specific construction jobs to complete, but on occasion he and some others were required to inspect a structure for the locals, such as a school or a government building. Those assignments were the most interesting, but also the most nerve wracking, because they made the soldiers involved so vulnerable.

Those were the times he actually saw children and regular people out and about. The few he had contact with seemed glad he was there. As big a mess as things seemed from a larger, abstract level, it was hard not to feel he was making a difference and having a positive impact there when looked at from the ground. His contributions felt worthwhile and compassionate, as difficult as that was to explain to people like Claire who couldn't conceive of compassion paired with the rifle on his shoulder.

It felt good, too, to finally apply skills he'd learned in his years of training. As much as he was hoping not to have to fire his weapon, it was remarkable to be in an environment where he was expected to be prepared for such a thing. It reminded him of talks he'd had with Claire about jujutsu. They had admitted to each other that there were times they almost wished someone would attack them in the real world so they could test what they'd practiced. They were preparing for something that likely would never happen. Without that practical application, their skills seemed reduced to a ceremonial status that rendered them unsatisfying on some level. Now at least with his Army skills, they were all coming into play and it was rewarding. He felt completely outside of his normal context and more real.

There had been some completely terrifying experiences, usually on the few occasions they'd had to convoy somewhere. Even when there weren't any bombs someone usually fired on them with some kind of small arms. They were certainly not technically on the front lines, but you'd be a fool to ever let down your guard and feel safe anywhere. The way Alex slept had completely changed because of that. He used to sleep soundly almost anywhere. Now he slept very lightly and in small bursts. He didn't always reach for his rifle, but any stray sound got his attention.

Alex had mentally prepared himself for being on active duty for a least a year or more, and he fully anticipated that this wouldn't be his only deployment. He hadn't talked to Beth about it much, but the fact that he hadn't been called up earlier was unusual, and the need for people with his skills was high. There was a good chance he would be back again. And again.

On the day of the bombing that took his arm, he'd been thinking especially hard about which chunks of time he would be missing from his children's lives. It was difficult, but it was a sacrifice he was willing to make for what he saw as a bigger purpose. He hoped it was a sacrifice that wouldn't be rendered meaningless by poor decisions from higher up.

Alex was remarkably lucky that a field operating room was within fifteen minutes of where the bombing happened. He didn't want to remember much about it because some pain was worse than physical pain. The physical pain was shocking, though. It was so huge it almost stopped registering as pain. He didn't think he'd passed out, but either that had happened, or his mind had erased certain experiences to spare him from the ordeal in retrospect. There were sounds that came back to him at odd moments from that frantic period. Doctors talking or shouting about addressing a cut on his leg that had been overlooked as they stopped the obvious bleeding from his shoulder before getting him on the helicopter. The whole thing didn't feel like it was happening to him, but that he was being forced to stay there in the middle of everything and observe against his will.

By the time Alex reached Walter Reed in Washington D.C. he was finally getting a grip (a left-handed-only grip, he thought bitterly) on his situation. They were efficient at Walter Reed, and kind, but clear. He was one of many, and they had a routine for dealing with each new soldier who was brought there. He was going to receive counseling and that was a direct order. They would do any other surgeries or medical procedures deemed necessary, and then he would start physical and occupational therapy. He would remain on medical hold (a sort of active duty limbo) until he was declared fit to leave by both a psychologist and a medical doctor. When he reached a point where there was nothing more medical science could do, the Army would discharge him and his service to them would no longer be needed.

As far as the injury to his right shoulder was concerned, the doctors in Germany had done an excellent job, and there wasn't anything else to be done about that. They had sewn over what skin he had left in the area and it was healing as well as could be expected. There was no residual part of the arm left. It was clean gone.

There was a lot of discussion at Walter Reed about a prosthesis, but Alex didn't want to hear anything about it. Thanks to the wars in Iraq and Afghanistan, where more soldiers were surviving serious injury than in any previous conflicts, the technical advances in prosthetics was booming. They were lighter and better, and one doctor in particular kept trying to persuade Alex that since he was entitled to one, he should at least be fitted and talk to the right people. Alex was having none of it. Since there was nothing left for him to use to control such a thing, he didn't see the point. The only function a prosthetic could really serve in his case was to make him appear whole at a glance to strangers as he walked down the street, or to fill out a long-sleeved shirt. If this was who he was now, in his mind he should be that and get used to it. He was so stubborn on the issue the doctors gave up on the idea earlier than he suspected they would have liked.

A plastic surgeon addressed the remarkably small amount of harm that had happened to the right side of his neck and face (his helmet had done its job). There was going to be a large scar on the lower half of his right leg that would be impressive under other circumstances, but seemed like the last thing anyone would notice now.

The complicated part for the doctors at Walter Reed was tending to the less visible injuries he had suffered. He had some kind of inner ear damage that was disrupting his sense of balance.

And then there was the counseling. Therapy didn't carry the same stigma that it once had for American soldiers. People accepted now that suffering in silence about the horrors of war was not noble but dangerous and unnecessary. However, Alex had his own problem with it. There were things he was not ready to say, and if they kept him there until he did, he would never get home. He made a decision to share as much as seemed reasonable, but he was not going to get bogged down in counseling and never see his kids again. If he couldn't be in Iraq, he wanted to be home.

Fortunately or unfortunately for Alex, the demand for qualified Army counselors had skyrocketed, and the man assigned to him was fairly new. He apparently took Alex's swearing about his arm as a sign that his progression through the various stages of grief on that issue was on schedule, and he seemed unable to detect Alex was keeping anything from him. Alex was open about his frustration and pain, and since he appeared more practiced at talking about his emotions than was typical of many men, the counselor deemed him more mentally fit than he should have.

Alex didn't sleep well at the hospital. He wondered if he would ever sleep well again. Most nights he lay awake and tried to picture his life without his arm. Could he drive now? He probably could, but would he be allowed to? He should probably ask someone, but certain questions never crossed his mind in the daytime. That, or he couldn't imagine asking anyone about certain things regardless of the time of day. Like sex with Beth. How awkward was that going to be? And jujutsu was over. He'd always figured at some point when his kids were bigger, he could make time in his schedule for that and finally get his black belt. It was ironic, because the time he would get back being out of the Reserve opened up enough room in his schedule to make martial arts possible again. Could he still bike his kids to the park in the trailer? Could he catch Caitlin jumping at him off the top of the slide? What about his job?

Despite all the worry and physical pain he suffered at Walter Reed, his hardest moment came when he realized he was expected to use the phone by his bed to call his family. He knew Beth had been contacted once he had arrived in Germany. There were people in the Army who specialized in such calls, and it made Alex glad he was a carpenter. But he had the option of calling anyone now on his own if he felt like it, and he didn't know whom to call first. It should probably be Beth, but he had a bad feeling about it. He was afraid to call his mom because she was so emotional, and he didn't know if he could deal with that right then. He wanted to call Claire, but didn't know what to say to her either.

He put off calling anyone until he'd been in the hospital for a full week, and at that point he decided if he didn't hear Caitlin's and Conner's voices he would go crazy, so he dialed home. Beth answered on the first ring.

"Hello?"

"Beth?"

"Alex! Oh my God, where are you? I've been worried to death because we haven't heard anything since the call after you were hurt and I didn't know what to do!"

It was good to hear her voice and he felt stupid for having put off the call. She was his wife and she loved him, and she'd taken vows about sickness and health and for better or worse, so surely everything would be okay.

"I'm in Washington D.C. at the hospital here. I'm sorry you've been worried, it's just that...it's hard here and I was hoping I could come home soon, but it looks like I'm going to be here about two more months. That's what the doctors are telling me today, anyway. How are you doing? How are the kids?"

"God, Alex...I'm okay. Better, now. The kids are fine. Conner's got a nasty bump on his forehead because he and Caitlin are always jumping on the couch and he took a dive yesterday, but they were both jumping again today."

Alex smiled at the image. He wanted to be there and not in Washington hooked up to an IV drip.

"Alex?"

"I'm still here. I miss you."

"I miss you, too. Can I come visit?"

"Yeah, anytime you want. I, uh...they don't allow kids under twelve in the patient's rooms so I wouldn't bring them. I don't know if the kids should see me yet anyway. It might be too scary here."

Beth paused. "How...? They told me it was your arm. Are you...? How are you?"

"My right arm is just gone. All of it. And I have some

balance problems but that's the main thing the doctors here are trying to correct if they can. The rest of it's not even worth mentioning, really. Cuts and bruises kind of thing. I'm...I'm going to be okay." He didn't know if he believed that as the words came out of his mouth, but it seemed like the right thing to tell Beth.

He thought he heard her crying on the other end of the line. It sounded as if she had her hand over the phone.

"Beth?"

No answer.

"Beth, Honey, we're going to be fine, okay? Okay? Beth? I love you, please talk to me."

Beth finally managed to say with great difficulty, "I love you, too," but he could tell she was a disaster. Maybe he shouldn't have called. There was no way to know. There were probably tears no matter what he did.

"Beth, are you going to be okay? What do you want me to do?"

Beth continued to cry into the muffled phone and Alex decided to wait her out. Eventually she said, "Alex? When do you want me to come out there?"

"Whenever you want. I'm going to call my mom next. Maybe you can come out with my parents or something."

"Maybe."

Beth was quiet for a moment, and Alex could hear her trying to breathe more normally. Then she said, "I kept thinking maybe it was a mistake, that someone would call back and say there had been a mix up or something."

"No mix up."

"So... so you're really an amputee?"

"I guess. But I'm still just me." He didn't think that was true anymore, but again he felt a responsibility to say something Beth needed to hear. He thought he heard a retching sound in the background. "Beth? Beth are you okay?"

He didn't hear anything for a moment as apparently Beth had finally figured out the mute button on the phone. When she came back on, he asked, "Beth, are the kids there? Can I talk to Caitlin?"

"No. No, Alex, they're at my mom's for a bit so I can do the bills and stuff. Can we call you back later?"

"Sure. I'd really really like that." Alex gave her all the relevant information about his address and room number and what extension to try. He told her he loved her and then there was silence at the other end of the phone until eventually the dial tone kicked in.

He called his mom next, and she was so distressed and weepy that Alex decided he was done with the phone for the day. He was starting to dread actual visits.

The next day, however, he did get to talk to Caitlin and Conner. It made him homesick in a way that was tangible, but they were so sweet he hated when the call was done. Connor babbled long strings of words, most of which were impossible to interpret over the phone without visual cues. When the little boy finally relinquished the receiver to his sister, Caitlin went on and on about some coloring book that came with special stickers as if it were the only topic worth discussing. Listening to her made him happy, but in a way that also hurt somehow. And then Caitlin asked, "Do you still have my key?"

"I don't actually know, Honey. I was wearing it with my dog tags the whole time, but all my stuff I think is in the closet here and I haven't had a reason to dig through any of it. I'm pretty sure they took your key off me when they had to operate."

"Did the operate hurt?"

"A bit. But I'll be okay."

"Can you still make Mr. Bunny Face do chasing with the pointy teeth when you come home?"

"Oh, you know I can. I wish I could come do that now."

"Why can't you come now?"

"Because I still need to get a bit better first."

"I think you should come home, Daddy."

"I'm working on it."

"Daddy?"

"Yes, Honey?"

"I don't like it when you're gone."

"I know. Me either. Can you tell me about the stickers some more?"

"Yes! There is a princess on every page and there are stickers to match and you have to know Mulan gets the sword and that Belle has a book and that...." Alex shut his eyes and listened to Caitlin go on happily about stickers and princesses the whole rest of the call until Beth decided it was enough. As much as he had enjoyed talking to Caitlin, the conversation also set his stomach churning. His kids were so innocent, and he worried about disrupting their safe little world when he returned. He wasn't sure how his appearance would do anything other than scare them. Alex stared at the now silent phone in his lap, loneliness starting to fill his lungs and creep up his throat.

That was when he finally decided to call Claire. Alex had to ask a nurse to dig his notebook out of his things to find the number, because he'd never called her at Eric's place before. (He also had the nurse find Caitlin's key while she was at it, and he put that on the side tray to his left so he could pick it up and hold it when he wanted to.) It was odd not to picture Claire in the apartment they had shared together that initial summer out of college.

The first time he called he got the machine and hung up because he couldn't imagine what sort of message to leave. When he tried again later, he got Eric. He could hear Claire in the background, and they sounded as if they were just getting in from somewhere like the store because there were crinkly bag sounds and cabinets opening and closing.

"Hello?" said the unfamiliar male voice.

"Hi. Is, uh...is Claire there?"

"Sure, may I ask who's calling?"

"This is Alex."

"Whoa, how are you doing? Are you—? Wait, I'm sorry, you don't even know me—so, just a second." He called Claire over and another moment later she was on the line.

"Alex! Where are you now?"

"Hey, Claire!" He felt calmer than he had been since he'd left for Iraq. "I'm in Washington."

"At Walter Reed?"

"Uh-huh. Yeah, I'll be here for a while still. How are you?"

Claire laughed. It was a relief to hear someone over the age of four laugh finally. "What kind of question is that? I'm worried about you, but other than that I'm completely and perfectly fine. When are you coming home? Do you need anything? How can I help?"

Alex closed his eyes and wasn't sure how to say that she already had. This conversation finally felt like home.

"I'll take more cookies anytime you want to send 'em," he said. "And I guess you could put chocolate chips in them again since they won't turn into a gooey mess over here."

"Yeah, sorry about that first box. I should have thought of that, but at least you e-mailed me before I could do it again. I guess the heat affects a lot of things you don't think about."

"Yeah. I guess it does. So that's Eric?"

"That's Eric. He's great to live with and doesn't steal my body wash. And he always asks before he eats my ice cream."

"Wait, he's actually allowed to have some?"

"Yeah, of course. All you ever had to do was ask."

They were quiet for a moment, and then Claire said, "It was weird letting go of your apartment."

Alex laughed a little, which made his whole right side hurt. "It was yours way longer than it was ever mine."

"I know. That's just how I thought of it."

"Yeah, I guess I never really stopped thinking of it as ours either, kind of."

There was another pause, then Claire said, "So, your arm, huh?"

"Yeah."

"Which one?"

"The right one," he said.

"Does it hurt still?"

"Yeah."

"I'm sorry, Alex."

"Yeah, well...."

Claire waited a moment, then asked, "Can the other one still block a groin kick?"

Alex smiled to himself. "I guess it's going to have to."

"So, where do I send those cookies?"

Alex gave her the information, she slowly repeated all of it back, and they said their goodbyes. Alex was relieved to have had a moment that felt so normal. He was glad he could count on Claire for that.

What he didn't know was that about halfway through the conversation, Claire had gotten so dizzy she'd had to sit on the floor. She knew the last thing her friend needed was to feel as if he had to tend to her somehow, so she'd simply tried to sound as natural as she could. She'd repeated the address information slowly so Eric could write it down for her on the dry erase board they kept in the kitchen. When she hung up, Eric sat with her on the floor, his arms around her. He wiped tears from her cheeks with no understanding of what that really meant.

*

Beth drove out with Alex's parents to see him the following week. Visiting hours were between eleven in the morning and nine at night. Alex was looking better the day they arrived at the hospital around noon. His face was healing well, and the stitches had been removed from his leg the day before. His shoulder was still heavily bandaged, but the hospital gown covered it well. He made himself smile when they walked in.

Alex's dad put on a brave face, but his mother looked stricken when she saw him. Beth's eyes immediately traveled to the place where his arm should have been, and then to the remains of the wounds on his face and neck. By the time her eyes met his, she had masked her initial revulsion with a smile and came over to give him a kiss. Alex couldn't tell if the chaste feel of the kiss had to do with his condition, or the fact that his parents were in the room.

Alex almost wished they hadn't come. The visit was tense and strange. Beth was rattled and his mother kept crying and his father didn't know how to handle either of the women in the room and still try to talk to his son. They all made an attempt at being pleasant for a while, and everyone asked all the obvious questions. Alex wanted updates on the kids, and Beth provided him with a new stack of photos, along with one in a frame of Caitlin and Conner together. His mom wanted to know if he was eating well. His father asked about the doctors and quoted him statistics he'd read about how qualified they were there, apparently to reassure himself and his son that Alex was in good hands. Alex didn't know how to tell his dad that the quality of the inpatient care he was receiving was fine, but his observations of the outpatient care were downright disturbing.

The whole experience made Alex tired. His parents decided to give him some time alone with his wife before they all went out for a bit and came back later to join him for dinner, once Alex was done with his mandatory counseling session.

His mother kissed him on the forehead. "Oh, my sweet boy, I am so thankful to God that you're alive."

"Yeah, it's His fault I suppose, isn't it?" muttered Alex.

"What?" His mother looked confounded as her husband led her out of the room to the visitor area where they would wait for Beth.

"Nothing. See you in a bit, Mom," Alex called after her.

When he was alone with Beth they simply stared at each other for a moment. Then she came over and stood by his left side. He wondered if he still resembled the husband she remembered from the left side, and consequently she would be spending more time there.

"So..." she said finally, "When do you come home?"

"Well, they're not sure. They're not making much progress on the inner ear thing, but they want to try everything before they give up."

Beth seemed as if she were steeling herself for something and took his hand. "Is everything else...you know, are you okay everywhere besides all that?"

"Yeah, Beth. I'm pretty sure if you still want four kids, we can have four kids."

He thought she looked disappointed briefly, but

decided that couldn't be right. His head hurt and he didn't want to go to counseling. It was exhausting finding things to say there that satisfied the therapist but still maintained his privacy without tipping anyone off.

Beth frowned a little and glanced down at his hand. She traced the back of it with a finger slowly. "Alex, some people get those...those artificial limbs and they can make them look pretty good. I was looking into it, and they can—"

Alex was annoyed. "No."

"But, Alex! You could walk down the street and look like you—"

"No. I don't want to look like something I'm not."

"But maybe with it you'd look normal!"

"Yeah, to people who don't know me."

"But that's the point!" she said helplessly.

"Beth, why should I care what people think who I don't even know?"

"But—"

"No."

So they were stuck and had discovered yet one more thing to argue about. Beth looked as if she might cry, and Alex sighed. He told her to close her eyes a moment and he guided her face close to his with his hand. He stroked her cheek lightly with his thumb. He kissed her gently until she started to kiss him back.

"Beth, I don't know what to tell you yet," he said softly. "It's going to be hard and I'm not sure about anything except that I just want to come home. I don't want to fight here, okay?"

"Okay."

He kissed her goodbye and watched her go out the door to meet his parents. What a fun group that must be, he thought to himself sarcastically. He didn't know how his mother and his wife hadn't strangled each other by the end of such a long car ride. Maybe they simply fell asleep to whatever deadly dull audio book his dad had probably insisted on playing the whole drive.

The orderly arrived with the wheelchair to take him down the hall. The physical therapist still didn't want him walking on his own yet, even though the IV drip was gone and he wouldn't be tripping over that. He wished he weren't being treated as if he were going to break. Unless there was an IED in the hall, he couldn't imagine what they felt he needed protection from at that point. If he wasn't going to be dead, he may as well be learning how to walk without leaning over and falling down.

The visit after dinner went better, and he spent a long time with his mother alone the next afternoon as he tried to reassure her he was going to be fine and he got her to catch him up on what his kids were doing now. He had a brief chat with his dad about nothing personal, but that was how they were.

He spent one last stretch of time alone with Beth where she refrained from bugging him about anything. He thought she seemed more relaxed by the time he kissed her goodbye, but he could tell she couldn't wait to get out of Walter Reed. She'd made the mistake of walking Alex down to the big physical therapy room that afternoon, and the sight of so many other soldiers suffering from various levels of dismemberment and trauma had made her look ill.

Alex didn't know how he felt about the whole visit. He was glad to have the new pictures of the kids, but he wondered if Beth should have simply mailed them. And his mom remained shaken regardless of whatever he said to assuage her worries about his future.

A couple of weeks later, Claire had arranged with Pammy for the two of them to fly out together and see

Alex for themselves. It was a welcome arrangement. Pammy was in grad school in Arizona and living with her boyfriend who was also a student. Claire hadn't seen her in a while, and they were glad to spend time together and catch up. Pammy was still studying anthropology and she loved living in the Southwest. Claire told her about Eric and the new classes she was putting together at the dojo, and how Sensei was considering expanding into a second location and putting her in charge of it. The pleasant conversation made for a good distraction from the uncomfortable purpose of their trip.

They flew into Ronald Reagan National Airport in plenty of time to check into their cheap motel and catch a cab to Walter Reed during visiting hours. They were nervous as they approached the hospital, but they had discussed at length the need to make Alex feel like himself, so they tried to remember how to act normal. The report from Mrs. Sullivan after her return from Washington had been concerning, and was still fresh in their minds. Claire needed to see Alex for herself, but was apprehensive, and thankful she had Pammy with her for the visit.

"Hey, you!" said Pammy as she walked boldly into Alex's room. "Do you get all the pudding you can eat in this place?"

"Hi!" Alex sat up straighter in bed and smiled. "Mom said you guys were coming but she didn't say when! Hey, Claire!"

"Hey, Alex."

Pammy purposely then ignored the entire hospital setting, and launched into chatting with her brother as if it were any other family reunion. He told her about the phone conversation he'd had earlier with his kids, and she told him about her field research and her TA position. Claire was quiet. She kicked off her shoes and settled herself in on the end of the bed cross-legged, and Alex moved his legs to make room for her while he continued to direct his attention toward his sister.

Claire studied him as he talked. There was some scarring on his face and neck, which in time wouldn't be too bad, and his left half in general seemed fine. But the absence of his right arm was really a shock to see. He had a light bandage over his shoulder area, and she wondered what exactly was under it. What a pain, she thought, to lose your dominant hand. She wondered what tasks he'd been able to successfully transfer to his left already, and how many to learn remained.

Watching Alex talk to Pammy about nothing that had anything to do with his situation seemed to be making him happy, but Claire decided she couldn't do that. For her to ignore his condition would be fake, and that wasn't what their friendship was like. Eventually he did turn to her, and the look of gratitude on his face at her mere presence made the entire trip worthwhile.

"So what's up with you?" he asked.

"Oh, you know...punches, kicks, rolls. Hey, one of the new classes I'm designing is for little kids. I'm thinking like around Caitlin's age next year—the five to six-year-old crowd. I'm going to blow bubbles and have them pop them by kicking, and all kinds of fun things. It might be fun if Caitlin signed up. You could help her out at home, so she'd get good pretty fast I bet."

Alex laughed a little. "I don't know, Claire. She's a pretty girlie girl. Big into the princess thing right now. Maybe Conner in a few years...but I wouldn't count on my help for anything."

"Why? Just because of your arm?" asked Claire. Pammy shot her an uncertain look.

Alex gave her a smirk. "Well, no kidding, because of my arm! I can't imagine why that would be a problem. Oh yeah, because as I recall, all that sparring we ever did required two of them. Unless I grow a new one, I think I'm out of commission. That black belt is officially not going to happen for me now, so we can scratch that off my to-do list."

Before Claire could respond to that, the nurse arrived to help walk Alex to occupational therapy, so they had to clear out for a while. They said their goodbyes, and then Pammy and Claire spent a few hours walking together on the Mall, looking at monuments and admiring the cherry blossoms which were in full bloom by that time in late April. Pammy wanted to visit the Lincoln Memorial, but before they reached it, they found themselves at the Vietnam Wall.

They'd both read about it, but never seen it, and they were stunned by its true impact. It was subtle enough, to start. The wall cuts its way into the earth down by your feet, and you start reading names because there aren't that many on that first, small slab of polished stone. But the farther you walk, the deeper you go, until the wall stretches beyond your reach and the names are impossible to take in because there are far too many. And it keeps going. And then it hits you that the names are people and it's devastating. By the middle of the walk through the memorial, Claire realized Pammy was crying. Claire put her arm around her, and they stood there for a long time.

"God, Claire, what did they do to my brother?" she finally said. Claire wasn't sure which "they" Pammy was blaming, but it didn't matter. She wondered if the President had been required to offer up his own arm as a sacrifice to the war gods, if he would have thought differently about going into Iraq.

CHAPTER ELEVEN

When Claire returned home, she spent several days contemplating an idea. She was worried for Alex. There was a general sense of loss emanating from him that was bigger than the arm. It was everything that had been blown away with the arm, like his ability to write easily, or to eat with a knife and fork...or jujutsu. Claire didn't think she could offer him much, but she did feel competent to provide him some kind of martial arts training, assuming he was interested. She believed if Alex could retain that part of his past, he might recognize himself better, even in his new form.

She talked to Sensei about her concept for left-arm-only jujutsu. He told her that it wasn't out of the question at all to modify the techniques to accommodate Alex. They would have to think about everything thoroughly and take good notes to remain consistent. He was willing to work with her after hours to figure it out on any evening he was free.

So the first night Sensei was available, they met in the dojo ready to work. Claire put her right arm inside her gi and had Sensei tie the belt tightly around her. She was shocked at how instantly vulnerable she felt by having that arm unavailable. It was scary. She started to appreciate with greater clarity how daunting Alex's world may have become. She wasn't even sure how he would manage the belt himself, but Claire would worry about such details later. Right then they had other things to figure out.

She and Sensei bowed onto the mat.

"Where shall we begin?" he asked her.

"I suppose at the beginning, Sensei." But even as she said it, all the white-belt techniques flashed through her mind and seemed insurmountable. There were rolls and breakfalls and stances.... There was a cartwheel you were supposed to at least marginally master in order to pass that level, and Alex hadn't been good at that with two arms. Even the list of bows required both hands as far as she was concerned.

Sensei considered every technique with great care. They went through each posture and bow, and he told Claire if she presented her body with the correct intention, the arm would not be missed.

The breakfalls were hard for Claire to master with one arm, but she knew Alex was far stronger, so he would probably fare better with those. The forward and side rolls from the left side weren't hard to adapt to, but the right side made Claire nervous. She could feel her arm involuntarily twitching to break free every time she aimed herself toward the floor without it there to brace her. She wondered if Alex's phantom arm did the same thing every time he needed it.

A backward roll when starting from the floor was unbalanced and harder to control, but possible with practice. The blocks and strikes were peculiar to negotiate, since typically one hand was up in order to deflect incoming blows, and the other in a defensive position near the ribcage preparing to strike if necessary. Did it make more sense to keep her one arm closer to her body in preparation for delivering a strike, or to extend it outward to block one? It felt dangerously exposed to extend her only arm, but Sensei said the first priority had to be defensive. The one arm would have to perform both functions, which was not instinctual at first, but could be done. The kicks were a relief, and only the blocking element needed to be addressed there.

Wrist locks were a challenge. She figured at least with Alex's larger hands—*hand*—he would have an easier time controlling someone else's. She and Sensei found ways to do all of the locks, but some were more difficult than others, especially from a particular side depending upon the technique.

Changing sides was an adjustment martial artists thought about regularly. Most people were comfortable learning a technique on the right side until they understood it, and then worked on performing its mirror image. The left side seldom felt as natural unless you were dedicated enough to make it that way with repetition. When Claire had run classes where she instructed people to only work on their left sides, she was always met with quiet groans. Even experienced martial artists often had a moment of hesitation when an attack came from the "wrong" side. The running joke was that if you had to fight someone with martial arts training, you should punch with your left.

Alex now had only the left side, so he was at a weird kind of advantage in a small way. But simply translating everything into a mirror image wasn't possible. For nearly every technique Claire and Sensei attempted, switching sides meant modifying the details all over again. That meant Alex was going to have to learn nearly twice as many techniques in every kyu level.

When they took a break from the mat, Claire freed

her arm to take notes. Once they had composed a proper set of instructions for left-arm-only jujutsu, Claire planned to have Eric come in and take key photographs so she could compile a complete binder for Alex. If this was still an element of his life that he hoped to preserve, she wanted it to feel real, with something official to hold onto. She didn't know if Alex would even be open to it or not, but preparing the binder made her feel less helpless about what to do when he finally came home.

Alex was discharged from both the hospital and the Army in late June. His shoulder didn't hurt anymore, but the sensations he was having on that side were odd. He could still feel the arm, and it often itched or ached. There was some connection between that and the weather—more specifically, the humidity. Alex hadn't determined a pattern yet, but it came and went.

In his dreams he still had both arms, and Alex was surprised every morning when he went to move them that the right one was gone. It was for the briefest of moments, but between the time he knew he was awake and the time he opened his eyes, he was himself, and he was whole, and he didn't remember anything. It was his favorite time of day. Then the rest of the day would begin.

His leg and face had healed well. The inner ear problem had been addressed as far as anyone was able, but without much improvement. The doctors told Alex he would always have balance issues, but physical therapy had taught him how to compensate. He learned to read visual cues from his surroundings to keep himself upright. Other than the missing arm, he appeared to be a healthy, strong, 28-year-old man. Inside was another story.

Beth flew out alone to get him. Alex had made it crystal clear he did not want a fuss about his homecoming, and she was not to call the paper or a local news crew. She appeared greatly disappointed, but agreed, and didn't even organize a family party. She simply helped him gather his things at the hospital, and took the pamphlets of information they gave her about continuing help available to Alex through the VA. The staff recommended the support group for returning and injured soldiers in his area, as well as an occupational therapy program and more counseling. Alex wanted nothing to do with any of it, but he saw Beth tuck all of that material into her bag. The plane ride home was quiet.

Beth's mother was at the house with the kids. Caitlin had recently turned four, and Conner would be two the following month. When Alex arrived home, Conner was napping, but his little girl burst out of the house to greet her daddy. She was all smiles and told him "thank you" for the stuffed unicorn and magic wand he'd sent her for her birthday from the hospital gift shop. Alex had tears in his eyes and could barely believe how old his daughter looked at four.

Caitlin touched the loose sleeve of his t-shirt and asked, "Where did your arm go?"

"Remember I told you on the phone that I had to leave it in Iraq?" he said, trying to not make it sound like a big deal.

"Why?"

"It got too hurt to keep, so you'll have to help me stay super careful of the other one, okay?"

"Okay. Come see my new princess stickers!" And she started bouncing toward the house.

It certainly wasn't the end of the discussion, because Caitlin was, in fact, confused about the whole thing, and continued to ask her dad at odd moments about his arm. Alex didn't want her to be afraid, so he always answered her matter-of-factly, and that seemed to work. The missing arm attracted her attention because it was a change, but she wasn't frightened. It was a pleasant surprise, overall, how well the kids adapted to his condition. Conner didn't seem to notice, and Caitlin having asked her questions was quickly satisfied that her dad was still her dad, even if he'd left his arm in Iraq for some reason. She started assuring him when she came back from play dates or her grandparents' house that she had remembered to bring both her arms and he didn't need to worry.

Alex wanted so badly to do everything with Caitlin that he used to, but his balance was not right, and some things seemed too risky. She wanted him to spin her around on the lawn like he had before, and that was impossible. But then came a moment when Conner was napping and they were out in the yard when Caitlin asked Alex, "Can we do a new pick-me-up game?"

"I don't know, Honey. It makes me really nervous to carry you now because something in my head makes it hard for me not to tip over."

"So it's like the dizzy game, but you don't have to spin first?"

"Pretty much. Sometimes it's kind of like someone spun me around a bit and I have to think about what I'm doing before I move."

"But if you pick me up I can be dizzy with you."

"It doesn't work like that, Honey. It's like I'm pre-dizzy and I don't want to risk falling while I'm holding you."

"I'm not scared."

Alex smiled. "I know. You're never scared, are you?"

Caitlin smiled back at her dad proudly as she shook her head. "Not even of spiders or of worms or of monsters!"

Alex ruffled her hair a little. "It's okay to be scared

of some monsters, though. Everybody gets scared, and being scared or sad is sometimes a way of knowing we care about something."

Caitlin didn't appear interested in considering that. She only wanted Alex to lift her up again. "Daddy, I'm not scared and if you pick me up I can jump and I can save myself so it's okay, see?"

"Like a superhero jumping off a building?"

"Yes! Mr. Bunny Face and I can jump off."

God, he loved that intrepid girl. "Okay," he said, "let's figure something out."

They wound up inventing what they called the "Save Yourself" game, where Alex would hoist Caitlin up in his arm and practice moving around with her, but if he were scared he was starting to tip he would say, "Save Yourself!" Then Caitlin would spring off him, arms spread wide like a bird, and land on the ground where she would make sure to step back enough of a distance that he wouldn't land on her if he fell. He showed her how to fall safely, how to tuck her chin and roll so she wouldn't hurt her head. She got grass stains all over her pink princess outfit, but neither of them cared. They were having too much fun to care.

By the end of the afternoon, Caitlin was good enough at safely launching herself out of her dad's arm that he didn't worry about trying to carry her anymore. Conner would be another story, however, so he told Caitlin they should only play Save Yourself when her little brother wasn't around so he wouldn't insist on trying it too.

Time with Conner was all about reading books and hooking together wooden toy trains. Alex never ceased to be amused by the kinds of things Conner thought his trains should be hauling—usually things he picked up from the yard like dandelions and violets and pebbles.

All of the time Alex spent with his kids was

everything he wanted. He loved sitting on the floor with them as they crawled over him, and how they snuggled in his lap as he read to them, and rolled in the grass alongside him while they all laughed. He even got to sneak Caitlin out once after dark when she couldn't sleep, and they looked at the stars and made up constellations together. (Although there were far more princesses up there than he had ever suspected.)

But everything else about being home was distressing. Beth was impatient, and didn't want to make accommodations for anything Alex might have to do differently. She didn't seem to understand that even skills that could be accomplished with one hand, he had to relearn because it was now the wrong hand. Unlocking the front door felt unfamiliar, holding a glass of water felt new, even the remote control for the TV seemed weird in his left rather than his right. To make matters worse, Alex was starting to discover how much of the world was designed around right-handed people in general. He was beginning to suspect that even when he got more comfortable using his left, certain things would remain unwieldy regardless.

Getting dressed took him forever, and he simply started wearing Army sweatpants and a t-shirt every day because it was the easiest outfit he could reliably do in the time Beth allowed him. She expected Alex to change Conner's diapers, which, if the boy were feeling wiggly, he could only manage with Caitlin's help. Beth complained that she had to do all the driving but wasn't willing to let him practice with her car, and his was a stick-shift which was now out of the question. She whined that his writing was illegible when he added things to the grocery list. It felt to Alex as if Beth were trying to negate his injuries by denying she should hold him to a new (less preferable) standard.

Part of their trouble was that Beth had gotten into a

new routine that didn't include Alex anymore, so even without his injuries it would have been hard making the adjustment to having him back. She had become accustomed to making all of the decisions for their household alone, and resented any of them being questioned after so many months.

They fought about daycare for the kids, because even though Caitlin and Conner enjoyed it, Alex didn't want them going there. He was home, and it would be a while before he went back to work, so he didn't see the point. Alex thought she let the kids watch too much TV. Beth thought he was too strict about bedtimes. Alex believed Caitlin should be picking up her own toys at the end of the day. It drove Beth crazy when Alex gave Caitlin treats at odd times. Beth neglected to stock the foods he liked. Alex didn't like her method of paying the bills or the number of credit cards she'd acquired in his absence. Beth couldn't stand that he kept leaving his shoes in the hallway like he used to. There seemed to be no end to the list of irritations between them. Alex knew they'd had problems before, but re-acclimating to each other under one roof after Iraq seemed to multiply them tenfold.

Alex overheard Beth explaining on the phone that the adjustment to having him back was bigger than the resumption of sex, which was all her friends were apparently focused on when imagining what couples reuniting after such a long stretch apart were interested in. He couldn't figure out why she was even implying to others that they were having sex. He certainly wanted to touch Beth like he used to, and feel closeness and acceptance and pleasure again. He'd hoped being intimate with his wife would help him forget, and make him feel whole, but Beth couldn't be a party to that yet.

The first night Alex was home, Beth made sure to go

to bed after he was asleep so she wouldn't have to deal with him. The next night he made a point of staying up with her so they would go to bed together, but she claimed to not be feeling well, so he left her to sleep. She lay rigid as he tried to snuggle close to her.

The third night Alex finally asked her directly if she ever intended to touch him again. She denied there was any problem, but Beth wasn't good at hiding the disgust she felt about his disfigurement. They made an attempt at sex in the dark. It didn't go well. It seemed to Alex that she'd consented purely out of some sense of spousal obligation, and if Beth wasn't enjoying herself there was no way for him to. He could think of plenty of ways that his missing arm shouldn't make any difference at all in bed, but Beth behaved as if she were mentally someplace else and merely lending him her body. He struggled with finding a position that worked for him, but Beth's lack of cooperation or good humor added to his frustration. Alex had been deprived for so long, he decided to push ahead regardless. Then he discovered sex brought out odd sensations in his phantom hand, which didn't help, so he finished and rolled over and didn't bother Beth again.

Alex hadn't anticipated a life without sex when he returned home. He tried to put himself in his deployment mindset, which was the only time he'd ever not had access to sex when he was interested. But the idea of having to live in that state indefinitely was more than a bit unsettling.

By far the hardest thing about sharing a bed again, however, was the actual sleeping. Alex could not sleep through the night anymore. He woke at every noise. He'd panic if he couldn't find his rifle, and then Beth would have to remind him he was home. A lot of nights he simply got up after only a few hours of thrashing around. He would stand in the doorway of each of his kids' rooms and watch them sleep, safe and sound. On clear nights he would go outside and study the stars. Occasionally he'd sit alone under the tree with the tire swing and cry. Before Beth got up in the morning, he'd crawl back in bed and get some rest in fits and starts. But decent sleep like he used to know was impossible.

Alex called people to come visit and welcome him home in stages. He started with his parents, who came out for dinner his third night back. Next, he wanted to see Claire and finally meet Eric. Beth was resistant, but the fact that Claire would be bringing a boyfriend for a change caused her to relent.

Claire and Eric came over on a Sunday afternoon for a late lunch. Beth told Alex they were going to do hamburgers and hot dogs on the grill, and he was in charge of it. He wasn't sure how she expected him to do that, but he was tired of fighting, so he agreed. Beth dressed the kids in clothes that were extra cute, and made potato salad and cut up some watermelon.

Alex was standing by the grill when Claire and Eric arrived. He was trying to get a sense of how to handle the tongs and the flipper with his left hand before attempting to do anything with actual meat.

"Alex?" he heard Claire say, as she came around from the driveway and directly into the back yard. He turned to see her coming toward him, smile on her face, and a guy to her right holding a container of food and with some sort of bag slung over his shoulder. Alex set the tongs down and jogged over, lifting her off the ground with his arm as he hugged her tightly. She laughed, and Alex held her close as her feet dangled and said, "God, it's good to see you." Then he started to tilt.

Caitlin came running through the back door at that point, saying to Claire in a happy and excited tone, "You have to do Save Yourself! You have to jump off him and roll away when Daddy starts to do the dizzy thing!" Alex was already steadying himself without a problem, but Claire smiled at Caitlin, slipped off her friend into a basic back breakfall, then did a graceful backward roll and hopped up several feet away. "Like that?' she asked the little girl who was watching her in awe.

"No, you jump high like a superhero. But now I want to do that thing you did! Daddy, can we do that backward thing? Can you show me?"

Alex smiled at his daughter. "You know what? Claire is a really good teacher and I bet she would be happy to show you while I work on the food." He looked over at Claire and said, "You mind working on your day off?"

"Not at all. Caitlin, you want to go over with me to the grass and try?"

"Yes! But I have to get Mr. Bunny Face so he can learn too." And she disappeared back inside the house again.

Claire cast Alex an amused look. "Mr. Bunny Face?"

"Yeah, I know. It's that *Holy Grail* rabbit you gave us as a wedding present, and damn if that wasn't the only name I could think of."

The man next to Claire said, "Well, your daughter has good taste in movie rabbits. I'm Eric." And he shifted the food container over to his right hand so he could extend his left.

"Nice to finally meet you," said Alex, shaking Eric's hand as Caitlin reappeared, bunny clutched in her arms.

"Daddy, can we show them Save Yourself? How we do it?"

Alex glanced back toward the house to see if Beth was coming out yet, and when he decided the coast was probably clear he said, "Sure, just once real quick, but then I have to figure out the grill so I can make you that hot dog I promised, okay?"

Caitlin nodded and then handed her rabbit to Claire saying, "Can you hold Mr. Bunny Face to watch?"

Claire obligingly took the rabbit, which Eric viewed curiously. As Alex moved onto the grass with his daughter, he heard Eric ask Claire quietly where the big pointy teeth were, and she stuck her finger into the bunny's mouth to show him. Eric smiled when the eyes turned red.

"Are you watching?" asked Caitlin anxiously. "You guys and Mr. Bunny Face are supposed to be watching!" Her dad scooped her up in his arm, while Claire obediently turned the bunny to face them.

Alex smiled, then pretended to be worried and said, "Oh no! Caitlin, I might be starting to get dizzy! Save Yourself!" The girl laughed as she launched herself out of his arm and hit the ground with a slight bend to her knees. She then carefully placed her hands in a sort of T shape on the ground in front of her, looked back over her shoulder while tucking her chin, and did an imperfect but recognizable forward jujutsu roll away from her dad, where she scrambled to her feet again, appearing proud.

"Caitlin!" said Claire, "That was a nice roll! I'm really impressed. You know, if we tweak a couple of things, we can make it super duper quiet. Want me to show you?"

Caitlin nodded as she came over to pull Claire onto to the grass. "And the one that goes backward, too?"

"Sure thing," said Claire, smiling behind her at Eric as she was led away.

Alex walked back over to grill and sighed. Grilling was not his thing. It was his father-in-law's thing, so Beth's dad had made sure his daughter's new home had a big gas grill when they first moved in. Alex hadn't felt competent at it with two hands, and was not looking forward to attempting to manage it with only one. He wondered vaguely if Beth was hoping to embarrass him by insisting he try.

Eric walked over, glanced from Alex's face to the grill and the associated tools, and after a moment he said, "Hey, you know, we never had a grill like this when I was growing up, so I never got to learn how to do something like that. You want to maybe talk me through it so I could try? I mean, if you'd rather, obviously, you do it, but, um... you could also just take it easy and give me a chance. If you want. You'd be doing me a favor."

Alex was relieved and said, "No, be my guest! I can go in and get the meat and then you can totally do as much as you want." He glanced down at the container in Eric's hands and said, "Can I take that in when I go? What did you bring?"

Eric handed Alex the container saying, "It's sholeh zard. It's Claire's favorite thing my mom makes so I've been trying to make it for her myself. I'm not as good at it yet, but Claire gave this batch a thumbs up. It's a dessert—a rice pudding with saffron. My little cousins love it, so I thought your kids might like it too."

"Thanks," said Alex. "Can't wait to try it." He scrutinized the bag over Eric's shoulder as he took the container and said, "Did you bring a camera?"

Eric smiled and made a small shrug. "It's hard for me to go anywhere without a camera, but in this case, I was thinking if you guys were interested, it might be nice to get a few shots of all of you as a family again. I mean, it's been so many months apart, you could probably use a few nice photos you could frame that show you all in one place finally. You know, all at home."

"Huh," said Alex.

"It's just a thought," said Eric. "If you don't need

anything like that, I could just get some cute shots of the kids or something, but—"

"No, that would be great. I was trying to think of the last time we had our picture taken all together, and I think it was before I got on the bus to Fort Atterbury. Conner was screaming because it was way past his nap time, and Caitlin wouldn't look at the camera because she was hugging my leg and crying.... Not exactly the kind of shot that makes a good holiday card."

Eric laughed. "No, but it sounds real. Some pictures aren't supposed to be art or even decorative, they can be a visual journal and that's enough to make them worthwhile. Sounds like a pretty good picture to me."

They heard Caitlin squeal on the lawn, and they both glanced over to see Claire rolling backward as the happy girl chased her. Then they heard Beth emerge into the back yard saying, "Caitlin! What are you doing on the grass in your nice dress?" She had been holding Conner in her arms, and she set him down and put her hands on her hips. Conner raced with a wide grin directly over to his father, and Alex set the container he was holding down in time for Conner to start grabbing at his arm. Almost as a reflex, Alex pulled his arm up to lift his son off the ground, and then swung it as if being a human jungle gym was second nature. He kept his eyes warily on his wife the whole time.

"Mommy," Caitlin said, "did you see me? I can do a —"

"What I see is you getting grass stains on that new outfit," complained Beth, "and I have enough to do around here without wasting time with—"

"I'm sorry, it's my fault," interrupted Claire, taking Caitlin by the hand and leading the reluctant child back onto the patio. "I'll pay to clean the dress or wash it for you if you like."

Beth didn't look impressed with the offer, but as she

turned toward her husband, she finally spotted Eric and her eyes opened a little wider.

Alex said, "Beth, Claire's just being nice. I'm the one who took Caitlin onto the grass first, so if you want to be mad, be mad at me. Anyway, this is Claire's boyfriend, Eric."

"Nice to meet you," said Eric, walking forward a few steps and extending a hand. Beth looked briefly as if she didn't like the idea of taking it, but then she put on a smile and shook his hand lightly. "That's a beautiful pair of earrings you've got on. Are they lapis?" he asked.

Beth seemed a bit startled, then put a hand up to one of her ears as if to recall what jewelry she was actually wearing. "Yes, I got a real deal on them."

"Well, they go really well with your top. I was just telling Alex that I brought my camera to do a family portrait if you're interested. I'm a professional photographer, and I thought it might make a good welcome home gift. We could do a couple now, if you want, before we eat and the kids possibly get dirty."

Beth brightened a little at the idea, and motioned Caitlin to come over to her so she could dust her off and inspect the offending dress more closely to see if it should be changed. She eyed Alex, and then said to Eric, "I would love a nice family picture, finally. But Alex? I want you in your blue shirt."

Alex had stopped swinging Conner since he was starting to tip again. He was noticing a pattern of his vertigo being stress related. "The... the one with the buttons?"

"Yes the one with the buttons. It's a dress shirt, and you're the only one not properly dressed," said Beth looking irritated.

"I think he looks fine," said Eric. "I can work with it, we just put the kids in his lap and—"

"Alex?" said Beth, giving her head a slight jerk toward the house.

Alex paused where he was, looking stricken, and then he muttered as he started to move, "Well this will be a while."

Claire couldn't quite believe what was happening. The world had become a very strange place if a shirt could elicit an expression of slight terror on her friend's face that way. Every instinct she had was telling her to follow Alex and help him with those damn buttons, but she wasn't sure how to get away with that. She glanced worriedly at Eric, who seemed to grasp her concern as his gaze followed Alex walking into the house. He looked thoughtful for a moment. Then he started getting equipment out of his bag and said to Beth, "You know, you have some lovely flowers out front. Can I get a few pictures of just you and the kids for a sec? Conner's outfit is really adorable. I shoot a lot of weddings where the ring bearer isn't dressed half this nice. My aunt can't find anything like it for my cousin who is about the same age—where do you shop?"

Beth appeared pleased as she touched her hair in a couple of places. She herded her children out toward the front of the house with Eric, who cast a glance back at Claire with a small grin before he disappeared around the corner.

Claire ducked into the house and started hunting for Alex. She found him in his bedroom staring down at a dress shirt on the bed, all of the buttons undone. He looked as if he'd been asked to lift a tank with his arm.

"Hey, Alex," said Claire from the doorway.

Alex glanced up, smiled briefly, then frowned back down at the shirt. "She undoes them all before she hangs them up. Every time. Caitlin buttons them about halfway up for me because she wants to help, even

272

though it takes her a while, and then I can get the damn thing on and only have a few left to do myself. But Beth? Beth always undoes them all and then wants me to do them in the same amount of time that I used to."

Claire was feeling pissed, but that wouldn't fix anything in the moment. "Can I just help? I'd rather have you out there with us than stuck in here."

Alex sighed. "Yeah, that'd be great."

Claire helped him slip the shirt on, but wasn't sure what to do with the empty sleeve on his right. "Do people clip this? Cut it off? What do they do?"

"I don't fucking know. I just don't wear long sleeves."

Claire studied the sleeve a moment, then decided to roll it up and clip it in place with a simple brooch she saw lying on Beth's half of the dresser. She started work on the buttons, careful not to misalign the two sides of the shirt like she often did with her own. She wondered if Eric believed she did that on purpose so he could enjoy standing close while he redid them for her.

Alex looked down at Claire's hands, working together to carefully do the buttons as if it were nothing. She was close enough he could smell her body wash, but there was an unfamiliar scent in her hair. Maybe saffron? He'd find out when they got to dessert. Dessert seemed very far away.

Claire smiled up at him as she finished the button a couple from the top. She thought he looked better with his collar open. He smiled down at her in return, but appeared rather pained. "Thanks," he said. "That was nice of you."

"I'm always nice," she said, as she used both her hands to smooth out the front of his shirt. She then gave him a single pat on the chest and said, "Let's go get you photographed, and then maybe we can eat. I'm starved."

Beth was coming down the hall as her husband and his female friend were coming out of the bedroom together. Beth stopped dead, and Claire didn't think she'd ever seen her angrier. They all simply stood there a moment, and as Alex started to speak there was a shriek from Caitlin outside. With no thought to anything else, Alex simply bolted toward the back door, even as Claire could already hear Eric calling out, "It's all good! Conner stepped on her bunny—Nobody's hurt!" Claire was left in the hall with Beth, who glared at her.

"Why do you have to interfere in everything?" Beth finally asked.

"I wasn't, I—I just want to help my friend."

"Well *husband* trumps *friend,* so *butt out.*"

Claire made herself breathe as evenly as she could. Eric faced bigots enough that she'd asked him how he kept from blowing up all the time. He'd told her that that wasn't who he wanted to be, and it merely escalated things anyway. When he had to control his temper, his strategy was to grab onto a thought that couldn't make him mad. His current go-to image was of her being knocked backward from a sitting position by a small but enthusiastic dog during a shoot at the animal shelter. She'd been laughing too hard to resist it. She tried to picture Eric hopelessly pushing a cat out of his lap so he could work.

"Sure," said Claire. "Didn't mean to step on your manicured toes."

She was past Beth and halfway to the back door before Beth asked, "Why would you bring an Arab here, anyway? Don't you think we've been through enough? I mean, isn't that just insensitive of you?"

Claire turned to face her best friend's wife. She had never wanted to clock Beth in her perfectly made up face more. *Eric and the cat,* she thought to herself desperately. *Eric and the goddamned cat.*

"He's Persian," Claire answered. "Unless you want to get technical, and then he's an American." She headed outside, shaking a little.

She kept her distance from Eric as he was working so as not to distract him. He was happily directing the kids this way and that, and laughing when they didn't quite get it right. Alex was sitting on the ground, his legs crossed, Conner in his arm, and Caitlin filling the space where his other should be. Alex looked genuinely happy in that moment, and Eric caught it frame after frame.

Beth came over and said she wasn't going to get on the ground, so Alex stood up and tried to smooth out his clothes again. Beth positioned herself in front of him in a way that neatly obscured the right side of his body. She tried to hold Conner still at her feet as she put on a practiced smile. Caitlin had her arms around her dad's leg and was grinning up at him. He affectionately rubbed her shoulder, his face tilted down at her with an expression that suggested he was about to laugh.

"That's great," said Eric from behind his camera. He kept clicking as he changed position, instructed everyone to look his way, and turned the camera twice. Then when he said he thought he had something and was done, he smiled at Caitlin and said, "You're free now! Run!"

Caitlin laughed, and she and her brother started running in circles on the lawn. Eric grinned as he watched them, then searched for Claire. When he caught her eye she saw his expression change to one of concern. He gave her a questioning look and she shook her head a bit. He walked over to her as they could hear Alex and Beth starting to bicker quietly near where the kids were laughing. Eric frowned slightly as he looked at her.

"What's up?" he asked softly.

Claire shook her head again. "I don't think I can do this."

Eric continued to frown as he studied her face. His jaw shifted almost imperceptibly. "Then we go," he said. He turned back toward Alex and Beth. "Hey, um, I am so sorry to do this to you guys, but, uh...checking some stuff on my camera a second ago I realized I forgot something for another job, and I think if we stayed to eat I might be cutting it close in terms of my deadline. Totally my fault."

Alex glanced from Eric to Claire and his brow creased. "You sure? I mean, it shouldn't take me that long to get the grill going and stuff."

Claire wasn't looking well. Alex started to take a step toward her until Beth put a hand on his only elbow. Eric gently guided Claire in the direction of the car, and as they were walking said, "Yeah, as I say, really sorry, gotta run, but enjoy the dessert, okay? Next time you can come to us, all right?"

As Eric gave Alex and his family a small wave, Caitlin finally noticed they were leaving and ran ahead to intercept Claire while holding her bunny.

"Aunt Claire! Where are you going?" she said, taking her hand as if to lead her back.

Claire bent down to Caitlin's eye level and smiled at that cute face. "I don't feel great, Sweetie. We can roll more a different time, okay? And keep Mr. Bunny Face away from any bottle rockets." She gave the bunny a little tweak on the nose, then hugged Caitlin, and got up as she waved back toward everyone else. She cast Alex an apologetic look and headed with Eric toward the car.

Alex pulled his arm from his wife's loose grip to jog

ahead to Claire and put his hand on her shoulder. She looked him in the eye without smiling and said, "I'm sorry."

Alex frowned at her, then gave her a hug that he felt was inadequate with only one arm, and said quietly in her ear, "Thanks for trying." She nodded a little as he let her go. He waited with Caitlin bouncing at his feet as he watched Claire and Eric drive off.

As they started down the road Eric said, "Do you want to talk about whatever that was yet?"

"Not really," said Claire. And after a moment she smiled at him and said, "I can't believe you lied for me. That's so not you."

"I didn't lie. I do have a deadline. I was just planning on being up all night to get it done, and now I don't have to. No, the only thing I kind of lied about was pretending I can't work a grill. I mean, technically, I've never worked a grill like *that* before, I only know charcoal."

Claire looked out the passenger side window at the fields and houses as they passed. She put a hand on Eric's thigh and he covered it with his own hand, which was warm. "You were good with those kids," she said.

"They're good kids, so that was easy."

"Yeah, well, I bet ours one day will give them a run for their money." Eric gave her hand a squeeze. Claire was starting to feel better. She just wished she felt things were going better for Alex.

But nothing was going better for Alex. After a month back home, things had gotten so tense between him and his wife that it finally came to a head one afternoon over seemingly nothing. Both the kids were napping at the same time for a change, and Alex decided to work on cleaning out a storage closet. He came across a box of fall and winter clothes, and Beth came in as he started tossing all of his right-handed gloves into the wastebasket.

"What do you think you're doing?" she asked as if she were scolding Caitlin for something. Alex didn't appreciate it when she used that tone with their daughter, either.

"I'm baking a cake. What the hell does it look like I'm doing?"

She snatched one of the gloves out of the waste can. It was Italian leather and she'd bought it for him two Christmases ago.

"This is a perfectly good glove!" she said angrily.

"That I'm never going to wear again, so why should it take up space?"

"But we could give it away or—"

"Beth, who wants one fucking glove?"

She glared at him. "Maybe someone dumb enough to get his arm blown off."

The statement made Alex so angry that he finally lost it and started to yell.

"Damn it, Beth. you think I chose this? That I wanted this to happen or something? 'Cause hey, I got all the way to Iraq and thought, what would piss Beth off? Oh sure! I'll get my goddamned arm blown to bits and that'll show her! It was all just to screw with you!"

"Well at least you would have been thinking about me instead of yourself! You joined the Army without telling me! You just announced you were running off to do all your training! I never asked to be an Army wife! Why did you think you were the only one with a say about risking your life? I mean, where even am I on your list of priorities? I'm already below the kids, and your sense of duty, and Claire, and—"

"Leave Claire the fuck out of this, she never did anything to you! And why do you have to make everything here so fucking hard? I felt like back in OT that all this might not be so terrible but, every damn

278

day here it's like you want me to fail!"

Beth threw her arms up and yelled, "Oh, quit whining already! You're as bad as the kids! It was bad enough that I had to handle everything by myself for months on end, but then you had to come back and make more work for me with—"

"So, what are you saying? You wish I'd been completely blown to bits and then your life would be a fucking paradise? God, do you even have a clue, Beth?"

"Hey, at least I'd have gotten a big fat government check that way and no one dragging my life down!"

"Well, I'm sorry the payoff isn't better for getting killed in stages, one motherfucking limb at a time!"

At that moment Alex spotted Caitlin standing in the doorway with tears in her eyes and clutching her beloved stuffed bunny. As he looked at her, he realized she'd never heard her daddy shout in anger before. She'd never heard him swear. She seemed truly frightened. Alex and Beth had always done all of their fighting in private away from the kids, but even that had never escalated to this. He went cold.

"Caitlin? Honey?" He started to move toward her, but she became more upset and backed away, tears streaming down her face. He thought he could actually hear his heart cracking as it broke.

Beth seemed to sense an opportunity and took it. "So now you're going to scare the kids to death? Why should you even be around if you're going to ruin their lives, too? She was fine before you came back! And now she has to see you like this!" she yelled, gesturing at his injured right side. "Look at her face! She's terrified! And who can blame her? If you really cared for her you wouldn't be so selfish, just thinking about what *you* want! You'd do what's best for *her*!"

Alex didn't answer Beth. He merely watched in dismay as his daughter started to wail and run back to her room. If he couldn't control himself he shouldn't be there. He'd rather have been killed in Iraq than hurt his kids. Maybe he shouldn't be around them yet. He had worried about that all along, but the look on Caitlin's face convinced him. She deserved better. She had to save herself and roll away.

He quietly grabbed a duffle bag and started tossing some of his clothes into it. He couldn't zip it with one hand, so he held it level enough that nothing would fall out. Alex didn't say another word to Beth that day, but he watched her glare at him as he called his mother to ask if she would mind coming out to get him, and could he stay for a while. He couldn't bring himself to see Caitlin or Conner before he left. He didn't trust that he wouldn't scare them. He didn't trust himself with anything.

Alex was at his parents' for almost a week before he called Claire. He wasn't proud of having run back to his childhood home, and he wasn't sure where he was headed anymore. He felt pointless.

Claire went to visit Alex soon after she got his call. It was peculiar to see him back in his old room. His posters were gone and replaced with framed pictures of quilts that his mother preferred, but the furniture was still the same, and the wall color was the same pale blue it had been since high school. There was a fake plant on his old desk instead of the jumble of notebooks and pens she always associated with his living space.

Alex was lying on top of the bed, his arm over his eyes. Claire couldn't tell if he was sleeping or not, so she knocked softly on the open door. He moved his arm enough to see it was her, then sat himself up.

"Hey, Claire."

"Hey."

He didn't look at her and he didn't say anything.

"Can I come in?" she asked cautiously.

"Sure, yeah, I'm sorry. I'm just distracted. Um, how are you doing?"

Claire kicked off her shoes and climbed onto the end of the bed where she sat cross-legged. "Good, I guess. Busy."

Alex nodded. He seemed depressed, which, when Claire thought about it, he would be crazy not to be.

"How is it going here, with your mom and all?" she asked.

"Good, I guess. I don't know. She doesn't let me do anything. I had to put up a big fight about actually bathing myself, if you can believe it. I told her I was not going to let my mom give me a sponge bath, but she won't let me take a real shower because she's convinced I'm going to lose my balance and hit my head and die in a wet heap in there."

"She's just scared, Alex."

"I know, but, God! At home Beth was no help, and anything I tried to do to modify stuff so I could start to do things on my own would give her fits, and here I'm not supposed to do anything or my mom starts to cry."

Claire listened sympathetically. She wanted to ask him what had pushed him out of the house, but she knew the only thing it could be was that he felt he was somehow doing it for his kids. She couldn't imagine how, since it was obvious his kids needed him, but something must have happened to convince him otherwise. Home was a problem, but his parents' house was obviously not working either. It was all wrong. Alex needed to feel free to work out new ways of functioning in the world while not being made to feel like a freak or a baby. She was worried for him, and decided maybe it was a good time to tell him about the work she had been doing at the dojo.

"Well, Alex, I have something for you to try if you're

interested. It might at least get you out of the house."

"What's that?"

She pulled a binder out of her bag and handed it to him. He took it with interest and started paging through the pictures and instructions. He looked back up at her, seeming both astonished and disbelieving.

"What is all this?"

"Sensei and I have been reworking the jujutsu techniques from ninth kyu all the way through Sho-dan. Every single one has been approved by the Grand Master in Japan, and if you want to, you can do a condensed test of the basic levels, and then test for black belt. Assuming you still want to."

Alex was quiet as he studied the notes. It was all there, and it was beautiful. There were instructions carefully typed in a clear font, and color photographs of Claire (right arm tied under her gi) in key positions with Sensei where more visual explanations were needed. Some of the techniques were as he would expect them, and others were surprising and ingenious. He was overwhelmed, and his eyes started welling up. He'd never been more keenly aware that he hadn't ever seen Claire shed a tear.

"I...wow. Claire, I don't even...."

"There's no pressure," she said. "It can just be something interesting to look at if you don't want to try it."

"No, I do. I can't believe.... This was a lot of work, Claire. Thank you."

"Hey, what are friends for, right?"

He glanced down again at the notes and wiped his eyes with the back of his hand.

"When can we start?" he asked.

They started that day in the back yard. It went pretty well, until Mrs. Sullivan returned from her errands and saw what they were doing, and cast them disapproving looks. The confrontation she had with her son after Claire left caused Alex to retreat to his room early. He didn't know how to convince his mother the activity wasn't dangerous. The more he persisted in going off to work with Claire, the more uncomfortable his mom tried to make him when he returned home, and the more time he ended up spending alone.

Claire believed it was a positive step that Alex was getting out and doing something he enjoyed. She thought things had been going well, but when she stopped by to pick up Alex one afternoon, his mom said he wasn't interested in going out. Claire went up to look for him and found him lying on his bed with his back to the door.

"What's up?" she asked from the entrance to his room.

He turned to look at her. "Nothing. I just don't want to do anything today."

"What does that mean? You haven't been doing anything at all?"

"I don't know. I've been reading. And it got me thinking is all, and now I just want to lie here, okay?"

Claire was concerned. "What have you been reading?"

"Whatever stuff Mom gets me. The stuff on the desk."

Claire knew his mother had banned certain movies and the evening news. Mrs. Sullivan had apparently experienced too big a scare nearly losing her only son and was trying to keep any more misery at bay. Claire sifted through the books on the desk: all upbeat things, some historical biographies, the *County Vet* books by Catherine Devin that were so light. But the one on top was a Devin novel called *Bending Chance* that she didn't know. His mom had probably assumed being by the same author as the things she'd read already that it was in the same vein. Something about it disturbed Claire, even though the cover was nondescript.

"Can I borrow this?" she asked, picking it up off the pile.

"Go ahead. It's not as fast a read as you'd think, though," said Alex.

"You're sure you don't want to get out today?"

"I'm sure. I don't feel.... Yeah, tell my mom I'm not hungry, either, on your way out, okay?"

"Okay. Call me if you need to, all right?"

"Yeah."

Claire drove away frowning to herself. Alex needed a change. All of his mom's overprotective care was not useful. He needed to know he could do things and that he had a purpose. Alex needed hope.

Claire arrived home to an empty apartment. Eric was out on a shoot and wouldn't be back for hours. She grabbed some leftovers from the fridge, and then curled up on the couch with the Catherine Devin novel. Within a few pages she was glued to it. It wasn't anything like the cute *County Vet* books that she knew Mrs. Sullivan had pulled off of Pammy's old shelves. This book was complicated and somewhat scary.

There were about a dozen characters, each in a situation they hoped to influence in order to have some control over their fate. The basic premise of *Bending Chance* was that even if you could alter your destiny, there were too many other people around you whose fixed destinies forced the outcome of your own. If everyone around you let themselves be controlled by fate, there was no wiggle room left in that scenario for you to exert any control over yourself. None of the characters knew one another, but their lives were intertwined in ways they couldn't see, and those other lives sealed the fate of the rest in some fundamental way. They were all struggling with something. One man was cheating on his wife, another was stealing money legally through a corporate loophole, a mom secretly hated the youngest of her four children, and so forth. Each story was compelling, but the most troubling one that stood out for Claire was about a young man named Keith.

Keith had hit his head in a diving accident and was confined to a wheelchair. He brooded over his situation and wanted a normal life, but he was destined for failure and worried about suicide, and the way the book seemed to be headed, Claire was afraid to see how things would end for Keith. The book was intricate and fascinating, but it left one with no sense of hope. It almost seemed to obliterate the idea of hope entirely.

When Eric got home after dark she was nearly finished with the book, and Alex's mood was making more sense. She could not think of a worse thing for him to have been reading.

"Eric, have you ever read this?" she asked, as he bent down to kiss her once he'd set his equipment down.

He glanced at the cover. "Never heard of it. I think they're shooting a movie based on one of her other books, though. Why, is it good?"

"It's very good, but...well, it's dark."

"Dark can be fun in its own way," he said. Eric headed into the kitchen and started pulling out the necessary assortment of things to assemble a bowl of cereal. By the time he came back into the main room to sit with Claire while he ate, she was sitting up with a serious expression on her face.

"Hey Eric?"

"Yeah?"

"If this is too much to ask, I understand, but could I bring Alex here?" asked Claire.

"Why do you feel you have to ask me to do that?"

"No, I don't mean for a visit, I mean to live here for a while."

Eric stopped in mid-chew for a second. Then he swallowed and set his bowl in his lap. "Why? I mean, sure, I suppose I don't mind, but isn't he getting help from his parents?"

"Kind of. He's living there, but I think it's making him more depressed. I just feel like I should be doing more to help, and that I'd have a better shot at that if he stayed with us."

"Well, if you think he'd be comfortable and you really think it could help, sure. Would he be okay on the couch?"

"That's what he did the whole time we lived together, so I don't see why not."

Eric looked thoughtful. "Claire, I'm glad you want to help your friend and I'm happy to do what I can, but make sure you know what you're doing. Alex has been through a lot, and I don't know if you're really equipped to handle him right now. I've read that many returning soldiers have all kinds of post-traumatic stress symptoms, and there might be better people for him to get help from."

"Yeah, I know. It's just, since Beth won't help, and his mom is making things worse, and he won't go to counseling, I feel like I may be the last person left he might listen to. I can't leave him like this and I'm worried."

Eric continued to eat. When he finished, he got up, rinsed the bowl and left it in the sink. He came back out and started to strip his shirt off. He looked down at Claire on the couch and said, "Well, I'm really tired, but if our privacy is going to be compromised for a while, we should have some noisy fun while we can, so let's go!"

Claire laughed as he pulled the book out of her hand and set it on the table, then grabbed her gently by the wrist and started pretending he was going to drag her to the bedroom. The notion that he could actually drag her anywhere was preposterous since she knew about two dozen wrist escapes and he'd seen how well they all worked. Claire had planned to go straight to sleep that night, but now she decided she was not so tired.

"Thanks," she said as they turned out the lights and headed for the bed.

"Don't thank me yet!" he said, leaning in to kiss her as they reached the bed, his hands working their way under her shirt.

Claire giggled. "No! About the Alex thing, and letting him stay here if I can get him to do it."

"Well, don't thank me for that yet, either. We'll see how it goes, okay?"

Claire smiled as she undressed. "You know I love you, right?"

"You say that, but I'd like some proof, please."

Claire laughed as she crawled under the covers and into Eric's arms where she felt she belonged.

The next day she was only scheduled to teach a few private classes in the morning, and afterward she changed and drove straight to the Sullivan house. Alex was up at least, and sitting on the porch. He hadn't shaved and he looked irritated.

"Hi," he said as she walked up and took a seat next to him on the bench.

"Hi. Are you doing any better today?" she asked.

"I guess. I came out here to get away from my mom because I was trying to make myself a sandwich and she wouldn't let me open any jars. Why is it so hard to let me simply do something? I mean, so what if I have to take an extra second to sit down so I can hold the thing in my knees to turn the lid? What difference does it make to her? She keeps saying she's there to help, so why don't I let her help." He looked tired. Claire tried to remember the last time she saw him smile. Not since she'd seen him with his kids.

"Alex, come live with me."

He looked at her with surprise. "What?"

"I talked to Eric about it last night and he doesn't mind. I think until Beth.... Well, things aren't working for you here, and maybe at our place you could get back on your feet."

"You don't have to do that."

"Yeah I do. I'm ready to pack you up this minute and go."

As Alex sat there, Claire could see some of the liveliness she knew in her friend return to his eyes as he considered her offer.

Then he turned to her and said, "Let's do it. Right now before my mom can guilt me out of it."

They went into the house and started throwing his clothes onto the bed for packing. He left Claire to arrange things in the bag because he knew she was better at it (even before he lost an arm), and Alex went to gather his things from the bathroom. His mom appeared in the doorway as they were finishing up and asked what was going on.

"I love you, Mom, but I'm going to go stay with Claire and Eric for a little while, okay?"

"But, Alex! You—"

He kissed his mother on the forehead as Claire was zipping up his bag. "Mom. Thank you for everything, but I need to do this. Tell Dad, 'thanks,' too. I love you."

Mrs. Sullivan shot Claire an accusatory look as they passed her in the doorway, and then the two friends headed down the stairs, out the door, and into Claire's car. It felt like a prison break, and on the drive they both had the vague sensation they were going to be stopped at any moment.

When they got inside the apartment, Alex stood by the door and glanced around. "Where should I put my stuff?"

"Well, you're on the couch, so I guess next to it on the far side is most out of the way."

Alex started digging through his bag to find his razor. He had an electric one now, because he'd cut himself too often with the regular kind trying to manage it left-handed. Claire went into the kitchen to throw together some kind of lunch. Without Eric there, it felt almost instantly as if she and Alex were roommates again, only in a slightly bigger, nicer apartment. Alex found it interesting that he felt more normal in this completely new place than he had in his childhood home.

He went off to shave in the bathroom, and Claire set up a lunch spread like they used to do as roommates. She put out bread and jars of condiments and whatever lunch meat seemed edible and lettuce and a cutting board with a tomato. Alex came out and had a seat at the counter and she handed him an unopened can of Coke, then took a seat across from him.

"So, what kinds of regular things in your life are hardest still? You know, to manage with just one arm?" asked Claire.

Alex thought about it. "Toothpaste. The couple of times I tried it myself I made a mess of it, but then I haven't had a chance to practice. Every night I've been coming into the bathroom and my mom would have put the toothpaste on the brush already, and at home Caitlin wanted to do it, and I couldn't tell her 'no' because it was so sweet, so I haven't bothered to figure that one out yet."

"Would the kind of toothpaste that comes in a pump

be easier?"

"Maybe. I don't know. There's a lot of stupid stuff that slows me down and makes me feel...." Alex sighed. "Beth would freak out about how long it took me to put on my shoes, but I can't tie anything with one hand. I leave 'em laced kind of loose so I can just jam my feet in, but I can't go running like this. And I want to drive again. And writing with your left hand is fucked up! Everything gets all smudged, and it's hard to keep the paper still, anyway. And I need to get some left handed scissors, but again, how am I supposed to hold the paper? Or whatever it is I'm trying to cut? And buttons *suck*. And even zippers are hard because they don't want to work if you don't hold them still while you do them. And, I mean, in one way it makes sense to use, like, Velcro or, like maybe that toothpaste pump idea. But at the same time those other things are still out there, and I feel like I should find ways to deal with them as they are."

"I get that," said Claire. "Well, let's make lunch and see how you do."

Alex looked warily at the tomato on the cutting board, but started by getting himself out a couple of slices of bread and putting them on the plate. Next, he got out some ham, which wasn't a big deal, but the package had already been opened before, and he wondered how he would tear the seal if it were new. Probably with his teeth. Lettuce wasn't hard, mayonnaise wasn't that bad....

Claire tried not to appear as if she were watching him too closely while she put together her own sandwich. She was tempted to try everything with only her left hand, too, because it was much more challenging than she would have imagined. She'd never thought about how much you need another hand or arm for leverage or support sometimes for ordinary things. But she didn't want to make Alex more self-conscious than he already was, so she went about her business and would be there when he needed her.

Alex paused. "I guess I could learn to like sandwiches without tomatoes. Any suggestions?"

Claire considered the problem. "That is tough." There didn't seem to be a way to brace it on the cutting board with his arm so that his wrist could bend enough to reach it with the knife. His lap was no help in this case. "I suppose you could kind of hold it with your foot while you slice it, but then I don't want any of it."

"Thanks."

They stared at the tomato together and thought.

"How about this?" he said after a moment. He stood up and lightly set his knee on the cutting board and he butted the tomato up against it. The slices he made weren't pretty, but they were slices. He put them on his sandwich.

"Huh. But what now? It would get too messy to keep doing it that way the farther you got into the tomato," said Claire.

"But I could turn it at this point, right?" He flipped the tomato onto its flat side and held it down with some of his fingers while he carefully sawed in small motions with his thumb and index finger. Again, not pretty slices, but slices nonetheless.

Claire took the extra slices and put them on her own sandwich. They each put the final slice of bread onto their respective meal and started to eat.

Then Claire asked, "Alex, would a prosthesis help? I know you rejected it as useless, but wouldn't it have solved, like, the tomato-bracing problem just now?"

Alex shook his head. "No fake arm. In my case it doesn't do enough good. If I had enough arm left that I could control, like, one of those grasping hooks, that would be useful. But I don't. I'd rather give up tomatoes than lug something purely cosmetic around."

"Fine! Just asking. Hey, do you think we could slice a tomato on the grater? Wait, they're too smushy for that, and it only shifts the problem of what to hold. Hm...."

Alex was eating his sandwich while staring at the cutting board. It was wood with some rubber grips on the bottom that kept it from sliding. And then he stopped eating a second and said, "Claire, do you still have that tool box I left in the old apartment?"

"Yeah, sure, under the sink. You want it?"

Alex nodded. "I'm pretty sure I left a bunch of those really long finishing nails in there from the weapons wall project. Do you mind if we mess with your cutting board?"

"I don't care," she said, as she slid some things around under the sink and came out with a black tool box. "What do you need?"

"I think just a hammer and those nails. A pilot hole would be smart, but you don't have a drill here, do you?"

"Uh, if we have one it would be Eric's, and I wouldn't know where to look."

"Well, let's try it anyway."

"Try what exactly?" said Claire.

Alex flipped the cutting board over and extended a third of it past the end of the counter. Then he fished a long nail out of the tool box and positioned it in the middle of the extended part of the board. "You start it with the hammer, I'll hold the nail."

"Um, not to sound like your over-protective mother, but I don't want the responsibility of possibly smashing your only hand, so let me start it, and then if you want to take it from there go nuts."

Alex smiled and handed her the nail. "I'll be the human clamp then." He leaned his weight into the part of the board on the counter.

Claire carefully tapped the nail in the spot where Alex had put it before, and once it was firmly in place, she handed the hammer over to him and she took over the job of holding the board down. Alex took one or two tentative taps, then in a couple of heavy strikes had the nail all the way through. When they flipped it back over it was now a cutting board with a spike sticking out of it a couple of inches.

Alex looked pleased. "Okay, I think we need at least one more, like an inch or so over."

They repeated the whole procedure and now had two spikes. Alex grinned as he took the rest of the tomato and impaled it on the nails. He picked up the knife, and after scoring the tomato's skin, cut off a decent slice. He added it to what remained of his sandwich.

"I like it," said Claire. "Very Spanish Inquisition."

"And *No*body ever expects *them*," said Alex. He took another bite and chewed while in thought. "I think," he said as soon as he'd swallowed, "that with, like, three nails spaced right, I could brace or impale a ton of things. I mean, it's not a solution for out in the world, but I'd only use a cutting board at home anyway, so who cares?"

"Actually, modifying the cutting board reminds of that thing-a-ma-jig you have in your workshop. The little thing you made to brace stuff you want to saw?"

"Oh, the bench hook. Yeah, a little wall at the end of the board, or maybe one on each side of a corner...."

Claire took another bite of her sandwich, which was tasting better. "I'll bet there are any number of jigs and stuff we could make in your shop. If you had a little cutting box, like your miter box, but for vegetables or cheese.... And you have those 'quick grip' clamps, right? The ones you can do one-handed? You could use those to clamp stuff down and to brace things against."

Alex thought about it. He hadn't had the heart to go back in his basement wood shop when he got home because he assumed that was another element of his life that was over. But he'd forgotten about the clamps that he'd still be able to manipulate with one hand.

"You know, Claire, that's not bad. Even the clamp alone just now, I could have clamped the cutting board to the table and had the clamp itself to brace the tomato against. Or if I used a light enough touch, possibly even clamp the damn tomato down. And, actually, with clamps to replace simply holding things with my other arm, maybe I could do lots of things, including work in my shop again. Learning to run the tools left-handed sounds annoying, but I'd get used to it."

He looked at Claire appreciatively. This was progress. This was hope.

They ate lunch in a familiar silence after that. They both wondered independently what would happen when Beth found out about this new arrangement.

They took a long walk for the rest of the afternoon and tried to pinpoint other skills he was concerned about, and brainstorm solutions. It was comforting to have someone he trusted simply help tackle those ideas. Alex tried to ignore the way people couldn't help staring at him on the street. In theory being seen by strangers didn't make any difference, but actually being out in public and feeling on display was another matter. It bothered him more than he felt like admitting, even to Claire.

Alex did tell her about how his instincts were still to use the arm that was gone. He had been lucky so far that he hadn't smashed his face in a fall yet, since his first reaction was always to do a two-armed breakfall. The modified version Claire had taught him worked, but it still wasn't automatic. Not adjusting in time when objects were falling was a more common problem. His reflex of trying to catch things with his once dominant hand meant he was usually too late.

As they crossed the park, Claire said, "Oh, we can address that." She scooped up a stray ball abandoned near the tennis courts and tossed it to her friend. He smiled as he caught it, and they continued passing it back and forth between them as they went. Claire figured most of Alex's retraining was going to take time and practice, but it didn't all have to be work.

As they walked, Alex would have to stop and essentially realign himself with the world periodically. The inner ear issue was bad enough, but with his arm gone that changed his center of gravity. It was awkward to have one side of his body be about ten pounds lighter than the other, which could cause him to miscalculate how much of his weight to lean where, and he'd start to tip.

When they got back to the apartment it was getting dark, and Eric was already making dinner. There was some kind of rice with lentils and sautéed vegetables and chicken. Alex couldn't remember the last time he'd looked forward to a meal, and this one looked really good.

"Hey, Alex. You guys hungry?" he said as they walked in. Claire went over to where Eric was working by the stove and gave him a kiss. He smiled and kept her there happily with one hand on her waist for a moment as he continued to nudge vegetables around with a wooden spatula.

"Smells great," said Claire as she reached into the hot pan and tried to pick out a piece of red pepper.

"Stop doing that! You're going to burn yourself," said Eric in mock annoyance. She smiled as he kissed her on the cheek before turning his attention back toward the stove. "Did she ever bug you while you were trying to get stuff done in the kitchen?" he asked Alex.

"I don't really cook. But I did watch her burn her tongue a dozen times because she couldn't wait for the cookies she made to cool."

Claire smiled and blew on her piece of pepper. "What did I do to deserve being ganged up on? I'm a very nice roommate!"

Eric kissed her again. "Yeah, well, you can improve your roommate score if you help me tackle all the laundry that needs folding that's on the bed before we go to sleep tonight." Claire laughed in a way that made her seem more like a girl than Alex ever thought of her. Alex was happy for Claire, but it was strange to see her so clearly settled into a new routine with its own banter and flow. She seemed to have found her place, and it wasn't with him.

"What do you want to drink?" Eric asked as he started moving food onto serving dishes and Claire began setting the table.

"Anything room temperature," said Alex. "Too hot or too cold and it feels like it's pouring into my phantom arm. It's the weirdest fucking thing."

"So you still feel that arm?" said Eric. "I mean, if you don't mind my asking. If I say something stupid, please shut me down."

"No, it's fine. And yeah, it still feels like it's there, and a lot of the time it hurts, especially by the end of the day. I can feel...." Alex seemed to be someplace else for a second, but then he focused in on Eric again and tried to remember what he was saying. He cleared his throat. "They did this weird thing at the hospital with a mirror so I could sit at a table and see my left arm in the reflection, and it would somehow register in my brain that my right arm was back, and that would help the pain for some reason for a little while, but it never stuck."

"Whoa, that must have been really strange," said Eric.

"Yeah, well, you get used to strange."

As they ate, Claire and Alex shared with Eric the ideas they had come up with that afternoon. Eric told them he'd once edited an instructional film for surgeons about tying knots with one hand and offered to find it. He also suggested they all go out together and play ping-pong sometime to heighten Alex's left-handed reflexes, and that sounded fun.

After dinner Alex decided he needed to call his wife. He asked if he could take the phone into the bedroom for a minute.

"Sure, Alex. Do what you need to," said Claire.

He started punching the buttons with his thumb as he carried the phone with him to the next room and pulled the door closed behind him with his foot. Eric and Claire tried not to overhear, but the walls were thin. They washed the dishes together and let the sounds of the water drown out as much of the one-sided phone conversation as they could.

"Beth?" Alex said, when she finally picked up her end of the line.

"What is it?" she asked in a flat tone.

"I just needed to tell you that, uh...I moved out of my parents' house."

There was a pause. "Where are you?" Beth finally asked.

"Beth, I want to come home."

"Where are you?" she asked again.

Alex hesitated. "I'm at Claire's place, with her and Eric."

Beth was silent so long Alex would have thought they'd been disconnected if it weren't for the sounds of cartoons playing in the background.

"Beth, I couldn't stay at mom's anymore because I was just getting into a worse and worse headspace and at least Claire wants to help me figure out how to do stuff with the one arm but I really want to come home and figure it out there. Can I talk to Caitlin for a sec? Because I—"

"How can you do this to me?" she finally yelled.

"But, Beth! I want to come home! I don't want to be here, but Claire's at least willing to work with me and try to get me—"

"So I'm supposed to be happy you ran back to your old girlfriend? When after all th—"

"God, Beth, Claire was never my girlfriend! You know that! And Eric is right here, anyway, so what possible fucking difference could it make? You have no reason not to trust me!"

"No reason? You joined the Army without telling me and you think I have no reason? Claire even got to know about *that* before I did! Really, Alex? Like you think I don't know you used to make late night calls to Claire all the time when you thought I was asleep? Is that enough of a reason? Or that your mom sees Claire on a regular basis but she's never shown any interest in helping me when I've needed it? And then sh—"

"You're going to drag my *mom* into this now? Oh for fuck's sake that is—"

And on it went like that for far too long. Alex closed his eyes and sat on the edge of the bed near the heap of clean clothes. It was no use. Beth was really angry and only succeeding in making him angry as well, and there was nothing he was going to be able to say during that conversation that was going to help. They yelled pointlessly until Beth finally hung up on him.

Alex stayed where he was for a while. He didn't feel like trying to be good company at the moment. He felt like crying and decided against it. He felt like punching a wall and decided against that, too. He couldn't go home yet. It would kill him to have Caitlin witness another ugly scene between her parents, but that was all he and Beth seemed to be capable of. Alex didn't know what to do, which layered despair on top of the sense of guilt he already carried for merely being alive.

When he did finally emerge from the bedroom, Claire had already made up the couch for him, and Eric had stepped out to pick up some supplies he needed for a wedding shoot the next day. Claire was curled up on the end of the couch with part of the comforter over her feet, and reading a book. She looked small and delicate like that.

It made Alex think of the summer Sensei had them perform in a demonstration at the state fair right after Claire's first black-belt test. There were maybe a dozen students involved, about half of them black-belts, and Sensei had asked Claire to watch over all the equipment while everyone else set up the mats. She hadn't changed yet, and she was perched on a bench in her street clothes next to all the bags and weapons, swinging her feet and gazing up at the sky. The thing about the scene that struck Alex and stayed with him, was how using Claire to guard everything appeared more like setting a trap than anything else. She didn't look as if she could protect anything, but anyone who knew her, knew better.

Claire noticed him standing there and she looked up at him with concern on her face. "How are you doing?"

He shrugged and sat down on the other end of the couch. "I don't know, Claire. It's all...it's hard." After another moment he added, "Are you sure you want me here?"

"Of course I am. If I could have my way, I'd store you in the closet and pull you out whenever I'm up for a decent argument or need a bug moved outside."

Alex smiled. "Eric's not good with the bugs?"

"No. He'd rather pretend they're not there, so I'm getting used to it."

"I have to confess, half the time I squished 'em anyway."

"No!" said Claire.

"Yeah. And I kind of miss arguments that aren't so...personal. You and Eric don't disagree much?"

"Not really. I mean, he's got his own take on things, obviously, but he's pretty liberal, and most of the time our opinions are similar. And he's just...fun. He's really easygoing, and we get along all the time. Probably looks kind of nauseating, huh?"

"No, it looks, I don't know, like you get each other. It looks good on you, being happy like that."

"I'm sure something will come up someday that we'll have to hash out, but Eric is so sweet I can't imagine him not trying to find a calm way to deal with whatever that might be. It takes a lot to get him mad, and even then he doesn't lose his perspective. Anyway, so far, day-to-day stuff? There's nothing really to argue about. We just like being together."

Alex considered it. He wondered what that kind of relationship would be like. He recalled his mom trying to convince him it would be nice to have a romantic relationship with his best friend. At the time it felt like the equivalent of asking him to have sex with his sister, and it was too disturbing to contemplate. Now it didn't sound so odd. It sounded less stressful than the path he had taken.

He sighed. "So, what should we do while I'm here? They're not ready for me at work until the new year because my replacement is under contract, and I don't want to sit around like I did at my parents'."

"I've been thinking about that," said Claire. "I cleared it with Sensei to use the dojo when everyone leaves so we can train any night you want, which I think would be good for you. Also, I think we should make a real list of stuff you need to relearn how to do and get to work on it—like using a computer again and putting on your work clothes by yourself and writing and basic chores—and we'll brainstorm them one at a time like we did today with the tomatoes. How does that sound?"

"That sounds like a real start, finally," said Alex. He looked relieved.

CHAPTER TWELVE

As the days turned into weeks, Claire began to realize how complex things with Alex really were. He was different. In most ways he was still the friend she knew, but there were times she suspected he might be playing that friend out of habit or necessity. Claire was starting to understand a little better what had probably frightened or frustrated Beth.

She knew Alex well enough to know when he wasn't being honest, and all signs pointed to the likelihood that he was keeping something to himself. Whatever it was seemed to be slowly killing him. Claire thought she saw glimpses of it at night when he thrashed around. He seemed to be reliving something awful, which she assumed was the bombing of the convoy.

The first few nights with Alex in the apartment, Claire got no sleep at all, because he often cried out and she would go to help. Sometimes she would sit up with him and keep him company until he was ready to try and sleep again. However, if he was still out when she responded, she was scared to wake him. What if Alex didn't know who she was? How dangerous could he be? As she concluded that sounds from around the apartment building were disrupting his sleep, she set Alex up with a white noise machine. It had worked for her brother's kids, and she was glad to see it worked for Alex, too. Eric wasn't thrilled with the rain forest setting that seemed to do the trick, but Claire suggested that it masked even sounds the two of them might make in bed at night, and he decided he could live with it after all. Alex still had nightmares, but at least he was sleeping. Claire couldn't tell if the sleep was worth it if that meant Alex was staying in the nightmares longer.

From Alex's perspective, his most disturbing chronic problem was the nagging feeling he'd forgotten his weapon. From the moment his rifle was issued to him at Camp Atterbury, until the moment of the bombing, he was responsible for keeping it constantly at his side, and that was hard to unlearn. Every time he got up from his seat, or moved into a different room, he felt a stab of panic as he searched briefly for his M-4. The sensation reminded him most closely of the feeling he had not long after Caitlin was born, when he would occasionally drive somewhere without her and catch a glimpse of the empty carseat in the rearview mirror. He would experience an instant of terror that he'd left her somewhere by mistake.

At first, Claire was tempted to try and transfer his obsession onto a new object, such as his wallet, or the clamp he now kept in his back pocket (which came in handy for bracing things against or holding down paper that needed signing, like receipts). But in the end, she thought it was healthier to let it go, however uncomfortable that was in the meantime for him. Some things had no easy solutions.

As the weeks turned into months, Alex became far more independent in terms of manipulating things in the world. He learned to tie a basic knot with one hand

and could put on his own dress shoes. Claire convinced him it wasn't a cop-out to get sneakers with Velcro that would stay on tightly enough so he could start running again. Claire's car was an automatic, and she let him practice driving it until that got comfortable. (They did research and found out when he was ready to get a new car for himself, he could have it modified so that all the controls around the steering wheel could be operated from the left side.) His handwriting was getting more legible and fluid. For clothes with long sleeves, Claire figured out a cute way for him to reach through the unneeded one and pull it inside so it didn't dangle. He could type on a computer at nearly his old speed. He became a fan of electric can openers. He mastered toothpaste in no time at all.

In many cases, the thing Alex was really wrestling with was speed. There actually wasn't much he couldn't do with only one arm once he set his mind to it, he simply needed additional time because there were more steps involved. Like zipping up a jacket. He figured out pressing himself against a wall to hold one side of his jacket still as he zipped it worked fine. It was just markedly slower than throwing a jacket on and zipping it up as he walked, the way he used to when he had two hands.

Claire also learned that with some struggles, such as shirt buttons, the real obstacle for Alex was pride. There was a tool he could use—a sort of stick with a wire loop at the end for grabbing and pulling buttons that they'd given him in OT at Walter Reed, but Alex was determined at first not to be dependent on it. At least on men's shirts the holes were on the left side, so he discovered he could put his thumb in the hole and use his fingers to force the button through. However, he could only do that with any speed if it was one of the buttons high enough on his shirt that he could hold the fabric still with his chin. Once Claire convinced him to finally accept the use of the tool to do the lower buttons, they were able to check that skill off the list.

For the most part, Alex was up for every challenge. He doggedly went at each problem Claire presented to him until he conquered it. The only exception was jujutsu.

Alex was actually doing pretty well with his training, which they did after hours at the dojo. But Claire came to realize that it was the one arena where he allowed himself to let loose his otherwise bottled up frustrations. She sensed Alex didn't feel he belonged there anymore. His focus wasn't good. He used the time they spent in the dojo to try and shake off his anger about not seeing his kids, or his irritation with his wife...or whatever that final thing was that gnawed at him. It was the one place he allowed himself to fail, and Claire wasn't sure what to do.

She tried to talk with Eric about it, but he was at a loss. He had been remarkably patient about having a such a complicated long-term guest, but Eric thought they were out of their depth when it came to Alex's struggles and depression. As they moved through Thanksgiving weekend where Alex spent most of it trying to get Beth to let him talk to his kids on the phone, Claire could see Eric become more troubled. She asked him for his thoughts one night as they were settling into bed.

"I mean, Claire, you've done a lot, working full-time and still accomplishing so much with Alex, but I'm worried you're wearing yourself out, and that you're already near the end of your list and he's still not really better. I know you thought once he gained certain skills it would make him happier, but it's like he has a temporary burst of confidence, and then his attitude slides backward again. He can joke around with you, and he's pleasant enough company over dinner, but seriously, underneath that? Something's way off."

Claire considered it, then said, "Well, maybe there are important things he's worried about doing that aren't on the list. Like, how awkward do you think sex might be compared to what he was used to? But I don't think I can bring that up. That one really sounds like something he should talk about with a guy."

"Well, that guy isn't me. I really don't think he would appreciate my bringing that up, like, ever," said Eric. "And I like to think of myself as pretty supportive, but, uh, I'm playing the boyfriend card and saying I don't want you working with him on that one."

Claire cast him a *Don't be ridiculous* look, then sighed. "I feel like I'm running out of ideas and it worries me."

Eric kissed her, then turned away to shut off the light on his nightstand. "I'm sure you'll think of something. Just don't beat yourself up if you can't."

When December rolled around, Claire evaluated her friend's progress. Alex was doing better on a lot of levels, and would probably function fine at home if Beth would let him come back. Claire wanted Alex home with his kids for Christmas. His job was starting up again in mid-January, and it made sense for him to resume his real life before then.

Claire thought he should be taking advantage of the support groups and counseling available to him, but she knew Alex well enough to understand certain things had to be dragged out of him. And the worse it was, the more tightly he held on. Whatever was plaguing him, he was not going to trust to a stranger or his wife. Her own attempts to get him to talk hadn't worked.

Claire decided she had to try something drastic.

So late on a Friday, when Eric was out doing some

editing that would probably take him all night, Claire suggested to Alex they head over to the dojo together. He agreed, and he even drove. When they arrived, Claire unlocked the door to the darkened building, then locked it again behind her. Once inside, she turned on a light, but left the blind on the window down. Alex took off his coat and his shoes and tossed them in a corner. Claire went into the back and put her things in her private changing area. She unplugged the phone.

Claire had a spare gi in the back, but only put on the top half over her t-shirt, and left on the workout pants she was already wearing because they were flexible enough. Alex was in a t-shirt and his Army sweatpants. They both took off their socks.

Alex muttered to himself as he bowed onto the mat, annoyed that he was never there in the proper uniform. If he ever did test for his black belt he'd have to buy a new gi. It was a big "if" in his mind. Claire had faith in the reworked techniques, but Alex was uncertain. They seemed aberrant to him, no matter how graceful Claire might make them look. The more he tried to adapt what he'd originally learned into something so different, the more it seemed wrong to custom tailor an ancient art to fit his new, incomplete form. Probably better to throw up his hand and admit defeat. But Claire had other ideas.

"Okay, show me what you've got," she said, as she took up a loose but defensive stance on the mat.

Alex bounced lightly in place to warm up. He assumed his modified stance when he was ready, and warily eyed Claire. She made a small jab, and he blocked it. She tried again with the other arm and he blocked that too.

"Try a lock this time," she instructed. She punched. He traced his hand along her arm the way they had practiced. He caught her hand and did the lock until she slapped out. She came at him with the other arm, but that side was trickier. Claire slipped out before he had time to do anything. She gave him another chance, and he struggled briefly, but he did it. The next lock didn't go as well.

"Claire, I can't do it. Maybe you and Sensei can do this one with only one arm, but I can't, okay? Let's move on to the next one."

Claire was irritated. "No. If you want your black belt, you're not going to get to skip things. You can do the lock, you just have to try harder."

"Claire, I told you, I tried and I can't! Drop it already!"

She looked at him as if she were calculating something in her head and weighing her options.

"No. I don't think so." She came at him suddenly with a technique he'd never seen before that resulted in her locking his shoulder. He forgot sometimes since she only used techniques with him that they'd trained on together, that the three yellow stripes stitched into her black belt meant she knew many more. She was using them now. He slapped out with his foot since his only arm was incapacitated, and she released him.

She creased her brow slightly and made another small jab, this one frighteningly close to making contact with his face. The block this time was real. Alex was annoyed.

"What the hell was that? I thought we were going to review kyu levels."

"I did too, but you wussed out." Without warning she was coming at him with a kick to the knee that he only barely managed to escape.

"Cut it out, Claire! That wasn't—"

But this time she stepped into him and cracked into his ankle while she caught his arm and took him down in a hard throw. She braced his only arm against her leg and slowly rotated her wrist. This time it took him a moment to remember he didn't have another hand to slap out with. He gritted his teeth and started thumping one of his feet on the floor.

"You want up?" she asked.

"Stop it, Claire! Shit that hurts."

She looked down at Alex on the floor and relaxed her grip just enough that he thought he was going to be able to get up again. Then she wrenched it sharply.

"Ow! What the fuck are you doing? Let me go!"

"No."

He grimaced a bit and looked up in astonishment.

"What do you mean 'no'?" The pain shooting up his entire arm was unbelievable. He was seriously concerned about the damage she might be doing to him. Ironically "jujutsu" meant "gentle art," because with much of it you could inflict pain without doing permanent harm, but Alex was starting to doubt that concept was relevant when taken to an extreme.

"I mean 'no.' If this arm means anything to you—if anything means anything to you—you're going to have to fight me for it."

He stared at her in bewilderment that quickly turned to anger.

"I'm not going to fight you! Why would I—Ow! Damn it! Holy—"

"I can take it, Alex. If I can't keep down a one-armed guy with bad balance, then I don't deserve the belt I'm wearing. Take back your arm if you can, and if you can't, I'll break it and you won't have any."

The pain was unbearable, and the insulting tone she was using put him over the edge. He briefly feigned he was passing out, which distracted her enough that he was able to catch her leg in a brutal sweep. He cracked into Claire's shin so hard she knew it would leave an impressive bruise. She'd experienced worse, so she paid it no mind. In her time at the dojo she'd survived one concussion, two broken ribs and more sprains than she could count. She didn't care about bruises.

Claire hit the ground hard in a well-practiced breakfall, and moved to get the advantage. She studied him closely as he got up and decided to aim for the side of his ribcage that was unprotected.

Alex figured out quickly what was coming because it was the same thing he would have done, and moved to protect himself by angling his body with his arm toward her. He did it almost too late and he barely missed a very scary looking kick.

"Claire, I am serious. I don't know what the fuck you think you're doing but I—"

Claire ignored him. She made a brief feign to the left and then socked him straight in the eye. Alex reeled backward and saw stars. "Holy fucking—Have you lost your mind? I'm not going to fight you, but—Ow!" While his defenses were down she'd gotten in an excruciatingly painful strike between his ribs right under his arm.

She started to kick him in the chest but he caught her leg and twisted her around. Claire knocked the wind out of him for a second with her free leg and rolled away when he relaxed his grip. She hopped up and searched for her next opening.

"Claire!" It was disconcerting to Alex on top of everything else how she continued to say nothing and had no discernible expression on her face. She got in another painful strike to the ribs. "Claire, I don't want —" She tripped him and sent him sprawling. He didn't trust her not to kick him while he was down, so he scrambled up quickly, just in time to receive a painful chop to the neck. "I don't want to hurt you!" he finally managed to get out. Although at that moment it seemed like a ridiculous thing to say, since he was the one experiencing the pain and abuse.

Claire didn't care. He needed to defend himself for real or nothing he did on the mat would mean anything to him anymore. She was not going to let him decide he wasn't going to try. She was going to give him no choice but to try. She went for a hard groin kick but he blocked it fiercely.

She could feel his anger, but it wasn't enough yet. Claire grabbed his arm and rotated it into a searingly painful position, and he cried out. She ignored the slapping he instinctually did with his foot. Right when he was getting scared for his arm, he turned and got her to release the lock by force as he knocked her off balance with one of his legs, then picked her up and threw her. She remembered to tuck her chin as she hit the floor, which saved her from smacking her head, but the rest of her felt sufficiently smacked. She hopped up again as quickly as possible and kept at him.

Claire realized what a dangerous thing she was doing, but she didn't care. The unbridled strength of a man, even with one arm, was unbelievable. Terrifying, actually, and Alex was going all out at that point. She could outmaneuver him for a while, and in single techniques she could outperform him, but the strength it took to keep going without pause was wearing her down. He was simply stronger than she was. And he was mad.

She wasn't even sure how well he was seeing her at that stage. He was swinging at her so savagely and with such fury that she figured she'd merely become a symbol for everything that caused him pain. That was fine. That was what she wanted. Alex wasn't going to talk to anyone until he got past some of that, so she would be the punching bag. She gave him a chop by the ear that made his head ring and caused him to bleed.

311

Alex didn't know what he was doing for a while. He really did forget briefly it was Claire he was fighting, because she came at him so relentlessly he didn't have time to do anything but react. Every blow she landed on him was so serious that he didn't have a choice but to come at her in the hope that he might take her out to spare himself some pain.

When he simply went at her with stupid brute force, she found openings to exploit, and she took advantage of them every time. When Alex relied on the real techniques she had shown him and combined that with his greater strength, he managed to make some progress against her. He could feel her fatigue, but it only made her somewhat sloppy, not slower. He deflected blows to the point where his arm was beyond registering the pain, but she kept coming, and he finally decided his only way out was to trick her.

Alex turned so his weak side was exposed, knowing she would think he'd screwed up and left himself vulnerable. As soon as she started to adjust her position to strike him in the ribcage, he beat her to it and kicked her as hard as he could square in the chest. Claire clenched her teeth as she crashed backward against the weapons wall. There was a clattering sound, along with the thud Claire's body made, and a hanbo hit the floor. She started to stand up, but couldn't. She slumped back against the wall.

Alex stood over her, breathing hard. Claire sat on the mat gasping. She was quite sure she had a broken rib and it hurt like hell. She remained very still and looked up at Alex. He rubbed his hand on his face briefly and he started to cry. She tried to stand again, but it hurt too much, so she stayed where she was. Alex eventually sank down to his knees next to her, wiping his eyes with the back of his hand.

"God, Claire, what am I supposed to do?" he said,

his voice cracking.

She sat there with her eyes closed for a moment, and then she reached out and took his hand. His only hand, she thought sadly. The one with the ring still on it. What the hell was wrong with Beth? She'd wanted a big church wedding but the actual vows apparently hadn't meant anything. Beth was supposed to be the one trying to put Alex back together, and letting him know he was still useful and loved and needed. Evidently it was up to Claire to mend him and make him feel whole again, and Beth would take him back when the hard work was done. Beth had never deserved Alex less in Claire's opinion.

"Did I hurt you, Claire?"

"Doesn't matter," she said softly, and forced herself to sit up a little straighter so as not to worry him. If Alex was going to talk, this was the only moment he was going to do it, and she didn't want him distracted by her own pain. "Tell me what happened over there, Alex."

Alex slumped down next to her and closed his eyes. Claire thought about all the time they had spent together on that mat. She thought about the cocky boy's arm she had wrenched around that first time they were paired together, and about the journey that had turned him into the strong yet broken man beside her now. "Talk to me, Alex," she said.

"What do you want me to say?" he asked quietly.

"I want the part you haven't told anyone else yet. The thing that haunts you that is keeping you from your family. Whatever it is, let me know it, and I'll live with it, too. I know there's something you're not telling anyone because I know you."

Alex sat still for a moment, and then he absently rubbed his thigh a little where she'd kicked him so hard that he'd cried out.

"There was a little girl."

"A girl?" she repeated.

Alex's eyes were still closed. "Yeah. There were lots of little kids running around the war zone, because the whole damn place is a war zone so where else are they supposed to go, you know? It's their home and, and, we come through and they want things. Things all kids want, like candy, and whatever we're willing to give them. I always kept a stash of something like that in my pockets just in case, right? Like at home with my kids, 'cause Caitlin likes chocolate so much, and it's fun to hand her a treat if she's been extra good to her brother or something. And she is good to her brother, Claire, you should see her. She's so...."

He paused, but Claire remained silent.

Alex took a deep breath and continued. "So, the day of the, the...accident, we were on a convoy. I know everyone knows that part, but it's so hard to explain what that was like. It doesn't mean anything to anybody here. There'd been a report about another possible bomb but those were like, all the time, so you got less vigilant about it some days. That's not true, exactly—more like, you just accepted it. If you die you die, and if you think about it you can't get anything done, so you...you just accept it and do your job. My job was to provide security in that situation. So we were moving at a good pace and it was hot because it was always fucking hot, and...and the truck two vehicles ahead of me was hit by a bomb. In that scenario we were designated to stop and rescue crew members, so I got down...."

Alex paused again and looked at his hand. He turned it over and studied both sides of it. Claire simply waited until he started talking again.

"I took up a position so the wreckage was behind me and I was looking out, but like, twenty yards away was this injured girl. She had to have been about the same age as Caitlin and so sweet...she...she was so scared and no one was coming for her. She was crying. I realized I could change positions without it affecting what I was supposed to be doing, so I went over while still looking out. She was bleeding and crying and she reached up for me, so.... I mean, she was scared! Where were her parents? They could have been dead or hurt or...I just...I went to scoop her up and once I had my arm around her, that's when the second bomb went off."

Alex started to cry again, and he put his hand over his face. Claire put an arm around him and ignored the screaming pain in her side as she did so. "What happened, Alex?" she said as softly as she was able.

Alex looked directly at Claire and said, "When the bomb exploded it blew her up and ripped my arm off at the same time. The first doc said if she hadn't been there to take the brunt of the blast, I'd be dead."

He looked up at the ceiling. "How am I supposed to live with that, Claire? Am I supposed to wake up grateful every day that Caitlin's Iraqi alter ego got blown apart in my face? There were pieces of her.... and I.... I have to see this space where my arm is supposed to be, and the last thing I remember feeling with it is that girl and.... Because, Claire, that's what I feel now. My arm still feels like it's there, but stuck the last way it was before it got blown off. It's wrapped around that girl all the time. Sometimes it feels like my fingers have fallen asleep and they tingle, and sometimes there's pain, but always my arm is forward a little, bent at the elbow, my wrist, my hand pressed tight so she won't...she won't.... How am I supposed to be glad to be alive, Claire? What does that make me?"

He started to cry again, but it was more of a choking sound this time. Alex lowered himself weakly and laid

315

his head in her lap. Claire stroked his hair until he fell asleep. She needed sleep, and possibly an x-ray, but after all Alex had suffered the least she could do was be a safe place to rest for a while.

They stayed that way until morning. There were no nightmares. Claire had eventually passed out sitting up, her hand settled on the spot where her friend's right arm should have been.

When he woke, Alex sat up slowly and realized he felt like a train had hit him. At first he thought he was back in the hospital in Germany, but then he saw the first hint of daylight coming in around the blinds on the window of the dojo, and he remembered. He remembered everything.

"Claire?" He shook her slightly. "Claire?"

She reluctantly opened her sleepy eyes to look at him. "Hey, Alex," she said, her voice scratchy.

"Hey."

He got up and slowly made his way downstairs to use the bathroom. Claire sat where she was, but then she saw Eric come rushing to the door. She heard him yell to her through the glass. She started to stand, but her circulation was suffering in a few places, and she stumbled twice on her way to let him in.

"Jesus, Claire! I've been worried sick about you! Have you been here all night? Why didn't you answer the phone here? I'm getting you your own cell phone finally and I don't want you to argue about the expense this time. Why are you all bruised? What happened?"

Claire could feel Eric was a jumble of panic and relief all mixed together. He'd obviously been up the whole night. She wasn't ready to answer his flood of frantic questions, so she smiled a little to reassure him, and gave him a kiss. "I love you," she said contentedly, and she kissed him again and felt some of his panic begin to subside.

Right then Alex reappeared. He stood and watched them a moment, unnoticed, as Eric gingerly put his fingertips to Claire's cheek with concern and she smiled calmly. Alex was glad his best friend had found such a good guy. He liked the kindness they showed one another with every touch and gesture. He cleared his throat a bit, and Eric and Claire both glanced his way.

Eric looked from Claire to Alex and back again, apparently trying to make any sense of what the evidence in front of him suggested. Alex had obviously been bleeding at some point from one ear, and an eye was swollen nearly shut. There were bruises forming on his neck and all over his entire arm. Claire appeared less battered from the neck up, but she winced with every turn of her body. She could feel a protective rage rising in her boyfriend as his eyes like slits turned on Alex who simply stood where he was, unguarded and limp.

"Don't," said Claire to Eric softly, putting her hand to his cheek and turning his gaze back onto her.

"But, Claire—" he started.

"No," she said, again softly. "I love you. Take us home now, okay? Just take us all home." Eric nodded but didn't look at Alex as they stepped out of the dojo into the morning light and cold air. They left Claire's car where it was, and Eric drove them all back to the apartment in silence with the exception of his suggestion that he take them to a doctor instead, which they both declined.

Eric helped his girlfriend painfully make her way up into their apartment as Alex followed slowly behind. When Claire got into their bedroom she began her damage assessment. One cheek was a bit bruised and swollen, but not terrible. The real Technicolor display was only visible once Eric helped her get her shirt off.

There was an impressive number of bruises on her sides and back, but the worst of it was one nasty bruise in the middle of her chest roughly the same size as Alex's foot.

"Claire, this is serious," said Eric with a grim expression.

Claire was completely unconcerned and shook her head. She felt along her ribcage gently to try and pinpoint any specific breakage. She grimaced now and then, but was starting to think any fractures were of a hairline variety, and probably not anything a doctor could help her with. She was simply going to have to put herself out of commission for a while. It was time to use up the sick days she'd been saving.

Eric ran her a hot bath where she soaked for a while and tried not to notice all the places she felt sore. He brought her tea and a cookie. He sat on the floor beside the tub so Claire wouldn't have to tilt her head up to look at him.

"How's Alex doing?" she asked eventually.

"He's asleep."

"Good," said Claire, and she shut her eyes. She opened them after a moment and said, "Eric? When he wakes up, can you offer him some tea, too?"

Eric looked irritated and shifted his weight slightly. "If you want me to."

"Eric, don't be mad at Alex."

"What do you want me to say? I mean, look at you, Claire! What is wrong with the guy?"

"I made him do it. I hit him first. Don't blame Alex."

Eric sat there a moment, brooding, and finally he said, "Yeah, well, no one could make me do that. I'd let you beat me to a pulp before I'd ever even think about hitting you back."

"And that's why I love you and you're stuck with me for life, okay? But be nice to Alex, please. This is nothing compared to everything he's been through. And I don't...I can't.... I think he'll be going home soon."

Eric frowned and cast his eyes down into his lap. Finally he sighed and said, "Do you want to lie here another minute, or do you want to go to bed?"

Claire thought about it. "I wish I could figure out a way to do both at the same time, but I can't. I suppose I should get out and get some rest. The pruney thing is not adding anything positive to my new look."

Eric helped her out of the tub, dried her off, and got her into a t-shirt. Claire was passed out against her pillow before he could even get the covers on her. As she drifted off, she felt him brush his fingertips over the bruise on her face, then he kissed her lightly and left her to sleep.

Alex was starting to stir when Eric came back out into the living room, where he sat down in a chair across from the couch, facing his guest. Alex sat up slowly. He winced as he moved his arm to rub his neck and realized he couldn't lift it that far.

"Would you like some tea or something?" asked Eric evenly.

Alex shook his head and winced again. "I think I'd like a shower, actually."

"Hey, whatever. I've been instructed to show you hospitality so that's what I'm going to fucking do."

Alex studied Eric carefully. He respected the way Eric appeared as if he were two seconds from whaling on him.

"Look, Eric...I don't know what to say. If you want to take a couple of shots at me at this point, I don't blame you. Just do it already and then I'll take my shower and cough up any blood in there, okay? I couldn't fight back right now even if I wanted to, so it would cost you nothing. I won't even tell Claire, since I know she's the only reason you haven't decked me by now."

Eric glared at him. "It is really fucking tempting to blacken your other eye so they match, but what's the point? I mean, if Claire actually wanted you permanently hurt, I don't really think you'd be sitting here conscious."

As brutal as the fight had been, Alex knew Claire had held back enough to refrain from doing anything that would cause lasting injury. Although there was no way of telling that to any part of his body at that moment. He was in a lot of pain. But less so in his mind and his heart than the day before.

"Yeah, well, I'm not as skilled as she is, so I don't know what I did to her," said Alex apologetically. "I don't know how to explain what happened, Eric. I don't know anything anymore. I'm sorry you had to.... I'm just sorry."

"Just take your fucking shower."

Alex worked at pulling his shirt off with his arm that didn't want to move as Eric watched him struggle. When Alex did finally remove it, Eric actually gasped. Alex's torso was as battered as Claire's, but something about the size and placement of the bruises was additionally disturbing. The wounds were all tight and specific and looked incredibly painful. Alex rested, trying to get up the strength to make it to the bathroom.

Eric muttered something in a language Alex didn't understand, and finally said, "Okay, I am so fucking beyond pissed right now I barely know what to do with myself. But Claire is somehow at peace with this madness, so I have to be, too. I'm going to go run you a bath because I'm not sure you can stand very long, and if you collapsed in the shower or something, Claire would be upset, and she doesn't deserve to be upset about one more fucking thing. She's the only part of this that matters to me. So just wait there, and I'll tell you when the goddamned bath is ready." He got up and started walking toward the bathroom.

"Thanks," said Alex. "Claire was right about you."

Eric paused to look at him with curiosity in addition to his anger. "What do you mean?"

"In her letters that I got in Iraq. She was crazy about you, like, really really early. She said she wanted to be more like you, and that you helped her be a better version of herself. She said that I'd think you were a good guy. It meant a lot to know when I was over there that she was happy. You make her really happy."

Eric hesitated where he was another moment, and when he turned toward the bathroom again Alex said, "Eric?"

"What now?"

Alex shut his eyes and finally noticed one of his teeth was a bit looser than it was supposed to be. "Eric, have you ever seen Claire cry?"

Alex could hear the exasperation in Eric's voice as he answered, "What the fuck kind of question is that? Of course I have! Like once a week since the call about your arm! I feel like I spend half my life wiping away her tears related to you and your drama."

Alex's eyes were still closed, so when he grinned he didn't see Eric's reaction, but he could sure hear the heightened irritation in his voice.

"Is that funny to you? What kind of friend are you, anyway?"

Alex opened his eyes again and noticed that Eric's fists were clenched tight, thumbs properly tucked outside along his fingers.

"I'm her best friend," said Alex. "But you're a better one and I'm glad."

Eric frowned, but seemed suddenly disarmed, as if

his anger were ratcheting down quickly. He unclenched his fists, let out a slow breath, then went to run the bath.

Later that day, right before dinner when both Alex and Claire were up and moving around a bit again, Eric left them to go grab some takeout. Alex sat on the couch, and Claire was trying to find a comfortable way to sit in the chair across from it.

Alex smiled. "You look like hell," he said.

"You should see the other guy." She smiled back.

"I'm surprised you didn't land a groin kick."

"Hey, it's not like I didn't try! You really learned your lesson about that back in high school. You landed one though."

"Yeah, not real effective on whatever's in your pants."

"Well, it's still not pleasant, I can tell you that much."

Alex tilted his head slightly and squinted at a really beautiful picture of his friend doing a high kick that was hung across the room. "Claire, you want to know something weird?"

"What's that?"

"I think my balance problem is better now."

"What?"

"Yeah, I think you may have knocked whatever it was out or off or over or something. I mean, maybe it's temporary until some swelling somewhere goes down? But, like, right now if I could run? I don't think I'd have to work so hard to compensate all the time like I have been."

"Whoa, that is weird. Let's hope it sticks. If it does, you think they'll want to hire me at Walter Reed?"

"Yeah, I don't think they want people looking worse going out of the hospital than they did coming in from, you know, the war. But, hey if you want a character reference...."

They sat quietly a moment. Claire couldn't get comfortable where she was, so she went and sat next to him on the couch. She leaned on him.

"You need to go home, Alex."

"I know," he said softly. "I miss Caitlin and Conner. And I miss Beth, too, even though you don't get that. She's not...you don't know how...."

"You don't have to explain it to me. I believe you."

"Thanks. I like Eric, by the way."

Claire smiled. "Yeah, well, he wants to kill you twice if that were possible, so I don't see us all getting together for another cookout anytime soon."

"I know." They were quiet another moment, and then Alex said, "Beth isn't...when I go back, she.... Claire, I don't think you understand how mad she is that I'm here."

"No, I do. I'm prepared for how this might have to go."

Alex sighed.

"Are you going to be okay to get some real help, now?" asked Claire. "Because you need to work through that nightmare. It's too horrible. It's too much."

"I've been thinking about it. Those counseling programs we talked about before might not be a bad idea. Less dangerous than your kind of help anyway." Alex paused. "It was good to finally say it, though. As bad as it is, now it doesn't feel so...impossible. It's so beyond fucked up. But just knowing you know makes a difference."

"Good," said Claire. "I've been thinking about how...how you still feel her...and I can't imagine what that's like to literally carry around a ghost or a memory like that. But Alex? There's no way to know how that scenario would have played out if you hadn't done what you did. She might have died anyway, but the last thing she felt was your arm around her. Maybe in her last moment she felt safe. Maybe you should carry that thought with you instead."

Alex swallowed hard as he rested his head against hers. They sat that way for what seemed like a long time, and then Claire brightened.

"You know what I want to do before Eric gets back?" she asked.

Alex raised an eyebrow at her, then realized even that hurt.

"I want a picture."

"Of us?"

"No, of the fucking Easter bunny. It would be a good companion to that prom picture. I still have mine, and it would be nice to have them in one of those matching double frame things."

"You are demented."

Claire laughed, and then she grimaced as she touched her side. "Just a sec, I'm going to get my camera."

She disappeared into the bedroom for a moment and came back out fiddling with her own personal camera. "There's a way to get it to be on a timer...."

"Here, let me try," said Alex, reaching up painfully with his arm. He placed the camera in his lap and started manipulating the tiny buttons. Claire admired how he was adjusting to the single hand so well.

"There," he said after a moment. "I think I can do it. Where do you want us to be?"

"If you put the camera up on the TV and we stand over here with the wall behind us, that could work."

"Charming. You're sure you want to do this?"

"Yes. It might be the...." She changed her mind about sharing the rest of that thought, and instead said, "I'll pay for it, and I can give one to your mom for

Christmas."

"Oh God, I will pay you *not* to do that!" said Alex, laughing.

"Okay, let's go. Eric will be back any minute, and this is a picture I can't ask him to take."

They set up the camera, and did one test shot that wound up being them discussing how long the timer was going to run, and then they did a few more until they got one Claire liked. They smiled as she stood with her back to him, his single badly bruised arm around her waist.

By the time Eric returned with the food, Alex and Claire were laughing on the couch recounting their prom night together. If they hadn't appeared like they'd been in a bar fight, it would have been a sweet little scene. Eric still didn't look happy, but he did join them to eat and watched them swap stories. The more Claire laughed, the more relaxed he became, until Alex started to believe Eric could eventually forgive him, even if he likely would never trust him again.

Alex and Claire's recovery routine in the apartment over the next couple of days involved watching Eric's *Monty Python* DVDs over and over, laughter, a few serious discussions, and sandwiches. They would periodically inspect each other's wounds, Alex softly touching her face to check on her bruise, and Claire gently taking his arm in her hands to see which parts were still tender. They worked together on a plan to get Alex home.

Late one night in bed, Claire turned to Eric and said, "I think once he goes back to Beth I'm never going to see him again."

"You've been friends too long for that to happen."

"No, Eric, Alex needs to be with his kids again, which means his marriage has to work. That's only going to happen if I get out of the picture," admitted

Claire sadly.

Eric was quiet for a moment before finally saying, "Well that's not fair, but you're probably right. Beth wants things to match some picture in her head. You don't fit into that picture, and I'm sure never did."

Claire scowled. "What is her problem anyway? I mean, what did I ever do that got in her way?"

Eric shook his head. "It's not.... Look, I don't know what kind of filter you and Alex have on that you don't see each other, but you're beautiful in a way she can't touch with all her makeup and the way she starves herself to fit into those tiny clothes. And Alex is...." Eric flinched slightly, as if the words he was about to say hurt. "Alex is sexy and shit, Claire. He's probably never had a problem landing a girl in his life. Even with the arm missing, Beth probably feels insecure about how other women look at him. Seriously, when we're out at that bar and he's crushing it at ping-pong, are you missing the number of women who seem to wind up hanging out on the sidelines by Alex? She doesn't trust other women near him, and you can call yourselves 'just friends' all you want, that doesn't make you not another woman."

Claire was trying to picture Alex objectively and decided she really didn't know how he looked. He wasn't a guy to her, he was a construct of their history. His ears stuck out a little and there was a bump on his nose, but maybe it was a good bump? He just looked like Alex. She shook her head. "It shouldn't matter what he looks like. It should be obvious that's not the kind of relationship Alex and I have."

Eric glanced away from Claire a moment, then shook his head again as he turned toward her. His expression suggested she wasn't hearing him right.

"But you and Alex don't have normal boundaries at all. You hang off each other more than most actual couples I know. I mean, I can handle it—most of the time anyway—but I don't know many guys who could. And Beth.... How much do you really expect of Beth? She didn't finish school, she doesn't have a job, she doesn't really have something of her own that I can see —other than her role as a wife and mother, and she ended up in that way too early. She needs Alex to be something for her that fills that space. And she probably wanted him for things that in the end don't mean much, the stuff on the surface that seems nice from the outside. But you don't care about that stuff, so you're not as, I don't know, fragile. Of course she feels threatened when you're around. You scare her because she doesn't scare you. As much as it looks like she's running things, Beth's dependent on Alex for everything, and you and Alex are real with each other in a way that leaves everyone else out."

Claire looked at him with concern. "Do you feel left out?"

"Of course I feel left out," said Eric. "That's an insane question. You guys practically read each other's minds." He gave her a smirk and added, "I would never challenge the two of you to charades."

"We do rock at charades."

"No doubt. But, I mean, I get why Beth can't handle it, the way you guys are. I'm jealous too."

That startled Claire. "Why haven't you ever said anything?"

"Because you're not doing anything wrong, so it's my problem. I'm just grateful that at the end of each day you choose me."

Claire kissed him. "It's not a competition."

Eric shrugged. "Well, sometimes it feels that way. And Beth knows she'd lose, so when things get hard she doesn't want to play. She's probably ashamed she doesn't know how to help Alex and it was easier to push him away than figure it out. It's messed up, but people do some crazy shit when they're scared."

Claire considered it as she snuggled in closer to her boyfriend. He was wrong to ever think there was a comparison to be made. The relationships were too different. Alex may be protective of her, but Eric was considerate of so much more. It would never occur to Alex to offer her his jacket in the cold the way Eric did, or to make sure to leave her the last cookie in the jar. And sure, she and Alex could finish each other's sentences, but it didn't mean they agreed. She liked to be challenged, but she liked better to be understood. Alex was familiar. Eric was home.

She sighed. "I love you, Eric. Thanks for your patience with all of this."

"Anything for you," he said, wrapping his arms around her but with care not to cause her pain.

At the end of the week, when their bruises were turning a ghastly shade of yellow and Alex's black eye was essentially healed, they started preparations to get Alex home. They approached Alex's mom with the assurance that he was intent on patching things up with Beth. He asked to move back into his childhood room so he could truthfully tell his wife he wasn't staying with Claire anymore.

Once that was settled, Alex started calling Beth. She hung up a lot at first, but he had flowers sent to her every day. He mailed her the beautiful prints Eric had made of their family taken on the day of the aborted cookout—photos that made them look like the beautiful, happy family Alex hoped they could be if they tried.

Eventually Beth started listening. Alex promised her that he would get counseling from the VA. He told her he loved her and he missed the kids. He lied and said Claire had lost interest in him since he was useless in the dojo without his arm, and jujutsu was all she really cared about. He lied further and said now that Claire was living with Eric, she didn't want to make time for him the way she used to, and they couldn't talk like they once did. With that out of the way for the time being, they started to talk about the deployment, and how traumatic it had been on Beth's end.

"Do you know how terrifying it was living with the idea that you could die while you were over there?" Beth asked him.

"I know. I'm sorry."

"I mean, I spent every day worried that men in uniform were going to come to the door to tell me you were dead. I started taking the kids out all the time because being home near our stupid door was too stressful. And then I couldn't tell people outside of the family readiness group that I was scared of our door, because if I complained about anything even a little bit, I would get an earful about how it didn't compare to whatever you were probably going through. I swear, if one more person said to me while I was struggling with the kids that 'at least you're not the one at war' then I, I don't—"

"No, that sounds hard in its own way. It's hard to be scared for someone and not be able to do anything about it," said Alex, and he meant it.

"Well, it was," said Beth, sniffling. "And...and it's really hard for me to say this, but I'm not as good with the kids as you are. They don't listen to me like they do when you tell them to do things. They never make you crazy and you never yell at them and then I feel horrible all the time when I can't handle it."

"That's not fair to you Beth. I've never had to care for them alone for months on end under stress like that."

"No, but we both know you would have dealt with

them better than me. And part of me hates you for it, and part of me is just glad they have you."

Alex was impressed with her confession. It was honest in a way that left her vulnerable, and that was new. Maybe they could learn to really talk. He was going to need someone to talk to. "But that's why we shouldn't be apart now that we don't have to be," he reasoned. "We can do this together as a team, like we're supposed to, so you don't have to do it all. I want to come home. I'll try harder not to be a bother."

"You're not a bother," said Beth quietly, sounding regretful.

"Well, I can do stuff better now. A lot of stuff is kind of slower so you need to give me a little more time for things like taking out the garbage, because there are a few extra steps, but I can do it. I can be helpful again, especially with the kids. How are they today?" he asked, trying not to sound more interested in them than in her.

Beth sighed. "Alex, they.... Actually, they really need you home. I haven't been straight with you about that when you've called before. Having you back again and then away after only a month, it.... It kind of threw them for a loop and it's been a mess here. I keep thinking it will get better but it doesn't. We had a whole routine while you were in Iraq, and now they won't go back to it. Conner cries and looks out the window for you, but at least I can distract him with a snack or a video. Caitlin, though.... God, that girl has always preferred you from the day she was born. No matter what I do, no matter what cute outfits I get her, or dolls, she just wants that damn Mr. Bunny Face and *you*. I think she hates me now because she thinks it's my fault you're not here, and if you never came back...."

"So imagine what a hero you'll be in her eyes if

you're the reason I come back," Alex offered. "Wouldn't that be good? She needs both her parents. Whether you think that or not, she does."

There was a pause, and Alex felt he was so close. Then Beth said,"What about the arm?"

"What about it? I mean, what do you expect me to do about it, Beth?"

"A prosthetic so you look more—"

Alex gritted his teeth and held the phone tighter. Claire never once made him self-conscious about his missing arm in a way that left him feeling grotesque or lacking. He certainly missed his arm, but he no longer felt as if he couldn't be a whole person without it. The fake arm was a step backward. "Beth, I really don't want—"

"Just for, like, church or something. Or if we want to go out."

Alex closed his eyes. "Fine."

"Fine?"

"Yeah, I'll look into it." At least he knew in his heart that Caitlin didn't care how he appeared on the outside. As long as he could be himself around her the concession would be worth it. He opened his eyes again and studied the back of his hand. He could do it for his daughter.

There was silence on Beth's end for a moment, and then she said, "Okay."

"Okay?"

"Okay. Give me, like, a day to kind of get things ready here. The tree is up and stuff got moved around for it, and.... And you can't see Claire anymore," she added abruptly.

Alex didn't say anything. He'd known that was coming.

"Alex, did you hear me?"

"Yeah."

"*Yeah* you heard me or *yeah* you won't see Claire anymore?"

"Yeah to all of it."

He heard Caitlin come into the room where Beth was, suddenly clamoring at her mother's feet asking if that was her dad on the phone, and saying she wanted her dad and please please please please please she'd be good if she could just have her dad back. Alex felt his heart shatter as Beth shooed her away, and he could hear his daughter whimpering in the background. Caitlin needed him there whatever it took. She was too little to really save herself. He shut his eyes tightly. He clenched his fist, then slowly relaxed it.

"Whatever you want, Beth. You can have whatever you want."

"Okay then." She sounded pleased. "We'll see you when you get here. I'll make you a cake or something."

It was less than a week before Christmas, and when Alex told Claire that he was finally going home she realized she had never been happier and sadder in such equal proportions in her life. Alex didn't talk to her about the specifics of whatever arrangements he'd come to with his wife, but Claire had her suspicions. And the bottom line was she knew he desperately needed his kids, so it didn't make any difference.

Claire helped Alex pack his few things at his parents' house, which reminded her vaguely of helping him do the same before he left for college. She thought about how back then he'd left her a prom picture. She'd decided not to share the picture of the two of them in their bruised-up version of the same pose. She wanted Alex to have a copy, but that was too dangerous on too many levels. She liked to think maybe someday they could look at hers together, and they could laugh at more than just their hair. She couldn't imagine when that day might be.

Alex and Claire got into her car that he'd helped her buy and they headed off in silence.

They pulled up in front of the tiny house decorated brightly with Christmas lights. It was the shortest day of the year, so the sunlight had gone long before they got there. They could see motion through the curtains, and the shadows of children bouncing on the couch in the cool glow of a TV set. They sat watching the oddly sweet scene for a minute or two.

Finally Alex turned to her and said, "So...Claire, it may be quite a while before I see you next. I don't know...I...." He looked back at the shapes of his children in the window, and noticed their shadows were dancing along on the snow outside. As if his children were matched with silent partners they couldn't see.

When he returned his gaze to her, Claire smiled and said, "It's okay. You're still my best friend even if...." She wasn't feeling well, but she kept smiling anyway. She took a deep breath and tried again. "You're still my best friend, Alex. You go do whatever you need to do and come find me anytime when that works for you, okay?"

He looked at her a moment and realized he was tearing up, but she was not going to cry. That was Claire. He loved that about his best friend. He loved her.

Alex took one of her hands in his remaining one and kissed her in the palm, then wrapped her fingers closed around it as he would with his daughter. Claire realized as well as she knew his body and its flaws and its strengths, she'd never felt his lips before. They were soft.

"Thanks, Claire."

"You're welcome."

Alex stepped out of her car and went up the walk.

He hesitated briefly, pulled something out of his pocket, and walked back to Claire's side of the car where she rolled down her window. "Here," he said, and he handed her Caitlin's key that went to nothing but her heart.

"But, Alex—"

"I don't need it anymore. I'm home. You keep it for me until I can see you again, okay?"

"Okay. Bye, Alex."

"Goodbye, Claire."

Alex then went straight up the walk and didn't look back. Claire watched him knock at the door. When it opened, light flooded onto the snow, and she heard two excited little voices shout, "Daddy's home!" over and over and over.

Claire took her necklace off—the one with the friend pendant—and she slipped the key onto the chain as well. She put the necklace back on, and tucked the pendant and the key together inside her shirt.

Claire started up her car and drove home to Eric. She trusted he would put her back together again when she arrived and fell apart in his arms.

ACKNOWLEDGEMENTS

This book was the third of three I wrote in rapid succession several years ago when I first decided to try my hand at fiction. I wanted the challenge of seeing if I could create relatable characters and tell interesting stories, but found quickly it was a good way to explore issues knocking around in my head so I could be more at peace with them.

The first novel, *Almost There,* was a way for me to work through my worst fears about being responsible for small children as a then mother of two. My second novel, *Seducing Cat*, gave me a space to consider questions of sexual needs as we age. Since the second book focused on two people who were together who shouldn't have been, I decided to make the next book about a pair of people who could be a couple and weren't. I then also used that story as a way to work through my fears about my husband possibly getting deployed.

My husband was called up for his first tour in Iraq while I was still finishing the first draft of *Just Friends, Just War*. We had six days notice before he was scheduled to leave for the first leg of his assignment in Texas, and I was two months pregnant with our third child. My first thought when he told me (after "No!") was, "But I haven't worked through all my feelings about this yet in my novel!" I really had hoped to have puzzled out how to feel, what to think, on all questions about deployment before it happened to us.

So, the first obvious acknowledgement (always) is to my husband for not only providing me necessary details for the Army elements of this story, but for reading through the draft on the plane to Kuwait and giving me feedback at a time when anyone else would have said, "I'm busy." There are not many things I know in this world, but that my husband loves me is one of which I'm certain. He also did all my formatting because he's great.

My wonderful brother, Barrett Klein, did the design work for my cover, and found many typos to fix. My other wonderful brother, Arno Klein, designed my author website, and helped make sure my story telling was clear. I have the world's best brothers.

Thank you to Michael Coleman for somehow getting uncoordinated-me all the way to black belt way back when at the Futen Dojo. You continue to impress and inspire me with your creativity and energy.

Thanking my original test readers is tricky because it was long enough ago I will forget someone, but I know they include my parents, Alice Peck, Julie Snyder, Nancy Weisser, and Gabriella Hanna. Thanks for wading through the rough version and making me feel it was worth polishing.

Thanks to my mom for everything, and being my biggest fan.

I appreciate more than I can describe the input and encouragement of my test readers of the final draft: Julie Gardner, Kate Gomoll, Gretchen Leanna, Fernanda Moore, Laura Rooney and Robyn Sullivan. Each of these women makes me feel like a real writer in a way that without their support, I would not.

This is the last of my novels my dad got to read in any form. I think my grandma would have liked this book, and I would have loved to have discussed it with her. I miss them both.

Thank you for reading. You complete the cycle, because writers need to be read. I appreciate that more than you know.

ABOUT THE AUTHOR

Korinthia Klein was born in Detroit, Michigan, studied music at The Ohio State University, and went on to graduate from The New World School of Violin Making. She currently lives in Milwaukee, Wisconsin with her husband, Ian, and three children: Aden, Mona and Quinn. She and her husband run a small violin store called Korinthian Violins and an Airbnb above it. Visit her author site at korinthiaklein.com for links to more of her writing, including her first two novels *Almost There*, and *Seducing Cat*.